The Casebook of Sam Spallucci

A.S.Chambers

This edition published in 2018.
First published in Great Britain 2012 by A.S.Chambers.
Second edition published 2014 by A.S.Chambers
Copyright © 2018 Basilisk Books.

Cover art © 2017 Carolyn Edwards.

ISBN 10: 1480278688
ISBN 13: 978-1480278684

DEDICATION

This book is dedicated to all the wonderful people I have met over the past few years who are proud enough to call themselves my fans.

You have my eternal gratitude. If you had not been there, I would not still be at this.

ALSO BY A.S.CHAMBERS:

Contents

Introduction

My name is Samuel C. Spallucci. I am an investigator of the paranormal. As I sit here typing at my laptop, the moon hangs full and white in the night sky that envelops Dalton Square, Lancaster sometime after two in the morning.

In the last week, I have witnessed visions of what seem to be the past and the future, seen three dead bodies, been abducted twice, knocked unconscious (also twice), conversed with supposedly mythological creatures and had at least seven people eagerly expect my death.

Oh, and I think I may have also gunned someone down in cold blood.

So would you like to know some more about my first few days on the job?

You would?

Okay. Walk this way...

The Case of The Satanic Suburban Sitcom.

So, may I ask you what is the weirdest question you've ever been asked? You know the sort of thing. You're normally sat in a quiet corner of your favourite bar or pub (the Borough, in my case, as it's just over the road from my office) supping away at your favourite brew, enjoying the peace and solitude of your own inner ramblings when you notice that someone is stood next to you.

Even before you look up from your alcoholic musings, you just know that it's going to be trouble. There's that air of "Oh, dear God," hanging in the air, but you do the polite thing and look up at the person looming into your personal space whilst smiling expectantly.

Now, if it was a normal person stood there, perhaps wanting to share a table due to the lack of space or wanting to ask you what the time might be as their watch had stopped, then they would smile back and make polite conversation.

No, the sort of person stood there now does not smile, they gawp. They have that faraway look in their eye that tasted far too many magic mushrooms in their youth or tells of a childhood climbing electric pylons on long, hot summer days. Also, they tend to dribble somewhat, don't they? Not much. Just a drip from the corner of their slack-jawed mouth.

Then they pop the question.

There's no reason or rationale to their request. It's just totally random. It might be something like, "I hit badgers with teaspoons. Wanna join in?" or "You wanna see my collection of belly button fluff? The yellow ones are really interesting."

Yeah. Weird. Really weird.

Well the other week I got asked a question that topped all of those: "Will you investigate the cast of a high-profile sitcom? I think they're all Satanists."

I suppose it began as an ordinary day. It was a mundane Monday morning in October and I was in the process of readying myself for opening up to the public at large. I had finally gotten around to assembling my desk. Well, when I say "assembling" what I really mean is swearing loudly and throwing pieces of chipboard around my office in Dalton Square. I guess the internet is a wonderful thing, but when you use it to buy flat-pack furniture, you really ought to check that the instructions come in your native language or at least with a phrase book for Mandarin or Cantonese. Also, why is it that those long black screws they supply always seem to have the knack of lurching to the side just as you try to screw them in so that you gash your hand with a Phillips screwdriver? Until I saw *Revenge of the Sith* I was convinced that Anakin Skywalker would end up as the suited Darth Vader after a near-fatal wrestling match with a self-assembly hi-fi unit from the star system of Ikea.

So it was that my screwdriver was making a satisfying clattering noise as it smashed against the far wall when my office door opened and a diminutive, grey-suited man shuffled in. He stood in silence, peering through his large, dark-rimmed glasses as he tried to decide whether it was worth his life to enter what was quite obviously an unofficial war zone. After a brief pause he ventured, "Mr Spallucci?"

I looked up from my DIY carnage and smiled. "That's me." I stood, enthusiastically brushed my clothes down and stepped over the wreckage of the victorious desk before sticking out my hand. "Samuel C Spallucci, investigator of the paranormal." At last, some semblance of relief from the frustration of fascist furnishings. A little bit of normality, I thought.

Then he asked his question.

Well I have to admit that it threw me somewhat. I mean, it's not the sort of question that one might expect from a chap who looks like Moleman out of *The Simpsons*. Now, "Can you help me find my biro?" or "Is this the public lavatory?" Those I would have expected, but "Will you investigate the cast of a high-profile sitcom? I think they're all Satanists." Well that is just what Grace, the young bar-maid at the Borough, would call somewhat "random."

I was rapidly becoming aware of an ever-increasingly embarrassing silence permeating the room, so I shoved some evil pieces of Chinese wood out of the way with my shoe and motioned for the man to come in.

"Thank you," he mumbled. "Mr Spallucci, my name is Roger Philips. I'm the producer of the television series *More Tea Vicar*. Perhaps you've heard of it?"

I nodded. Of course I'd heard of it! Everyone's heard of that little gem. It has single-handedly revived the fortunes of Wednesday nights on prime time commercial television. What was once the domain of dull, mundane repetitive soaps or banal, obtrusive docu-dramas has now been transformed into a comedic jewel in the schedules. "Please. Please come in," I gestured once more, sweeping some deadly, black screws off the comfy sofa. It would not do to impale a potential client.

Philips shambled into my office. He was quite obviously a man on the edge of a nervous breakdown. He constantly fiddled with the frayed cuffs of his cheap, grey polyester suit and his eyes fidgeted around the room taking in my "obsession".

"You seem to have a lot of clocks," he commented, gazing up at the old railway station time-piece that hangs on my wall opposite the main door.

"I like to know what the time is," I shrugged noncommittally, patting my trousers for a packet of cigarettes.

Philips' mouth hung open as his eyes passed from the station clock to the long-case clock, the brass carriage clock, the library clock and the napoleon hat – to name but a few. "But so many? How many are there?"

I extricated a pack of Luckies and tapped one out. "Dunno. I lost count years ago." That was somewhat of a lie. In the office there are, in fact, twelve. Upstairs, in the flat, another ten. I think.

"He stood agape for a minute watching the slow swing of the pendulum in the long-case before saying what everyone else has always said when confronted with my collection. "But doesn't the ticking drive you mad? All that noise?"

I flipped the Lucky into my mouth and lit it with my Zippo. "Trust me," I said, "There are far worse noises you can listen to all day. Now," I gestured to the comfy sofa, "why don't you tell me exactly what it is that I can do for you?"

Philips shambled over to the brand new, soft-fabric sofa and studied it as if it would sprout some sort of demonic mouth and devour him. His sad eyes looked at me as if seeking reassurance.

"It's okay," I volunteered. "It's not an Auton."

He smiled slightly and perched himself on the edge of the comfy chair, smoothed out his trousers, coughed and began to explain his situation. "Mr Spallucci, like I said, I am the producer of *More Tea Vicar*. It is a somewhat successful situation comedy that has turned my company, John O'Gaunt Media, into a rather profitable venture."

"I'm familiar with the story," I nodded, seating myself across from him in my swivel chair. "You singlehandedly badgered the executives at ITV to take on an idea that they described as 'insanely outdated' by offering them the show gratis for three months. It subsequently torched all the soap-opera and reality shows in its back-draft as it rocketed up the ratings. They are now saying that you have single-handedly altered the way that the public view mid-week television. Quite an achievement for someone who started out with not much more than a simple idea and a hand-held video camera. You're based over on White Cross aren't you?"

He nodded. "For now, yes. We hope to move to larger premises soon, what with all the promised redevelopment down on the quay."

"You said 'we'?"

He gave an embarrassed smile. "Yes. Contrary to public belief, John O'Gaunt Media is not just one man in a suit. We are actually more of a partnership of five: myself, Malcolm Haversham, Howard Baines, Maggie Sothwell and Melanie Brande."

"The main cast of Vicar?" I raised an eyebrow. "I wasn't aware of this?"

"Not many people are. We keep our business dealings very close to our chest."

I tapped the nails of my fingers against my teeth. "And you think that your partners are Satanists? I can see how that would be awkward at a church tea party, but in the echelons of high business..? Not really an economical sin, just a cardinal one."

Philips shook his head, frantically. "I know what you mean, Mr Spallucci, and normally I would say live and let live, it's just that it appears Haversham has been abducted," he rummaged inside his jacket and produced a long envelope, "and this was left in his dressing room."

I took the manila envelope and studied the front. It was embellished with a five-pointed star drawn in black ink. I looked back up at Philips. "If this is evidence, why don't the police have it?"

He scratched his ear and stared at the floor.

"Shit," I groaned. "They don't know, do they?" I waved the letter at him furiously. "This is a criminal matter. If someone has been kidnapped, then the police need to know. You can't just come running in here and expect me to bypass the due process of law!" I stood up sharply and thrust the letter towards him. "I think you'd better take this back."

Philips raised his head and his rheumy eyes behind those large glasses looked absolutely pitiful. "Please, Mr Spallucci, read the letter. I know I should have gone to the police, but the things they say in there..." He shook his head and buried it in his hands. "It's awful. Absolutely awful. I can't go to the police. They say they will sacrifice him tonight!"

I looked back at the five-pointed star. It looked so neat, so stark – one point facing up, two on either side. It didn't look like it had been penned by a lunatic that wanted to sacrifice a TV vicar, but then apparently Jack the Ripper's handiwork had also been very neat.

"Why do you think the rest of the cast are involved?" I asked.

"Recently there has been unrest, dissent between the partners," he explained. "I don't know the ins or outs of it but yesterday Haversham telephoned me to say that he had worrying news about the others and that I should meet him in his dressing room this morning. When I got there..."

"You found this instead?"

He nodded.

"I still don't see why you haven't gone to the police."

"I told you, they say that they will sacrifice him!" he wailed. "They also said that they have eyes everywhere and would know if I went to the authorities. I used to know the old Detective Chief Inspector quite well, but the new chap who's filled his shoes is somewhat of an unknown quantity." Philips paused. "Besides, he's a, you know?"

My mouth fell open. I couldn't believe what I was hearing. The new Detective Chief Inspector, Jitendra

Patel had taken up his position just two weeks ago and the local rags had already fanned the flames of latent racism that burnt in the uneducated masses, but to hear it from an allegedly intelligent man such as Philips made me see red. I didn't say a word. I couldn't say a word. I just dragged him up by his lapels, manhandled him across my office and jettisoned him down a flight of stairs before slamming the door behind him.

I lashed out at the partly-assembled desk, swore as I barked my shin and slumped into my swivel chair before catching sight of the thin, white rectangle that lay discarded on the floor. It was Philips' envelope. I picked it up and stared at the five-pointed star, licking my lips as my mouth felt dry. I needed a drink. I picked up the phone and started to dial.

I think the thing I like most about my office (and also my flat, which is situated just upstairs) is the handy location. 15a Dalton Square is close to just about everything that I really need. It's a three storey building with my flat on the top floor (although there is an attic space which I might find a use for at some point), my office on the middle floor and the Paradise Dragon Chinese restaurant on the ground floor, opening out onto Dalton Square. The Dragon is owned and run by one Mr Harry Kim. Now any *Star Trek* nuts out there will be jumping up and down at the coincidence of my landlord having the same name as the chief of engineering from *Voyager*. Trust me, even though he talks incessantly about his folks back home, I have never seen him fall disastrously in love with either a hologram or a shape-shifting alien. Harry is just Harry – a damn decent bloke. I mean, who else would let me take up so much room rent free? Okay, I did rid his kitchens of a poltergeist a couple of months ago for which he was, and still is, eternally grateful, but that gratitude goes both ways as a lack of monthly rent certainly helps my finances stretch that bit further.

If you come out of the stairs leading down from my office to the side of the Dragon, then turn either left or right, you can follow the road round into the centre of town. Lancaster is not the biggest of cities and is easily navigable by foot, which suits me down to the ground as my 1983 VW Polo Classic is somewhat temperamental. I sometimes wonder if it is possessed, but then I shrug and think, "Nah. Stephen King's already done that one."

If you cross over the one-way road in front of the Dragon, then you are in Dalton Square proper. This was the direction I had taken after making one quick phone call and stuffing the dratted envelope in my mac pocket. Now most people would normally cross over the road using one of the two sets of pedestrian crossings at either end of the square, but I prefer the more direct route. Why not live life to the max, I say. The cars that screeched to a halt and blasted their horns did not seem to agree. I just thrust my hands in my mac, kept my eyes straight ahead and hopped onto the opposite path. I was now on the island that makes up the centre of Dalton Square. It is, as it were, a small park decked out with four large flower beds, recently renovated benches and a large copper statue of Queen Victoria which faces the Town Hall. I carried on walking past the late queen and hurried in the direction away from the local politicians towards my ultimate destination: the Borough.

The Borough lounges on the corner of Dalton Square and Sulyard Street. Look for it on Google Maps.

You'll see it immediately. It's one of the few pubs that are actually marked on there. Quite right too as it's my little haven of calm and worthy of such recognition. I bounced up the front steps, pushed the doors open, breathed in the warm, welcoming atmosphere and smiled.

I was home.

I slipped off my mac and lay it on the back of my chair near the window then popped my fedora hat on top before wandering up to the bar. It was about mid-day so it wasn't too busy. I smiled at the barmaid. "Hi, Grace."

Grace beamed her infectious, little smile straight back at me. She's a nice kid, a post-grad at Luneside University down on the Quay. Like most students, she is normally broke and hence supplements her funding with a few hours here and there working behind the bar.

"Hello, trouble," she grinned from under her woolly brown hat that never seems to be parted from her curly red hair. "You on your own today?" She reached under the bar and pulled out a bottle of Jack Daniel's and one crystal tumbler.

I shook my head. "Nah. He'll be here in just a bit. You know Spliff. He'll be late for his own funeral, that one."

Grace chuckled and reached under the bar again. This time she produced a bottle of Gordon's as well as another tumbler. "That chilled?" I asked as I poured myself a whiskey.

"It bloody well better had be!" boomed a clipped baritone voice from behind my shoulder as I heard the doors swing open and shut, "but then that gorgeous little pre-Raphaelite picture knows just how I like my gin..."

"Chilled and straight, just like your men?" Grace

grinned, pouring a measure of alcohol.

"Exactly!" beamed Spliff as he downed the drink in one. "Much more of a challenge. Now Samuel, dear. What seems to be the problem on this fine autumnal day?"

I smiled, raised my eyebrows at Grace and took my drink over to our table in the bay window where the portly frame of Reverend James Francis MacIntyre (or "Spliff" to his friends) joined me. He slumped down into his chair opposite and slipped his dog collar from out of the slit in the neck of his clericals and flipped it onto the small table between us. "Off duty," he smiled and raised his glass to me. "Your good health, Sam. Now, what's got your g-string all knotted up around your testicles?"

I reached into my jacket pocket, pulled out the envelope and slid it across the table. Spliff's grey eyes twinkled as he picked the item up and turned it over in his hands.

"A valentine's card? It's not even Hallowe'en yet, let alone Christmas. Mind you, I always knew you'd come round to my way of thinking."

"Behave," I sighed. "What do you make of that? I got given it this morning?"

Spliff held the envelope between his thumbs and index fingers and smiled. "Was the deliverer of this a good, god-fearing Christian?"

"I didn't get the chance to find out. I threw the bigoted little racist out of my office." I sipped at my whiskey. "He said he was sent it by Satanists."

Spliff harrumphed.

"What? What's the matter?" I asked.

He turned the envelope around, making sure that it was facing the right way up. "Samuel, what do you see here?"

"A pentagram," I shrugged.

"Indeed. Now tell me which way it is facing. Where is it pointing?"

"Upwards. The point goes up."

"Exactly." He tossed the envelope onto the table and downed his gin before waving the empty glass in Grace's direction. "That's no devil symbol there, Sam. It's the five wounds of Christ, a Christian symbol. They drew it the wrong way up, the imbeciles!"

Grace approached the table with our bottles of drink. I flipped the envelope face down. She's a sweet kid. I didn't want to freak her. "You do know it's only you two who get waitress service in here, don't you?" she smiled.

"Ah, and what lovely service it is, my dear," Spliff beamed.

Grace giggled. "Stop it, you old queen. Now what else can I get you?"

"DRPs?"

"No probs. Coming right up."

She trotted off to the bar and returned shortly with a bowl of peanuts. After she had returned to work, Spliff palmed a few nuts into his mouth and asked, whilst chewing, "So what does it say?"

"Hmmm?"

"The letter? What does it say? Really Sam, I do sometimes wonder how you managed a first back at uni."

"Oh. I don't know. Like I said, it was given to me this... Hey! Spliff!"

He yanked the envelope out of my reach as I lunged forward to stop him opening it. He whipped the enclosed letter out, slipped on his spectacles and peered gleefully at its contents. "My, my," he murmured. "Ooo, nasty. Urgh. Wouldn't have done that in front of my mother, that's for sure. Is that physically possible?" When he had finished, he waved the letter under my nose and said, "Well they may not have much knowledge of arcane imagery, but they certainly have a graphic imagination. James Herbert would be proud of them. Want to see?"

I snatched the letter from his hand and glowered at him before having a read for myself. As there might be children reading this, I won't go into too much detail, but let's just say that the writers of the letter seemed quite determined to ensure that the next time Haversham ate a three-course meal he would be able to watch it travelling all the way down his oesophagus, into his stomach and then onto his bowels. Nice. "Sick bastards," I grumbled. "You think they mean it?"

Spliff had been steadily munching his way through the bowl of nuts and was now tipping the dusty remains into his hand. "Who knows?" he shrugged. "But can you take the risk that they don't? If I had a student come to me in floods of tears saying that their teddy bear had been stolen and had found this in its place then I would tell them to stop whinging and get a new teddy bear," (I always admired Spliff's loving touch and pastoral care for his charges as a university chaplain), "but this is a real-life person, albeit a hack, has-been actor who had to marry into money to save his dying, lack-lustre career."

"Tell me again, why they appointed you? Was it your ability to empathise with those in need or just your, kind, caring manner?"

He leant forward and grinned, "Sam, you know it

was because the bursar couldn't take his eyes off my finely-toned arse. Now, what are you going to do about that poor hack, Haversham?"

I sighed and pulled out my mobile. I had another phone call to make and a good dose of humble pie to eat.

One hour later I was munching on a falafel panini I had grabbed in Market Square and I was making my way up Penny Street towards the White Cross industrial estate where John O'Gaunt Media had its offices and studios. I was feeling somewhat perplexed. When I had rung Philips I had been expecting the cold shoulder treatment. I had thrown him unceremoniously out of my office, after all. Instead he was very warm and welcoming. He understood my anger at his silly off-hand comment. He had come from an old working class background, he explained, and deep prejudices were hard to be relieved of even in this cosmopolitan age. So he had arranged for me to visit the studios and meet with the three other members of the production team: Baines, Sothwell and Brande.

I wrapped my humble pie in cling wrap and stashed it in the freezer for a later date. My stomach, however, had been rumbling at the lack of more tangible fodder following my mid-day drink, so I had opted for the panini and quite delicious it was too. I was just finishing it when I crossed over the lights from Penny Street to South Road with the imposing stone built edifice that is White Cross Industrial Estate looming in front of me. Like many of the older buildings in Lancaster, it has a link to the Victorian mills. I think this one used to be a linen mill, but I might be mistaken. I'm not from round these parts originally and my local history is somewhat patchy. It was revamped in the eighties and split up into numerous offices and warehouses. John O'Gaunt occupy the main building on the front which overlooks the main road that crosses the canal bound for Preston and Glasson Dock.

It was quite a blustery day and I pulled my coat up tight to keep out the chill. The number two bus was just dropping gaggles of students off on the opposite side of the road outside the infirmary. Looking at the young, fresh-faced learners made me think of my desk in pieces back at the office. What was I going to do about those infernal instructions? Could I get an English set off the internet?

I froze. A chill ran down my back that wasn't being directed by the wind. I glanced over my shoulder and saw a youth stood a few metres behind me. He looked like he had come up the canal tow-path and was leaning casually against its stone entrance by the rambling ivy. I was sure I hadn't seen him as I'd passed it, but then my thoughts had been somewhat elsewhere. I stopped in my tracks and let my eyes study him. He was of average height and seemed slim of build, clothed in shabby jeans and a grey hoodie. What really grabbed my attention were his pale, grey-blue eyes that just stared at me from under his mop of dark, brown hair. I'm sure he didn't blink once.

I started to take a step towards him when I heard someone calling my name. I spun round towards the source of the voice and saw Philips hurrying towards me from White Cross. I flicked my eyes back round to the canal tow path and, surprise surprise, the boy was gone. I swore under my breath. I don't like mysteries and I don't like being spied on, but there was nothing that I

16

could do about it right now, so I fixed my professional smile on my face and walked over towards my host.

I have to say that the John O'Gaunt studios were not at all how I expected them to be. I guess it was Philips' slightly careworn appearance that had somewhat coloured my expectations, but the insides were rather quite swanky. The producer showed me in through the main entrance where I was smiled at and greeted by a pretty young receptionist who handed me a visitor's badge. Various bodies were milling around, traversing from one important location or office to another. I had to dodge quite a few people in my journey across the foyer. Philips led me down a bright, white corridor past a number of purple doors. "What's behind these?" I asked.

"Oh, these are our sets." He explained. "We have a limited amount of space here, obviously, so we only use five rooms and rotate the sets in them. The rest of the time the sets are stored away in the props department. They're sort of flat-pack, I guess."

I cringed at the use of the term "flat-pack", thinking once more about my desk-shaped nemesis, but he didn't seem to notice. I pointed to the nearest door. "So what's set up in here at the moment?"

"That would be 52, Acacia Drive – Mrs Haddock's house."

I looked blank.

"Mrs Haddock is played by Maggie."

"Ah," I said, and opened the door. Philips bustled behind me explaining that we really ought to go straight to his office as the actors were very busy and were waiting for us, but I just ignored him. I'd never been on a film set before so I wanted to have a look. It was a rather weird experience. When I walked through I was directly behind the cameras (there were two of them). Beyond that was a room that looked for all intents and purposes like my mother's living room: photos of relatives on the wall and toby jugs in a small corner cabinet.

"Mr Spallucci, time really is of the essence. We should be..."

Philips continued to blabber on as I entered the living room. I smiled. Yes, it really was like my mum's house. There was the gas fire and the hearth rug. There was the faded three-piece suite facing the telly. The curtains were drawn back and held in place with little ties.

I sat down on the sofa and stroked my chin. Well this certainly didn't feel satanic at all did it? I was suddenly aware that Philips had stopped yammering on. He was just stood staring at me. "Is there a problem? I asked.

"Mr Spallucci, I know that you are not accustomed to this environment, but please, please don't touch anything. Every item here will have been set out at the end of the last take and will be prepared for the next shooting."

I raised my arms, slightly worried that I may have inadvertently ruined the artistic forming of the sofa. "How come it's not being filmed on today?"

"Because its occupant is currently waiting outside my office," he sighed. "Now if you would kindly follow me?"

I stood up, making sure not to do anything as clumsy as kick the hearth rug and made to follow Philips. Just as I was passing the fire-place I stopped and glanced at a small ornament on the mantel. Now, on my *mum's* mantel, you will find a profusion of Leonardo figurines or china dogs. I was sure that she had never owned anything quite like this. It was a silver piece about ten centimetres tall. It seemed to be a lion with a long, serpentine tail and an extra head in the shape of a goat. Instinctively, I reached out and picked up the little figurine.

"Mr Spallucci!" Philips stomped over, grabbed the ornament and very carefully set it back in its exact position. "I told you not to touch anything. Now please, can we go?"

I gave the statuette a hard stare then nodded and walked out of the set.

Philips' office was not too far away – just through a couple of double doors and down a bending corridor. My sense of direction is not very good at the best of times and, away from natural light, I was completely lost. However, I knew that we had arrived before he could say anything, just by the sight that met my aching eyes. At first I thought I was imagining things. There in front of his office door, bickering maniacally was a woman who had been cloned and then subsequently been both aged and rejuvenated so that there were two versions of her – one in its late sixties and one in its early twenties. Not only that, but every seemingly decent cell had been sucked from her body and replaced by ones which screamed "Strumpet!" Such were the phenomena of Melanie Brande and Maggie Sothwell.

"Philips!" screeched the younger actress, Brande. "Where the hell have you been? I've been waiting ages. I haven't got all day, you know? I have a function to attend in two hours and I have to get myself ready." She shot

19

me a filthy look. "Who's this perv? He looks like a dirty mac man."

"This is Mr Samuel Spallucci. The investigator I told you about, Mel," Philips explained in a placatory manner. "He's here to talk to the thr-" He stopped short and frowned. "Where's Howard?"

"He's gone home, dear," said Sothwell. "Said he had important business to attend to. You know how impatient he can be." Her eyes fell on me and I saw an unmistakable twinkle in their pupils that made my libido want to run screaming for the middle of the Antarctic. "Well, hello, Mr Spallucci," she purred, offering her bejewelled hand. "Wonderful to meet you."

I politely shook her hand whilst my libido continued to hurriedly pack its belongings into a large suitcase. "Pleased to meet you too, Mrs Sothwell."

"Oh, please, young man. Call me Maggie," she giggled in a coquettish manner.

I smiled the smile a terrified rabbit gives the headlights of a large, oncoming truck and looked hopefully at Philips.

He coughed. "Perhaps, you would like to start by asking Melanie a few questions in my office? I will try to track down Howard whilst you do so."

I nodded quickly, gave Sothwell another quick smile of fear and rushed into Philips' office, followed by the sulky Miss Brande.

"You got a cigarette?"

"Pardon?" The question caught me off-guard. I was still trying to accustom myself to my latest set of surroundings. The office was small but impeccably neat. There were photographs of Philips posing with various actors plastered across one wall and awards displayed on another. The third wall was home to his desk and a number of filing cabinets. There were two chairs: Philips' desk chair and a red, leather sofa. Brande had folded herself onto the sofa and crossed her legs provocatively. I could not help but notice the top of a stocking peeking out from under her incredibly short skirt.

"I said, 'You got a cigarette?' You a retard as well as a perv?" She crossed her legs again.

I blushed and fished into my mac, drawing out a pack of Lucky Strikes. I flipped the lid and offered her one. She took it without so much as a thank-you. My guess was that Miss Brande was not very forthcoming in gratitude.

She popped the cigarette in her mouth and lifted an eyebrow expectantly? "What?" I asked.

She sighed and removed the cigarette. "A light?"

I reached into another pocket and retrieved my Zippo. I tossed it over to the brunette and sat on the desk chair. "Knock yourself out. Please," I grumbled.

She lit the Lucky then studied the lighter. "Fancy. Quite esoteric," she commented. "I've always liked pyramids. So... potent." She threw the Zippo back. I had better explain that it has a design of a pyramid with an eye emblazoned across the front wall. I've had it since it caught my eye as a student. It was a gift from... well let's just say "a friend" for now, shall we?

I pocketed the Zippo. "Well, here we are," I said.

"Indeed we are," Brande blew a smoke ring. "One young starlet and one ageing dirty mac man. Do you get over to Rylands park much?"

I ignored the quip and pressed on. "What can you tell me about Haversham?"

"Apart from the fact that he was a dirty old man?"

I groaned. "Do you think all men are perverts then?"

She shrugged and the shoulders of her red dress rose and fell causing her necklace to glint in the light of the office. "Only those over twenty-five. Those under are normally quite buff."

Buff? Did people still use that as a description? I shook my head and continued. "So? Tell me about Haversham." She opened her mouth to speak and I held up my hand with the smoking Lucky between my fingers. "Without any comments about his perviness."

Brande grimaced, inhaled heavily on her cigarette and pouted. "Not much to tell really. He was quiet, boring. Kept himself to himself really."

"What about his interests?"

"Dunno. Like I said. He kept himself to himself."

I was getting nowhere fast. "When was the last time you saw him?" I asked.

"On set two days ago. He seemed somewhat anxious." Brande fiddled with the hem of her red dress.

"What do you mean by anxious?"

"He was fidgety, jumpy. He kept snapping at us."

"Us?"

"Me, Maggie and Baines."

"What about the rest of the cast? What about the crew?"

She shook her head. "Nope. He was okay with them. Perhaps he was just having a luvvie fit?" She looked at her watch and stubbed the cigarette out on Philips' desk. "Can I go now? This is boring."

I had to admit that I was hardly enthralled myself. I nodded and stood up. As the actress made to stand, she leant forward and her pendant glinted in the light once more. I frowned and reached out, grasping it in my hand.

"Hey!" she shouted. "Get your filthy hands off of me!"

I twisted the pendant around and dangled it in front of her green eyes. "Do you know what this is?" I demanded, my face in front of hers.

"A necklace," she sneered and tried to wriggle free.

I pulled tighter. Brande gasped as the chain cinched around her neck. "Don't get smart with me. A man is missing and I have to find him." I pointed to the two-headed creature made from silver. "This is a chimera and I've seen another one of these quite recently."

There was a sharp slapping sound as Brande's palm connected with my cheek and I staggered backwards, dropping the pendant. She spat at me, turned and stormed out of the room. As I wiped her spit from my face I decided that perhaps the interview could have gone somewhat better.

I collapsed onto Philips' desk chair and groaned inwardly. This was sheer lunacy! What was I doing here? Earning a living, that's what, I told myself. It couldn't get any worse, I told myself. It couldn't.

There was a gentle knock at the door.

"Come on in!" I called.

The door swung open and the ageing figure of Maggie Sothwell swept in, a radiant, beaming smile filling her heavily made-up face. "Mr Spallucci, darling," she flounced, "I have been dying to meet you."

I bet you have, I thought.

"Roger has told me all about you."

"Roger?"

"Roger, darling. Roger Philips."

"Ah," I nodded. My *chat* with the fiery Brande had obviously disturbed my memory. "Please, Mrs Sothwell, take a seat." I waved towards the sofa.

Sothwell luxuriated herself down onto the forgiving upholstery. "Please, darling, like I said before, call me Maggie. Oh, this is so exciting. A real-life detective, here at our little studio. Have you solved many crimes, Mr Spallucci?"

I coughed and mumbled something placatory. I hardly had the heart to tell her that this was my first professional case since setting up in Dalton Square. "Well, Maggie, as you know, I'm investigating the disappearance of Malcolm Haversham. What can you tell me about him?"

"Oh, Malcolm was a delightful man. So attentive," her eyes glimmered.

I shuddered at just how attentive Sothwell liked her men to be. "You said 'was'. Do you think he's dead?"

"Who's to know, darling?" she shrugged making her voluminous bosom ripple under her tight–fitting dress. "I would imagine that things don't look very good for him though?"

"Why would that be?"

She leant forward conspiratorially, "Because of a phone call I overheard the other day, that's why?"

I nodded for her to continue.

"Well, darling, it was before we were about to go on set and Malcolm was missing, so I volunteered to go and find him. I was just about to knock on his dressing room door when I heard raised voices. I stood and listened, trying to make out the words, but it was no good. My other faculties may still all be there, but my hearing's not what it used to be. Then I heard him stomping up to the dressing room door so I hid round the corner. He came out in quite the fury, darling. He was shouting obscenities into the mobile and just before he hung up he said something like, 'You don't scare me. You're all mad, I say. Mad!' Then he pocketed the phone and marched off to the set. Most peculiar, don't you think?"

I tapped my teeth with my nails. Peculiar? I wasn't so sure. Convenient seemed more likely. I could smell a proverbial rat. Something here was about as phoney as a sun-tan in Lytham-St-Annes.

I asked Sothwell a few more questions and dodged a few of her more personal inquiries then graciously allowed her to get on with her life. I picked my hat up from Philips' desk and twisted it round and round between my hands. My investigation was moving in a similar direction to my fedora: in circles. Two interviews and all I had achieved was an overwhelming feeling that the two female leads of *More Tea Vicar* were more concerned with their sex lives than the disappearance of Haversham.

I stood up and kicked the sofa. I was frustrated. Totally frustrated. There was nothing, just spurious hints and futile dead ends.

Except...

As I made my way to the office door I turned over in my mind the image of the two-headed chimera. Brande had the necklace and there was the statue in Sothwell's fictional home. Was there a connection?

I didn't know, but if Baines appeared to possess such a symbol then perhaps... just perhaps. I walked out of the office and went to hunt down Philips. I needed Baines' address.

Sociologists may argue against me, but I believe that Lancaster can be divided into four really distinct social groups. At the bottom and, as in most cities, most prolific are the working class. This is itself split into two groups. There are those who are either looking for or have jobs (such as in the high street shops or on the numerous industrial estates), then there are those who don't want a job and will never look for one until the day that the council throws them into a pauper's grave. The workers/work-seekers in this group are the salt of the earth. They may not be the most academically intelligent but they are grafters and make sure that their families are well-fed and cared for. The work-shy ones, well, how can I put it politely? Hmmm. I can't. They're losers. They will harass you for a quid with some sob story about needing to save up for a train ticket or a meal and then go and piss it up a wall or shoot it up their arm. Both of these sub-groups tend to live in areas dominated by small terraces or semis that used be council housing but have been gradually sold off to make quick capital for the permanently broke local authorities. The former group hate the latter and the latter just don't give a shit.

The second class of Lancastrians tend to be the imports. They are, on the whole, the liberal middle-class. Normally, they are university graduates who liked the area so much that they decided that it would be a wonderful place to settle down, co-habit and raise three bratty children called Louis, Penny and Lyle. In the early eighties they were solid Labour. Now they are true Green and would happily have solar panels on every inch of the roof of their converted Victorian terrace house if it wasn't going to look just so very unsightly. I don't have much time for this class, the pompous, sanctimonious floating voters. In fact, I probably have to say I prefer the jobless winos to these folk-singing, arran clad, body-shopping hypocrites.

Anyway, onto the third class. These are the ones whose families have been here the longest. These are the old money in Lancaster. They vote Tory but I just can't hold it against them as they quietly get on with their lives. They will normally have a rambling pile out in Scotforth somewhere or a family farm on the edge of the city. I will never be able to agree with their political views but I respect them for holding true to what they actually believe rather than following the latest fad or trying to stab someone in the back to climb up the social ladder. Which brings me onto the fourth class.

These are what would have been called the bourgeoisie many years ago. Marx would have hated them. These would originally have been in the working class or the middle class. However, somewhere along the line, the greed for money and power has infected them. They have turned their backs on those who supported them when times were hard. They have scurried off to a private estate somewhere and surrounded themselves in their own personal red brick fortress complete with a trampoline for the snobby offspring. These they ship out to Cumbria for schooling rather than pollute them with anti-social ideas from local children. They shop in Preston or Manchester and the husband works even further afield whilst the wife stays at home to cook, clean and drink gin.

Needless to say, when I drew up outside Baines' spacious mock Tudor house, my view of him was already somewhat coloured. As I crunched my way up his winding gravel path, I glanced over my shoulder at my 1983 Polo and sighed. Perhaps my animosity to this sort of set up was jealousy. Perhaps it was a feeling of injustice. Whatever it was, I knew that I would end up giving the guy a hard time and thoroughly enjoy it. I rapped the ornate door-knocker and waited a few moments until the door opened. A tall, grey man with a slight stoop peered down at me with a condescending glare. No, honest! He was! I'm not letting my prejudices colour your first encounter of him. He had the look of someone who feels that everyone else is totally beneath him. "Philips said you were coming," he sneered. "I suppose you'd better come in."

So I did.

I have to be truthful here, the inside of the house was rather nice. I had expected fake wooden panelling and a roaring fire, but it was quite minimalist with a distinct lack of clutter accentuated by crisp, sharp edges. Nice and tidy, just how I like my living spaces myself. "You were late at the studio so I had to leave," Baines explained as he walked ahead of me, giving me plenty of opportunity to study the back of his stooped, black-clad figure. He really was quite tall, a good head height above me. It was no wonder that he stooped. "Damned inconsiderate keeping us all hanging about like that. I really don't see what all the fuss is." He opened a stark, white door and gestured for me to enter.

"I would have thought that you would be

concerned for Haversham," I commented as I entered the room which was a mixture of office-cum-study. There was a large grey desk positioned slap bang in the middle of the floor with one wall full to the brim of books opposing a wall that was complete glass, overlooking an expansive garden.

What really caught my eye, though, was a sketched drawing mounted in a large frame on the wall behind the desk. I crossed the room, all thoughts of Haversham momentarily swept from my mind, my eyes fixed to the picture.

"You like that?" Baines asked, a touch of warmth in his voice. "Curious piece, isn't it? It was a gift. Apparently it's from Greek mythology. It's a..."

"Chimera," I finished as I let my eyes skip from the goat's to the lion's head and down the serpentine tail. It was truly a fine piece of work. I could make out every muscle, every sinew down the twisting spine of the creature as it rose up on its hind legs to attack me. "Who was it a gift from?" I asked.

"No one that you would know," Baines answered dreamily as he drew level and gazed lovingly at the piece of artwork. "I'm not normally one for receiving gifts as, all too often, they come with a price – but I just couldn't say, 'No,' to this. The picture was calling out to me. Does that make sense?"

I nodded, unable to speak as I continued to be drawn into every last detail of the artist's vivid imagination.

"It's not the first time I've seen this chap today." I whispered, "Melanie Brande wears one round her neck and there is a statue of one on the set of *More Tea Vicar*."

Baines turned to face me. "Really?" I tore my eyes away from the creature and studied his response. He seemed genuinely surprised. "That's funny. I've not noticed." He moved away and sat behind his desk, his hands clasped together. I gave the picture one last glance and walked back around in front of him.

"So why is it you're not concerned for Haversham?" I asked once more.

Baines gave a non-committal shrug of his rounded shoulders. "The man's an oaf, a drama queen. He will have suffered some sort of hissy fit and flounced off somewhere for a week or two before gliding back in all sweetness and light, saying how he has missed us all, his dear friends, so terribly, terribly much."

Baines' voice dripped acid and contempt.

"Are you saying this has happened before?"

"God yes!" Baines harrumphed. "A number of times. "The man is completely unreliable. Something normally sets him off and he goes walkabout."

I tapped my teeth and considered Sothwell's description of Haversham's phone conversation. It did seem to fit with what Baines was saying. I reached into my inside pocket and pulled out the envelope containing the letter. "What do you make of this?" I asked as I passed it over.

Baines peered down at the pentagram then slowly opened the envelope and withdrew the letter. He gave it a quick glance and snorted his contempt. "Did Philips give you this?"

I nodded.

He slowly shook his head. "That man is a complete cretin." He waved the letter in the air and said,

"I'd recognise this handwriting anywhere. It's Haversham's!"

By the time I slumped down into my armchair in my flat above my Dalton Square office, my head hurt. I grabbed the stereo remote and flicked it on. The calming sounds of Mike Oldfield wafted around my living room and I closed my eyes. I was stressed. I could tell this because the sound of multi-instrumental genius was not the only accompaniment playing in my ears. The infernal sound of the tiniest bells ever cast were jangling furiously in my head. I suffer from tinnitus. I've had it since I was a kid and it's more or less constant, but it's normally a background noise, a whisper that I hardly ever register. However, when things start to stress me out, it's all that I can hear, all that I really notice. Everything else gets swept aside in the rushing waves of tintinnabulation and my head screams for quiet. So as I sat there, my eyes clenched tight, I did what I normally do in this situation: I turned the music up loud and grabbed the bottle of Jack Daniel's from its space on the floor next to my chair. I poured a large measure and downed it in one then lit myself a Lucky Strike. The smoke sank deep into my lungs and I coughed, but it was a good cough, a satisfying cough. A deep harsh sound that could punch through those wretched bells!

I poured another glass of whiskey and sat deep in thought. Something smelt as fishy as the docks at Glasson. I pulled the now well-read letter out of my pocket and scanned its scrawling script once more. Baines claimed that this was Haversham's hand-writing. This meant one of two things: either Haversham had faked his own abduction or Baines was lying. As I sipped at the bourbon I considered both of these points. Brande hated Haversham, but then she seemed to hate most people of the opposite sex from a certain age upwards. Sothwell claimed that Haversham had been arguing on the phone the day before he disappeared. Was that connected? Was it fabricated? Philips claimed that Brande, Haversham and Sothwell were all Satanists. Was this true or just speculation?

The truth of the matter was that I had no hard and fast facts to base anything on. There was just a possibly fabricated letter and a bunch of hearsay. Marvellous! I drained the whiskey glass and looked outside the window across the square. It was getting dark, twilight. A good time to go snooping around when no one would spot you. If you try and snoop during the night, then you might as well wear a black and white striped sweater and carry a bag marked "swag". Someone will instantly spot you in the empty street and either call the police or confront you. If you venture out when day is just ending and night is falling, then there are enough people around for background cover. You can blend into the last stragglers as they wend their tired way home from a long hard day's work. You are just another faceless, nameless body swept along in the daily grind.

It was time for a good snoop around the John O'Gaunt studios. This was the only place I had which was tangible, which linked the players in my little drama together. I got up and made my way to the door when my mobile started to vibrate in my pocket. I fished it out and flicked it on. "Hello?" I asked.

"Mr Spallucci?" It was Philips. I raised an eyebrow. Don't you just love synchronicity?

"Speaking. What can I do for you Mr Philips?"

"I... I'm at the studio," he whispered. "There's something going on. There's something you ought to see. Please come quickly. Please... Oh no!" The phone clicked dead.

I stood staring into my mobile as if it could explain to me what had just happened. "The plot thickens," I muttered to myself and walked out of my flat.

I was back at John O'Gaunt studios in approximately ten minutes. The sky was turning a deep indigo shade of purple and Venus was hovering over the stone crenellations of White Cross Industrial Estate. Quite apt, I thought to myself, that the Daystar known in antiquity as Lucifer should be watching over a supposed satanic cult.

I cut away from the meandering traffic of late commuters and wandering students and made down the approach towards the entrance to the studios outside the main gate of the estate. I made sure that I did not look suspicious and refrained from checking over my shoulder before trying the front door – I was just another employee entering the studio on mundane business.

The door swung inwards and I was left peering into a dark corridor. "No lights on, but there must be somebody home," I muttered to myself and quickly stepped inside. I closed the door behind me and drew a small penlight out from my mac. The small beam flicked across the plush, carpeted floor of the main corridor and exposed no stumbling blocks or protrusions so I carefully ventured along the gloomy passage. The corridor was, dare I say, deathly quiet. The sound of my footfalls were cushioned by the pile of the well-trodden but immaculately clean carpet. All I was aware of was the sound of my breath and the tinny ringing in my ears. I'm not one for dark spaces. I used to wake screaming as a child, crying for my poor parents to turn all the lights on before I would even try to return to some semblance of infant slumbering. As I cautiously edged my way through the premises towards Philips' office, my mind kept telling me that creatures of unimaginable grotesqueness would leap out from around a blind corner and proceed to rip my head off then devour my innards. I could feel tension starting to increase in my body. My shoulders were starting to ache and I was aware of my heart pounding. This was not good; higher blood pressure affects tinnitus. I stopped for a moment as I drew near to Philips' office and leant against a wall. Sure enough, the ringing in my ears was gradually crescendoing. I concentrated and tried to slow my heart rate by breathing slowly, but it was no use, the old ticker was beating faster than ever.

Damn it! I swung the pen light around the corner and, after seeing nothing, decided I just had to press on regardless of the irritation in my ears. I leant up against the office door and pressed my already overloaded ear up against the purple painted wood. I could hear nothing apart from those noises that existed purely in my head. I swore and slowly edged the door open. It silently swung half way then came to an abrupt stop. I pushed a bit harder but it did not budge an iota. My hand was shaking as I swept the light around behind the door. First, it found a pair of black, highly polished shoes, then the legs of a grey suit lying limp on the floor. I rushed in and bent to grab Philips by the shoulders. I gripped the penlight in my mouth as I used both hands to turn his body over. It almost dropped from the grip of my teeth when he opened his eyes and smiled at me.

The next thing I knew was a heavy blow to the back of my neck, then there was just darkness.

When I came to, I realised that I was in a most unfortunate predicament. Aside from the fact that the back of my neck was throbbing, I was also somehow bound hand and foot to the floor. As I wrestled with my bonds I dared to move my head in order to survey my situation.

It was dire.

I was tied down in the centre of a pentagram.

The day just seemed to be getting worse.

As I tugged hopelessly I heard the steady, confident footsteps that I knew would be Baines. Even the sound of his shoes sounded as smooth as his crooning baritone. "Ah, Mr Spallucci. I see you are awake. Very good. We would not want you to miss the fun now, would we?"

"You call this fun?" I asked. "This is about as much fun as a Saturday night in Skerton. Ow!"

My left side erupted in pain as the sharp toe-end of a patent high heel shoe jabbed into me. "I grew up in Skerton, you old git!" The delightful Miss Brande.

"Well that explains a lot," I shot back. I received another sharp kick, but it was worth it to see her riled. I really hated that little bitch. Like Baines, she was adorned in a long, flowing scarlet red robe, although hers was cut short enough to show off a decent amount of leg. Didn't people only wear that sort of thing on dodgy websites? You know the sort – www.saucy-wiccans.com.

I could hear hushed voices from my right and turned my head to see the source. There was the miraculously not-dead Philips and the blue-rinsed Sothwell conversing with an elderly man adorned in a shock of white hair. "Ah, the eponymous Malcolm Haversham, I presume?" I called out cheerfully.

The white-haired man turned round and his blue eyes twinkled as they fixed on me. "The hardly-renowned Mr Samuel C Spallucci, I presume?" he returned as he bowed his head slightly.

I shrugged as best as I could with my arms at obtuse angles from my body, "It's been a short career so far."

"And it will remain so," Haversham commented as he held out his right hand, palm up. Baines shuffled up beside him and placed a cruel looking dagger in his grasp. "You see, Mr Spallucci, we really cannot allow a gentleman of your profession to wander aimlessly around our little city whilst we practice our dark, nefarious deeds, can we, hmmm? You might inadvertently cause us some sort of bother. So we decided that we ought to lure you here somehow to despatch you quickly and quietly. At first we thought that my abduction would suffice but, alas, our acting could not have been of great merit as you did not readily devour the bait. So we had to resort to another staged abduction over the telephone, and quite a performance it was too," he said towards Philips, who stood and beamed as the others actually began to clap him.

"No, please. You're too kind," Philips protested. "It was nothing, really."

I shook my head in despair. Apparently I was about to be sacrificed by a cult of self-congratulating luvvies. "But you had me here this afternoon. Why didn't you just kill me then?"

Haversham looked genuinely horrified at the suggestion. "What? In just the second act? Where would be the build-up? Where would be the suspense? No, Mr Spallucci, you had to leave us and go away to brood over the matter for a while whilst the viewer tried to piece the mystery together with you." He smiled the sort of smile an old uncle gives a young lad who is trying to ride his wobbly little bike down the street for the first time.

"The viewer?"

"Yes, the viewer, Mr Spallucci. It is always about engaging the viewer in the story. Anyway, you are now at the end of the show and about to be removed from the picture, as it were. No hard feelings."

My blood ran cold. "None taken," I croaked and began yanking hard at the fastenings around my wrists.

Haversham casually polished the wicked edge of the curved blade with a golden-coloured cloth. "I really wouldn't exert yourself, Mr Spallucci. Those fastenings are quite secure. You would only hurt yourself, and we wouldn't want that would we, hmmm?"

I stared at him incredulously. Wouldn't want me to hurt myself? What the hell did he think the knife would do? Give me a soothing back massage? The guy was a complete fruit cake! They all were. How had I managed to let myself be snared in by bunch of five imbeciles.

Five.

Imbeciles.

Those words rang a bell. Why? Why did they sound so vitally important? As the five Satanists rounded on me and Haversham started to chant in a low, menacing voice, I desperately tried to wrack my fear-stricken memory for a glimmer of hope. However, my memory was currently curled up in a dark corner gibbering into its jumper which was pulled up over its head. As Haversham raised the knife I imagined myself bending down to coax my poor little memory out of its paralysis with a small packet of peanuts.

Peanuts.

Dry roasted peanuts.

Spliff!

The Satanists were now stood at the five points of the pentagram. I double-checked the lines on the floor. My head was in one of the points and Haversham was behind me which meant the symbol was facing upwards, not down.

The knife started to arc down through the air of the film set.

"YOUR PENTAGRAM IS THE WRONG WAY UP!!!" I shrieked and closed my eyes.

There was silence and no searing pain in my chest - which I took to be a good thing. Tentatively I squeezed an eyelid open and peered through. Haversham's outstretched arms were being held in place by the strong grip of Howard Baines. It appeared that I had been granted a reprieve, if only momentarily. I would have to think fast.

"What do you mean that it's the wrong way up?" growled the deep baritone of Baines.

"I would have thought you would have done your research," I said, my mind racing ten to the dozen.

Haversham had now lowered the knife and was peering at me from a rather surreal upside down angle. "In what way, hmmm? It is the Sigil of Baphomet, a most dark image indeed."

I shook my head. "Sorry to disappoint you, but not the way you're using it. With my head here, it's the five

38

wounds of Christ. You have me tied down the wrong way."

Brande swore such words that were most unbecoming of a young lady and spat, "He's lying! The old git's lying to save his worthless neck."

Sothwell waved a pacifying hand at her to calm the firebrand down. "But what if he isn't dear? What if we make a pointless sacrifice? Surely that would displease the dark lord?"

Baines towered above me. "How are we supposed to believe you, Spallucci? Melanie has a very valid point. You could just be trying to trick us."

I smiled. "Surely one of you has a phone on you? Go online and check Wikipedia. I bet it's on there. There you go. Wikipedia, the fount of all knowledge, scientific and arcane."

"There's no need."

I turned my head and frowned. It was Philips that had spoken, but there was something about his voice. It seemed distant, far away.

"He speaks the truth. He is positioned wrong. We must move him," and in one graceful move he had knelt down and unhitched from the floor the clasp that held my left wrist. This would be my only chance. I gripped the fabric and whipped the heavy clasp around behind my head. It lashed around Haversham's ankles and I pulled hard. Normally, I don't think it would have worked, but he must have been caught off guard and he toppled over to his left into Baines who was too busy shouting at Philips to see the white-haired actor collapse on top of him.

I yanked my left hand free, lashing and all, and scrabbled to free my right hand. Just as my fingers had prised the clasp open I felt a weight pounce on me and a sharp set of nails dug into my neck. I rolled back and slammed Brande heavily onto the floor. She shrieked and fell limp, winded.

I pulled myself to my feet and quickly assessed the situation. Brande was winded. Haversham seemed to have struck his head and was out cold. Sothwell was staggering over to try and help Baines to his feet. Philips... Philips was just stood staring into thin air.

I shrugged. I had no time to wonder what was going on there. I caught sight of the knife and flew at it. Just as I grasped its cold hilt, a black polished shoe crunched down on my wrist. I yelped in agony then cried out as another shoe kicked me in the face. I fell back down on the floor and felt blood welling up in my left nostril as a fully recovered Baines reached down and prised the knife from my weakened grip. "Mr Spallucci," he menaced, "you appear to be far more resourceful than we had imagined. Sacrifice be damned! I'm finishing you now!" His face glowered as he fished a small revolver out of his robes and levelled it at my face. Then something rather peculiar happened. His aim faltered and he blinked as he dropped the gun with a loud clatter and backed off quickly. "No. No. No!" he shouted, waving his hands in front of him. "It can't be. You can't be that! It's not real. I only did it for the kudos. I never really believed in you." He was staring right at me and tears were streaming down his face as terror held him fast. He sank to his knees and buried his head in his hands and wept loudly. Puzzled, I drew myself up off the floor and instinctively slipped the revolver into my coat pocket before taking in my surroundings. Sothwell was the only other person not incapacitated or a gibbering wreck. She shot a worried frown at the gun-shaped bulge in my pocket before deciding that enough was enough and darted for the set's exit. She didn't get very far as the door was flung open and a group of uniformed policemen barged through, sending her flying. They raced into the room, batons raised and an authoritative voice boomed from behind them, "Nobody move! Police!" A tall, dark-skinned plain-clothes officer strode commandingly between the bobbies as they took up position around the varying members of the cast. "What the hell have we got here?" he demanded.

"DCI Patel?" I asked as I wobbled to my feet and stretched my hand out. "Sam Spallucci. Pleased to meet you."

Jitendra Patel grabbed my hand and helped me up. His dark eyes scanned the five actors then fixed themselves on me. "You have the office in Dalton Square, yes?"

I nodded.

"Would you care to enlighten me as to why we received a 999 call saying that you were about to be murdered here?"

I frowned and watched in a state of bewilderment as the policemen started to cuff my captors and read them their rights. Haversham took quite a bit of rousing and Philips seemed as if someone had laced his tea with Diazepam, but the most disturbing sight was that of Baines. As he was bundled past me he screamed in absolute terror. "Get me away from him! He will kill us all! He will kill us all!"

My spine felt icicles slide down its vertebrae. I looked back at DCI Patel. "I have no idea who rang you. I didn't tell anyone I was coming."

"It would seem that you have a guardian angel,

41

then, Mr Spallucci," he smiled.

I smiled back and grimaced. My face hurt. "Please, call me Sam." I stuck out my right hand, this time in friendship, rather than a call for assistance.

The detective took it and shook it firmly. "Jitendra. Pleased to make your acquaintance. Listen, you look pretty beat up and we have a few questions to ask, obviously. Would you mind if one of my men dropped you off at your place to clean up then bring you back to the station?"

I ran my hand through my hair. "Sure," I agreed. "Get it out of me while it's still fresh."

"That's the idea. We'll go over this place with a fine tooth-comb." He strode over to Brande and hoisted her to her feet. "Come on you. Time for another show, and no play-acting." Brande said nothing. She just scowled as Jitendra and another officer led her away. As they walked past I saw something glint and tinkle as it hit the wooden floor. I bent down and scooped it up. It was Brande's silver pendant of the chimera. I looked at the mythological creature and ran a fingernail over my teeth. This little fellow seemed to have been everywhere, but it seemed to bear no significance to the Satanists at all. No one was watching me so I slipped it into my mac pocket next to the purloined revolver and headed towards the door of the studio where a policeman stood talking on his radio.

Thirty minutes later I was walking stiffly up the stairs to my flat whilst a bobby was parked up outside the Paradise Dragon. I felt as if had spent twenty-four hours in a gigantic tumble-dryer. I was hot and sweaty and my muscles screamed at every movement. I fished my keys out of my pocket and made to insert them into my lock.

I paused.

There was an envelope tacked to my door. It was addressed, "Sam."

I groaned inwardly. I had endured my fill of mysterious envelopes for the day, but I pulled it down and thumbed it open. When I realised what it contained, I could not help but smile. Whether the smile was one of joy or worry I was not totally sure, but I was certainly glad of the item that I now held in my hand. It was the assembly instructions for my office desk, in English. Scrawled across the bottom was a short message. "Sam. If you are reading this then the police arrived in the nick of time." I groaned at the awful pun. "I hope this will be of use to you as you seemed very troubled on the matter of your desk earlier. We shall meet soon. Alec."

Alec?

Who the hell was Alec?

Then it struck me, the boy standing outside White Cross when I was on my way to meet Philips. I had been thinking about the desk when he had been watching me. But how had he known my thoughts?

I shuddered. It was creepy. Very creepy. Nonetheless, I apparently owed the young man my life and more importantly, I decided as I looked at the plans for the desk, my sanity. Yes, young Alec, I thought to myself, I look forward to meeting you soon. I opened my flat door and stepped inside. There was a policeman waiting for me downstairs and I still needed to finish building my desk.

The Case of The Vexed Vampire.

Needless to say, after my little escapade with the five bungling Satanists, I decided that I needed to relax, to chill out, to curl up in a ball and cry "Mummy!" So, after tightening up the final screw of my chipboard nemesis, I did what I normally do when I'm stressed, I slipped downstairs to the Paradise Dragon to eat until I felt fit to burst.

"Sam!" cried Harry Kim, the restaurant's owner, as I walked through the glass doors that were adorned with red and black dragons, "Good to see you, old man. How are you?" He frowned then said, "No, don't tell me. You look like shit!"

I chuckled and removed my hat and mac which the restaurateur went and hung up by the kitchens. "Observant as ever, Harry," I called as I wandered over to my usual corner just behind the reception area, giving me a clear view of Dalton Square.

A bottle of sake in a warming jug was placed on the table next to me along with a small china cup as Harry came and sat down opposite. "You been working too hard, my friend?" he asked, his face obviously worried. "Too many..." he wiggled his fingers in front of me like epileptic worms, "ghosties and goblins?"

I poured a cup of sake and downed it in one. "I wish," I grumbled. "Too many bloody actors."

"Actors? Actors?" Harry gave a feigned look of amazement. "Already you going into movies, my friend? You should write a book."

I laughed. Good old Harry. He always cheers me up.

"So what will it be then, Harrison Ford?" he winked. "Spicy bean curd and boiled rice, am I right?"

"As ever Harry." I downed two more cups of sake and waved the half-empty bottle, "Another one of these beauties too, eh?"

"Of course, my friend. I'm sure you've earned it." Harry bustled off shouting in Cantonese at waiters and kitchen staff alike, sending them into a frenzy of chopstick polishing and napkin arranging. I reached into my jacket pocket and pulled out a thin wallet that I had brought downstairs with me and pulled out my own personal chopsticks. Whereas most chopsticks are either a light type of wood or plastic, these are made from ebony. Their blunt ends are capped in sterling silver and their business ends are sharpened to a fine point, enabling even the clumsiest of diners to skewer the most difficult to grab piece of bean curd. I slowly polished them on my napkin before laying them down on the table next to my right hand. They were a present from my parents when I graduated. Neither of them had ever tasted Chinese food in their lives and had no idea as to why I loved the stuff, but they just accepted that it was my thing and they bought me the best present that they could afford. I clicked my teeth together and ran a finger along the sleek, dark wood. I thought about my mobile sat in my pocket next to my hip. I could get it out and speed dial number 2. I could talk to Mum and see how she was. I could ask about the neighbours and what the weather was like down there.

But I wouldn't.

She would want to talk about Dad. She always wanted to talk about Dad. It had been almost twenty years and still the conversation came back to him. So my phone stayed in my pocket and words were left unsaid.

Instead I finished off the first bottle of sake.

Half an hour later and I was feeling warm and content. I had a belly full of bean curd and a liver full of sake. I sank back in my chair and stretched my arms out above me. My Tissot watch slipped down my wrist into my shirt sleeve. I slipped it back out and glanced at the time. Eight thirty. The night was still young. It was only Monday but town would still be relatively busy in an hour or so. I peered through the entrance of the shop out towards Dalton Square. The sky was dark and the street lights were bright. A large pair of googly eyes was bouncing up and down the windows of the office block opposite. God, I hated them. When they built that monstrosity about four years ago, some idiot had the great idea to install programmable light bulbs on the windows. Not only is it a complete waste of electricity, but some of the designs they come up with are totally pathetic. Rain in April, snow in December, fireworks in November. Then for the rest of the year great big googly eyes wandering from left to right, staring inanely at passers-by. It's like big brother stoned out on the biggest ever joint of marijuana.

I had to get away from their lunatic scrutiny. There was only one obvious place to go. I slipped a tenner onto the table, grabbed my hat and coat, waved goodbye to Harry, lit myself a Lucky Strike and headed off towards the Borough.

Only a couple of cars had to brake and honk their horns at me tonight. Much fewer than normal. I waved cheerily at the angered drivers. It was the least that I could do. I finished the cigarette as I reached the Borough and stubbed it out on the bin outside the pub then entered inside. It was already quite busy. People were milling around and ordering drinks. I looked over to the window and my heart sank. There was someone sat in my chair. Now, normally when this happens I pull the old, "There's a phone call for you at the bar," routine. Tonight, however, the couple sat in the window seats did not look like they would fall for such an old line. They were a man and a woman. He looked like he was in his forties or fifties, immaculately dressed and a fine claret-coloured cravat adorned his neck. She seemed quite a bit younger with short, dark hair, pale skin and a youthful complexion. They were sat silently, watching the world outside, quite oblivious to the humdrum of the pub. They were firmly rooted. I was sure they would not move.

So I dragged myself disconsolately to the bar. This was even worse. It was absolutely heaving. There must have been a function going on upstairs as loads of suited and booted types were jostling for drinks whilst painted ladies preened themselves and gossiped over fancy handbags. I sighed and was about to give up hope when I felt a finger tap on my shoulder.

"Hey you!"

I turned and saw Grace's little face beaming up at me from under her woolly hat. "Hi," I said. I noticed that she was in her civvies. "You not working tonight?"

"Just knocked off," she said. Her eyes wandered over to the window. "Oh no! You, like, lost your seat. Bummer!"

"I know. Quite the odd couple, aren't they?"

Grace nodded, little bangs of ginger curls bobbing up and down from under her hat. "You can say that again. They came in about fifteen minutes ago, ordered their drinks and have just sat there not saying a word. Creepazoids, if you ask me."

I smiled, then looked back at the bar. It was still solid. I sighed.

"You could always come clubbing with me," Grace volunteered. "I'm off to the Sugar House in about an hour or so. I could come and call for you... if you wanted that is?" Her young, innocent face smiled up expectantly.

The Sugar House is the local student-run night club. It is full of loud, ramshackle music, sweaty bodies and herbal-smelling toilets. "Thanks for the offer, but it's not really my thing."

"Oh." Grace looked somewhat disappointed, then her eyes twinkled and she motioned to the crowd at the bar. "It's a rugby do. I've heard they're planning, you know, karaoke later."

I looked down at the grinning little face and laughed. "Why on earth would you want to drag an old fogey like me to one of your hip and trendy night-clubs? Won't I ruin your street cred?"

She shrugged. "Doesn't bother me. Besides, you'll be miserable if you stay here tonight and you know it."

I looked at the bar then at the two creepazoids and nodded. She was right. It felt like my sanctuary had been violated. "What time did you say?"

"Call for you about ten?"

I looked at my watch. It was just coming up to nine. "Okay," I relented, "but the first drink's on you."

The happy student grinned and flicked me a little salute. "No problemo!" she chirped. "I'll see ya laters!"

I smiled as she bounced out of the Borough. She really is a nice kid. I gave the busy pub one more miserable sweep with my eyes and walked out into the night air.

Half an hour later I had showered, smoked about four Luckies, downed a couple of glasses of Jack and sat on the edge of my bed looking at various arrangements of clothes. I'm not a big fashionista and I tend to keep it simple: suit, mac and fedora. That's all I've ever needed. They keep me warm and dry and to me that is the main function of clothing, but tonight I was apparently going clubbing and I felt that I needed to change my attire somewhat. I held up a pair of plain, black trousers. They seemed okay to me, but would they be somewhat formal? I held up a pair of jeans next to them. Am I too old to wear denim these days? I am almost forty after all. I clicked my teeth together as I mulled the quandary over, then thought, "Sod it!" and pulled the jeans on. I hadn't worn them for a while and was worried that they might suffer from middle-aged snugness, but the zip pulled up fine and showed no signs of going south on its own.

Okay, so that was the leg department. What should I wear on top? I was just evaluating the merits of a plain, green tee over a lightweight shirt with buttons when I heard a pounding from downstairs. I paused with the shirts in my hands and listened. There it was again. Someone was hammering on my office door. I dragged the t-shirt over my head and ventured to the door of my flat.

Now there was a raised voice accompanying the knocking. A male voice was calling out my name. Slowly, I opened the flat door and peered over the banister. The voice and the knocking continued, but I could not see far enough to make out who was the source of the racket so I had to venture down to the half-landing between my flat and the office level. The sight that met my eyes was not really what I had been expecting.

There, hammering on my office door was a tall man in his late twenties/early thirties wearing a basin cut dark-haired wig (at least I hoped it was a wig – would anyone have their hair cut like that?) a tattered tight blue top, black trousers that stopped above his ankles and (this is the best bit) plastic pointy ears.

I coughed loudly and the stranger turned to face me. His features were neat and angular and his shirt really was quite messed up. He fixed his eyes on me and stared up the staircase. Silence hung between us waiting for one of us to speak. He looked kind of nervous and worry creased his basin-topped forehead, so I decided to break the ice. I lifted up my right hand, spread my ring and little fingers to the right and said, "Live long and prosper?"

For a moment the stranger stood looking up at my hand then he just slumped to the floor and started banging his head against my door before burying it into his hands and sobbing loudly. Not the effect that I had hoped for, I had to admit.

Cautiously I descended the stairs and approached the crying man. I crouched down and reached a hand onto his juddering shoulder. "Hey, calm down. I'm sure it's not that bad," I reassured him.

He kept his face buried in his hands and wailed, "Live long and prosper! Live long and prosper! What a joke! What an absolute joke!"

"Sorry, mate. I didn't mean to upset you."

"It's not you. It's me."

"Why's that then?"

"I'm going to live long, that's for sure, but I don't think I'll prosper."

I was now feeling as confused as a dairy farmer at a Vegan Society convention. "Why do you say that?"

You know how they say that the cheetah is the fastest land animal on the planet? Well that night I think I broke the big cat's record when I shot back up the stairs into my flat after the crying man turned his face towards me, bared a very sharp pair of fangs and said, "Because I'm a vampire, that's why."

Okay, so I've read *Dracula* and I've seen *Buffy the Vampire Slayer*. Vampires can't enter your house without an invitation. I was just hoping that applied to rented properties too. I mean, it had to, surely? My name was on the lease, wasn't it? I had signed a lease. I was sure I'd signed a lease. I scanned my living room for something I could use to defend myself with. Holy water was out, as was garlic. A cross? As the sound of footsteps trudged wearily up the wooden staircase I darted across the room and took a wooden crucifix down from the wall. Not very big, but then size wasn't important was it? I certainly hoped not and if it was I would go and haunt the descendants of Sigmund Freud.

I turned and saw him stood in the doorway. He was shaking his head. "I was kind of hoping that you would respond a bit different to that," he sulked. "I thought you were a specialist in this field?"

"What? In bloodsuckers?" I asked, and held the crucifix in front of me.

The vampire looked at the cross then back at me and shook his head. He ran his long fingers through his black wig and groaned, "Oh, this is all going so wrong. I'm not here to suck your blood. I'm here for your help."

I slightly lowered the crucifix and said, "My help?"

He nodded and I could see small red rivulets forming in the corner of his eyes. "I had nowhere to go, no one to turn to. You seemed like my best bet. I got one of your fliers in my shop."

Now I was really confused. "Your shop? Vampires are in the retail business?"

The vampire sighed. "I've only just been made a vampire. I own the sci-fi book shop down on North Road. Last night I was hit by a car. The last thing I remember was an awful lot of pain and this woman bending down over me. Then tonight I woke up like this."

"She dressed you up as Zachary Quinto?"

He placed his hands on his hips and glowered at me. "No! I was on my way back from a sci-fi convention when the car hit me. I woke up as a vampire." He paused. "Anyway, for your information I am dressed as Leonard Nimoy, the original and true Spock, not some psychotic brain stealer from *Heroes*."

"Sorry," I apologised. Jeez, the guy had issues. "So what am I supposed to do for you then?"

He shrugged. "Help me find out what I'm supposed to do now. It's not as if she left me a manual or anything. I guess there must be certain rules and procedures."

My fingers drummed my teeth as I looked at the door-frame between us. "Yeah... rules and procedures." I looked at the crucifix in my hand. I looked back at the vampire. He didn't seem like a crazed blood-sucker and the ripped top certainly seemed to weigh out his story about the car accident. "Okay, I'll help."

He smiled slightly. "Thank you. Now hadn't you better invite me in?"

"Oh, because of the door thing?"

"No! Because it's very rude keeping me stood out here in the cold."

I hesitated as I processed this little snippet of information and he sighed, "Never mind," and just walked straight across the threshold. "You might as well put that away too," he commented, taking the crucifix out of my hand. "Apparently, apart from the sunlight thing, a lot of the myths about vampires are just that: myths."

I suddenly felt like a rabbit having invited a fox to afternoon tea in its burrow. For Christ's sake I had a bona fide blood-feasting monster in my flat! What the hell was I thinking? Would he turn on me and have himself a little night-time snack? Was I a walking pantry, full of delectable midnight feasts? I sincerely hoped not. I watched him intently as he paced around the living room, his eyes scanning his surroundings. "You have a lot of clocks," he commented. "Doesn't the ticking drive you mad?"

"There are worse things to hear," I shrugged.

He raised his Vulcan eyebrows in agreement and

placed his hands behind his back before rising up and down on the balls of his feet. "Well?" he asked.

"Well what?"

"What are you going to do?"

What was I going to do? Good question. I needed to think fast. "Well... First things first. What's your name?"

"Dave. Dave Nichols."

"Dave?" I creased my forehead in obvious disbelief. "Shouldn't it be something more like Vlad or Lestat?"

Dave placed his hands on his hips and gave a deep sigh. "Do I look Transylvanian or French? You really shouldn't believe all you read in books you know."

"And this coming from someone dressed as the science officer of the USS Enterprise?" I shot back. Dave was about to say something else when I heard the worst possible sound I could and my blood turned to ice as a thousand geese were strolled across my granny's grave.

It was a knock at the door.

My eyes locked onto the carriage clock on the windowsill. Five to ten.

Grace.

Shit!

"Oh, this is not good," I wailed. I looked at the door then I looked at the vampire. I grimaced. What was worse. That I had a vampire in my flat or a sodding Vulcan? "Bugger, bugger, bugger..."

"What's the matter?" Dave asked, "Aren't you going to answer the door?"

I gave him my best withering stare but it just slipped off his fixed Vulcan exterior. Either he actually had no social skills whatsoever or he really went for the method acting approach to role-play. My money was on the former. "It's a friend of mine. She's come to take me to a night club."

"You're going out on a date?"

"No I'm bloody not!" I snapped, temper suddenly flushing my cheeks, "I'm old enough to be her father. I think." I tried a quick mental calculation, but all the numbers were running around in the vacuous space between my ears waving their arms in the air and screaming, "Run away! Run away!"

The door knocked again. "Sam!" a female voice called. "It's me. You in there?"

I stared at the vampire and levelled a finger at him. "You owe me big time, mister," I said and opened the door.

"I thought you were never going to answer." Grace was adorned with her normal cheery smile and her woolly hat. She was also wearing a small denim dress over a pair of those thick black tights that seem fashionable today. "Were you on the loo?"

In spite of the insanity of my predicament I couldn't help but smile. She's somewhat infectious. "No," I explained. "I was just with a client."

Being somewhat shorter than me, Grace stood on tip toe and peered over my shoulder. Now whereas most people, if they saw a battered-looking Vulcan or indeed any other species from a 1960s sci-fi series, would probably take a double-take and make some sort of disparaging comment, Grace just waved cheerily and said, "Hi! I'm Grace!"

Dave gave a perplexed little wave back and introduced himself. "I'm Dave."

"Pleased to meet'cha," the perky little student beamed. "So, Sam. You gonna, like, invite me in?" For a moment I had one of those curious feelings of déjà-vu then I recovered and let Grace inside.

Her eyes scanned my obsession and she opened her mouth to speak. I held up a finger. "With *Doctor Who* it's 'Oh, it's so large.' With me it's 'What's with the clocks?' Why can't anyone ever say 'It's so large,' to me?" I stopped and realised what I had just said. Grace was snickering into her hand and Dave was looking at me somewhat perplexed. Apparently Vulcans (or is it vampires) don't get accidental innuendo.

When she had controlled herself, Grace just about managed, "Actually, I was going to ask you if you were nearly ready. We get into the Sugar House free before ten thirty."

I felt my ire deflate and started to smile, but then I caught sight of Dave and my amusement faltered somewhat.

Grace seemed to pick up on my thoughts. "Bring him too, if you like. He looks like he could use a good night out." I was about to say that was a really bad idea, but she had swept past me and grabbed Dave's hand, pulling him off in the direction of my bedroom. "Have to get you changed first. It's not a character night. You been to like a fancy dress thing already?"

Dave gave me a bewildered look that was an obvious plea for help and I just shrugged. One cannot stop a whirlwind that's in motion.

"You don't mind him borrowing these clothes, do you Sam?" Grace called out as she closed my bedroom door. I puffed out a long breath of air. It was going to be a long night. I needed a drink.

A little while later we were headed through town, swimming through the streams of clubbers as they made their way to the various late night hostelries. I kept casting a bewildered eye over my recently acquired client. It was weird enough seeing someone dressed in my clothes, let alone knowing that they did not possess a pulse. The idea of taking him out into the darkened streets was somewhat disconcerting. It wasn't as if I knew him. I didn't even know if I could trust him. Part of me kept expecting him to go all William the Bloody on me and start chasing blonde teenage girls.

He seemed totally in awe of his surroundings. His eyes did not stay fixed on one point for more than a couple of seconds. First he would watch a party-goer, then a lamp-post, then a shop sign. He seemed to be like a child taking his first steps out into the big, wide world. It was quite obvious that the change in him had heightened his senses and they were taking some getting used to.

Grace, on the other hand, was totally oblivious to my worries and Dave's voyage of discovery, bless her little cotton socks. She was whiffling on about her day at work and an essay that she was writing. I vaguely heard her say that she was really pleased that I had agreed to come out with her and that, perhaps, if I enjoyed the evening, we ought to do it again sometime.

I stopped and watched Dave as he came to a halt and his eyes stayed fixed on one particular shop front on North Road. I followed his gaze and realisation dawned. "Grace?" I asked.

"What?" she replied her eyes tracking back and forth from me to Dave. "Something up?"

"No. It just looks like there's a queue forming up there. You sure we're going to get in?"

The Sugar House was just up North Road from where we were standing and a line of people were already forming outside it back onto the main road. "It'll be fine," she beamed. "I'll just go and check, though. Okay?"

I nodded and she wandered off.

"That part of your life's gone now," I whispered to Dave. "You've got to let it go."

His hand touched the glass window of the sci-fi shop. "I can't," he said. "I just can't. It's all I have. You know? Like the Galacticans as they travel through space, all they really have is the Battlestar, all alone in the dark."

"Are we talking about the old *Battlestar Galactica* or the new one?" I asked.

"Oh, definitely the new one. It's far superior."

"I only watched a few. Found it a bit too post 9-11 for my taste. You know, reds under the bed and all that. I find the idea of people looking like us but actually being sleeper monsters quite disturbing. People you think you know suddenly turning then being complete killers."

"They would have to be rooted out and destroyed before they were activated."

I took a step back. "That's a bit harsh, don't you think?" Well this was a sudden and unexpected not-so-welcome turn to the conversation. His voice was at once firm and hard, most unlike he had been earlier.

Dave faced me and the streetlights shone yellow in his dark eyes. "They are everywhere. They have been sent to cause chaos and destruction. They appear harmless and look just like everybody else, but when the time comes their masks shall fall and death will come by their hands. They must be eradicated." He paused, breathing heavily for a second, then all tension seemed to leave his body as his features became softer, less cruel. His voice lost its edge as he smiled and said, "But you've got to admit Number Six is reason alone for watching the series though, haven't you?" His smile faltered. "Sam? You okay there? You look a bit pale."

"I'm fine, Dave," I reassured him, pulling myself back together. He hadn't even noticed. He had slipped into this other persona without so much as a skip of a heartbeat (or whatever it is that vampires used to measure small amounts of time), then once again it was gone and here was the mild-mannered sci-fi shop owner. What was going on inside his head? What seed had been planted in him to germinate and grow? "Look," I motioned over his shoulder, "here comes Grace."

Grace bounced back along North Road from the corner of Sugar House Alley. She was grinning and waving maniacally. "Come on, slow coaches!" she shouted.

I turned to Dave and shrugged. "I think she means us."

"I guess she does," he agreed.

We strolled leisurely up to the little red-head. "I guess you've got us all in then?"

Her grin was even wider than normal. "Oh yes! The Gracester strikes lucky. It was Barry on the door and he's a pushover. Just fluttered my little green eyes at him and, you know, putty in my hands." She giggled. "Now come on, before he so changes his mind."

Dave and I followed her around the corner and down the alley towards the entrance. We could see

Barry standing cross-armed on the door with a group of annoyed looking punters lined up against a graffitied wall. Dave paused. "Curious," he commented.

"What?"

"You don't normally see such grammatically correct graffiti."

The words were impressively large, covering most of the sizeable, grey wall. "Spud was here." it read. "I see what you mean," I agreed, watching Grace chatting to Barry out of the corner of my eye. If he had been any more closely related to a gorilla, he would have been sticking bananas up his nose and thumping his chest. "*Was* has been spelt correctly and they've even used punctuation," I noted, indicating the full stop.

"Are you two going in or what?" It was a crass-sounding voice and it emanated from an even crasser-looking female. She was stood with her mates in the queue who were all seemingly desperate to catch hyperthermia due to the lack of clothing. Her hair was dyed dark violet and her midriff seemed to ooze over the top of her impossibly small skirt. "Bit old for her, ain't you? Bloody paedo, I bet."

I was good. Very good. Normally, I'd shout something back. I'm very bad at controlling my temper like that, but Grace was there and I didn't want to show her up after she had gotten us into the nightclub. My mouth worked silently, trying to find something civil to say. I had to say something. Something. My eyes fixed on her voluminous belly and I frowned at the sight of the expansive, smooth skin. "Where's your belly button?"

"What?" the harpy shrieked. "Damn perv!" (What was it with women calling me a perv today?) "Get your filthy eyes off a me!" She tried to hitch her skirt up but failed miserably due to the fact that there was no way she could bend the laws of physical matter. I shook my head and set off towards Grace.

I realised that I was walking on my own. "Dave?" I called. "Coming?"

The vampire snapped out of some sort of reverie. He had been staring intently at the fat woman as she had started to talk to her friends again. I walked over and touched him on the elbow. "Dave? You okay?" I asked.

"Yeah. Sure," he whispered, his throat cracking. "Just... Nothing. Let's go."

I gently led him down the alley away from the queue of irate punters and precisely grammatised graffiti.

As I'm sure you have probably realised by now, nightclubs are not really my idea of fun. My idea of fun is more a quiet night in with a glass of bourbon, a take-away and something daft on the TV. Clubbing it, for me, is right up there with such things as letting rats eat your toes and shoving cocktail sticks coated in tabasco sauce up your nose. Why I had agreed to let Grace drag me along to this was quite beyond me, let alone why I had decided to bring a worrisome vampire with issues regarding his identity.

I knew from the start that it was not going to go well. I decided to just make sure my seat belt was secure, brace myself and await the oncoming crash.

Now, I have nothing against clubs, per se. If people want to spend a night bashing their heads away to incredibly loud music and getting hammered on drinks or high on other such stuff, then that's up to them. It just doesn't work for me. I guess it's probably the ear thing. I have enough going on behind my ear drums to assail the poor overworked timpani. They don't need anything else to barrage them. So it was that, after checking my hat and coat in at the cloakroom, I entered the main room of the club and the aching sensation started to niggle away at the front of my head.

Grace turned and grinned at me. She looked so happy she could explode with glee. She was obviously excited at the prospect of boogieing the night away so I returned the smile and forced myself to ignore the encroaching agony that I knew would undoubtedly follow.

"I'm gonna grab a drink," she hollered across the pounding beat of rhythmic music that was stamping on the egg shell of my ear-drums with a pair of size twelve Doc Marten boots. "You want one?"

I nodded and tapped Dave on the shoulder then mimed a drinking motion. He nodded then let his eyes wander across the busy room. I signalled to Grace that we needed two and, as she bounced off to the bar like a young lamb across a fragrant meadow, I turned my attention to the vampire. Ice seeped slowly down my spine. Watching him was like watching a wolf sat silently calculating how many sheep it could carry away from an unguarded pasture. He was stood rigid, his eyes wandering slowly from left to right across the mass of gyrating dancers. Not once did he blink. Not once did he flicker. He was silent, steady and cocked like the firing mechanism of a loaded gun.

What had I done?

"Dave?" I asked tentatively, waving my hand in front of those piercing eyes, "Talk to me. You in there, mate?"

He let out such a sigh that I had not heard for some time. It was the sound of longing, neediness and desire. I had sighed like that so many times when Caroline had walked out of my life. "It's just so...beautiful," he finally managed, his voice barely audible. "All this life. It's enthralling, intoxicating, Sam. I wish you could see it like I do."

"You're not going to go all fangy on me, are you?"

He turned to me, his face looked horrified. "God, no! That would be like going to the Dark Side and you saw how that turned out for Anakin, didn't you?" He shuddered. "No molten lava of Mustafar for me, Sam. These creatures are here to be protected. They have no idea what is coming, what awaits them."

"What's that then?"

He shook his head. "I have absolutely no idea, my friend. None whatsoever. Here come our drinks."

Grace joined us holding three drinks and managing to not spill a drop as she weaved through the crowd. Ever the professional, I thought. "I got you a beer, Sam. Sorry, no hard stuff here," she winked. "Got you one too, Dave. That okay?"

"Fine by me," he said and took a sip from the bottle. "Wow!" he cried as he pulled the glass container away from his mouth and stared at it in complete amazement. He then drained the rest in one fell swoop. "That was good! I need another," and he waded off towards the bar.

Grace sipped at her orange-coloured drink and gave a small grin. "He's a bit weird but rather sweet, isn't he? Where did you meet him?"

"He turned up at my place this evening," I told her, carefully watching Dave as he bought not one, but five bottles of beer.

"What's his, like, story, if you don't mind me asking?"

"It's complicated," I said, "and I think we'd better just leave it at that for now, okay?"

She nodded her little nod, her woolly hat bouncing up and down. "No probs."

I peered at the drink. "What's that? Vodka and orange or some strange sort of fruity cocktail that's lost its umbrella?"

"No, silly," Grace giggled demurely, "just orange. I don't drink."

"Oh." It was all I could say. The possibility that the young girl never touched alcohol had never crossed my mind. I suppose what with her working at a pub and being a student, I had just taken it for granted that she would party like there was no tomorrow, just like the majority of her peer group did.

"Here he comes."

I looked up and saw that indeed Dave was on his way back. He had already drained one of the bottles and was onto his third of the evening.

"I'm gonna dance," Grace said, backing up to the dance-floor. "You wanna, you know, join me?" Her head was cocked inquisitively to one side and her mouth radiated a pretty smile in the gloom of the club.

I laughed. "No. Go on, dance yourself silly. I have two left feet, you know. Besides, I think I'll be needed here." I motioned with an incline of my head towards Dave.

"Okay," she called out as she entered the heaving throng, "but I expect more later, Mr Spallucci."

Sweet kid, I thought to myself and smiled quietly.

"Christ, she fancies the pants off of you!" The rather squiffy vampire thrust another bottle of beer into my spare hand. I drank heavily from my original one then faced him. "Yep, she really thinks you're the bee's knees, that one. It's kind of like when Deanna Troi wanted to get back with Riker but she was all shy about it. She had to wait until Worf was off on DS9 and settled in with Dax before she could make a move. At least you don't have a beard to shave off."

I emptied my first bottle and sat it on a nearby table. "First," I counted on my now free hand, "you are way off the mark there. Grace is a sweet kid. There's no way she would fancy an old fart like me." I ignored the rude snorting noise that the vampire's rasping lips produced and continued, "Second, you are so, so pissed. Third, what is it with you and sci-fi?"

He shrugged, almost dropping two of his bottles of beer. "It's a life," he stated matter-of-factly.

"But it's all fiction."

"I didn't say it was my life, did I?"

I let him have that one.

"And she so does fancy you," he smirked, emptying another bottle. "I can smell it. Heightened vampire senses, you know." He tapped the side of his nose with a beer bottle and almost jabbed his eye out. "Improved taste too," he grinned and started on the next bottle.

"So I noticed," I frowned. "So what does your bloodhound nose tell you right now? That I haven't used the correct deodorant? That the group of students over there are smoking some very unusual mixture of tobacco?"

Dave harrumphed and drew his head back then

inhaled with great aplomb. Then his head snapped forwards and his eyes targeted on someone out of my line of sight across the dance floor. He was suddenly very still, completely focussed and quite eerie. For an instant, all traces of alcohol seemed to have left him, then there was a crash of glass as the beer bottles smashed to the floor and he was no longer stood by my side.

"Shit!" I cursed and started to scan the room. I had been a complete muppet and I'd let my guard drop. I just hoped that someone would not pay the price for my carelessness.

People. Lots of people. Most of them young, lots of them dancing. All of them unaware that an inebriated, undead killer was lurking in their midst.

As the pounding beat of music shook the room, hands waved gleefully in the air swaying to its deafening pulse and rhythm. My eyes squinted through the melee and my ears screamed in protest at the torture that was being inflicted upon them. The bells were ringing. Louder and louder they grew, making me feel like a modern-day Quasimodo. So high, so sonorous, so beguiling, dragging me away from the here and now, pulling me away from my purpose. I slapped myself around the face. "Get a grip! Get a grip!" I told myself. I had to find him. I had to concentrate.

Grace!

Where was Grace? She was in there! Somewhere in that throng of revellers, she was enjoying herself, oblivious to the danger that she was in. I had let her bring him. I had led him here like a friend, damn it! If he had harmed her...

I saw a flash of red under a green woolly hat and pushed my way towards it. There she was, side on, grinning away like a loon with a couple of other girls dancing and whooping like there was no tomorrow. Her friends saw me and shouted something to her which I couldn't hear under the din. She turned and smiled at me with her little radiant smile, then beckoned for me to join her. I shook my head and ploughed further into the crowd. I tore my eyes away from the look of disappointment that settled on her young face.

I had to focus.

I had to find the vampire.

I spun round and round frantically trying to spy him, but it was no good, there were just too many people in the way, spinning past my vision. I drew in a deep breath and braced myself. I was going to have to try and listen. I was going to inflict excruciating pain on my senses and open up my ears to the noise around me. I stood still and prepared myself, then above the pounding and the drumming of the relentless music I heard it.

A scream.

I bolted towards its source.

The crazy thing was, most people in the room seemed completely oblivious to the shriek. They continued to dance to the thumping and banging din that they called music. Most seemed wrapped up in their own little piece of heaven, grins on their faces and hands in the air. They didn't even protest when I barged past or elbowed them out of the way. They just continued to sway in time to the rhythm – totally blissed out.

One person who wasn't blissed out was the source of the scream, only now the scream seemed to have changed into a tirade of verbal abuse, all of it aimed at Dave. "You disgusting pervert! What d'you think you're bloody doing? Get your filthy hands offa me!" and so it went on and on. I won't burn your ears with the rest of the vitriolic outpouring.

I recognised the voice instantly. It was the badly dressed woman from the queue outside the nightclub. She was bouncing around inside her clothes that were at least two sizes too small and was jabbing a furious finger at the vampire who was stood to one side looking decidedly perplexed. With her other hand she had a tissue clasped to her neck. Even in the dim light of the nightclub I could make out a dark flower blossoming on the white paper.

"What's going on?" I asked as I made my way over towards Dave.

"Oh, I might've guessed *Paedo Boy* would be in on this!" she spat at me, her eyes rolling upwards.

I ignored the insult. Now was not the time for a slanging match. "In on what?"

"Here I was, dancing with me mates," she waved her free hand to her gaggle of cronies who were stood around with their arms folded and looks of disgust painted on their heavily made-up faces, "when I feel someone sidle up behind me. Well, naturally I think that me luck's in, what with being the stunner that I am." I refrained from laughing. "Then all of a sudden your pervy mate bloody well bites me neck." She turned back to Dave and lunged forward. "I'll have you for that! It's... it's..." I could practically hear the rusted cogs turning in her head as she tried to find the right word. "Bullying!" she shrieked. "Bullying! That's what it is."

I caught eyelock with Dave and raised an eyebrow. His shoulders shrugged and his face said,

68

"Help."

"Well, what you gonna do then? Ay? Ay?" she shouted at me. "Look at my neck. I bet it's gonna scar. I'll lose all my good looks, I will. I want compensation!" she bellowed.

I had had enough. I walked over to Dave then turned to face the overweight harridan. I took a deep breath, leant forward into her face and said, "Look. I'll tell you what you can do right now."

"What?" she asked, curious.

"Just piss off."

I turned on my heel, grabbed Dave and headed for the toilets. For the first time in a little while I actually felt like smiling.

"What the hell happened there?" My smugness at flipping off the overweight tart had subsided as I was now stood in the gents with a door wedged shut behind me and a shamefaced vampire in front. Could the night get any worse?

"I... I don't know," Dave stammered. He looked even paler than he had done earlier although there was a slight blush to his cheeks and his lips had a definite scarlet tinge to them. "I just knew that I had to attack her. I couldn't stop myself."

I leant against a sink and frowned. "What do you mean you had to attack her? You only had an inclination to take a chunk out of her neck and no one else's?"

"I swear to God, Sam. No one else. It was just her. I felt her from across the dance floor and I couldn't stop myself." Dave looked wretched. A slick sheen of perspiration had formed on his forehead. He wiped it away with the back of his hand then stared in horror at the result. His hand was smeared red. He was sweating blood. He fell very silent and looked like he was swaying slightly.

I recognised that look. "Dave? You okay?"

"I think... I think I'm gonna be..." He turned and bolted for a cubicle. Whilst he was getting acquainted with Hughie on the big white telephone I fished out a Lucky and lit it. This was insane. I had a newly-created vampire who seemed to attack people at random them threw up at the sight of blood. Bloody marvellous!

I finished the fag in four long puffs and stubbed it out on the floor before marching over to the stricken vamp. "You alright?"

The retching stopped and he managed to raise a feeble thumbs up. I shoved my hands under his arm pits and hefted him up. The pan was full of blood. "Don't look, just don't look," I urged him as I flushed the toilet and grabbed a handful of loo roll to wipe his face down. When I'd finished his ablutions, I flushed that away too and clapped him on the shoulder. "There we go, mate. Looking good, feeling great!"

Dave smiled weakly and there was a banging at the door to the gents followed by some cursing and swearing. "We need to get out of here," I stated, "and fast, I think."

Dave nodded.

I looked around. There was a fire exit at the far end of the cubicles. Perfect. "Come on. Let's get you some fresh air."

I half pushed, half carried the swaying vampire towards the fire door, then lifted a foot and booted the escape bar. The door swung open and an alarm started to shriek. The hammering on the other door stopped suddenly and I could hear screams of panic. Ah well, I thought, at least it created a diversion, and I heaved Dave out into the night air. We had barely gone three steps when we almost stumbled over something lying in our way.

"Shit!" I shouted as I toppled forwards and fought to regain my balance. Dave grunted as he landed in a heap on the obstruction.

I straightened myself up and heard my back creak. Oh, what a night, I thought, then I realised that Dave hadn't moved.

"You okay?"

Slowly, the vampire lifted himself off the obstacle before turning and running for a corner in which to be sick once more. I just stood and stared at the dead body of the overweight girl from the nightclub. There, on her neck next to where Dave had bitten her, was a deeper and much nastier, fatal wound. The night had just gotten even more worse.

"Sam! Sam! Is that you?"

My heart sank at the sound of the female voice. Grace! Bloody hell. I had completely forgotten about Grace! I glanced down at the body then at Dave vomiting violently before walking quickly round the corner to greet her. She bustled up to me brandishing our coats and my hat. "I thought it was you. I, like, heard your voice. Is your friend with you?"

Even now, although I had abandoned her in the Sugar House, she was still smiling out from under that woolly hat. She made to walk past me. I grabbed her by the arm and pulled her back. "I wouldn't go round there, if I was you," I cautioned the little student. "It's not that pretty."

"Why? What's up?"

I paused. What could I tell her? That there was a body round there that had been killed by a vampire and another creature of the night was busy throwing up blood in the corner of a yard? No. So I bent the truth a bit. "It's Dave. Those beers have sort of caught up with him, you know?"

Grace grimaced. "Oh," she said quietly, "Yuk. Listen, do you need any, you know, help?"

I could tell from her voice that the offer was the obligatory type from one friend to another which hoped it wouldn't be called upon. I smiled inwardly and shook my head. "No, I'll be alright. I'll get him back to his place and clean him up." I popped my hat back on my head and slipped into my coat. "Thanks for these, though." Then something dreadful crossed my mind. There was a killer vampire out there. "What are you going to do now?"

"Oh, I've met a couple of guys, you know. So we'll find somewhere to party." She rocked back and forth on her heels. "You could text me when you've sorted him out, you know? Come and join us?"

I smiled and shook my head. "No thanks. I think I'm partied out for the night, so I'll get Dave home then head back to my place. Just make sure you stay with the others, okay? Don't wander off on your own. What?"

Grace was giggling behind her hand. "It's okay, Sam. You sound just like my dad. That's a bit weird."

I turned to go back to the car crash hidden round the corner. "Look, I've got to sort this mess out okay? You just be careful, you hear. I know what you students are like. I was one myself once, you know?"

She flipped me a little salute, then ran off towards her mates who were gathered down the road. They giggled to each other and pointed at me as Grace joined them before they all wandered off together in the opposite direction. I chewed my bottom lip and went to find Dave. He had stopped throwing up and was sat in a heap on the floor by the body of the dead woman. "It wasn't me!" he moaned. "I didn't do it."

"I know, Dave. I know. You were with me remember?" His brown eyes looked up at me and red streaks were drying on his cheeks. I remembered that he cried blood as well as sweated it and puked it. "Right," I said, pulling him to his feet. "We need to get to the bottom of this. We need to find out just what's going on with you. I find it far too much of a coincidence that you are vamped then a dead body turns up the next night which is someone who you yourself had attacked a few minutes earlier. There has to be a connection."

He peered glumly at the pale corpse. "What are we gonna do with her?"

"She's beyond our help. Someone else can deal with the aftermath. You're my client, not her. I know somewhere safe I can take you. I have a friend who can help us."

Dave nodded like an infant does when they have been told that everything will be alright and someone would make it all better again. After wiping his face down with a handkerchief, I led him away from the scene of the murder and off towards Saint George's Quay – to Luneside University.

First, I rang Spliff's doorbell. The dulcet tones of *Ode to Joy* rang from within his apartment. Dave looked at me and raised his eyebrows. "Don't," I warned him. "If you were still wearing that wig you would look so completely Vulcan."

He shrugged and considered the various blue and white flags of Saint Andrew that hung on the stairwell. "Are these the property of your friend?"

"Uh-huh," I rolled up my sleeve and swore. "Shit, it's past midnight."

"Is that a problem?"

"Spliff values his beauty sleep. He'll be cranky if we've woken him."

"Oh."

I jigged up and down then tried the bell again and hammered on the glass door for good measure. There was still no reply. "Come on, you old sod. Where are you?" I fumbled into my pocket and pulled out my phone, unlocked it and hit speed dial. I heard the receiving phone ring in stereo; in my ear and in the apartment. It rang about seven times then an educated Scottish voice spoke into my ear, "You have reached the phone-line of Father James MacIntyre. This is not a recording. It is the middle of the night. I am very busy. It had better be good."

I grimaced and mouthed "cranky" to Dave then said into my phone, "Spliff, it's Sam. I'm outside your flat. I'm in a pickle. Please let me in. I need help."

"You need your bloody head read," he sighed down the phone. "It's past bloody midnight and I'm busy." There was a short silence which I didn't dare fill, then he continued, "Is it a matter of life and death?"

"Yes."

"Does it require the services of a middle-aged but still nonetheless rakishly attractive priest?"

I smiled. "Yes."

"Does it require doing unspeakable things with

half a cucumber and a tub of Chivers marmalade?"

"Sorry, Spliff. Not tonight."

Dave's face was a picture of bewilderment. I guess that was down to the vampiric power of a heightened sense of hearing. I winked at him. He shook his head a little and looked somewhat worried.

"Ah well, I suppose I really ought to help," Spliff relented. "The key's under the dead begonia, as usual. Let yourself in."

"Thanks Spliff." I reached under the blue pot that sat adjacent to the door and contained the withered stem of a once beautiful plant. A brass Yale key jangled on its small fob as I bounced it in my palm. Spliff has always had one stashed there ever since he went sleepwalking once in the altogether. It is also why he has the large Scottish flags. They just about cover the essentials if he's forgotten to replace the key and has to go and get help from the university porter's lodge. That reminded me; "Oh, by the way. I've got company, so you'd better be decent."

"I always am, dear boy," he replied. "I always am." Then he hung up.

I unlocked the door and let myself and Dave in.

So how can I describe Spliff's chaplain's flat atop Grizedale Block at Luneside University? One word will probably suffice: decadent. Most vicarages or rectories have that slight musty smell of old books and deadly committee meetings. There will be pretty little arrangements of roses and lavender or other English garden flowers decoratively vased around the rooms in an attempt by an ageing housekeeper to lighten the mood of the rambling house.

Spliff's flat has a decidedly different ambience.

"Oh, my!" Dave exclaimed when he came face to face with a life-size gold-painted statue of Michelangelo's *David* in the foyer. It had a long black coat draped over its shoulders and Spliff's Panama hat placed at a jaunty angle on its head. It had a couple of sagging helium balloons tied to its arm and was adorned with a leopard skin thong. "I take it your friend is hardly conventional?" Dave enquired, his eyes unable to part company with the underwear.

I chuckled. "That would be somewhat of an understatement. They tried him in a normal parish for a while but when you start to forget to turn up for services," I shrugged as I removed my hat and coat, before precariously balancing them with Spliff's on *David*, "people tend to be rather unforgiving. Oh, and there was an incident with the Rural Dean, a Chihuahua puppy and a stick of salami."

Dave paused, where he stood and turned to consider the front door. "If I leave now will he forget I ever came?"

I moved him back round and led him towards Spliff's living room. "Oh, you ain't seen nothing yet, my Vulcan friend," I grinned. Then the vampire's face fell as he passed through the vestibule and watched Spliff saunter through his living room. I wasn't sure what was causing the vampire more consternation: Spliff in his black silk kimono, emblazoned with a bright red dragon entwined around a naked geisha girl, or the general decor of the room.

First, there's the books, journals and newspapers. They are absolutely everywhere: on bookshelves, tables, chairs and scattered liberally across the floor. There is always a pile of discarded reading material in an unceremonious heap by the kitchen door. These are the ones that have offended Spliff and his own individualistic sense of morals. They have caused him to shout "Bollocks!" exceptionally loudly before tossing them across the room onto his "burn at midnight" pile.

Next there is the artwork. Spliff likes his artwork. It ranges from reproductions and photographs of the works of artists such as the aforementioned Michelangelo through to common little bits of tat that you can buy along the Prom in Morecambe at the height of summer. They all have one thing in common, though: nudity. There are more tits, willies and bums than you can shake a stick at in Spliff's living room, and if you did try to shake your stick at them all you would probably end up very sore and extremely blind.

Then finally there is the general mess. Apparently Spliff's last cleaner resigned when her doctor informed her that the marks around her ankles were not, in fact, a bad case of eczema but were in fact flea bites. That was about twelve months ago. The university has since given up. Apparently they arranged to have his carpets taken out and burnt whilst his room was fumigated, but mud sticks and no other campus cleaner has been brave enough to climb that flight of stairs since. I won't go into too much detail but needless to say that Spliff likes his cigarettes, his coffee and his fine alcoholic beverages but I don't think I've ever seen him use a sink let alone washing up liquid. There is a dishwasher in the kitchen, but it was never the same again after Dante urinated in there.

That thought brought me up short. I had brought a stranger into the flat. My eyes scanned the room quickly, but not fast enough. Dave screamed and started to hop wildly on one leg, whilst a black fury that was all teeth and claws started to shred my borrowed trousers. "Get it off!" he clamoured. "Get it off!"

Spliff bustled over and scooped the cat up in one easy gesture. It immediately turned into a black ball of soppiness, purring and pummelling at his neatly-trimmed beard. "Oh, my poor little fluffy-wuffy-puff-ball, did the nasty man fwighten you?" He glowered at Dave as he continued to tickle the black spawn of Satan's belly. "I mean what does he expect coming up here and disturbing us at this hour?"

"That thing's vicious!" Dave shouted. "It's got longer claws than Wolverine!"

Spliff was about to proffer a retort when a muffled cough came from his bedroom. "I'll... just settle Dante down in the spare room," he tried as a diversion, heading over the other side of the flat towards the vestibule.

I eyed my old friend up and down. "You said you were busy."

His eyes darted nervously to his bedroom as he shooed Dante out of the living room and shut the door. I groaned and marched off in the direction of his boudoir. "Sam!" he called out. "Don't!" but it was too late. I had already flung the bedroom door open and had marched in. A pretty young male was curled up under Spliff's red, satin bed sheets. "You made them leave, lover?" he murmured without even opening his eyes.

"Nope," I said, gathering up what I hoped were his clothes, "but you are." I dragged the sheets back and forcibly removed the butt-naked youth from the bed.

"Hey!" he screamed, "Who the hell are you?"

"Someone who knows jail bait when he sees it," I

shot back as I frog-marched him through the lounge and towards the open front door.

"Get your greasy hands off me!" he swore as I propelled him out of the flat.

"Glad to," I spat and threw his crumpled threads at him. "Now piss off back to nursery-school and don't come back you little arse-wipe!" I yelled and I slammed the door.

"Well that was uncalled for," Spliff commented sulkily as he meandered over to his drinks cabinet, "and after I agreed to see you at such an inconvenient hour. I need a brandy. Don't think that I'll be offering *you* one, though."

"Bloody hell, James!" I exploded. "How many times do I have to tell you? The young ones are trouble! Not to mention illegal."

Spliff half-filled a large brandy glass and swirled the alcohol round to warm it up. "For your information, he *was* legal. He's a first year."

"And that makes it okay does it?"

Spliff shrugged and proceeded to light a cigarette in a "Who gives a damn?" sort of attitude.

"You know what they say, you muppet." I stalked over to him and snatched the fag out of his hand and proceeded to punctuate each word with a jab of the small, white tube: "Don't stick your pen in the company ink!"

"Hah!" he flounced. "You're a fine one to talk!"

"And what's that supposed to mean?"

"They also say, 'Don't sleep with the daughter of the priest whose parish you're on placement with!' I know it's not as catchy, but it rings true doesn't it?"

I seethed with rage as I crumpled the cigarette up

in my hand. "Bastard," was all I could manage.

"Git!" he retorted, then, "Damn, you've made me hungry now." He pushed past me and headed off into the kitchen.

"Erm, I thought he was supposed to be helping us?" Dave tried, tentatively. He made to follow Spliff but stopped in his tracks as the priest flipped a one finger salute over his shoulder. "Sam?"

This was not going to plan, but then things rarely did with Spliff. I manoeuvred the vampire into a precariously small amount of space between some coffee cups and some old books on one of Spliff's gaudy red leather sofas. "Sit there and don't touch anything. You might catch something," I warned him. "I'll go and reason with the old queen."

Spliff was banging about in his tiny kitchen as he slammed a sliced bloomer onto the cluttered counter before kneeling down to rummage around in the overfull fridge. "Mayo, mayo, mayo... Where's the bloody mayo?" he chuntered to himself.

"In the bedroom?" I volunteered sarcastically.

The silk-robed clergyman stood up, pondered this and replied, "No. Today it was Philadelphia. I distinctly remember putting the mayo away last night. Damn senior moment! See what you've done to me, Sam?" He knelt down again and moved a jar of expensive-looking mustard. "Aha! Doctor Hellman's I presume!" he exclaimed and came out brandishing a white jar which he then proceeded to open and lather onto a thick slice of bread before stuffing it in his face.

I winced. "That is totally gross, you know? Most people put something else on the bread first."

"You're a fine one to talk, dear," he sniffed. "You

don't even eat eggs." He masticated for a few seconds then nodded past my shoulder. "So what's with him, then? A waif and stray you found down by the docks?"

I shook my head. "I'd ask you to sit down, but as there's not even any room to swing a cat in here... Not that I'd want to swing Dante, mind. He'd have my eyes out on the first pass." As you have seen, Dante is an exceptionally vicious tom cat. Vicious to everyone that is except for Spliff who coos over the furry razor blade and calls him his little "fluffy-wuffy-puff-ball." This little "fluffy-wuffy-puff-ball" is in the habit of sitting on the window ledge of Spliff's apartment and catching sparrows as they fly by. It is a fiend and a menace and I very rarely make it out of the flat without getting at least my ankles pounced on and punctured. Dave got off somewhat lightly considering its neurotic hatred and suspicion of strangers.

"Fluffy-wuff was just upset because you came and disturbed his sleep." Spliff finished his mayo sandwich and ceremoniously licked his fingers. "I know how he feels. Now, dish the dirt on Mister Dull and Uninteresting out there."

"Mister Dull and Uninteresting is actually called Dave, and Dave is a vampire."

"A vampire?"

I nodded.

"Called Dave?"

I nodded again.

Spliff peered over my shoulder at Dave who was still sat on the sofa. The priest smiled and wiggled his fingers at his nocturnal houseguest who gave a rather bemused wave back. "Crap name for a ruddy vampire," Spliff hissed through a forced smile whilst absentmindedly wiping mayonnaise from his beard with the back of his hand.

"I dunno," I turned and motioned for Spliff to follow me back into the living room, "there are vamps in *True Blood* called Bill and Eric. I mean, Eric the vampire? You've got to admit that's worse than Dave."

Spliff shrugged in a non-committal form of agreement and proceeded to re-enter the living room. He had finally calmed down and his curiosity had obviously been piqued. "So, Dave," he began as he sat himself down atop the pile of books on the sofa next to the vampire and started to inspect him quite closely, "Sam, here, tells me that you are, in fact, a vampire."

Dave nodded, hesitantly. "I am."

"Hmmm..." Spliff tapped an index finger against his lips. "Tell me Dave, can you prove this claim?" As I stood to one side I saw Spliff's hand slip down the side of the sofa and latch onto something. I made to speak, but he shot me a sharp glare with his grey eyes.

"Well," Dave started, "I have a pair of fangs." He opened his mouth wide and the sharp teeth slid out ominously.

"Impressive," Spliff pondered, "but my cat has fangs and he only drinks the blood of birds, small rodents and those who piss him off in the middle of the night." I made a snorting noise and those steel-grey eyes shot me another glare. "I think we need a bit more proof than that."

"Such as?" Dave asked."

"This," and in a swish of black silk, Spliff had pulled out a pair of dress-making scissors and had driven them into the back of Dave's hand.

"Ow! Jesus! You lunatic!" Dave shouted as he

jumped up and began to hop around the flat for the second time that night - this time waving his hand maniacally in the air. "That bloody hurt. That's gonna scar. It'll... It'll..." He stopped and stared at the back of his hand. So did Spliff and I. "Bugger me," the vampire whispered as the wound slid shut and the blood absorbed back into his skin.

"Not tonight, dear," Spliff purred. "Not tonight."

So I brought Spliff up to date with the events of that night: Dave turning up at my office with his story of the female vampire at the car accident, biting the girl at the Sugar House and finding the same girl dead from a vampire attack shortly afterwards. "Obviously, I don't believe that Dave killed her," I said, "as he was with me at the time of death."

Spliff lounged back in his armchair and ponderously stroked his small, dark goatee beard. "So it would seem. So it would seem," he mused. Then he leant forward and addressed Dave, "So you know nothing about the vampire who," he formed quotation marks with his fingers, "created you? You'd never seen her before or had any previous contact?"

Wearily, Dave shook his head. "I just run a small sci-fi bookshop. I may read fantasy, but I'd never dreamed of actually becoming part of that world. Hell, I never even thought it existed."

"Oh, it exists alright, Dave." Spliff looked over at me. "You'd be surprised what we've seen before now, old boy."

I quietly nodded my head. I remembered the first time we encountered the paranormal back at university. It had been a hell of a shock and was still an unresolved matter in my book, at least.

"Can you help me?" Dave pleaded. His hands were clasped tight together and his skin was as pale as the moon and as taut as his nerves. "Please. You've got to help me."

I walked over and sat on the edge of the armchair. "It strikes me that we could do with knowing more about the vampire that created you. Like I said earlier, it seems quite a coincidence that there should be a vampire attack the night after you were made. Perhaps she was involved. If we knew her identity, then perhaps we could track her down."

"But I don't know her name."

Spliff spoke in a soft, soothing manner. "You may think you don't, Dave, but you were at the centre of a traumatic experience and very near to death. Your mind had other things to deal with at the time. However, your brain may have picked up on something and it may be buried in your subconscious. We could try to extricate it."

Dave's eyes narrowed as he thought this over. "You want to hypnotise me?"

Spliff nodded.

"It didn't work when Doctor McCoy used it on Kirk in *The Prometheus Design*," Dave protested.

Spliff sighed. I groaned. "Look, I don't care what you've been reading or watching in your little Trekkie world," Spliff snapped. "That's fiction. This is reality. Hypnosis will help you relax and help you open your mind to me, allowing me to share your thoughts."

Dave suddenly perked up. "You mean like a mind meld?"

Spliff's mouth dropped open and was about to let loose a vile expletive so I pre-empted him to diffuse the situation, "Yes Dave. A mind meld. Spliff will perform a Vulcan mind meld on you just like Sarek performed on Jean-Luc Picard in *Star Trek: The Next Generation*."

There was silence again as the vampire thought this over then he grinned. "Cool!"

Spliff's eyes narrowed and he sidled up to me. "Never took you for a Trekkie," he observed.

"Insomnia and re-runs on late night TV," I whispered.

"Ah!" He turned towards Dave and attired himself in his most serious looking face. "Now, then, I'm going to need you to lie back on this couch and relax."

The sandy-haired vampire did as was requested once Spliff had made some space by pushing the various bits of detritus onto the floor. He slipped a pink furry cushion under Dave's neck as the patient lay out on the red leather sofa. "Be careful with that," Spliff warned, gesturing to the cushion, "It's Dante's girlfriend."

Dave looked somewhat horrified at the idea that a cat's love-toy had been placed under his neck and I glowered at Spliff. The portly priest ignored me and carried on: "Now, Dave, I want you to focus on this." He slipped a ten pence piece from a nearby coffee table and held it in front of the vampire's face. "It is really, really important that your eyes do not leave this coin. Do you understand me?"

Dave nodded, silently.

"Good boy," Spliff patronised. "Sam, could you be a dear and dim the lights please?" I wandered over to the light switch and did as I was asked. The room was suddenly lit in the sort of manner that Spliff reserved for entertaining young, male students with an essay crisis. "Look at the coin, Dave." Spliff continued in a low, soothing baritone voice. "See how the light glints off its finely polished surface. See how it dances over my knuckles." He started to flick the coin over the back of his hand. First to the left, then back to the right. Over and over it went. Back and forth across his knuckles. I sat down on the edge of the coffee table and watched the coin bob up and down. I had seen Spliff perform this neat little trick a number of times, and it always fascinated me. "See the coin walking up and down, Dave. See it walking over my fingers, just like it walks from person to person in its little, impersonal life. From one wallet to another. From one cash register to another. See it bobbing up and down, faster and faster. Then slower and slower." Dave's eyes were fixed on the coin. I could see in the glint of the dim lights that his pupils were tracking its path. They were glued to the shiny, silver metal disc.

"Imagine this coin is your life, Dave. Lots of little steps making one big journey. Lots of little steps bringing you right here now to this room, to this sofa."

"Lots of little steps." Dave's voice was not much more than a murmur.

"That's right, my dear. Little steps. Your mind is my mind."

"My mind is your mind," Dave whispered.

"Spliff!" I hissed. "Behave."

"What?" he protested. "I'm tapping into his subconscious. Jungian archetypes and all that."

"You're dicking about, more like."

He shrugged. "Same difference. Anyhoo, he's deeply under now. Where do you want to begin?"

"At the beginning I guess. When he was knocked down."

Spliff nodded. "Dave?"

"Uh-huh?" His eyes were completely glazed over and seemed to burn a deep red in the dim light.

"I want you to tell me about your accident the other day. When the car hit you, what were you doing?"

"I was walking down Caton Road."

"Why were you there?"

"There was a convention at the Holiday Inn. I was on my way home after handing out some fliers for the business."

Spliff looked at me for confirmation. "Sounds about right," I concurred. "What with the book shop and all."

Spliff continued the interrogation. "Where did the car hit you, Dave?"

"Outside the Holiday Inn. It jumped the lights. Didn't even see it until it was under me."

Spliff and I both grimaced. "Ouch!" Spliff whispered, then asked, "What happened next?"

"I was lying on the pavement. I could feel a lot of pain in my chest and I think I was bleeding from somewhere. Then I knew I wasn't alone. Someone was with me. I could hear voices."

Spliff gave me a warning look. I inhaled and let my breath out slowly. This made something quite clear. There must have been more than one vampire.

"Tell me about the voices," Spliff asked, his Scottish baritone soft and coaxing.

"There were two. One a deep-sounding male. Very refined. The other a female. Sounded quite young. They were arguing."

"What about?"

"Me." Dave frowned. "The man said they had to

go, but the woman said that they couldn't just leave me there. The woman came over to me and placed her fingers on my neck. She said that my pulse was weak."

"Dave, did you see the woman?"

"Yes. She was very pretty."

Spliff raised his eyebrows. "Aren't they always? What did she look like?"

A soppy smile filled the vampire's dreamy face. "T'pol."

Spliff paused and looked at me with a contorted look of confusion on his face. "What?" he mouthed to me.

"The science officer on the Enterprise," I whispered.

"I thought that was Spock?" Spliff whispered back. "Does he cross-dress these days?"

I smiled. "It's from another series," I informed him.

"You really need to get out more, Sam," Spliff muttered as he turned back to Dave. "What does this T'pol look like? Apart from the pointy ears."

"Petite, slim, nice... you know..." I gesticulated appropriately with my hands, "and short, dark hair."

"Sounds adorable," Spliff huffed.

"Ideal insomnia fodder," I smiled back at him.

"Quite. Now, Dave. What happened next?"

"The man said they had to go. He said others would be there soon. She said that I was near death and she had to save me. He wasn't happy about that. She said, 'Stop being so stuck-up and keep watch.' Then she bent over me and sank her teeth into me. I felt really light headed. I thought I was going to pass out but she placed her wrist over my mouth and I felt her blood seeping into my mouth. It tasted sweet, like honey."

"Lovely," Spliff grimaced. "What happened next?"

"There was the sound of a car and the man shouted, 'Nightingale! We have to go, now!' She pulled her wrist away and looked worried. 'He's not finished,' she said, but the man was insistent. She gave in but bent over and whispered instructions into my ear."

"What were they, Dave?" Spliff asked, then out of the side of his mouth, "Live long and prosper? Make it so? Ow!" He rubbed his leg where I'd kicked him. "Uncalled for, Samuel."

"She said, 'Find the Eternals. Protect the Twins. Await the Divergence.'"

Spliff gave me a puzzled look. I shrugged. It meant nothing to me, either. "Ask about the male vampire," I whispered.

Spliff nodded. "Dave, did you see the other vampire? The one with Nightingale."

Dave nodded wearily. "Yes. Just after she had whispered in my ear he came over and grabbed her by the arm to pull her away."

"What did he look like? Captain Kirk?"

I slapped my hand to my head and groaned.

"No." Dave's voice was still far away, oblivious to sarcasm. "He was taller. Grey hair and well dressed. I remember he had a red cravat."

I recalled the man and the woman sat in my window seats. "Damn!" I cursed. "I saw them earlier today in the Borough."

"Seriously? What were they drinking?" Spliff asked.

"Well it wasn't blood, that's for sure. I need a fag." I patted my pockets. "Bloody hell, where are they? You got any?"

"Silk Cut."

"You pissing about? You know I hate those."

He shrugged.

"I'll pass. I think you'd better wake him up."

Spliff grinned wickedly. "Dave I'm going to count backwards from five and when I reach zero you will..." he shot me a quick grin, "be a Klingon warrior with a hunger for *gagh*."

"Spliff!"

"Okay, okay. Dave, time to wake up baby," he cooed, "Up we get. Time for school."

The vampire yawned and rubbed his eyes. "Hey guys. We learn anything?"

I got up and stretched my arms. I was suddenly rather tired. "Yep. We sure did. It would appear that you were taken out of the oven before you were fully baked."

Five minutes later we were all sat in silence, each holding a very large brandy. Dante, retrieved from the spare room, was curled up asleep on Spliff's knee and Dave was staring out into space. "Well I guess that's just bloody typical," he eventually sighed as he upended his wide-bowled glass. "Not only do I get hit by a car, but a vampire does a Friday night special on me." He gave an involuntary shudder as the expensive cognac slid down. "Bugger!"

Spliff and I exchanged glances. The sandy-haired vampire seemed exceptionally down and there didn't seem to be anything that we could really do about it. We could neither finish the job nor reverse it. We had reached a somewhat unexpected impasse. Spliff scratched his black cat thoughtfully behind its ear as it purred loudly. "My concern," he mused, peering through his little, round glasses at Dave, "is that these vampires are still out there. Think about that dead girl at the Sugar House, hmmm? Goblins and fairies didn't do for her, did they? No, I think your saviours are still out there."

I nodded. "I agree. Don't forget, I saw them in the Borough. For all we know, they could have been watching my place, waiting for you. They might have second guessed that you would look for help."

"What do you think they would want with me?" Dave asked.

"My guess," said Spliff, "is one of two things. They would either want to finish the job, or..." he paused a bit too dramatically.

"What?"

"How might one put it?" Spliff stroked his beard and grinned wickedly from ear to ear. "Correct their mistake?"

Dave's face fell. "You think they might want to kill me?" he wailed. "Why on earth would they do that?"

"Loose ends? Cheap kicks?" Spliff shrugged and stood up, causing an annoyed cat to tumble to the floor. Dante shot his owner a dark scowl then began to vigorously wash his privates in annoyance. "How should I know? I'm not a vampire."

"I think Spliff has a point," I interjected. "We don't know how they think, do we? Also, we have to presume that my place is off limits for you. So I have a suggestion. We hole up here for the night and keep watch over you, then tomorrow, when it's light, Spliff and I can safely do a bit more digging. I can find out if there have been any more deaths recently and he can, I don't know, look into other stuff." I yawned and looked at my watch. It was past one in the morning. I was starting to feel dead on my feet.

"You don't look fit to keep watch over anyone, Samuel, old bean," Spliff observed, pouring himself another brandy. "Look, why don't we take it in turns? You get some kip for a couple of hours and I'll wake you up at, say, three a.m.? Then I'll take a turn at shut eye. That way we'll both be fresh in the morning for our little field trip."

I yawned again and nodded. "Sounds like a plan. You okay with that?" I asked Dave.

My client's thoughts seemed momentarily elsewhere, but he snapped back to us. "Yeah. Sure," he said. "It sounds fine, I guess."

"Okay," I said, settling down into my armchair, "wake me at three." I was asleep as soon as I shut my eyes.

I felt an insidious chill bite into me. I shivered, drew my trench coat tighter and hung onto my fedora as the wind tried to tease it away. An old, stained newspaper skipped along the pavement: "Spud was here and chased by Cylons!" the headline read.

I realised it was a dream. I decided to go with the flow.

I was walking down Cheapside. I passed Burger Bob and his grill whilst wondering what he was doing selling burgers in the middle of the night. I waved cheerily at him. He screamed and ran off down Lower Church Street. Curious, I thought.

The wind was screaming up Damside Street as I walked past the Wetherspoons pub. Lots of people were sat stock still at the tables. They all held empty glasses. There were no cars around so I walked over North Road and looked into the window of Dave's shop. It was dark inside and I could see next to nothing. There just seemed to be piles and piles of books. They all had the same title: "It's Coming." There were big books, small books, pamphlets, comics. There were even games still wrapped in their cling-filmed boxes. They all bore the same title: "It's Coming."

What was coming?

"Wouldn't you like to know?"

My heart jumped into my throat and I jerked out into the road. It was a good job that there were no cars there. I would have been hit and, dream or no dream, I'm sure it would have hurt.

"Yes, I would like to know," I said to the dead woman. The bite mark on her neck looked deep and ragged, but no blood seeped from it. Curious.

She laughed. Her laughter was joined by that of a milkman who was getting out of his float and a postman delivering letters to the shops along the street. All around me, normal looking people started to point at me then laugh. I turned to run. I wanted to get away, to leave this dream behind, but I knew I couldn't escape.

"It's coming!" they all shouted as I tried to drag my way away from them in the wet clay into which North Road had transmuted.

"It's coming!" they screamed at me as the viscous material dragged my legs down into the ground.

"It's coming!" they proclaimed as a loud roar snapped me from my sleep.

"Jesus!" I swore as I rolled out of the armchair and tumbled onto the floor. The floor, a nice solid, carpeted floor. No clay, just a fibrous pile of nylon with the occasional crumb of bread or pretzel. Praise the Lord of synthetic materials and midnight snack detritus.

I heard the roar again and flipped myself onto my back in panic, then smiled as I recognised its source.

Spliff was splayed out in his armchair, his head lolled back and his mouth open. That guy can snore for Hibernia.

My mouth straightened. Where was Dave? The sofa was empty apart from Spliff's usual junk. There was no other sound in the flat apart from Spliff's reverberating palate. I ran into the bedroom: empty. The kitchen: various bacterial life forms, but otherwise empty. The hallway: empty and the door open.

I stormed back into the living room and hefted a firm kick into Spliff's thigh.

He yelled and woke with a start. "What? What? Wasn't me? Who? Where? Sam?" He looked at the empty sofa. "Oh. Sorry. Shall I make some coffee?"

I raised a finger and started to shout.

Fifteen minutes later I was sipping the most lovingly made cup of coffee that I had ever tasted. I was sure that every drop was filled with the essence of absolute contrition and apology. There was also a decent slug of brandy in there for good measure.

"Sun's coming up," Spliff observed.

I said nothing and just stared out the window at the long shadows creeping their way out westwards.

"Is your coffee nice, Sam?"

Again I said nothing.

Spliff sat quietly, his fingers silently drumming on his leg, then he tried, "Perhaps he just popped out for a breath of fresh air? What do you think?"

I glowered at him from across the top of the coffee mug. "And perhaps he'll top up his tan whilst he's at it, do you think?" I snapped. "Jesus Christ, Spliff! All you had to do was stay awake! It's like Uni all over again. 'You grab five winks, Sam. I'll watch over the ghost, Sam.' Bloody hell, what was I thinking? You lost us that one and now you've lost us a neurotic, new-born bloodsucker. If he attacks anyone, God help me..." My words faltered at the sight of my best friend looking totally crest-fallen.

"Do you really think he could attack someone?" Spliff asked. His words were faint and weak. He looked pale and sick behind his goatee.

I sighed. There were white hairs in his beard. I hadn't noticed them before. A subtle sign of age creeping up on my best friend just as it was stalking me, too. A reminder that we were both, after all, only human.

"I don't know," I admitted and finished off the coffee. "I don't think he'd want to, but last night, he just homed in on that woman. There's stuff going on that we know nothing about, Spliff."

"Where do you think he's gone?"

I tapped my fingernail against my teeth and thought about this long and hard then words from the previous night came to me: "It's all I have." I placed the empty mug on the floor and stood to leave. "I think he's gone back to his mother ship," I said. "I'll see if I can find him. He can't go out in the daylight."

"You want me to come with you?" Spliff asked?

I looked at the sad, middle-aged cleric in the silk night-robe and the greying beard and shook my head. "No. It's okay, buddy. You get some proper sleep, okay?"

"Okay."

I turned and left the flat.

Lancaster is quite a calming place first thing in the morning. As I traipsed back along the river Lune and into the city centre, I watched the varying people going about their first-light business. Small trucks darted along the one-way system hurrying to deliver produce to local shops. Street cleaners whupper-whupped the gutters, hoovering up the detritus from the previous night's revellers - some of whom were shambling along the half-deserted streets back to their homes, back to where they belonged.

I was heading to where Dave thought he belonged. His life. His business. His obsession. I turned down Cable Street and walked past Sainsbury's as an articulated lorry pulled in to drop off its delivery. Opposite, I could see Sugar House Alley. I shuddered at the thought of the grim discovery Dave and I had made last night, then I frowned. Something was wrong. Where were the police? Where were the bands of blue and white tape? Where were the circling lights and the probing, inquiring reporters?

My feet picked up speed and I jogged down to the imposing, stone Gillow building that stood majestic in front of the Sugar House before venturing around to the rear car park. Surely someone must have stumbled across the body by now? But even before I reached the back yard, I already knew the truth. The body was gone. The yard was stark and bare, the whitewashed walls clean and scrubbed. There was not a drop of blood, no sign of the murder that had occurred just a few hours before.

Someone had been here.

Someone had tidied up. Meticulously.

I heard a rustling noise behind me and I spun around a hundred and eighty degrees. A familiar pair of eyes met me from under a mop of dark hair.

"You!" I shouted, "Come here!" and I ran for my teenage stalker only to stop short after just a few paces, my heart in my mouth.

He had vanished.

Right in front of my eyes.

"What the...?" I removed my hat and ran my hand through my hair in confusion. He had been there. He had been there, the boy from in front of the White Cross.

Alec.

I reached into my trench coat and fished out a Lucky. I flicked my Zippo and inhaled deeply. Things were getting creepier and creepier and I needed to get out of the yard. I walked over to where he had been stood just a second ago and looked at the ground. There was nothing, not a trace. It was as if he hadn't even been there. Had I imagined it? Was I creeping myself out?

I closed my eyes and listened. At first there was just the light jingling of my own internal church tower with the background thrum of early morning traffic on North Road, but then, as I concentrated, I started to hear something else, something faint.

Breathing.

I opened my eyes and scowled. "I know you're there, Alec, but I don't have time for these games right now." I finished my cigarette and tossed the dog-end at where he had been standing then I walked out onto North Road and headed for Dave's shop.

Okay. So here goes, I suppose this is the appropriate time to confess something that you may have already guessed. I, Samuel C. Spallucci, am into sci-fi. Now, when I say *into*, I don't mean the sort of *into* that involves stalking cast members of *Star Trek* or dressing up as Spock (unlike a certain missing vampire). No, my sort of into stems from the memory of being a seven-year-old sat in a flea pit cinema with my dad watching a huge grey triangular star destroyer zoom into view from over my impressionable little head and blast the living daylights out of the Tantive IV before Darth Vader swaggered his black-suited arse into a clinically white corridor and captured the sexily demure Princess Leia.

I remember sitting in awe and wonder at the flashing laser bolts and thrumming lightsabres.

I remember grinning up at my Dad as he affectionately tousled my hair.

It was the last time we ever did anything together that was really fun. The last time that we did anything together before he got ill.

So yes, I'm into sci-fi, but not in the obsessive Trekkie kind of way, but in the way that a seven-year-old sees the world before it all goes horribly pear-shaped and gets turned completely on its head. As you get older you can hide yourself in your bedroom and watch Blake and his freedom fighters outrun Servalan whilst you ignore the shouting downstairs. You can watch Q running rings around Jean-Luc Picard on a flickering screen whilst the smell of disinfectant seeps into your nose in a hospital ward's day room.

You watch all of this knowing that there are other

lives out there. Other lives that are not yours and you so want to be a part of them.

Anyway, time marches on and so do television schedules. Special effects improve and CGI rules as the great god of fantasy. One of the first sci-fi programs that embraced this new technology was *Babylon 5*. I won't bore you with the details, but needless to say it was a drama about life on a space station and one of the central characters was Commander Susan Ivanova played wonderfully by Claudia Christian. As I stood outside Dave's shop in the early light of the morning I pondered over the possibility that the newbie vampire might have a *thing* for the former commander of the *Babylon 5* space station. Sure there were pictures of other characters adorning his frontage, Kirk, a couple of Skywalkers, Rog Blake and the eponymous Number 6, but over and over my eyes were drawn to the blue-suited, brunette-haired figure of Commander Ivanova. There were at least ten posters of her not to mention a handful of framed and signed photographs and collectible cards.

As I knocked on the door I couldn't help but smile.

At first there was no answer, but then, as I lifted my hand to knock again, a voice called out from within, "It's open, Sam. Come on in."

I twisted the handle and the door swung in easily. It was dim inside. There was no illumination and the posters and paraphernalia in the window were blocking out most of the encroaching daylight. "Shouldn't you be asleep?" I asked as I carefully closed the door behind me.

Dave was hunched up in the far corner of the shop as far away as possible from any stray sunbeams.

"Apparently not," he noted. "Would you mind?" he motioned with his head towards a set of blinds on the front window. I nodded and rolled them down. The vampire noticeably relaxed somewhat.

"So how goes the very long night of Dave the vampire?" I asked.

A smile touched his pale lips. "Oh, very good. I thought you were just an insomniac." He stood up and brushed his clothes, sorry, *my* clothes, down. "Not many people know that episode was originally penned for Ivanova."

"You must have been gutted when she left before the fifth season."

He sighed. "Things change, I guess. It's just so hard to let go."

I scanned the shop. It wasn't very big, about the size of a suburban living-room, but every available space was crammed with books, games, memorabilia and much, much more. The stock must have been worth a considerable amount. "I guess you've put a lot of work into this place," I volunteered. "I can see why you wouldn't want to leave."

Dave picked up a plastic model of Boba Fett and absent-mindedly flicked a speck of dust from the bounty hunter's Mandalorian helmet. "It's not just that," he sighed. "It's the unknown. How am I supposed to find my way when I have so many questions left unanswered?"

I was about to say something when some primeval early warning system prodded my subconscious and my head turned to the back of the shop, allowing me to see a petite, dark-haired female lower a voluminous hood down from a black cloak that covered her from head to toe.

"Well," she smiled, "it's a good job that we're here to answer them then."

On registering the word "we" I made to move but felt two vice-like hands gripping my arms immobile from behind as a refined baritone voice purred, "I really wouldn't try anything stupid Mr Spallucci. It would be your last act, I promise you."

I was fluidly deposited in a nearby plastic-backed chair and the hands remained on my shoulders, keeping me safely prisoner. I sat motionless knowing that trying to escape would quickly cost me my life. I hadn't even heard these creatures enter the shop. Dressed in their long, light-shading, cloaks they had slipped silently onto the premises without so much as a whisper. I did all that I could for the moment and that was look at the female vampire in front of me as she smoothed the creases out of her cloak. She was fairly dainty - about five foot two, I would have estimated. She had short, brunette hair and looked in her early twenties, but then looks, I guessed, could be deceptive. "I would have said Dax, myself," I said to Dave who was stood motionless across the room, his mouth agape.

His head turned to me and he frowned, momentarily confused as to my meaning.

"Nightingale," I nodded towards the female vampire. "I'd say she looks more like Ezri Dax from *DS9* rather than T'Pol. She's cuter," I grinned disarmingly.

"I think I'll take that as a compliment, Sam," Nightingale smiled as she walked over towards Dave. "I wasn't born in the last few decades, so I don't find the term *cute* offensive. Although," she tapped a slender finger against her slim lips, "there are colleagues of mine who would have ripped your throat out for less." She placed a hand softly around the back of Dave's neck and peered up into his eyes. "How are you, my child?" she asked, her voice brimming with concern. "I have been so worried."

"I... I'm okay, I think," the infant vampire managed. He pointed in my direction. "Sam has been good to me. He has looked after me well. Please, please don't hurt him." He turned to me. "You won't do anything," a quick glance to my captor, "stupid, will you Sam?"

I gave as much of a shrug as the hands of steel would let me. "No more than normal," I volunteered.

Nightingale gave a wry little smile and nodded to her counterpart. "Marcus, if you wouldn't mind?"

I felt the weight leave my shoulders and I was able to stand up, stretching my arms. "Well," I began, "now we all know each other's names, perhaps someone could enlighten me as to what exactly is going on and just why a dead woman has vanished without a trace this morning?"

"Don't push it, Mr Spallucci," rumbled the deep voice of Marcus. "You are in no position to be flippant."

I carefully edged away from the tall vampire and let my eyes wander over him. Under the cloak, he was once more immaculately dressed, a tweed suit, highly polished brogue shoes and a silk cravat. Quite the English gentleman. All he needed were a couple of hounds and he could have been off to shoot a few defenceless birds, although I guess the prey he hunted were normally quite a bit bigger than a partridge and ran on two legs. "For your information, Marcus, old bean, I'm not being flippant in the slightest. Last night I found the body of a woman who had quite obviously been killed by a vampire. This morning, said body was gone. Poof," I

102

flicked my fingers in front of me, "as if by magic, not a scrap of blood was left behind. Needless to say I find this quite disturbing."

"Looks can be deceptive, Sam," Nightingale said from behind me.

"Don't give me that crap, I know what I saw. Dave saw the body too, didn't you?"

He nodded slowly.

"I don't doubt you saw a body, Sam," Nightingale continued, "but just because it looked like one of your kind doesn't mean that's what it was."

"You're saying it was another vamp?" I frowned.

She shook her head. "No. Far from it, and right now it doesn't concern you. All I can say is that no innocent creature was killed last night. That is not what we do. That is not why we were created."

My mind ran back to Dave under hypnosis; "Find the Eternals. Protect the Twins. Await the Divergence," I repeated verbatim, then gasped as my feet left the floor and air struggled to reach my lungs.

"Where did you hear that?" Marcus stormed as I grappled with his hand clenched suffocatingly around my throat. Black dots formed in front of my eyes and everything started to turn grey.

"Marcus!" yelled a female voice from far, far away. Suddenly, air rushed into my burning lungs and my backside rushed into contact with the unforgiving floor. "That will achieve nothing."

"He is a threat, I tell you," the grey-haired vampire scowled, "I don't trust him."

Nightingale was next to my side, her cold hand calming my hot cheek. I hadn't even seen her leave Dave's side. "My apologies, Sam, but please tell us where you heard that. It's very important, as you might have surmised."

"Dave was talking in his sleep last night," I lied, not wanting to drag Spliff into this. "He mentioned you finding him dying and those were the words that you spoke to him before you left."

I could tell from the look on Nightingale's face that she knew I was hiding something, but after a short pause she stood up and helped me to my feet. "Then you probably already know that my child, here, is not fully born."

I nodded. "You were disturbed. A car drove past?"

"That is correct, so we have to finish the matter." The female undid the cuff of her jacket and rolled the sleeve up before biting down hard on her skin. Blood oozed through the puncture wounds and she offered the bleeding arm to Dave. "Here you are, my child. All you need to do is drink of this and you will become one of us. You will join our consciousness and all your questions will be answered. All your doubts will be banished away for good. If you do not drink then you will stay as you are, a bastardised halfling with one foot in the mortal world and one foot in the world of the Children of Cain. You will wander forever not knowing peace of mind. It will drive you mad."

"Hardly a choice," Dave murmured and he took Nightingale's wrist up to his mouth. He wrapped his hands tight around her arm and drank greedily, like a baby at its mother's breast. Marcus looked on with reserved concern whilst the female vampire slowly stroked at the new-born's sandy-brown hair. "There, there," she cooed. "Drink up. It'll be alright." Then slowly, Dave's slurping slowed down and his eyelids slid closed.

He sank down onto the floor and started to breathe heavily.

"Is he asleep?" I asked.

Nightingale held up a finger for me to be quiet. I could see the puncture wounds in her wrist healing shut before my very eyes. "Just a minute, Sam. Marcus?"

The tall male approached the slumbering infant and placed a hand on his forehead. "Still cold," he commented

"That's good," Nightingale nodded.

Then Dave's eyes shot back and I swore. Loudly. His sockets were pools of blood. A bright scarlet film covered his eyeballs. "They're everywhere!" he wailed. "Everywhere. There's too many of them!" His head twisted from side to side under Marcus' restraining hand as if he were looking in fear at invisible people or creatures all around him.

"Who's there, Dave?" Nightingale asked calmly. "Tell us who's there?"

"Monsters. Faceless creatures. They've risen up out of the ground and they've taken us prisoner." He writhed under Marcus' grip, desperate to flee.

Nightingale gave her partner a look that held recognition then held Dave's wrists and spoke to him again, "Who's with you? Dave. Who is with you?"

"The boy," he whimpered.

"What's his name?"

Dave seemed to ignore the question and carried on with his hallucination. "They've taken us to *him*!" he spat the word out with such venom.

"Not another one," Marcus muttered. I felt like I had walked into a play somewhere in the middle and had missed the bulk of the plot so I just sat and watched enrapt.

"He's so dark," Dave hissed. "A soulless man with the heart of a black dragon. NO!" he shrieked, his entire body bucking against the restraint of the other vampires, "NO! Not him! God! Not him! It can't be him!" Tears of blood were now trickling down his cheeks. I'm not sure I'd ever seem someone in so much distress before.

Nightingale looked up inquiringly to Marcus. Marcus nodded for her to go on. "Dave. Who is he? Tell us who he is."

Dave's head shook violently from side to side. He was breathing heavily and erratically now. The words came with great effort. "His... name... is... Kanor!"

Then hell broke loose. Dave screamed so loudly that I had to cover my ears and things around the room actually shook. His legs started to slam up and down as red foam oozed from the side of his mouth. "He's burning up!" Marcus shouted as blood started to pour out of Dave's nostrils and his ears. "Night, we're losing him."

"What's happening?" I asked across the din.

"His body's rejecting the vampire blood," Nightingale explained as she hung desperately onto her child. "We left him too long. We need to stabilise him."

"How do you do that?"

Her face fell dark. "You won't like it," she growled and the next thing I knew, she had snatched my wrist and ripped it open with her sharp teeth before pushing it into Dave's open mouth.

Having the liquid that provided my brain with oxygen drained out of my body was a most surreal experience. As Dave sucked hard at my punctured wrist, my brain was screaming for me to pull away and get the hell out of there. My body, on the other hand, was remarking that this was a wonderfully blissful experience and why hadn't I ever tried it before?

As bright lights started to flicker in front of my eyes I felt my legs begin to buckle and I fell limply into Marcus' arms. Dave must have finished drinking because I was being curled up quite carefully on the plastic chair. I closed my eyes. I needed to sleep.

With the sleep came dreams, patchy, incoherent ones. I saw rank upon rank of faceless creatures made from clay marching across a barren land to fight with angels clad in brilliant white. At the head of the angels was a man clothed from head to toe in obsidian black. His face was covered by an eyeless hood. I marvelled at how he could see. Then I was stood in an old church. It was a ruin and stank of death. I was aware of a faint susurration coming from behind as a man stood in front of me and my companion. His shoulders were bent over in anger. Rage seemed to emanate from his very soul. There was something familiar about him. I knew this man. If only I could catch a glimpse of his face I would undoubtedly recognise him. Slowly, he turned round towards me, his face creeping out from under the shadows...

A rough shaking roused me from my fitful slumber. "Sam? Sam? Are you in there?" It was Nightingale. "Can you hear me?"

I slowly allowed my eyes to ease open and looked up into her small, pretty face framed by her short, brown hair. She smiled. "Hello sleepy-head."

"Screw you, bitch." I winked then motioned over to the newly-born vampire. "How's the patient?"

"All the better, thanks to you," she smiled, relief

pouring off her. "Sorry about that. His body was dying. It was rejecting the vampire blood and needed an infusion of human blood to stabilise it. Normally the infant dies because there's not a willing donor."

I shifted myself up into a sitting position and looked at my wrist. Not a mark. "Nice trick," I grunted. "They could use you on the NHS, but I suggest you tell patients that you're going to operate first before you go in with the knife."

Nightingale took my wrist in her cold hands and examined her handiwork. "Our saliva contains a clotting agent, amongst other things. Think of us as glamorous, bipedal fleas."

I couldn't help but chuckle. A small snore from nearby made me ask, "So what happened before the rejection? What was he seeing?"

Nightingale's face frowned as she ran a finger lovingly over the back of Dave's hand. "The stories you read portray us as heartless creatures. Brash and foolhardy, afraid of no one." She sighed deeply. "That couldn't be further from the truth. When we are born to this life we suffer a vivid dream that we will not remember once we wake up. It is the moment that we stop being vampires. The moment that we die. You see, Sam, unlike a human child who comes into the world full of glee and mirth, unaware of their own mortality, we are born screaming in terror having seen the thing that will kill us." She wiped a red tear away from her porcelain cheek. "Oh, Dave. What have I burdened you with?"

"You knew what it was that he was seeing." I said. "What was it?"

There was a polite cough and Marcus said, "Many have seen the creatures of clay, and we know that they are deadly, brutal vermin, constructed to destroy us."

Nightingale glared at him and Marcus grimaced. He had obviously said something that was not for my ears. "I saw them," I said. "While I was sleeping just now."

The vampires looked at each other in stunned disbelief. "You saw them? Just now?" Marcus' voice was trembling. "What else did you see?"

I tapped my fingernail against my teeth as I tried to remember then continued, "I saw a man stood in a church. He felt totally evil."

"Sam," Nightingale was knelt in front of me, her blue eyes focussed intently on my face. "This is very, very important. What did he look like? Could you describe him to us?"

I shook my head. "Sorry, but you woke me before I could see his face."

Her head hung and her shoulders sagged in disappointment. "At least we know his name now," Marcus volunteered. "Kanor."

Nightingale nodded and stood up. "The thing is Sam, many of us have seen the image of the black dragon in our dreams, but none of us have actually met him. We feel he is important and extremely dangerous. We need as much information as is possible."

"I'm sorry I can't be of much help," I apologised. "All I can remember is that I was stood in an old, ruined church." I paused a moment. "Do you think they were actually my dreams?"

Nightingale shook her head. "No. They were undoubtedly Dave's. They must have passed through to you when he drank your blood." She stood and eyed the sleeping vampire with pure curiosity. "I wish he could tell us more, but when he wakes he will remember nothing. All he will have is what we can tell him."

I chewed at my lip and plucked up the courage to ask the obvious question. "What were you two told that you had seen, when you were born as vampires?"

A little smile touched Nightingale's slim lips. "Curious one for me. Apparently I saw a man dressed in black in an old barn with a pistol."

"Oh," was all I could manage at first. Then after a bit of thought, "But I thought bullets couldn't harm you."

"They can't. Sunlight, fire and extreme trauma to the heart or decapitation; that's all. We are impervious to everything else."

"Crosses? Garlic? Holy water?"

The female vampire shook her head. "Nada. Not a sausage."

"What about silver? The internet's full of silver hurting vamps."

"That's a very recent idea. I think it's down to *True Blood*," Marcus said in an informative manner. "Now if you were a werewolf..."

"Whoa! Werewolf?" I jolted upright so hard that I almost fell off my chair. "You say there are werewolves out there? Howl at the full moon and rip people to shreds lycanthropes?"

"I'm afraid the Bloodline of Abel is very much a reality, Sam," Marcus explained, his voice laced with informative concern, "and you should be on your guard now."

"Why?" I did not like where this was going at all. "What have I done?"

"You have helped one of the Children of Cain," Nightingale explained. "The Bloodline have eyes everywhere. They will know and they will come after you. Soon."

"By soon you mean, next full moon?"

"Sorry."

"Well you guys will be here to help me won't you?" I pleaded already fearing the answer.

"Sorry Sam. Our responsibility is to look after Dave, here," Nightingale placed a hand on my shoulder. "I truly am sorry, but we have to protect the infant, especially with what his dream showed."

I wrenched my packet of Luckies out of a pocket and lit one. "Talking of dreams... You didn't say what yours was, Marcus. Care to enlighten me?"

The tall vampire's normally serene visage took on a look of beatific adoration. "I saw the light of day," he whispered.

"Okay," I puffed on a Lucky, "but surely that's, you know, a bad thing?"

"Oh no, Sam!" His eyes twinkled in the light of the room and his whole body seemed animated. "Before I stepped out into the light I had met the most incredible person, a blonde girl filled with such presence. I knew that it was coming and that I was to be its harbinger."

I gesticulated with the cigarette, "What? What was coming?"

"The Divergence."

"Marcus! Watch your tongue. That's twice now," admonished the petite female.

"Ah!" I smiled. "Await the Divergence. What were the other two instructions again? Protect the Twins and find the Eternals?"

Nightingale glared at me.

I felt exceptionally smug and blew a smoke ring as

the strong tobacco cleared my mind. "So, would I be right in guessing that Marcus' little blondie is, in fact, one of the aforementioned twins?"

"You know too much already," Nightingale grumbled. "To tell you any more would have consequences far more wide-reaching than you could ever imagine." She wrapped herself in her cloak before stomping over to Dave and swaddling him up in a blanket and lifting his sleeping form clean over her shoulder. "It's getting busy out there. We must be gone. Take care of yourself, Sam. Watch for the moon." She made for the back door then paused and called over her shoulder, "One more thing. Cut down on the drink. Your blood tastes like a distillery." Then, in the blink of an eye, the three of them were gone.

Half an hour later I had made my way back to Dalton Square. It was rush hour and the traffic was busy, snarled all the way down Great John Street. I was glad to be on foot. I had taken a rather circuitous route, wandering up Cheapside and along Penny Street. I wanted to be among living, breathing people rather than alone in a sea of lifeless, mechanised cars.

Right now, people felt good. Living, breathing, heart-beating humans. Creatures of the day rather than children of the night.

When I stepped out of Gage Street onto Dalton Square I glanced up at the clock tower on the town hall. It was just coming up to eight-thirty. I needed a drink and there was nowhere open at this time in the morning. I would just have to use my filing cabinet reserves.

I trudged up the flight of stairs to my office and let myself in before throwing my hat down onto the sofa.

Wearily I meandered over to the filing cabinet and slid the top drawer open. I reached inside to grab the bottle of Jack Daniel's that resided therein and paused as my fingers alighted on something long and padded. My brow creased as I pulled the envelope out. In old, flowing and unmistakably feminine handwriting, my name was penned on its front. I slid the packet open and whistled as a large number of twenty pound notes fell out onto the floor along with a letter.

I squatted down on the sofa next to my hat and fished up the note. It read, "Sam, if you are reading this then you have just been very sensible and not angered Marcus too much. I apologise for his short temper but we have all been under a lot of strain recently. I just wanted to thank you for looking after my child. It is strange to think that I do not even know his mortal name yet, but that is of little consequence as he will have to choose a new name shortly. Anyway, as a token of my future appreciation, I have enclosed five thousand pounds in cash for your time and trouble. I trust that is a sufficient amount. I also enclose a warning in case I forgot or did not have chance to tell you of it: watch for the moon. Vampires are not the only supernatural creatures out there and others have much less of a conscience than we do. We, the Children of Cain, are in a continual struggle with the Bloodline of Abel. They have eyes everywhere and they will know that we have been in contact with you. They will seek you out and most probably try to hunt you down. For this I apologise, but it is a matter out of my hands. For now, I must tend to my new-born child. Take care and, once more, my eternal gratitude. We shall contact you again when it is possible. Regards, Nightingale."

I got up and grabbed the bottle of whiskey from the filing cabinet then downed five long slugs of its reassuringly harsh liquid. So, apparently, I had made enemies of some sort of supernatural crazy-gang. Brilliant. My eyes fell on the sea of money that lay at my feet. At least I had enough money to treat myself to a slap-up meal and a new bottle of whiskey, so the day wasn't going to be that bad after all.

The Case of The Fastidious Phantom.

I'm guessing that, by now, you're wondering how I got into all this sort of stuff? Was I traumatised as a child? Well, duh, yes, but aren't we all? Did I witness supernatural phenomena as an impressionable teen? Well, I saw Margaret Thatcher get re-elected time and time again when we all knew she was going to be really bad for the country, but I don't think that really counts.

No, I was not subjected to anything paranormal until my last term at Luneside University. I had lived your normal average life, with the normal average ups and downs that accompanied your normal average family. I was the only child from good, solid working-class stock and I worked as hard as I needed to in order to get the university place that I wanted. Then, for three years I worked as hard as I needed to in order to get my degree which would let me go off and start training for what I believed I was called to do.

I was going to be a priest. Does that surprise you? It tends to have a bit of a mixed reaction. Some folk go, "Oh yes. Of course. I see it now." Whereas others just say, "You pulling my leg or what?"

I'd felt the calling for some time and had regularly attended the Anglican parish church in my home town at least once a week. I had been involved with the youth fellowship and loved all the high church trappings. I was truly at home when the building was immersed in incense smoke and bells were ringing out (not the ones in my head, I might add). So I studied hard and got myself to university in order to obtain the degree that I needed before I could start the selection process for theological college.

Anyway, the first two and two thirds of my academic years were totally uneventful. Well, paranormally uneventful. I won't go into any detail here, but you've all heard as to what students get up to. Late nights, binge-drinking, friends duct-taped to statues and traffic cones deposited in the most unusual of places. That sort of stuff was commonplace and I participated in my fair share of it along with the thumping headaches of regret in the morning. But of ghosts, ghoulies and goblins I saw nothing.

That was, until I met Gerald.

Like I said before, I was in my last term. It was summertime, the skirt lengths were high and the work to attention ratio was low. We were down to our last few lectures and exams were imminent. We could taste the end of university approaching on the smorgasbord of life and it was skipping across the palate rather nicely. I was living in halls for my final year and there were ten of us sharing the corridor with a communal kitchenette area at one end. I had actually vowed never to live on campus again after my hell of a first year, when an American student named Kyle decided that it would be absolutely hilarious to get totally bladdered every Saturday and ram a loo roll down the toilets before flushing them. I spent the last few weeks of that year kipping on a mate's floor in town rather than shoulder the depression that such childishness caused. However, my second year proved to be even more of an absolute pain, as living in town meant trekking backwards and forwards to campus with bag loads of heavy books which damn near put my back out a number of times.

So, come the final year, I asked the campus residence officer if there was anywhere on campus where I could live without the threat of blocked toilets and loud flat-mates. So it was that I ended up in Borrowdale Hall.

There were ten of us in total. I won't drag on with the details, but we were all finalists studying a mixture of subjects. There were three physicists, one English major, a mathematician, one chemist, one performing arts and three theologians. The theologians consisted of me, Spliff and a guy by the name of Malcolm Wallace. I'd known Spliff since fresher's week in year one and we had sort of become acquainted with Malcolm over the next couple of years. I would like to have said that we "befriended" him, but that would be somewhat of an exaggeration as he didn't seem to make friends very easily. He kept himself to himself, studied hard and, unlike the rest of us, didn't spend the evenings in the bar. He had spent his second year living in rented rooms with an elderly spinster. This had seemed to suit him fine, so I was amazed when he approached Spliff and me towards the end of the year saying that he had heard we were coming back onto campus and asked if he could tag along. The others on the corridor paid him no attention whatsoever. I sometimes wondered if they even knew he existed. I have to say that I had never made it past the plain, brown wooden door into his room.

When I wasn't studying or letting off steam in the evening, I'd normally spend time in Spliff's room when he wasn't earning himself a bit of cash in the manner that gained him his nickname. Needless to say, he was never out of pocket and was always flush for the weekend. His room wasn't as untidy as his lodgings would be in later life, but looking back on it, this was probably just because he had not accumulated as much stuff yet or become a master in the art of acquired detritus.

His room, like mine which was next door, had a great view over the green quad area between Borrowdale and Windermere halls. I was always amazed when I looked out over this that the whole area had once been a hub of Victorian industry – it was built on the site of the old Williamson linoleum works down between the Marsh and Saint George's Quay. A lot of the campus consisted of recycled mill buildings such as warehouses or factories and it was dominated by the huge lecture block that stood near the old chimney house. Both were splendid examples of Victorian industrial architecture at its best: functional, but strangely worthy of awe and adoration.

It was on a day in late May, when I was sat on Spliff's bed watching clouds drift by the top of the chimney-stack behind Windermere, that the first of two things that would occur over the next couple of days and would change my life came about. I had just grabbed our mail from Stewart, the elderly porter at reception, and

Spliff had filed his in the usual manner (dumped it with the accumulated heap on the edge of his desk over the top of the bin – the unimportant ones dropped to their doom and he eventually got around to doing something about the surviving remnant). I was opening the one letter that I had received that morning. It was in a heavy-weight manila envelope, so I had guessed it was important before I had looked inside.

"Now if it was me who had received an envelope like that," Spliff observed as he sipped on a strong cup of Earl Grey, "it would undoubtedly be a bill or some kind salesman inviting me to part with cash in a bloody timeshare apartment in Southern Spain. Whereas you, Samuel," he took another sip and grinned, "are the son of a gambler who has passed his luck on through your genes."

I smiled. "If I didn't know just how much my parents like you, I'd knock your Scottish block right off your... oh crap!" I sank down onto his bed and showed him the letter.

Spliff put his tea down, read the missive in silence and repeated what I had just said, "Oh crap indeed, Sam. What are you going to do?"

It had been a letter from the DDO: the Diocesan Director of Ordinands – the guy who oversaw those who wanted to wear their collars back to front and enter the clergy. He had written to tell me that my parochial placement had fallen through. I was supposed to be spending the three weeks after my exams trailing a local priest about his parish, but it seemed that said vicar had been caught in bed with the church-warden's wife and all hell had broken loose in the parish. Consequently, it would not be a suitable place for a raw recruit. Now, in

119

most dioceses, the DDO is a kind, caring sort who holds the ordinands' hands and gets them ready for selection conference and the big wide world of the parish. Ours, however, was a self-righteous, self-serving git. None of the potential ordinands liked him. We all saw him for what he was - a promotion priest. He was young and wore his hair in the fashionable style of the day whilst rising quickly from curate to parish priest to rural dean. Now he was a canon at Blackburn Cathedral. Everyone was tipping him for a pointy hat in a few years' time and pity those who stood in his way.

"He says that you'll have to find another placement on your own," Spliff read out from the letter. "What a sod! He knows you haven't got time to do that right now, what with finals."

I shook my head. "He's never liked me. He's a pompous arse." I let myself fall back onto Spliff's bed, clutching my head in my hands. "What the hell am I going to do?"

My friend seemed to ponder this for a moment then said, "Call out for a she-male hooker? That would take your mind off it?"

I laughed. "Not tonight, buddy. I think I'll settle for a few beers around campus. You gonna come help me drown my sorrows?"

Spliff shook his head. "Unfortunately, my only idea of joy tonight will be the companionship of Messrs. Marx, Engels and Lenin." He waved his hand at a pile of text books that lay strewn around a sheet of empty A4 paper.

I winced. "You still not finished the Marxism paper?"

He shook his head.

"But it's due in tomorrow."

He nodded. "And hence the lack of coming out with you to ritually burn an effigy of our beloved DDO. I'm afraid this wee Scotsman will have to hitch up his kilt and write like fury all night."

I hopped off the bed and made to his door. "Okies. I'll have one for you, then. I'll just go and see if any of the others are up for a drink."

A few hours later I was climbing back up the stairwell of Borrowdale Hall. I had succeeded (without much effort, might I add) to persuade four of the others from my corridor to go out for a beer that evening then I had headed off to a terminally boring ethics lecture (to this day I do not know for the life of me why I actually took that course) before spending a couple of productive hours engrossed in the library. Apart from the letter, the day was following the course that most of my university life took. I worked hard and I played harder. By day I would be secreted away in some secluded corner of the library, multi-tasking amongst piles of dusty old books and the shiny, sparkly highways of the new-born love child of the *Encyclopaedia Britannica* and Alexander Graham Bell - that wonder known in hushed tones of awe as "The Internet". I had an obsession to unpick all the words from every text that I studied. I wanted to understand how the author had arrived at his or her particular conclusions, then I proceeded to challenge them and ultimately try to overturn them with the latest ideas that were bouncing around the end of the Twentieth Century. Later, as the afternoon would wear on, and my eyes began to scream, "No more! We can take no more!" I would shut down my terminal, tidy up my books, stuff my scrappy notes into my back pocket and saunter back to my room then get ready to frequent one of the uni bars, where I would chug my beers down with great gusto until I was the last man standing.

A typical day.

I guess I don't need a dramatic pause here, do I? If this day had been a typical day then it would be rather tedious watching some shmo going about the same old, same old before yawning loudly, scratching his backside and slouching off to bed.

No. Not a typical day.

As I rounded the corner of the stairwell onto our corridor, my stomach rumbled. I glanced at my watch. Six thirty. Christ, I had completely lost track of time. I needed to eat before heading out.

I diverted into the kitchen area and wandered over to the cupboards. When I was a first year, it had been terribly unadvisable to store one's food in the kitchen. If you did that, then it would be gone by the morning. All that would be left would be a few pitiful cornflake crumbs and some mouldering pieces of fruit. This year, though, was quite different. We all had our own shelves in the cupboards and no food ever got swiped in the middle of the night when someone had an attack of the munchies from some of Spliff's products. Also, amazingly, the kitchen was always spotless. Now, normally, when you group a bunch of late teens-early twenties males together, you are wading through crud, pants and unspeakable crunchy stuff that adheres itself to your feet. Our kitchen was always spick and span – never a dirty pot, never a tea towel out of place.

This meant that I was able to quickly find a sparklingly clean spoon for my pot noodle as the kettle boiled me some water. I poured the water on and let the snack stand before lifting the lid and deciding that I had in fact made it a bit thick, so a fork would be better for eating the snack. I grabbed a fork and turned to leave the kitchen when I realised that I had left the spoon on the side. Deciding that I had best keep the kitchen in the manner to which we were all accustomed, I turned and made to put the spoon away.

The work surface was empty. There was just the kettle. I frowned. I was sure I had put the spoon down there. I had a quick scout around and saw no obvious pieces of cutlery. I shrugged to myself, deciding that I had obviously put the spoon back in the drawer when I had taken the fork.

Munching on my pot noodle I meandered back to my room planning in my head what beer I was going to drink and where later on that evening.

The next morning my head hurt like hell. I banged and clattered my way along the corridor and stumbled into the gleaming, bright kitchen. Instinctively I shaded my eyes from the debilitating sunlight that bounced inconsiderately off the pristine surfaces. I reminded myself to knock back some paracetamol when I got back to my room.

"Morning sleepy-head," chirped a bright, Scottish accent from around a mouthful of muesli. "Good night last night?"

"I think so," I managed as I shambled across to the fridge. "I don't really remember much about it." As I crouched down to look for my milk, the room swayed. "Whoa! Who moved the planet?"

There was the gentle sound of chuckling from behind me.

"Knock it off, Spliff," I moaned as I stood up with my carton and started to hunt for some cereal. "Damn it! It's too bright in here for me to think straight."

"Hmmm," my friend mused. "It is rather perky isn't it? What time did you and the others pile in last night?"

I managed to tip most of my cereal into a nearby bowl. Some of the cornflakes waterfalled onto the counter. I made a mental note to clean them up later, when it wouldn't feel like I was trying to scrub out the guts of a hippo. "Dunno. About four? Five?"

Spliff finished his breakfast and thoughtfully placed the spoon in the bowl. "And it is now about..." he glanced at the kitchen clock, "nine thirty."

"Don't remind me," I grumbled around my cornflakes. "I've got a ten o'clock."

"I guess you grabbed a bite to eat before you came back?"

"Yeah. Chinese I think. Might have been Indian, though." I squinted through my heavy eyelids. "Look, what's up? Why the questions?"

Spliff leant forwards across the dining table. "I take it you left your discarded packaging and other such things here to tidy up in the morning?"

I nodded. I winced. It hurt to move my head so much. "What of it?"

"Where are they now?" His eyes scanned the pristine room. Mine tried to follow, but gave up half way.

"The cleaners must have come in."

"As you know, I had an appointment last night with the leaders of the revolution. Aided by sheer stubbornness, self-control and a steaming hot pot of tea – oh, and some rather delicious hob-nobs – I managed to rattle out three thousand words before midnight. After this I slept like a baby only to stir vaguely when a bunch of drunken hoo-hars bumbled along the corridor in the wee hours."

"Sorry," I mumbled.

He waved his hand dismissively. "Even with this nocturnal noise I was able to wake bright and early feeling refreshed and rejuvenated." He looked me up and down. "Unlike someone else I might care to mention."

"Looking good, feeling great." I vaguely lifted my thumb up to illustrate the point but let it drop back down again with a crash after the exertion of too much effort.

"Indeed," Spliff continued. "Anyway, I have been sat here since seven a.m. enjoying the beautiful rays of our god-given light and the pleasure of my own company. Not a discarded scrap of your refuse was here when I arrived and I have seen neither hide nor hair of a cleaner. In fact, I have been the only living soul in the room." He paused. "Make that the corridor."

My head was starting to pound and I was losing the will to live, let alone the appetite for my cereal. I staggered to my feet and walked over to the bin where I deposited the remains of my breakfast. "Look, Spliff, I really don't get what you're driving at. I've gotta go and get ready for my lecture."

"Okay," he smiled, "but hadn't you better clean up those cornflakes you spilt, first?"

I grunted and turned to the worktop, grabbing a damp dishcloth on the way.

I stopped.

I stared.

I looked at Spliff, still sat at the dining table sipping his tea and smiling in a fashion that appeared both benevolent and smug.

I looked back at the spotless work-surface. There wasn't a crumb in sight.

"How?" I croaked.

"Tell me Sam," Spliff grinned, "do you believe in ghosts?"

"Do they have good painkillers?" I asked.

Spliff sighed and slipped a packet of paracetamol onto the kitchen table. "I thought you would need some of these."

"Thank you." I downed two and swallowed them with a swig of water.

"Now leave the glass on the side, sit down and watch," my friend instructed.

I did as I was told. I placed the half-full tumbler on the work surface, sat down at the table and watched in amazement as it simply vanished before my eyes.

"Jesus!" I shouted, leaping to my less-than-steady feet, then regretting the outburst as my synapses wept in agony.

"Serves you right for such blasphemy." Spliff placed his empty cup on the table.

I stuck two fingers up at him as the cup also disappeared.

This was far too much for my alcohol-abused grey matter. I was having difficulty focussing on the here and now let alone any apparent ghostly goings-on. "Where've they gone?" I finally managed when the pounding in my head had started to subside. Thank you, you great god Paracetamol!

Spliff rose to his feet and walked over to the crockery cupboard. "Allow me. I don't think you could tolerate any more sudden surprises this morning." He opened the melamine-coated door and there, washed and dried were my glass and his china cup, neatly positioned with all the rest. "Have you not wondered why this room is so clean and tidy, Sam? Look at it. It gleams brighter than Tom Cruise's teeth when he prattles on about Scientology!"

"I just thought that everyone tidied up after themselves," I shrugged pitifully.

Spliff shook his head in despair. "So bright, yet so naive. Honestly, Sam, one of these days someone will see you coming and squeeze you like a toddler squeezes a tube of toothpaste until there's nothing left inside. Have you ever put anything away in here?"

I thought about it then shook my head.

"Have you ever washed up?"

Again I shook my head.

"So why on earth would you presume that anyone else must have done so, either? You really do need to develop a more cynical side to your nature, young man."

The paracetamol was really starting to kick in now as I could open my eyes properly and was starting to be more capable of a logical thought process. "So have you seen this happen before?"

"Nope." He reached into the fridge and grabbed a square of white sliced bread which he proceeded to munch on. "I've always thought it a bit peculiar, but it wasn't until I came in this morning and saw the place spotless that I decided to investigate. I must have still been in the inquisitive zone from essay writing last night. I made myself a pot of tea and left the teaspoon on the side. I sat down and, when I looked up, the spoon was back in the drawer, clean and polished. Naturally my curiosity was piqued so I tried a few more things. Mugs:

back in the cupboard. Cheese: stored in the fridge. Spilt food: in the bin. Everything neat and tidy, all where it should be."

"And you think it's a ghost?"

"You got any better ideas?"

The painkiller allowed me partial access to the depths of my consciousness. The rational side of me wanted to explain it away. It wanted to find something substantial to wave in the air and shout out "Poppycock!" as loudly as possible, but there was nothing. There was nothing that I could counter Spliff with whatsoever.

In the end I slowly shook my head. "But why?"

"I think, Samuel that is for you and your little bouncy brain cells to find out. Why don't you start by asking the one person we all know who's been here the longest?"

The porter's lodge was just inside the main foyer of Borrowdale Hall. It was a cramped little afterthought of a room that had been split into two. The front contained a small desk and the external mail pigeon holes. The back was crammed full with piles of sacks and an assortment of tool chests that seemed to envelop a small, overstuffed armchair. This was where I found Stewart, his head in a trashy crime novel.

"Sam!" the old boy crowed when I walked in. "Good to see you. Saw you wandering over to the bar last night. Had a good one?" He winked conspiratorially.

I chuckled. Stewart didn't miss a thing. He was the hub of the residence. Anything that happened always fell within his radar: the drunkenness, the partying, the celebrations, the commiserations. He was privy to everything and divulged nothing. There may have been a counselling service set up by the powers that be, but anyone with a real problem went and talked to Stewart. It was like having a friendly uncle on demand. The sort you went to unburden yourself to when your parents were at each other's throats again and home was unbearable. The sort who would sit and listen attentively whilst you just rambled on and on about how life was awful and pointless and how you had just about had it up to here with everything. The sort who, after they had sat listening to you for half an hour without saying so much as a word, just gave you the feeling that everything would turn out alright in the end.

"Well, I don't remember much..."

He spread his arms wide. "Says it all then. You not come down for your post?" His eyes twinkled knowingly.

"Actually, I was kind of after some information."

The old man rubbed his bristly chin. "Now you know I'm not one for gossip, Sam," he said, his brown eyes dancing like a ballerina fifty years his younger. "What gets told in this room, stays in this room."

I held up a pacifying hand. "No, no. I understand. It's not about anyone in this residence." I paused. "Well no one living that is."

Stewart seemed to ponder these words, half closing one eye as he absentmindedly patted his jacket pockets. "You know, Sam, I think it's time I went and got some fresh air." He fished out a battered packet of Golden Virginia and some Rizlas. "Perhaps you'd like to join me?"

I nodded.

He accompanied me out of the lodge, locked the door behind him and stuck up a sign saying, "Back in ten minutes."

"Eee it's warm today." Stewart pronounced "warm" as "wahrm" as most long-lived Lancastrians do.

"I think it's set in for summer now," I observed after taking a pull on one of the roll-ups the porter had made for me. I made sure I didn't cough my guts up. There was more tar in there than on the surface of the M6.

"Nah, lad. Storms are coming, I reckon." He tapped his tobacco packet against his left knee. "This 'ere tells me so." He drew heavily on his roll-up, causing it to burn brightly, then he blew a long smoke ring before saying, "Anyways, you didn't come to seek me advice on the weather, did you Sam?"

"How long have you been here, Stewart?" I asked.

He let out a long breath and scratched at his beard. "Well now, let's see. It was a few years after the place opened. I was just out of the army. Bert was retiring... Must be getting on forty years, I reckon. Why's that?"

"You seen anything odd?"

The old man let out a deep chuckle. "You mean apart from young lads walking home with their pants on their head or girls trying to climb stairs on their hands?"

I grinned. "Non-drink related events then."

He peered at me again through his half-closed eye. "I might have, Sam. It depends on what you mean."

"What about on our corridor? In the kitchen?"

A warm smile formed under Stewart's beard. "I think I know what you'd be getting at, Sam. You're referring to a kitchen that, no matter how untidy you leave it, always appears to be clean and spotless a short while later? Am I right?"

I nodded.

"Nothing to worry about there, young'un," he explained. "It's just old Gerald."

I waited for the porter to continue as he finished his cigarette and proceeded to roll up a new one.

"Yep." He tapped some tobacco into the paper. "Gerald's been dead some twenty-odd years now." He gently prodded the brown flakes down and moistened the gummed edge. "He was the best cleaner we ever had in the halls. You could see your face in any surface that he polished." His small, disposable lighter ignited the end of the cigarette and he took a long drag. "So clean. So proper, he was. Always on time. Never dawdled. Yep. The best cleaner I ever knew." He blew out some smoke and stared off into space.

"What happened?" I asked, when it became apparent that his thoughts were off hiking up a distant mountain. "How did he die?"

"His heart gave out, apparently," Stewart finally said, tapping ash off the small roll-up. "Nothing suspicious. Nothing unnatural. He just died." He turned and looked me in the eye. "In your kitchen, no less."

The look on my face must have been a picture as he chuckled quietly to himself before letting his thoughts ramble off again.

"Why's he still here?"

Stewart shrugged, finished his cigarette and made to stand up. "Not got a clue, Sam. Why don't you ask him yourself?"

The rest of the day just dragged. We were nearing the end of our university education and exams were looming. Rather than letting up on us, our lecturers were determined to cram in as many revision seminars as possible. I had five that day alone; each of them in a small, stuffy lecture theatre surrounded with other students all who kept giving wistful glances out of the window to the grounds of the converted linoleum factory.

It never ceases to amaze me just what the planners of the university managed to do with the old derelict grounds of the Williamson works. Many conversions of Victorian and Edwardian architecture tend to end up looking like the love child of two completely incompatible parents. Stone brick is encompassed in gaudy steel and neon giving you a migraine as you try to work out just where the main entrance to a building is or whether said building is an office block, an art museum or a public urinal. Luneside University, however, kept the heart of the old complex and sort of went with the flow. Those buildings that could be restored were perfectly renovated and those that were beyond repair were levelled in favour of tasteful lecture halls and grassy lawns. It's not a very large campus, but it does seem to have the TARDIS effect. You are constantly amazed at just how much stuff fits within its walls and how much space was created in its conception.

It is a great place to stretch out and relax on a warm summer's day. The sort of day when you just do not want to be stuck in a seminar going over and over the same material that you read up on only a few months ago. I knew that I would be better off curling up under a tree with a few books and a cold can of something fizzy and alcoholic rather than listening to the incessant drone of some old fart who loathed students and thought that undergrads were just an inconvenience that stopped him from his own research.

There was one student, I noticed, who was still lapping up these little hours of hell and that was Malcolm Wallace. Whereas the rest of us were adopting the fashionable stance of the apathetic slouch, he was upright, pen in hand and eyes transfixed on the latest lecturer. As I watched him, I noticed that not once did his pen touch paper, but his eyes never left the speaker. He was enrapt and enthralled. I cast my eyes over to the front of the lecture hall to see what had got him so unusually keyed up.

The lecturer was babbling on about the concepts of free will and predestation. The names of various philosophers and theologians were scribbled unintelligibly on the white board and he was pointing from one to the other with a big stick.

I raised my eyebrows. This was old hat. We had gone over this last year. Why was Malcolm so on tenterhooks about it? I shrugged and went back to inward speculation on the two subjects that were currently bugging me: the ghost of dearest Gerald and my lack of parish placement. I guessed that something would crop up for a placement. I could do the ring round or have a chat with the campus chaplain. I was sure that they had protocols for such things. Now, the ghost was a completely different matter. What was I going to do about that?

Should I do anything about it? I mean, it wasn't as if he was malevolent or evil, was it? In fact, he seemed quite the opposite; fastidious in his nature, constantly tidying up after us. That was no mean feat in a student halls of residence. I chuckled slightly as I imagined

Casper the friendly ghost wandering around wearing a frilly pinny and a pair of Marigold rubber gloves. I was suddenly aware that the room was silent. I looked up and saw the lecturer scowling at me. I shrank further down into my seat. He coughed and carried on.

I decided that it would be best to save my ponderings on Gerald until later. I didn't realise just how fast things were going to move after the lecture. I really should have paid more attention to the concept of predestination and destiny.

The sun continued to beam down as I wandered back from the lecture rooms towards the halls of residence. Wallace had joined me and was in quite a chatty mood for someone who was normally so withdrawn that he usually made a wallflower look like John Barrowman's hyperactive twin brother. "That was fascinating, don't you think?" he beamed, the sun reflecting off the white streaks in his hair. "The notion that we are not really in control of our own actions, but at the beck and call of higher powers?"

I shrugged somewhat noncommittally, "It's old news, surely? I mean, right back to the Greeks and even before that, we were supposedly at the beck and call of the gods."

Wallace shook his head, "Yes, but what about today? What about the good old, post-modern here and now?" His eyes, with their curious hue of orangey-brown, were practically on fire with enthusiasm. The lecture had well and truly got him stirred up. "You ask a priest if they really believe that their god controls their life and they will cite 'free will' right back at you. They would say that we have the power to decide our own destiny and that nothing or no one can make you do otherwise."

"So?" I couldn't really see where this was going.

"Well I think it's baloney!" he exploded. A group of girls who were walking past us turned and giggled into their folders. Wallace was unperturbed. "Of course we can be controlled. All something needs is the power and the focus to achieve it."

I smiled and shook my head. "I think I'll leave that to the almighty. Perhaps he can steer me into the path of a parish placement?"

Wallace calmed down and looked at me seriously. "I thought you had one?"

"I did," I explained as we approached the glass doors to the foyer of our halls, "but it fell through. Besides, in hindsight they were probably a little bit too evo for my tastes."

"Ah, the 'God is a squirrel' brigade."

I paused with my hand on the door. "Pardon?"

He grinned. "You know the sort. When they talk to God, they do it with the wistful look in their eyes whilst they peer up into the trees or up at the rooftops, as if God was a squirrel nibbling on his nuts."

I chuckled. "Nice one."

"Thank you. Listen, if you're stuck, I'll have a word with the priest at my placement. With a bit of luck, I might be able to persuade him to take pity on you."

"Really?" A cool air-conditioned breeze wafted over us as we entered the stone building. "What's the church like?"

"High as a kite and barrels full of smoke," Wallace smiled. "You'd be right at home, Sam."

"Sounds perfect."

Wallace looked over his shoulder towards the

porter's lodge. "I'm just going to check my mail. I'm waiting for something."

"Okay. See you upstairs later?"

He nodded agreement. "I'll take you to the parish tomorrow if you like? Oh, just one thing."

"What?" I asked, my voice suddenly wary.

"Watch out for his teenage daughter," he winked before he headed off to the porter's lodge. "Apparently she's a bit of a man-eater."

Looking back on that moment I wonder perhaps if I should have refused his offer, but I didn't and, anyway, Caroline is a story for another time and another book.

Isn't it great when things just seem to fit together. You feel like there's a purpose to life. All is hunky-dory and there's not a grey cloud on the horizon. The birds twitter in the treetops, no one shot Bambi's mother and Buffy settled down to a happy ever after with Spike. Okay, perhaps I should have stopped at the Bambi reference, but you know what I mean. You get that warm feeling deep down inside of you that doesn't feel like indigestion and you can't help but smile.

I think I even whistled as I made my way upstairs. That's how good a mood I was in. I don't do not being in control. I like all the pieces of my life to fit snugly and neatly together. When they don't, well things just fall apart. So, hearing that Malcolm could sort me out with a placement was a big deal to me. Things were back on track and everything was how it should be.

It's funny how life comes and punches you in the gut so quickly.

I dumped my stuff in my room and sauntered down the corridor to Spliff's door. I knocked three raps and let myself in, grinning.

Spliff was sat on his bed.

His glasses were held loosely in his hand and his eyes were red-rimmed.

The twittering birds fell quiet as the gunshot rang through Disney Forest.

"Oh Sam..." he started, his voice cracking as he held back more tears.

"What?"

"Sam... It's your dad... I'm so sorry."

I was sat on something. I didn't know what. It was hard and my knees were bent so it was probably a chair. It could have been a large rock for all I knew right then. There was a mug in my hand. It was exceptionally hot. It must have contained tea or something. I neither knew nor cared. The heat was burning my hands, scolding them.

I let it.

It felt real.

Disturbingly comforting.

The painful sensation on my hands.

It felt real.

Nothing else was real. It couldn't be.

It couldn't be.

Arthritis doesn't kill people. It just doesn't.

Does it?

I looked down into the brown liquid. Yes, it was tea. I could smell it. Strong, brown tea, piping hot in a white mug that was burning my hands.

That was real. That was real.

Arthritis doesn't kill people. It makes them sore and cranky. They have operations and take medication. They don't die.

"Tell me again what she said."

Spliff sighed as he steeled himself again for the umpteenth time. "Sam, perhaps you need to rest for a bit."

"Tell me!" I snapped, my eyes staring down into the brown liquid. "Just... tell me."

"Your mum said that the doc came round this morning. He told her there was nothing they could do. There's a build-up of crud on your dad's lungs caused by him being immobile. It's called pulmonary fibrosis..."

"Are you saying it's my dad's fault he's dying?" Venom. Pure, spiteful venom.

A pause. A breath. "No, Sam. It's just a complication. A bloody awful, dreadful complication. They tried him with oxygen, but that's only making him more comfortable."

I wanted to smash the mug of tea. I wanted to press my hands so hard that it would shatter, spilling hot liquid onto the carpeted floor and driving shards of ceramic into my hands. I wanted it to hurt. I wanted it to make me bleed. I wanted it to shock me.

I wanted to enjoy the pain.

My dad had been in pain so long. So long.

That was going to end soon.

Pause. Breath. I put the mug down on the floor away from my feet. "How long?"

"Not long. Probably a few weeks at the most. He's quite advanced."

"Is he toilet trained? Does he know his alphabet? Can he count backwards from a hundred? That's advanced, Spliff. Dad's not advanced, he's dying!"

"I know he is. I'm sorry, Sam. I truly am."

I opened my mouth to let something awful loose

into the face of my friend, saw his wet, grey eyes and pressed my lips together.

Pause. Breathe. "I know you are. I know you are. I'm just..." I waved my hands around hopelessly then slapped them down on my knees.

"I know what you mean, Sam. There's nothing we can do."

Something prickled where my head met my neck. A thought clambered its way up into my brain. "Yes there is. We can talk to someone who's already been through it."

"You mean our friendly neighbourhood..." Spliff wiggled his fingers in the air.

In spite of how I felt right then, I laughed. The old bugger's the best friend a guy could ever have. He's always there for me when I'm down as well as always being keen to knock me back before I make a tit of myself. I don't know what I'd ever do without him.

"Our OCD ghostie? Yeah. I mean him." So I filled Spliff in on what Stewart had told me while he made a fresh pot of tea.

"I don't know, Sam," he said as we sat drinking more Earl Grey. "It all sounds a bit dark arts to me, you know?"

"It's not like we'd be raising a corpse or anything," I countered, "and he hardly seems malevolent does he?"

Spliff sipped his tea and nodded his head from side to side. "Okay, point taken, but how do you plan to go about communicating with the deceased? Hmmm? You ever spoken to the dead before? And stoned philosophy students don't count. Technically they still have a semblance of brain activity deep in their cerebral cortex."

"Well I guess we hold a séance, don't we?" I looked at him for approval as I brushed my fingernails over my teeth.

He looked back at me, his face a portrait of incredulity. "A séance? The two of us? Now I'm no expert, but we do seem to be a bit thin on the numbers, don't you agree? And would you know where to begin?"

"I'm sure you could think of something appropriate to say."

He nearly choked on his tea. "Me? Why me?"

I shrugged. "You're better with words."

Spliff half shut his eyes and glared at me. "I could take that as your way of saying I talk too much. Okay. I guess I could think of something, as it's you, but I still think two is a lame number."

I nodded then thought back to a conversation on predestination and destiny. "I think I might know someone else who would be willing to join in."

I knocked rather tentatively on the door to Malcolm's room. At first there was no reply and I made to leave, but then I heard the sound of approaching feet and it opened just a crack. The quiet student's face appeared and, as the doorway framed his face, I noticed just how much white was starting to appear in his dark hair that framed those light-coloured eyes.

"Hello Sam," he said. "Can I help you?"

I ran my fingers through my hair. "Yeah, Malcolm. It's just, it's a bit..." I looked up and down the corridor. There was no one else around at the moment, but I didn't want to risk anyone stumbling onto our conversation. "Delicate," I finished. "Would you mind if I came in?"

The recluse hesitated as he mulled over the possibility of letting a stranger into his inner sanctum. Just when I thought he would refuse, he silently nodded and opened the door enough to let me in. I quickly stepped across the threshold before he changed his mind. The room was almost exactly how I imagined it to be; absolutely neat and pristine with classical music playing quietly from a small CD player. For a moment I actually wondered if Malcolm had his own little supernatural cleaner, but then I told myself off for jumping at ideas – he was obviously just a very tidy individual.

He was also quite the reader.

"Wow!" I gasped as I surveyed the numerous bookcases filled with hundreds of books of all sizes and appearance. "I thought Spliff was bad for books, but this..." I waved my hand towards the impressive library as my words trailed off, unable to complete the sentence with anything able to describe what was going through my head.

"I like to read," Malcolm shrugged. "You would be amazed at what one can uncover."

My head nodded slowly as I continued to let my eyes wander over the collection. I noted some large, leather-bound tomes on the bottom shelves. "Some of these look pretty old, and are those scrolls?" There was an expensive looking glass box with what looked like rolls of parchment sealed inside it. I turned my face round to Malcolm who was grinning with obvious joy.

"They're exceptionally old." He reached up and brought the box down with due reverence. Carefully he placed it on his over-sized desk and unsnapped the catches. The unmistakable smell of centuries wafted up to greet us. He slid a pair of protective gloves onto his hands and pulled out a couple of the ancient documents. As he rolled the first one out, I saw the unmistakable stylised pictograms of Egyptian hieroglyphs.

"This is genuine?"

He nodded. "It dates from the time of Rameses the Great. See, there's his cartouche." He pointed to a series of small symbols enclosed in a flat-sided oval.

I could make out a disc, a man sat on a throne and a wiggly line. The rest was all, well... not exactly Greek to me, but you get my drift? "I'll take your word for it. What's on the other?"

"Oh this," he was whispering now like someone venerating at a holy of holies. I felt like we should be burning incense and lighting candles whilst we perused the scrolls. "This is my pride and joy." He unfurled the small document across the table. I think I may have involuntarily given a little gasp. It was obviously very, very old, but it was immaculate. There were no tears, no missing edges. It was covered in a script that I had never seen before in my life.

"Where's this one from?"

"Canaan," Malcolm beamed. "It's one of the earliest examples of Proto-Canaanite script."

"But that must be..."

"Priceless," he finished.

For a while we just stood and stared at the most valuable item I had ever laid eyes on and then I asked the obvious question, "How did you end up with it? A rich uncle?"

A look of beatific joy spread across his face as he rolled the scrolls back up and sealed them once more in the case. "My benefactor."

"You have a benefactor?"

He nodded.

"How come you never told anyone?"

Malcolm shrugged. "You never asked."

"Fair enough." My eyes started to take in the rest of the small room and they found a small table which was located discretely in the corner. It was dressed in a white cloth upon which stood five votive candles around a small upright pole that was entwined in two strips of ribbon; one red, one black. I walked over to the table.

"You haven't said what you wanted," Malcolm said, a touch of apprehension sounding in his voice.

"Oh, sorry. Spliff and I are going to do something tonight and we wondered if you might be interested. What's this?" I made to pick up the decorated pole.

Malcolm's hand was suddenly like a vice around my wrist. "Something that's not to be touched." His voice was firm and his orange eyes were like deadly daggers.

I drew back, quickly. "Sorry," I apologised.

Slowly, he released my arm and recomposed himself. "What is it that you have in mind?"

I faced him and decided that, probably, the direct approach was for the best. "We believe that the kitchen is haunted."

"You mean Gerald?"

I was gobsmacked. "You already know?"

"You never asked."

I winced. "Okay, I see a pattern here. Anyway, we intend to communicate with him tonight. I have some questions."

"I doubt he'll help you. He's not the chatty type, apart from the weather. He's always interested in the weather."

I made to say that he had never told us he had actually spoken to the ghost before, but the look in Malcolm's eyes told me the answer that I would get, so instead I asked, "How did you communicate with him?"

"Oh, that was easy. First I used an invocation ritual then I used the old tried and tested method." He pulled a wooden box out from under his bed and took something out which he offered to me. "You can borrow it if you want to."

It was the essential ingredient to every teen horror flick - a Ouija board. I took it from him. "Thanks." I turned the board over in my hands and peered at it from varying angles. It was light and thin with the alphabet inscribed upon it along with numbers zero to nine and the words "yes" and "no". I couldn't help but feel somewhat apprehensive. "Is this thing safe?"

"Sam, it's a piece of wood, not a gun. You can't load it with bullets and shoot your foot off by accident."

"You know that's not what I meant."

Malcolm shrugged nonchalantly. "I'm still here, aren't I? Still got one head, two nostrils and no green goblin hanging onto my shoulders."

"Fair enough." I frowned as I pondered what I was holding in my hand. "I imagine the DDO doesn't know about all of this." I gesticulated with the board. "I imagine he would freak out somewhat."

Malcolm nodded slowly. "I guess he would. What he doesn't know doesn't hurt him. I see it all as... research."

There was a slight awkward silence until I said, "So as you're lending us this little baby, I'm guessing you won't be joining us tonight?"

He shook his head. "I'd love to but I'm meeting up

with my benefactor. She's staying at a hotel in town so we'll go out for a meal and I'll be spending the night with her."

It actually took a little while for the inference to sink in.

Eventually, my brain prompted my mouth to say, "You're sleeping with your benefactor?"

Malcolm gave a little shrug. "It's complicated, but we both get what we want."

"Bloody hell," I swore, tucking the board under my arm. "It's always the quiet ones. Here we all are spending time in bars wondering whether some hot piece of skirt on the next table thinks we look cute and you've bagged yourself a rich, older woman."

"Older." Malcolm chuckled at the word. "Sam, you have no idea."

"Okay, so now you're creeping me out somewhat. I'm guessing that we're not talking late twenties, early thirties here?"

He burst into a fit of near uncontrollable laughter and had to sit down on his bed to bring himself to order. "No Sam, far from it."

Images of lustful nights spent in a quaint sitting room doused in the pervading aroma of lavender filled my head and I shuddered. "I'll take your word for it. Let's just leave it there, shall we?"

Malcolm spread his hands in a "as you wish" manner and changed the subject by asking, "So why do you want to talk to Gerald? Need a washer changing?"

"I wish."

Malcolm frowned. "What's wrong?"

"It's my dad. He's dying. I just found out. I just want to..." I wanted to what? I wasn't sure. It just seemed that I needed to do something, but I wasn't sure what. I felt impotent, and not in the Doctor Freud kind of way.

"You want to make sure that he'll still be around when he dies."

There it was. Plain. Matter of fact. I was terrified that, when Dad died, he would be gone for good, a piece of dust on the jacket of eternity ready to be scraped off with the Sellotape of time.

I needed to know that he hadn't been a waste.

I needed to know that he would go on forever. I needed to know that he would be there.

My mouth said nothing but my eyes must have spoken volumes.

"I know how you feel, Sam. I lost my parents when I was young. I was still at school. It was awful - a car crash. Some idiot rammed their car into a tree. They were burned alive. Burned alive, can you believe it? I went completely off the rails. I skipped school, spent my time in dive bars and got into all sorts of stuff that would make your toes curl.

"Then *she* found me.

"I was slumped on a park bench with a bottle of scotch in my hand and dubious stains down my shirt when she just sat down next to me and started to hum this tune. I can't for the life of me remember it now, but it sounded so good. It lifted all my cares away and I knew right there and then that she would save me. She stood up, took my hand and I followed her. She's been guiding me ever since."

"But you still don't know if your parents are, you know, in Heaven or whatever?"

He shrugged. "I don't need to. She's shown me that I don't need to worry about them anymore. I just need to live my life and follow my destiny."

I raised an eyebrow. "Your destiny? What might that be then?"

"Time will tell, Sam. Time will tell." He stood and pulled another box out from under his bed. It was full of tubs of herbs and various occult bric-a-brac. Definitely the sort of things that would make the DDO's coiffured hair stand on end. "For now, though, we need to solve your little problem, don't we?" He passed me a small plastic bag containing some brown powder. "This should help."

"It looks like something Spliff would sell," I said dubiously.

"It's althaea root. It attracts benevolent spirits. Burn it over a candle and say this enchantment," he handed me a piece of paper with writing on, "and Gerald will be bound. He won't be able to escape. That way you can ask him anything you want."

"This will definitely work?"

"Like a gem, Sam," Malcolm grinned. "Like a gem."

So the scene was set. The kitchen, as usual, was spotless. A white sheet had been spread over the dining table. The Ouija board was set central between myself and Spliff with a third, empty chair at the head of the table. (We weren't sure why we had set one for the ghost - it had just seemed like the right thing to do.) A large candle burned nearby and fragrant incense wafted around the room from some joss sticks that I had acquired from the Student Union shop a few weeks previous.

"You're sure we're not going to be disturbed?"

Spliff was polishing the board's glass pointer with the back of his t-shirt. "That would be a bad mistake."

"It's cool," I reassured him as I smoothed a small crease out from the white linen. "Greg and the guys are off at an all-nighter at the Sugar House. They've been banging on about it for weeks."

My friend nodded and placed the pointer on the wooden board. "Shame Malcolm didn't come. What did you say he was doing?"

I chuckled to myself. "He told me he has a date, so he's somewhat unavailable."

Spliff's eyes twinkled in the flickering light of the candle. "Malcolm Wallace?" he grinned. "A date? Well, bugger me sideways with a ten-foot barge pole! The sly old dog. What's she like?"

I shrugged. "He wasn't for giving. Apparently she's older."

"A lecturer?"

"I don't think so. He wouldn't tell me, exactly. Apparently it's been going on for some time now. He says she's fascinating."

A low whistle left Spliff's lips. "I bet she is. You'll have to grill him tomorrow when he takes you to that parish." He stroked his downy chin. "Which one was it?"

"Dunno. He didn't say and I sort of forgot to ask."

"Bloody hell, Sam." Spliff shook his head in despair. "Sometimes you can be so crap at squeezing info out of people." He placed a finger on the glass pointer and tested that it slid smoothly. "When we contact this guy, just let me ask the questions, okay?"

I smiled and nodded then placed my finger next to Spliff's. The glass felt unnaturally cold to the touch. I took a deep breath and looked up at my friend. He looked back and raised his eyebrows. I nodded. It was time to start.

Spliff cleared his throat, laid his spare hand next to the Ouija board and lightly closed his eyes. "We beseech the invisible powers that walk amongst us to make themselves known this day."

I stifled a laugh. It burst into a short snort.

Spliff's eyes snapped open. "What is it?"

I smiled. "Beseech?" I asked. "Come on Spliff. The guy we want to talk to only died about twenty years ago. I think he understands modern English."

"You were the one who said I was good at the talky stuff. Besides, there is such a thing as protocol, Samuel." Spliff sounded rather sniffy. "One has to follow the rules as they are lain down. We are dealing with the supernatural here, not the bra strap of some first year sports science student."

"Hey!" I protested. "Those things are dangerous. Get it wrong and they could have your eyes out!"

"Quite. Get this wrong and you could lose your soul." He closed his eyes again. Matter over. "Shall we continue?"

"Sure." I made sure that my finger was in place on the pointer and my chuckle reflex was locked up tightly in a box.

"We have come here this night to communicate with a restless spirit that walks these halls. We wish to commune with this lonesome soul and ask if there is anything that we can do to assist its passing over." He paused. "Is there anybody there?" His right eye opened just a crack and lanced me with accusation.

I was very good. I looked down at the pointer and was about to hit my chuckle reflex over the head with a cricket bat when I felt movement under my finger and the glass pointer slid across the board to YES.

My head snapped up - my mouth open, about to tell Spliff to stop dicking about - when I saw the look of shock on his face. He has never been a good liar and I could tell right then that he had not moved the pointer. "Spliff?" I managed. "What's happening?"

He ignored the stupid question and carried on. "Thank you for making yourself known to us, restless one. Please tell us what your name is."

The pointer moved again G...E...R...A...L...D. I let out a low breath and started to feel sweaty under my shirt. This was really happening. We had contacted the dead cleaner. My spare hand slipped into my trouser pocket. It brushed against the piece of paper and packet of althea root. For some reason that I was unsure of, I had failed to inform Spliff about them. Something was bothering me. Something was niggling at me. I wasn't sure what, I just felt like I needed it as a backup plan. Obviously I had presented him with the Ouija board, which he had taken great delight in, mincing around like a camp Dennis Wheatley, but the spell and powder... I had memorised the incantation, two words in Latin, and decided to bide my time.

My attention jerked back to the here and now. "We welcome you Gerald," Spliff was saying. "Please stay with us a while. We would like to ask you some questions."

The glass pointer did not move. My hand twitched on the packet of root as I remembered Malcolm saying that the spook was not one for small-talk.

Spliff's brow creased. "Gerald, are you still there?"

"Do you think it's cold for this time of year?" I

asked.

Spliff was about to admonish me when the slider slid over to YES, then rapidly:

"N...O...T...L...I...K...E...W...H...E...N...I...W...A...S. ..Y...O...U...N...G."

I smiled. *Thank you, Malcolm*, I thought.

"You must have seen a lot of changes."

"YES."

"Good ones?"

"S...O...M...E."

"Are the students much different?" I asked.

"No. S...T...I...L...L...U...N...T...I...D...Y."

I chuckled. "Well, thank you for keeping the place clean. It's appreciated."

"This is all very well and good, Sam, but what about your question?"

I frowned. Spliff was right. I knew he was. We had Gerald here for a more theological reason rather than to chew the fat over how things were better in the good old days.

"Gerald," I began. "I have a question to ask." The pointer stayed still. "I need to ask what it's like when you die."

The pointer hammered across to "NO."

"Please, it's important."

Again, "NO."

"Gerald, my father is dying. I need your help."

Spliff and I both swore in unison as the glass pointer suddenly super-heated. We snatched our fingers away as it spun maniacally before hurtling across the room and smashing against the wall.

Now was the time for the backup plan. I stood, grabbed the althaea root, sprinkled it over the burning candle and shouted, "*Spiritus manere!*"

There was a blinding flash and a force shoved me so hard that I toppled over onto the floor. Slowly, I picked myself up and looked over at Spliff as he did the same. We then both turned and looked at the other chair, which was now occupied, and I groaned.

I can't exactly remember what was going through my mind at that moment, but I know I was not exactly in a happy place. Our "visitor" for want of a better word was just sat there at the head of the table, his head slouched forwards onto his chest. He was dressed in a grey boiler suit which was immaculately clean. There were even sharp creases in the legs. His hair was dark but starting to thin and he sported a carefully combed moustache.

I kept expecting his head to snap up and for him to lurch towards us groaning, "Brains! Brains!" à la George Romero.

But he just sat there, motionless.

I looked over at Spliff.

Spliff looked at me.

"This is all your fault," I said.

He opened his mouth in shock. "My fault?" The Scottish accent lay heavy on the second word. "And how might that be, Samuel?"

"It was all your idea."

"My idea? In which alternate reality have you been living? Who was the one who suggested a séance? Who went and got this blasted Ouija board? The finger of fate points at you Mr Spallucci." He got up and walked over to the caretaker.

"What are you doing?" I hissed.

He poked a finger onto a grey shoulder of the boiler suit. The digit didn't pass through.

"Spliff!"

He ignored me and carried on with his examination. "Fascinating." He crouched down and cast his twinkling eyes over the visitor. "He seems totally corporeal if somewhat dated."

"Have some respect."

"Well, would you wear a 'tash like that unless you were a backing singer for the Village People?"

I ran my hand through my hair. This was not good. What had happened? "It wasn't supposed to be like this. I was supposed to get answers. Malcolm said..."

"What exactly?" Spliff's eyes were focussed entirely on me now. They were distinctly lacking in his usual carefree joviality. "What did the marvellous Mr Wallace tell you when you kindly leant him your ear?"

I squirmed. "He said that he could get answers for me. He said that the incantation would ensure that Gerald was bound here."

Spliff's eyes softened. "Oh, Samuel. So bright yet oh, so dim. What exactly did you think he meant by Gerald being 'bound'?"

I felt the blood drain from my face as realisation dawned from on high. Malcolm hadn't meant bound as in kept captive. He had meant bound to the physical realm. "What was I thinking?" I ran my hand through my hair again then tapped my teeth with my fingers. "I need a fag." I grabbed my pack of cigarettes and struck one up.

There was a polite cough. "Excuse me, sonny, but smoking's not permitted in the kitchen."

I dropped the match as it burnt down to my fingers.

Gerald's head was now up and his eyes sparkled under the fluorescent lights of the kitchen. "If you don't put that thing out, I shall have to inform the Dean."

I didn't say a word. I stubbed the cigarette out on a saucer.

"That's better," said the caretaker. His moustache wobbled from side to side as he seemed to be thinking. Eventually he asked, "Now will one of you two lads please tell me what's going on?"

I have to say that he took it rather well. Personally, I would have gone a bit mental, what with all the being dead and altered state stuff.

"So you two young lads contacted my dead spirit to ask for advice about Sam's dying father, and somehow I ended up all physical again." He ran his finger and thumb thoughtfully along one of his perfect creases.

"That's the gist of it," Spliff said as he placed a mug of tea on the table in front of Gerald. "Sorry for disturbing you. Sugar?"

"No thanks." He peered at the mug. "You don't think it will go straight through me, do you?"

"The bathroom's next along the corridor," I volunteered. "Oh," I said when I realised what he had actually meant. "No. You should be okay. You appear physical."

Gerald picked up the drink. He placed it under his moustache, inhaled and grinned. "Now that's a smell I've missed." He drank the brew slowly and lovingly. I noticed Spliff leaning back in his chair and peering underneath where the caretaker sat. There were no puddles. Thank heaven for small mercies.

"What was it like," I asked when he had finished the drink and wiped his moustache dry with a neat, folded hankie from his pocket, "being dead?"

His facial hair performed the little bobbing motion again as he mulled it over. "Busy," he finally said. "There was always something that needed tidying or fixing. Mind you, at least I didn't need to sleep. I could crack on at all hours."

"Thank you for that."

"S'okay," he shrugged. "It's all part of the job."

"But it's not as if the university are paying you anymore, though," Spliff pointed out.

"Not as if I have anything to spend money on either."

"Good point."

"Besides, it was always more than the money. Someone had to do the job. Someone had to clean out the blocked loos. Someone had to wipe down the pizza-strewn surfaces. Someone had to stop that annoying little drip which would bug you for days on end as it plinked into the wash basin." He shrugged again. "That someone was me. Always was. Always will be." He drained the cup, set it down neatly on the table and asked, "So what did you young chaps want then?"

"My father's dying," I blurted out. "I don't know what to do."

The caretaker's brown eyes held mine and I could see a sorrowful compassion deep inside them. "You poor lad, you must be devastated. How old is he?"

"Sixty-three."

"What's wrong with him, so to speak?"

"To cut a story short, his brain's being starved of oxygen. He only has a couple of weeks." I looked down at my hands. My knuckles were clenched and white. "I... I... just need to know..." I felt heat in my throat and warmth behind my eyes. My vision was blurring. "I just need to know that he will be..." My voice cracked and dwindled out. "...okay."

Gerald's hand came into my blurred vision as it slipped around mine and squeezed softly. I looked up and saw him smiling gently. "Surely I'm proof of that for you now, Sam? Surely I prove that he'll still be around once he's passed over?"

"But why are you here? Where do all the others go?" Tears were now running down my cheeks.

"Don't know why I'm here, lad. Guess I still have work to do, but let me tell you this, when people die, they do normally pass over. I've seen it."

"When?" Spliff asked. He had been so quiet; I had almost forgotten he was there.

Gerald got up and walked to the windows. He looked out over the rooftops to the top of the boiler chimney poking up at the centre of campus. "Last summer, one poor soul decided that he'd had enough. Don't know why. Don't want to know why - none of my business. He took himself up to the top of that chimney - God knows how he managed it - and the poor bugger jumped. No one can survive a fall like that. After he hit the ground there was this almighty flash of light and I saw him glowing bright then fade away. There was this wonderful sense of peace when his spirit left his broken body. It was his time, so off he went. I'm guessing that only certain folk - by that, I mean dead ones - can see that sort of thing. If everyone could, then the papers would be full of it, wouldn't they?" He gave a little chuckle. "I imagine there would be a whole TV channel devoted to it too. Anyways, Sam, don't you fret about your old man. When his time comes he will pass over..."

He paused. "Unless of course, he has a job to do here, like me, and if that's the case, don't you worry none 'cos I'm sure he'll be fine."

The kitchen was quiet for a short while. There it was, the finality of it all. There actually *was* life after death. We had proof sat in front of us.

Why would we need to worry anymore?

Why should we fear the unknown?

Why did I feel so cold inside?

Gerald coughed. "Well, if that's all you chaps needed to know, then I guess you'll be sending me on my way and all that."

The maudlin quiet turned to an awkward one.

"Ah," said Spliff.

"Ah," I echoed.

"Is there a problem?" Gerald asked.

"You mean I'm bloody well stuck here?"

This bit of news he did not take as well as the first. Gerald was storming around the kitchen like a pissed off tornado. He was waving his hands in the air, huffing, puffing and shooting us disbelieving glances.

"You stupid pair of numpties! Don't you know not to meddle in things you don't understand?"

"Things didn't exactly go as we'd planned," I tried.

"We?" Spliff spluttered. "Whoa there, cowboy! Don't drag me into this. You were the one who cocked up the spell."

"I did not cock it up. I read it exactly as it was written. We did everything to the letter."

"Making Super Mario here corporeal was not part of the deal. We were just supposed to bind him so that you could ask him questions. Why on Earth did you decide to do that? Tell me?"

"I didn't know that's what it would do!"

"You didn't know?" Gerald was totally stunned. "What sort of boy are you that uses magic spells that he doesn't know what they do? You could have turned me into a pig!"

"Malcolm said that the spell would tie you to this plane so that I could... just... ask..." I stuttered to a full stop as I saw Gerald's moustache twitch in his thinking manner.

"Malcolm?" Gerald asked. "Quiet lad. Dark hair going white? Funny looking eyes?"

We nodded.

Gerald twitched his moustache once more. "I think you've been had, sonny. He's been to see me a few times and each time it's with the 'What's it like on the other side?' or 'Do you feel you're not in control of your destiny?' Personally he gives me the creeps."

Two minutes later we were stood outside Malcolm's door whilst Spliff and I tried to work out our next course of action.

"We could knock."

Spliff shook his head. "One: he's out with the lady in lavender, remember? Two: as it was he who gave you this magical dumb-bell, do you really think he's going to be kind enough to bear the load? The smug little shit's probably sipping chamomile tea and eating bourbons with his..." he spun his hand maniacally trying to think of a suitably derogatory term, "his... sugar mummy whilst regaling her with a quaint little tale of how he duped a pair of ignorant Philistines."

I tapped a nail against my teeth. "Point taken. So how do we get in?"

"You could always break the door down," Spliff smiled viciously.

"Me? Why me?"

"Oh, I just thought all the lead that you keep in your brain case instead of grey matter might be heavy enough to smash through plywood."

"That's uncalled for." I wagged my finger at my spiteful friend. "He took advantage of me. I was in a state."

"Why don't I let us in?" Gerald suggested. "I could open the door."

Spliff squinted at him. "What? You think you could go all Casper the Friendly Cat-burglar, float through the wall and unlock the door from the inside? But you're corporeal! Solid!"

"Yes I am, which means I can use these." He fished around in his overall pocket and jangled a set of keys in front of Spliff's face. He turned to the door, selected a Yale key and inserted it into the lock. "Needs a touch of oil this. I'll have to sort it later." There was a click and the door swung inwards. "There we go. Let's have a look shall we?"

I followed him in and looked around. The room was more or less how it had been that afternoon: neat, precise, full of books and an aromatic pall of incense hanging in the air. Spliff was straight over to the bookcase. "Wallace, you old bugger, what have you got here?" He started to pull books off the shelves at random, flicking through them.

"Spliff!" I hissed. "Focus! We need to find what we came for. Stop messing his room up."

He ignored me and continued to paw over Malcolm's things. "Oh, hello."

I recognised that little croon. He had found something interesting - something that one would not expect to have found in a certain situation. You know, like a condom in the Pope's wallet - that sort of thing. "What is it?" I walked over to the desk and looked at what he was holding in his hand. It was the small stick of wood that had been decorated with coloured ribbons. "I saw that earlier. He was very protective of it."

"I'm not surprised. It's not really the sort of thing someone considering the clergy as an occupation should really have. It's an asherah."

"And that is?"

Spliff shook his head in despair. "Samuel, Samuel, when will you learn that religions are founded on their histories and not on what we pontificate about in the modern day. You've read the Old Testament?"

"Some of it."

It was my turn to receive a Paddington Bear stare. "You know the Canaanites? They inhabited the Holy Land before Moses and his bunch kicked them out."

I nodded. I wasn't completely illiterate. "Malcolm showed me an ancient scroll written by them."

"Humph. Nice bit of bed-time reading I'm sure. Well they had this rather fun practice of *erecting*," he savoured that word a bit too much, "big wooden poles then decorating them and dancing round them butt naked in the moonlight."

"You sure that's not your perverted imagination there?"

"Okay, okay, let's just go for scantily clad. But the Hebrews hated this so either made them convert or wiped them out. The whole thing was a fertility ritual. Freud must have loved it - big sticks and all that."

"Rather like a maypole," Gerald suggested.

Spliff nodded. "Exactly. It's all giving back to Mother Nature and that sort of crap. Anyway, the pole was called an asherah and, incidentally, so was their goddess."

I took the stick and frowned. "So what the hell is Malcolm doing with an ancient fertility symbol?"

Spliff shrugged. "God knows, but my guess is that it has something far more to do with his lady-friend than the Church of England."

I grimaced and placed the asherah back down where it had been lying on top of a large tome that was open on Malcolm's desk. I frowned. The book was open at "P" and there was a pencil mark in the margin next to an entry. I read it over and suddenly felt rather sick. "You'd better see this."

Gerald and Spliff peered over my shoulders and read the passage for themselves.

"Oh," said Gerald.

"Bugger," said Spliff.

The passage in question, to paraphrase, was regarding psychopomps. Psychopomps, explained the author of the encyclopaedia, were things that were used to guide the souls of those who have not fully passed over to "their final resting place on the other side". So all we needed was a psychopomp and that would be that - Gerald could wend his merry way on into the afterlife and we could get our lives back to normal.

There was, however, just one teensy-weensy, little problem.

A psychopomp was, itself, the soul of someone or something that had also died. Not really something that we had on our person - excluding Gerald of course.

There was only one thing that I could think to say at that moment: "I need a drink."

Apparently ghosts did have a problem with drinking after all. Gerald could touch things and manipulate things here on the material plane, but liquids did appear to pass straight through him. Not literally straight through him - puddle on the floor style - but it would seem that a ghostly bladder had no memory of what it was supposed to do. So, as soon as he had downed the first can, his distraught phantom insides caused him to run quickly to the toilet.

"Guess we'd better have his." I took a fresh can and passed it over to Spliff who ripped it open, necked it and held his hand out for another. I obliged. This time he drank more slowly.

"What about a pigeon?" he mused between sips.

I lowered my can. "Why? Are you hungry? Won't a frozen pizza suffice?"

"No, you dingbat! Not to eat. As a psychopomp."

"Can't say I've got any to hand."

"Campus is full of 'em." He nodded towards the kitchen window. "What say we nip out and, you know..." He waved his can in front of his neck.

"What? Offer it a beer?"

Spliff groaned theatrically and sank back into the kitchen chair. "For God's sake, Sam. I mean go and neck one. Use it as a psychopomp."

"Oh. I see." I finished my can as I mulled this over. "Not sure that would work. One: how do you propose we catch said pigeon. Two: if we did, would you have the balls to wring its feathery little neck whilst it sat there cooing cutely up at you. Three: if we did slay the little sky-rat, who's to say it would actually do what we wanted in its afterlife. If I was a dead pigeon, I would be more likely to want to go and evacuate ghost droppings in the eyes of my killers."

"Good point, Watson." Spliff waved a finger in the air. Then reached for another can. "Hadn't thought about that."

"Hadn't thought about what?" asked Gerald as he re-entered the room.

"The downside to using a murdered pigeon as a possible psychopomp," I explained, finishing off my own can. "Far too risky."

Gerald nodded slowly and sat down in a spare chair. "True. Dirty little blighters. Always making such a mess. Perhaps I could just spend the rest of eternity stalking the campus and exterminating the vile little fiends with their beady eyes and pointy beaks..."

I held my hand up. "Okay, okay. We get it. You don't like pigeons."

"You could be the Death of Pigeons," Spliff volunteered. "Make yourself a long, black cloak and go around throwing about bits of bread soaked in cola."

I looked at my rather drunk friend. "I beg your pardon? What the hell has that got to do with anything?"

He chuckled to himself. "You must have heard of what happens to pigeons when you feed them cola, Sam? Surely?"

I shook my head.

He whooshed his hands apart making an exploding noise and spraying beer liberally about his person.

"I'll take your word for it," I said, then yawned loudly.

"You tired, Sam?" Spliff asked, sipping more beer as I nodded. "Why don't you get forty winks? Gerald and I are still good to go. Perhaps we can figure something out?"

Okay, so you sort of know what happens here, but I was really, really tired. My shoulders were aching and my eyelids were drooping. I needed no encouragement to rest my head down on the kitchen table for five minutes.

Besides, Spliff was there to make sure nothing happened, wasn't he?

Yeah, right.

As I dozed, I was aware of everything spinning. I knew that the earth spun on its axis as it spun around the Sun that spun around the centre of the galaxy that most likely spun around a primal hub of the universe; but was I supposed to be so aware of it?

I tried to open my eyes.

I gave up.

I just lay there with my head on the nice, cool dining table whilst everything around me spun in a perpetual drift of the universe.

I swallowed and the contents of a dozen cat litter trays burnt their way down my oesophagus. I groaned. No more. I would imbibe no more lager. Why had it betrayed me? It had tasted so good when I had been drinking it just a while back. Now it was like the sandpaper-encrusted toilet paper of Satan's bottom. I'd have to change my drink of choice. No more artificial fizz for me. I'd take it neat and straight. Yes, whiskey in future. Nice, mellow, pure whiskey like my dad used to drink.

Dad.

I kept my eyes closed. Not even the welling tears could force me to open them as the weight of despair sank down into my alcohol-sodden stomach. How was I going to cope? He had always been there. Now he was going to be taken away from me. And what about Mum? He had done everything for her: brought in the money, paid the bills, decorated the house, burned the Sunday lunch. I managed a little smile at the reminiscence of my dad grinning proudly as he carved into the remains of a charred cow, whilst my mum looked on in dread.

This little piece of positive thinking gave my eyelids the smallest amount of strength they needed to jack themselves apart from one another. It was as I pried them open and the smallest of tears trickled down my face that I heard the most abysmal noise.

It was a deep, threatening roar. At first, I thought a lion had stalked into Borrowdale Hall, but I soon chided myself for such a stupid idea. Only an idiot with the hangover from hell could possibly think that. Then, through a misty blear, I saw Spliff sprawled on his chair, his head slung back, his jaw slack and the mating call of a hippopotamus resonating from his mouth.

At first I smiled, amused at the sight, then I felt a wave of panic waft over me as I remembered Gerald. I spun my head round one hundred and eighty degrees without it losing contact to the table, felt my stomach lurch and closed my eyes once more to try and still the motion of all creation.

When I opened them again, I was aware that we were not alone. There was a fourth person, a man, stood in the kitchen. He was talking quietly to Gerald who was listening intently to what the newcomer had to say. My brain was having trouble catching up with what my eyes were telling it, so it adamantly refused to help out. All I could do was watch as a yellow glow enveloped the dead caretaker. Then, before my bleary eyes, he dissipated and became one with the mist which drifted up into the air and faded away.

I must have grunted or made some sort of noise because the stranger turned and looked straight at me. I tried without much success to focus my eyes, but the muscles around the sockets were playing havoc with my vision. I was sure that I could see straight through him and he seemed somewhat blurred. I could not make out his clothes or fully define the features of his face. I tried to speak, but he shook his head as if telling me not to exert myself, then the fog around his face cleared and I recognised his features.

They were the same ones that I saw every time I looked into a mirror.

My brain decided that it was now completely overloaded and gave up the ghost. I passed out.

I was to stir, albeit rather briefly, one more time - can't a guy sleep off a drunken stupor in peace? I heard the slow, precise clicking of heels on tiles. They were the sort of heels which said, "Hello boys," and were worn by the sort of woman who would devour a man either as an object of desire, a morsel of nutrition or perhaps both.

They were what I refer to as "praying mantis heels". They are normally glossy black or tart red and they are confident in their approach. There's not the slightest hint of wobble, no uncertainty. They are heels with a purpose, heels with a mission.

And they clicked to a stop right next to me.

By now, my brain had packed its bags and left for Acapulco. I didn't even try to move or open my eyes when I felt long, manicured fingers run up my neck and into my hair. "This one's rather cute," murmured their owner who owned the sort of voice that matched her dress sense: deep, slightly cruel and ever so sexy.

I was aware of someone else walking into the room and mutter something just out of earshot. Then the woman stroking my hair started to hum under her breath and lights suddenly exploded in my head. It was wonderful! I was in heaven! Paradise was my giving in to her every whim. All I had to do was follow her, obey her...

"Stop that!" hissed her companion, who sounded male and rather annoyed. "We don't have time."

The humming stopped and suddenly I was feeling like crap - empty and drunk on a hard kitchen table. There was a rustling of paper and something was thrust into my hand. I heard the man walk off, anger and jealousy resonating in his hard footfalls.

My head was stroked one more time and there was the scent of the most amazing perfume - fresh and warm at the same time, a blue ocean washing over a sun-baked sand dune - as the woman's mouth bent down to my ear and her lips whispered just one word. "Later."

Then she was gone, her killer heels carrying her out into the corridor.

When I awoke, the sun was streaming in through the large kitchen windows and my senses were being soothed by someone cooking eggs and bacon. I winced as the dining table clung desperately to my face and my back cracked harshly when I sat up. Spliff was no longer slouched, snoring in his chair. He was now over by the hob, industriously pouring love and contrition into my breakfast. He turned as he heard me stirring and said nothing. He dished up the aforementioned duo of food along with fried bread, grilled tomatoes and even some lovingly reheated baked beans. Quietly, he slipped the act of penance onto the table and laid out a knife and a fork. As I tucked into the food (I didn't turn vegan until a few months later), the kettle boiled and he poured us both a cup of coffee. I noticed that he shovelled six sugars into his. Boy, he really was full of self-loathing this morning.

He placed my mug next to me and I took a small sip then continued to fill my stomach up with something other than alcohol. Spliff sat down in his chair and waited.

I continued to eat.

I'm not a spiteful person by nature but that morning I wanted him to stew longer than my mum's extra-strong red label tea.

When I had finished the breakfast and was sat sipping my coffee, I let my eyes fall on him. My friend shifted uncomfortably in his seat and his eyes cast down to watch his hands clasped around his own mug.

"I fell asleep," he finally managed, his voice not much more than a whisper.

"I know," I said.

He hesitated, unsure how to proceed. His eyes glanced over to the empty chair and his face reddened with embarrassment.

"Gerald's gone." His eyes finally looked up at mine and the fear in them was pitiful.

"I know."

Spliff looked somewhat perplexed. "You don't sound too unhappy about it," he said.

I shrugged and winced as I un-kinked my neck a bit before sipping some more coffee. "There's not a lot we can do about it is there? And we were trying to help him on his way, weren't we?"

"But what if something happened to him? Something bad?"

"I don't think that's the case." I went on to explain what I had seen during the night during Spliff's little nap. "I think he's at peace now, so to speak."

"You really think that was you?"

I nodded. "I could hardly be mistaken about my own face, could I?"

Spliff stroked his cheek, his brain cells ticking over. "How old?"

"Sorry?"

"How old did you look?"

"Dunno. I'm crap with ages," I said. Then I frowned and looked down at my hand. "There was something else. Did you see a piece of paper lying around?"

"No. What was it?"

I started to look around the table. "There were other people here later. One male and one definitely female. They put something in my hand." I looked under the table. "Ah, there we are. It must have fallen out." I bent down, picked it up and opened it out. It was a note written in neat, cursive handwriting. Malcolm's handwriting.

"Samuel," I read aloud for Spliff's benefit, "if you are reading this then you have successfully sent your

169

ghostly visitor on his way and I have left your life for the time being. I hope you got some answers to your questions, I truly do. I know I have. I have been asking questions for a long time now and, at last, someone will show me what I am yearning to know and understand - things that academia and the church could never satisfy my curiosity for. Talking of the church, I am sure that my placement will gratefully take you on now as I have no need for it. It's Saint Cuthbert's out in Caton. I hope it works out for you. Give them a ring but, like I said earlier, watch out for the vicar's daughter. She's rather feisty.

"Until we meet again, Malcolm."

"Well," said Spliff.

"Well," I agreed. "The old bugger. Didn't see that coming.

Spliff drained his coffee. "You think the woman with him was his benefactor."

"I guess so. She sounded rather hot."

"Well."

"Well."

So we sat there for a while finishing our coffees before sorting ourselves out for the morning. At nine, I gave Saint Cuthbert's a ring and arranged to visit them that afternoon.

That afternoon was probably even more momentous than the previous night.

That afternoon I met Caroline.

But that's another story.

The Case of The Paranoid Poltergeist.

The next day I had the hangover from hell. Now, I know what you're thinking, "Sure, Sam. We've all been there. A bit too much hard stuff and you have a dry mouth and a bit of a throbbing head." Well, let me tell you this, when it gets to about nine in the morning and the sunlight streaming through the open window is burning into your retinas when your eyelids are shut and the noise of passing traffic sounds like the four horsemen are partying on your eardrums, then you have a true hangover, my friend.

The worst of it was, the phone was ringing.

I was aware that there was this very loud, insistent din screaming at me and making my world shimmy and shake worse than a belly dancer atop of the Leaning Tower of Pisa, the trouble was that I could do nothing about it. I tried to move my hand but there were no muscles there, just jelly - fat wobbly jelly clinging to my heavy, heavy bones. Without opening my eyes, I put all my effort into my shoulders and tried to heave myself over.

I succeeded.

I fell off my office sofa and crashed downwards, smashing my nose on the floor.

I staggered to my feet and realised that there was blood dribbling from my left nostril. I weakly raised a finger towards it in a vain attempt to staunch the flow, whilst I reached for the phone with my free hand.

Where was the phone?

It had been on the desk yesterday. I was sure of it. I half staggered, half crawled across the room in search of the screeching little harpy, then tripped over one of three empty whiskey bottles. I crashed in a heap and nearly shoved my finger right up my nostril when I saw the dratted device lying on the floor at the foot of the sofa next to an empty Chinese take-away box.

As I fought back a rising tide of sweet and sour bean curd I grabbed the handset to my ear. "Sam Spallucci," I croaked down the line. The blood was now flowing quite freely out of my nose and I was trying to stop it from splattering onto the mouth piece with my handkerchief.

"Hello?" came a faint voice from a very long way away. "Is there anybody there?"

"Hello!" I shouted back, "I'm here."

"Hello? You're very faint," the other voice said.

I scowled, swayed, then noticed that I was talking into the ear-piece. I fumbled the phone around and asked, "Is this better?"

"Ah, yes. Much better."

"Sorry about that. You know what modern technology's like." I patted my pockets and found a crumpled packet of Luckies. The person on the other end said something as I fished one out and tried to light

172

it. "Sorry?" I apologised. "Could you repeat that, please. I missed it."

"I said, 'Do you investigate matters of a paranormal nature?'"

"D'uh, I'm an Investigator of the Paranormal, read the sign" said my head. "I do. What seems to be the problem?" said my mouth.

"It's difficult to explain over the phone. I'm ringing from Edmund Campion School on Ashton Road. Would you be able to come and speak to me in person?"

I was having no luck at all lighting the damn cigarette and my nose was still streaming blood so I shoved the filter up my nostril to try and make a practical use of it. "Ashton Road? That's down by the RLI isn't it?"

"Yes it is."

I nodded. "Okay I should be there in an hour or so, I guess." On the way to the school I would pop into A&E and have someone look at my nose – kill two birds with one stone. Success!

Three hours later I was standing in the foyer of Edmund Campion High School with the receptionist eyeing me as if I was an unsuccessful stunt double for John Merrick. I have to admit she had every reason to view me with suspicion, the Accident and Emergency guys had done a real number on my nose. By the time I had staggered into the RLI my face had been covered in blood and my handkerchief had been sopping red (I had given the cigarette up as a bad idea when I sneezed crossing over South Road). They had taken one sniff of me and mockingly said that if they were to try and cauterise the inside of my nostril then my face might go up in flames from the alcohol vapours. Ha ha, medical

173

humour is so droll.

So instead of nipping the problem in the bud, so to speak, they shoved wadding the size of an elephant's suppository up my nostril and taped it in place with plasters of some sort. They hadn't been very gentle with the process and, as a result, finger-spaced bruising was starting to bloom on my cheek bones and forehead.

Oh yes, I looked quite the picture, and here I was asking to be let within striking distance of teenage youths. I'm thankful the receptionist didn't ring the police there and then. Instead she asked, "Who is it you have an appointment with?"

I grimaced. "I don't know their name. They rang me this morning, about nineish."

"They didn't give you a name?"

"I didn't ask." I nervously rubbed the side of my inflamed nostril. It hurt and I winced.

The receptionist tapped a biro against her teeth. "Just let me ring someone, okay?"

I nodded as she picked up the phone and began to speak in hushed whispers. I scanned the area looking for the quickest way out if I was to be pursued by a bunch of prefects, security guards or whatever they used in schools these days. From what I'd seen in the press it would most probably be riot police with cattle prods – wasn't that what they used in the classrooms now? The tabloids were always banging on about the hallowed halls of education being out of control and run by undisciplined, knife-wielding hoodies.

As it was, I was confronted by none of these, but something far more potent. For a split second I was transported back thirty years. I was an eight-year-old boy stood outside the headmistress' office waiting to be scolded for dipping Lizzy Powell's blonde pig-tails in red paint and proceeding to use them to create a sunburst picture on her desk. Mrs Enfield, all green-suited five foot five of her was peering over her half-moon spectacles at me and saying "Samuel, I am so disappointed with you."

"Sorry, Miss," I mumbled.

"Pardon, Mr Spallucci?"

I snapped back to the here and now and gawped at the simulacrum of my childhood nightmare then stuttered, "I... I said... 'Sorry, I missed that.'" I smiled. At least I tried to. It hurt rather, so I guessed I must have looked like I was leering somewhat.

The head teacher gave me a curious look and repeated her original statement, "I'm Lindsay Wetherington. I'm glad you could make it," she glanced first at her watch, then my nose, "at last. Please, come into my office."

I tried to smile again and followed her whilst mentally telling myself over and over again, "I am not in trouble. I am not in trouble."

Her office was quite opulent. The walls were lined with a mixture of book-laden shelves, certificates and pictures of smiling pupils following their glorious sporting triumphs. Large ferns stood to the rear of the room, framing a panoramic picture window with a commanding view of the rugby field. The main attraction, however, was the desk. A grandiose mahogany affair topped with green leather and numerous filing trays. Next to a name plate sat a wood block carved with the old Trumanism "The Buck Stops Here." I had a feeling that Mrs (I had noticed a plain wedding band) Wetherington was somewhat of a pro-active head rather than the pen-pusher types that seem to be quite prevalent these days. She was the sort who, when faced with a problem, would grab it by the ears and bellow loudly at it until it cowered into submission. Now, as she seated herself in her high-backed leather office chair, she was faced with me – a somewhat scruffy-looking chap who pervaded an aroma of whiskey mixed with mints and sported an assortment of unfashionable facial bruises complemented by a rather extravagant nose-bandage.

"I must say, Mr Spallucci," she commented over the tips of her fingers that were steepled in front of her face, "that you are not quite what I had imagined. Did you fall out of bed the wrong side this morning, perchance?"

I grimaced and shrugged. "An industrial accident," I volunteered.

There was a short painful silence whilst her eyes bored into me. "Quite," she remarked. Short, to the point and extremely withering. I think that summed up both her use of words and her character in general. "Well, as it happens, come what may, I am in need of your services. Tell me, what do you know about poltergeists?"

I exhaled sharply and said, "Well, for starters, I'm sure that they're not covered by the National Curriculum."

There was a frosty silence.

The clock ticked.

Wetherington glared at me.

Oops.

I tried a more formal approach. "The term 'poltergeist' comes from the German for 'rumble ghost' referring to the noises often made by an invisible being knocking things about or moving them. In documented cases it has often been mentioned that the manifestation is centred around an individual, usually a teenager or adolescent." I paused. "I'm guessing that you have a lot of those here?"

"One thousand two-hundred and eighty-nine in years seven to eleven and two-hundred and eighty-seven in the sixth form, Mr Spallucci," she rolled off without a pause. "They are all in my care whilst they are in these four walls and I will not let anyone or anything bring them to harm. You understand me?"

I nodded sage-like. Then, when no more information was forthcoming, I asked, "And you think that one of them is at the centre of paranormal activity?"

"About two weeks ago," Wetherington began, "members of my staff noticed little peculiarities. Things would go missing. They would put something down on the desk and a moment later it would have been moved away by a few centimetres or so."

I shrugged. "Not necessarily a poltergeist. It could be absent-mindedness or, at worst, latent telekinesis. It could even be a childhood prank. We used to do that sort of thing all the time when I was a kid."

"My students do not play pranks, Mr Spallucci," Wetherington simmered. "They know how to behave themselves. Besides, the matter did not stop there. Things rapidly progressed. There were knocking noises, chairs falling over, doors inexplicably slamming. Then yesterday, this happened." She slid a digital photo across her desk to me. I let out a low whistle. It was a picture of a large ornate window with every single piece of glass smashed out.

"That looks expensive," I said, "and dangerous. Was anyone hurt?"

177

The teacher shook her head. "Fortunately not, but you can see my predicament here. I have to make sure that this does not happen again."

I nodded in agreement. If that glass had hit someone, it could have been very, very messy. Then something struck me as rather odd and I enquired, "Why have I not seen anything about this in the local press? The rags love a good, messy story about schools and safety to pupils? They must be lapping this up."

Wetherington paused and, for the first time since I entered the room, I sensed a certain amount of hesitation shroud her. She placed her hands flat on the desk and stated, "There will be no comments on this matter in the press. Of that I can assure you, Mr Spallucci."

There was a light knock at the door. "Ah." She rose from her seat, smoothing down her immaculate green suit. "That will be your escort. Enter!"

A teenage boy walked into the room. He was about average height and bore a mop of wavy, blonde hair that sat comfortably above his steel-rimmed spectacles. His uniform was moderately neat: a slight crook to the tie, a trace of shirt peering out from under his blazer and small scuffs to his shoes. The normal attire for a teenage school boy. He glanced quickly at me then focussed on his head-teacher. "You wanted me, Miss?" he asked, fear of retribution apparent in his voice.

"John," Mrs Wetherington began to explain, "Mr Spallucci here will be staying with us today to investigate certain matters. I need you to guide him around. Take him to your lessons and assist him, so to speak."

At the realisation that he wasn't in trouble, the boy visibly brightened. "Oh. Okay." He smiled at me.

"Pleased to meet you, Mr Spallucci."

"Call me Sam," I insisted.

"He will call you Mr Spallucci," Wetherington interjected. "You are an adult. He is a child. Each must know their place."

I shrugged and slipped a covert wink to John. "Okay, Mr Spallucci it is then. Shall we be going, John?"

I immediately took to my young guide. John was the bouncy sort of lad who always seems to sport a lop-sided grin that can tease a smile out of the most mendacious grouch. As he led me along the stone corridors to his next lesson (Information Technology) he chattered on about school life and other such things. From the random little anecdotes that he leapt between like a frog on bouncy lily pads, I got the overall impression that Edmund Campion was a nice place to study. Sure, Mrs Wetherington was strict and bollocked anyone who vaguely stepped out of line, but, as a result, no one normally *did* step out of line so everyone bimbled along in their own sweet way going to lessons, enjoying the companionship of their peers.

"I'm in a band, you know," he said as we turned down what seemed to be the forty-second corridor – I was completely lost – "My mum taught me to play the piano when I was little and a few of us got together and started jamming at the weekends. It's well cool."

"Cool?"

"Yeah, you know. Cool." He frowned at me. "You do know what that means, don't you?"

I grinned. "I'm not that old, you know. I just thought kids wouldn't still be using the same words as I did when I was your age."

He quickly glanced over his shoulder as if checking the coast was clear then leant up towards me in a conspiratorial manner. "Are you here because of... you know?"

I raised an eyebrow then winced. It hurt my nose. "Because of... I know what?"

"The stuff that's been going on," he whispered. "Things going bump and that window breaking yesterday."

I stood still and carefully eyed the youth up and down. "You mean that window that was broken by a cricket ball?" I fished just to see what exactly he knew.

John snorted. "Cricket ball, my arse. That's not possible."

"Why?"

He counted on his fingers: "One, we don't play cricket in the autumn. Two, I was there when it happened." He crossed his arms and grinned. "So what do you think's going on?"

"Whoa, whoa cowboy," I shot my own furtive glance around the corridor. We were alone, for now. "Let's just rewind a bit here. You were there? When the window broke?"

"Uh huh."

"What happened exactly?"

"Well it was lunch time and a group of us were just hanging around, you know. Not doing anything. We weren't where we shouldn't have been. Anyways we were chatting and it just sort of broke. You know? Smash! Made a great noise."

I sighed. Oh brother! "And none of you threw anything at the window at all?" I asked.

"No!" He shook his head violently. "We'd be in trouble if we did that. But we ran away anyway 'cos we didn't want to get the blame." His eyes shot over my shoulder and he was suddenly silent as a pair of girls walked around the corner. "Come on," he said. "My lesson's just down here." He led me down the corridor to a blue-doored room.

The computer room was unlike anything I had ever known at school back in the eighties. As John led me in, I marvelled at the sheer spaciousness of the suite. Tall windows let sunlight weave its way through roman blinds catching the white surface of the huge interactive whiteboard at the front of the classroom. There were four rows of terminals: one down each side of the room and two back to back down the middle. Most of the monitors were slideshowing bright, colourful photographs of school life: smiling teachers, thoughtful pupils, that sort of stuff. Some terminals were already occupied by members of the class who had logged on and were industriously working away at spreadsheets and Word documents.

I frowned.

"What is it?" John enquired as he started to log onto a nearby machine.

"Nothing really," I replied, undoing my overcoat and removing my hat. "It's just that this is a far flung thing from the computing of my day. We were all networking and programming in dark, dingy rooms which stank of teenage body odour. This," I waved my hand around at the room in general, "seems more like an office than a schoolroom." I shook my head and tapped my fingernail against my front teeth in thought.

John shrugged. "I guess things move on." He

removed his blazer and adjusted his sleeves before he began to type. I noticed a lilac coloured band on his wrist which bore the legend, "Anything is possible..."

"What's that?" I asked, curious.

He paused his typing. "The wristband?"

I nodded.

"It's a society I belong to. Surely you've seen the posters around town?"

I shook my head. I didn't tell him that satanic actors and new-born vampires had made me slightly distracted from the day-to-day recently. "I've been busy," I said instead.

"Wow." The boy's face was a picture of incredulity. "I can't believe you've missed this. It's really big. A lot of us are members." At this comment, a number of arms were raised and flashes of lilac wobbled down teenage wrists. "Here," he rummaged through his bag and dragged out a three-fold A4 leaflet, "take this. It's got all about the society. It'll change your life."

I smiled politely. I had heard all this before, many, many times. It was the big build up before either a financial sting or a catastrophic failing of faith. I glanced at the cover of the leaflet. It bore a lilac coloured emblem on it that seemed to resemble an upper-case letter "T" which was wrapped around by two spiralling lines. "I'll read it later," I smiled, carefully filing it in my inside jacket pocket. "I'm a bit busy at the moment."

John nodded and returned his attention to his screen.

I took a seat in the corner of the room just as a shrew-like little man with a sparsely haired head stalked in and slammed his things on the teacher's desk. He glared at me suspiciously and marched over. "You must be the investigator, I presume?" he snarled, eyeing me up and down the way an exterminator does an unfortunate rat that he has happened across in a dodgy restaurant.

"Sam Spallucci." I stuck out my hand. He gave it a withering glance then fixed his eyes on mine.

"You don't look like an Eyetie," he surmised, his fierce pupils darting over my face.

I groaned internally. "I'm not," I explained. "It's a long story, but my Dad..."

"Can it!" the teacher snapped, obviously not interested. "I don't give a flying fig for your life story. I'm Mr Crash and this is my lesson. Don't you dare get in the way. If you so much as step out of line, I'll throw you out the goddamn window. Is that understood?"

Part of me wanted to jump to attention and snap off a salute whilst shouting, "Yessir! Nossir!" but the sane side of me reeled it in and I just nodded my head. This seemed to appease Crash who turned his back on me and began the lesson. Well, I call it a lesson, it was more like a military drill. The teacher would bark out orders and the pupils would follow the instructions meticulously to the letter. Any who didn't keep up or dared to ask for an explanation were publicly humiliated in front of their peers. Needless to say there was no chatter, just the diligent click-clack-click of keyboard typing punctuated by the guttural bark of Mr Crash.

As Crash ranted on about files, folders and syntax I let my mind contemplate more ethereal matters, such as what was causing the disturbances here. So far I had seen nothing untoward whatsoever. The pupils hardly stepped out of line let alone allow their subconscious manifest itself as some sort of malevolent force and as for the window, well John himself had said that a group of lads had been there *doing nothing* when it had shattered. I was just starting to consider the possibility that all this was some sort of teenage prank which the school management in its blind disciplinarian style was unable to accept as reality when I felt a buzzing in my trouser pocket. This was followed by the raucous voice of Tom Waits singing about *swordfishtrombones*. I fished for my phone, saw the caller as "Unknown" and bounced it to voicemail.

When I looked up, the room was silent and most eyes were on me, especially those of Crash. "Sorry," I said out loud. "Bugger," I thought inwardly.

I had the image of a minotaur readying itself to charge and blowing sulphurous steam through its flared nostrils as Crash regarded me with complete and utter contempt. He lifted his finger and was about to shout at me when a dark-haired boy nervously raised his hand. "What is it Swarbrick?" snapped the teacher, flashing his wrathful energy between me and the unfortunate boy.

The boy muttered something that I couldn't make out, but Crash obviously heard quite clearly. "Well you've obviously opened the wrong file," he spat with complete lack of sympathy as he threw me a parting glance that was packed to the brim with hatred and warning before descending on the unfortunate boy.

I pulled my phone out and quickly turned it off. I valued my life too much to let anyone else disturb Crash's lesson.

I closed my eyes and rested my head against the wall as my nose throbbed in a way that told me it was going to be a long, long day.

I have to admit that I wasn't the most industrious of pupils during my time at school, and, as the lesson dragged on, I could feel the soporific effects of the warm room and the droning baritone of Mr Crash taking their toll on me. I was suddenly transported in time to the back row of a computing lesson where the monitors were small and green and where no light could penetrate the smog of underarms and fetid kit bags. I was supposed to be concentrating on setting up a simple subroutine, but the numbers and letters just kept darting around the dim screen refusing to stay still. My tired eyes began to drag and my lids started to droop.

I woke to the sound of tentative giggling and was aware of a voluminous shadow blocking out the calming light.

"Snoring tends to distract the pupils," rumbled the shadow.

I snapped up straight. "Wasn't snoring!" I managed as my dry lips prised apart and my parched throat gasped for air. There was a solid thud as the back of my head connected with a notice-board behind me, sending leaflets about cyber-bullying cascading down onto the floor. I muttered an apology and started to gather up the glossy pieces of paper.

"Typical!" Crash snorted. "Just what I thought. A loser. A waste of space. Look at you man. You're a wreck. A mess. You shouldn't be here disturbing my lesson."

He went on and on, piling heap upon heap of insult on my reddening cheeks. I could feel the eyes of all the students fixed on me and I wanted the ground to swallow me whole. It was so embarrassing.

But then, as the laughing paused whilst Crash

stopped to draw a single breath, I heard a small voice say from somewhere in the room, "It wasn't his fault."

That was when all hell broke loose.

First, I felt a breeze rubbing against my cheeks, calming the flaming embarrassment, then I saw posters and carefully crafted work pulled free from the walls and start to spin around the air in the classroom. Next, the mouse on Crash's PC detached itself and flew at high speed before thumping him on the back of his head. He turned to see who had thrown it, only to be bombarded with every other mouse in the room as they levitated off the desks and rocketed towards him. He barely had enough time to cover his face from the barrage of plastic and cable. I grabbed the bulky man by the square shoulders and tried to drag him down, out of the way, but he shrugged me off and screamed, "Stop this, I say! Stop it at once!" He raised a finger to say something else, but a flying keyboard caught him on the temple and knocked him out cold. He fell like a stone that had been dropped from a great height and, quite appropriately, considering his name, crashed to the floor.

The uproar ceased and calm settled once more as pieces of students' work drifted down to the carpet. I glanced up at the bare walls.

Well, I say bare. *Almost* bare would be a better description. Here and there the occasional piece of work was still firmly attached and neatly presented for all to see. *Curious*: I thought, before venturing over to the sleeping teacher. I smiled to myself as I observed that it was now his turn to snore.

After the IT lesson, came lunch. John told me that he had a packed lunch so we went out of the school building onto the yard area where he rummaged around in vain. "It's in here somewhere," he said, his head immersed in the gaping mouth of the over-stuffed bag. "I was sure I packed it last night." I peered over his shoulder and saw a multitude of pen lids, worn books, an odd sock and an mp3 player but no lunch box. He zipped the bag shut. "Crap!" he moaned. "I must have left it on the kitchen side. Mum'll kill me."

"Always used to be my dad that bawled me out," I said. "Mum was the soft touch."

John shook his head. "It's just me and Mum. She works hard and I have to remember so much stuff. It keeps floating away." He mimed little clouds drifting out of his ears then slung the offending bag back onto his shoulder.

I looked over at the queue of students lining up by the canteen. "What's the food like here?" I asked.

"It's okay."

"Better than nothing?"

"Definitely better than nothing!"

I began to walk over to the queue. "Come on then, slowcoach. Guess I'd better feed you. Don't want you getting into trouble."

John gave his lop-sided grin and bounced along after me.

"So you think it's really a poltergeist?" John was talking around a large slice of pizza whilst wiggling a half-full tumbler of orange juice. "I mean what else could it have been this morning?"

I finished off a small jacket potato with beans and scanned the canteen. It was a hive of activity and not just in the physical sense. Various smells and aromas were jostling for attention in the distant memory synapses of my brain. There was the processed cheese, the over-boiled cabbage, the leathery beef and how could one forget that strange pink dessert. There they were, banging around in an old tin can and being poured over my face like a historical baptism.

Schools change. Pupils change. The food we feed them doesn't. It has to be quick, vaguely palatable and, most importantly of all, very, very cheap. People have tried to reform school dinners over the years but, at the end of the day, governments don't really give a toss. The kids don't vote yet and they will ultimately do what they are told. Sit down, shut up and eat or you go hungry - and there was a lot of eating going on here.

"Don't the teachers eat here?" I asked noting a distinct lack of adult presence. There were the odd one or two teachers prowling around, obviously on crowd control, but none were dining.

"They eat in the staff room, I guess," John finished the pizza and glugged the juice down. "But come on, is it a poltergeist?"

I didn't really want to go there. It was too early to say conclusively. "Things can sometimes be not what they seem, John," I explained. I took his unused napkin and held it out in front of him. "Look at this." I opened the napkin out and held it ready to drop down onto the table. John stared at it attentively, his brown eyes peering through his spectacles. I dropped the napkin and blew at it. The paper cloth wafted into his face. "Tell me, who moved that napkin?"

He picked it up, looked at the paper towel then at me, slightly bemused. "You did, of course. You blew on it."

I nodded. "Correct. Now watch again." I let it drop and this time I took my hat off and slammed it down on the canteen table. A number of heads turned at the sound of the noise whilst the napkin drifted off onto the floor. "Now who moved the napkin?"

"You did again... I think." He screwed up his face. "Is this a trick question?"

I grinned. "Sort of. When I blew the napkin I was willing it to move. It was my choice. When I slammed my hat down, that was what I was choosing to do. A violent, angry gesture. But it had repercussions and the napkin floated away because of it. A poltergeist isn't actually a thing, John. It's a by-product, as it were, of someone's emotions. They get angry and things happen that are inexplicable and may not be possible to directly trace to said individual. Me blowing is more like another example of a different phenomenon altogether – telekinesis. That's where an individual moves things with their mind. They are in control of their actions. Do you follow?"

He looked down at the napkin on the floor. "You're saying that the things that have been happening, we need to decide whether they were caused voluntarily or involuntarily by someone. Whether they wanted them to happen or whether it happened because they couldn't control it."

I smiled at the use of the word *we*. "Something like that. Now, when you've put that napkin in the bin, why don't we go take a look at that window?"

Our shoes crunched on cruel-looking shards of glass as we stooped underneath the red and white hazard tape. "Wow. Quite a mess," I mused, taking in the empty frames where the window had once been

189

glazed. "And you saw this happen?"

"Yeah." John hovered uneasily at the barrier.

"It's okay for you to be here, you know. You're with me. Official business," I winked.

He smiled and came further in, albeit somewhat hesitantly. "I know that. It's just it was a really weird thing."

I bent down and pulled a shard of glass from the floor. "I can imagine. I bet you were shit-scared." I tossed the fragment and picked up another one.

"It was so sudden. One minute we were talking. The next..." he fanned his arms out, "crash!"

"Crash indeed," I mumbled to myself as I studied the edges of the glass. Small conchoidal fractures perforated the surface, testament to its sudden impact. "Tell me. Who was here?"

"Me and a couple of guys from form."

I inclined my head and waited.

"Oh. You want their names?"

I nodded. "It's okay, John. They're not in trouble."

He shrugged. "You know. It's a bit weird."

I shrugged back.

"Well," he began, "there was Jack, Sam and Sally."

"Sally? A rose among the thorns?"

"Pardon?"

"A girl?"

"Oh! No!" he laughed, rocking back on his heels making the debris crunch. "No. Sally is Peter Salsworth. An old teacher named him Sally back in year seven and it stuck."

I nodded again. "What were you talking about?"

"Stuff."

I groaned and shoved my head in my hands. "John!" I cried in despair. "You've got to give me more than this, okay? How many times do I have to tell you? You're not in trouble, okay?" I levelled my eyes on the teenager and gave him my best Paddington stare. He smiled back at me. We both chuckled.

"Okay. I can't remember much, what with glass showering down on us and all that. It's a bit blurry. I think we were just talking about others in our form."

I tapped my teeth. "This... talking... would it have been favourable?"

John frowned. "What do you mean?"

"You know, was it 'Bert's a decent sort of chap,' or was it more along the lines of 'I hear Bert's got a one-inch dick?'"

John chuckled. "Ah! Gotcha. Yeah definitely the second one. We don't mean any of it, you know. It's just..." he shrugged his arms wide.

"Stuff," I provided.

"Stuff," he agreed.

"And there was no one else here apart from you, Jack, Sam and Sally?" I stood up and looked once more at the window, then down at the confusion of broken glass.

"That's right. No one."

"This glass isn't very thick, is it?" I mused, kicking at the rubbish with my shoe. "What's more it burst outwards from that window, not inwards."

John looked up at the window. "That's the staircase up to the study rooms. We all go up and down there."

"Can you hear what's going on outside whilst you're ascending and descending the stairs?"

"Yeah. Sure. Like you said, the glass isn't very... oh..."

The fact that I had realised just before him hit John as hard as if it had been the glass from the day previous. The glass had burst outwards because it had been projected away from the source and that source had heard what the boys had been talking about.

What's more they hadn't liked it one little bit.

Afternoon lessons began at quarter to two and I dutifully followed John to his next session: music. If I'd been impressed by the IT room, then I was completely bowled over by the music suite. There was a dedicated block of four rooms set apart from the main school. Two were the standard classroom set out: desks, chairs and white boards. The others were like something from a record producer's wet dream. One was a recording studio with a fully sound-proofed booth and complete mixing desk. The fourth room was a small practice area that seemed to have a whole philharmonic orchestra crammed inside. There were violins and other stringed instruments hung up on the walls. Trumpets rested next to flutes and clarinets. A double bass was propped beside four electric guitars. Then there was a big set of drums next to which stood a beautiful pair of tympani.

John noticed the look on my face as we entered the practice room. "Sam? You okay?" he asked, his brow creased somewhat in concern.

"All we had was a rusty tambourine, one and a half pairs of maracas and a glockenspiel that was missing an F sharp." I grinned at the boy. "We had to play just about everything in C."

He smiled back at me. "You musical then?"

"My dad taught me a bit when I was a kid, you know?" I walked over to the trumpet and picked it up. It had been a while, but the brass beauty sat comfortably between my hands. I placed my right fingers on the valves and wiggled their tips. The valves slid up and down like pistons on a well-maintained engine. I gave a little sigh and shot John a knowing look. I was desperate to give this horn a good old blowing.

"Knock yourself out," he said. "I'd like to hear you."

I could barely contain my glee. I inhaled and firmed up my diaphragm, placed the mouthpiece to my lips and burst into what I considered to be a fairly ragged rendition of Mack the Knife. I was in my own little world once more. I didn't think. I just let my fingers bob up and down and my lips buzz as all the noises in my ears were pushed out by the sonorous warmth of the trumpet's brassy song. I would pay for it later, I knew that for sure – that was why I had quit many years ago, the noise from the instrument always caused my ears to go crazy – but for now, I was just there, in the moment, absorbed by the encompassing arms of my brassy lover.

I pressed out the last few notes and lowered the instrument. I was aware of the fact that John and I were no longer alone. There were a few more students hovering behind him, but also in the doorway stood a slim, bespectacled teacher holding a selection of files. Her eyes were peering over the tops of her glasses and were twinkling with mischief. "Do I have a new pupil?" she asked of me.

I blushed, blew out the spittle from the trumpet and carefully replaced the instrument back where it belonged. "Sorry," I apologised. "I think I got carried away."

The mischief continued to dance in her deep blue eyes. "Okay, you lot," she shouted to the kids behind her, "concert's over. You've got work to be getting on with." They chatted to each other as some went into the classrooms, some the recording studio and some, including John, picked up instruments in the practice room where they started to warm up. "They're working on practical stuff at the moment," the teacher explained. "It'll keep them busy. I'm Abalone Morris, by the way." She stuck out her hand, which I shook. "You must be Mr Spallucci. What have you done to your nose? Did Philip hit you or something this morning?"

"Philip?"

"Sorry. Mr Crash. I know he's quite abrasive, but all the same..."

"No! No, he didn't. I had a bit of an accident before I got here."

"Ah. Looks painful." She stood, looking at me.

I think I was still blushing. "Erm... how many pupils are in this lesson?" I asked, desperately trying to get back on task.

"The usual," she said, walking through to the main classroom and dumping her files unceremoniously on the desk. "Just under thirty. These are a good bunch. Not normally any bother."

I looked around at the signs of studious industriousness. The room was a hive of learning. "What about any other trouble?"

Ms Morris' lips twisted up in a curious smile. "You mean of the inexplicable kind? No. Not with this lot. Not a flicker. Not a murmur. Not a flying keyboard," she winked.

My eyes wandered around the pupils as they

chatted, scribbled and composed. They rested on a girl with dark hair that was shot through with bright magenta streaks who was writing rapidly on a piece of music manuscript. "She wasn't in the IT lesson this morning. I would have noticed her."

"It's a different group," Ms Morris explained. "This is a top set music lesson. Philip's group were a middle set IT."

"And all departments are like that? Different sets for different subjects?"

She nodded. "It means that the pupils get quite a mix of different peers and it helps to stop little cliques forming. Also we can teach them at a more appropriate level."

"Have you had any supernatural bother?"

"Nope. None whatsoever. I obviously don't teach a ghost," she grinned.

I sighed. "It's not a ghost. It's a poltergeist."

"There's a difference?"

"Would you call a flute a clarinet?"

She cocked her head to one side in acceptance. "For now I'll take your word but perhaps you could explain the intricacies to me over a coffee some time?"

I was sure that I had now turned completely scarlet as her eyes continued to twinkle at me over her glasses. When it became apparent that I had been hit dumbstruck from being hit upon by a teacher, Ms Morris grinned as she quickly wrote something down on a scrap of paper and said, "Well, you know where I am if you feel like educating me. For now, though, I have to see to my students." Then, with a smile, she tucked the piece of paper into my chest pocket before miming a telephone at me then weaving her way expertly around the class like a queen bee in a hive, carefully coaxing the most out of workers who would quite obviously do anything that she asked of them.

At the end of the school day, John and I walked down the curved driveway that led to the main gate of Saint Edmund's. The sun shone brightly and seemed to bounce off the young lad's mop of blonde hair. For a moment he looked so very, very young, weighed down with an incredibly over-stuffed blue rucksack and his steel-rimmed spectacles perched on the end of his nose. He glanced up at me. "It's been an odd kind of day hasn't it?" he said. "Mind you, I guess you're used to all that sort of stuff."

"I've seen worse," I admitted, shivering internally as I recalled a drained body from behind the Sugar House two nights previous, "but this was rather intriguing."

"Yeah," he whispered, "it was. What will you do now?"

We had reached the large iron gates that sat open under an imposing stone arch and I paused as I saw a multitude of school kids fighting their way onto two large school buses. "Guess I'll go clean up a bit then grab a bite to eat and a drink."

"You gonna chase up any leads?" Palpable excitement was radiating from behind John's glasses.

I chuckled. "Later. I can't think on an empty stomach."

"Cool." Then suddenly he looked glum.

"What's up?" I asked.

He peered down at his feet and let his scuffed, black shoes doodle in the dust. "It's nothing. It's just, well, I never knew my dad and Mum never says much about him. Well nothing polite, that is. I just kinda wish he'd been a bit like you."

I was silent for a bit as I rubbed the bandage on the side of my swollen nose. "Really?" I said, finally. "Well I suppose something would be better than nothing."

We turned our heads in unison at the sound of a car horn blatting across the gabbling of teenagers. "Oh. It's Mum," John observed, "I've gotta go. See ya tomorrow, Sam."

"Yeah, see you tomorrow." I watched as he lolloped off across the road to a small sporty number parked down the way a bit. He waved cheerily as he climbed in the passenger seat and I saw him lean across to say something to his mother. There was a flash of light brown hair as she glanced in her mirror to peer at me, but she was parked facing away so I didn't really get to see what she looked like before they sped off down the road, narrowly missing a few school kids ambling out of their way.

I sighed. He wanted a dad like me? Either I had made a good impression or the poor kid was desperate. I turned round and headed back into town, fishing out a Lucky Strike. I would grab a bite and a drink at the Borough whilst I mulled over the events of the day.

My stomach was rumbling and my head was pounding to the sound of a thousand soldiers re-enacting a hundred different battles in my skull. The school dinner hadn't exactly been filling and my throat was parched. I needed a few hours' peace and quiet to calm myself and mull over the events of the day as well as replenish my energy reserves.

The IT lesson had been rather creepy to say the least. It certainly appeared to have been the subject of poltergeist activity. I smiled at the memory of the bully of a man being felled by a flying bit of plastics and circuitry. He'd had it coming. How long had this being going on for at the school? About a couple of weeks Wetherington had said. I was still somewhat surprised that the press hadn't gotten hold of it even with her confidence in the matter. This sort of thing would have made wonderful tabloid fodder. "Church School Home to Devil!" they should be proclaiming. Yet there was not a sniff anywhere. I'm an avid newspaper reader. I devour them daily, local and national, whenever I get the chance. I would have seen it. It would be bloody hard to miss.

Something, somewhere was wrong. Something was stopping the proverbial from hitting the fan. It just didn't add up.

I entered the Borough and the warm smells of evening service wafted up my one functioning nostril. Familiar aromas. Safety in olfactory indulgence. I saw Grace grin from under her woolly hat and pull my bottle up from under the counter before proceeding to pour me a very large measure. "Do I look that bad?" I asked as I downed the drink in one then refilled it.

"Who won? You or the door?" she giggled.

I started on my second shot and must have looked as confused as I felt until her small hand reached out and gently tapped the dressing on my nose. "Oh! That!" I said. "Neither, actually. It was the floor."

Grace winced. "Ouch. Sounds painful. You hungry?"

"Ravenous. What you got for me tonight?" I asked

as I squinted up at the specials board groaning inwardly. It was all dead, dead or dairy – nothing I could eat.

Grace cocked her head to one side. "What do you fancy, Sam?"

I sighed. My head was pounding and my stomach felt like my throat had been cut. "You still got any of those bean-burgers? And some chips?"

"Oh. Okay. I think we've got some."

I paused and looked her in the eye. She seemed suddenly less cheery. "You okay?"

"Yeah," the little redhead said, "just a long day. Spliff!" she suddenly called grinning over my shoulder. "How are you?"

I felt a warm hand clamp onto my shoulder and give it a friendly squeeze. "Fine, my little dust-devil," came the well-spoken Scottish accent. "Nothing that a good drink and a weekend with a Thai lady-boy wouldn't put right." He stopped and stared at my face. "Sam, how many times must I tell you? If you go sniffing around ladies' lavatories you will end up with a tampon up your nose."

"Don't start," I warned him. I turned to talk to Grace but she had gone. There were just our bottles on the bar. I took mine and headed over to the table. "I think there's something up with Grace," I told Spliff as we seated ourselves in the window.

He raised an eyebrow. "You don't say?"

"She seems..." I searched for the right word. "Distracted?"

Spliff sipped demurely at his neat gin. "My guess is it's man problems."

I frowned. "I didn't think she was seeing anyone?"

"She isn't."

199

"So how can it be..."

Spliff held up his hand to silence me. "Sam, Sam, Sam. You've always trusted me, haven't you?"

"Unfortunately, yes."

"Well, just trust me on this one. Our little friend is obviously pining over someone who has no interest in her whatsoever."

I wracked my brains. A man? Grace had never mentioned anyone to me before. Surely she would have said something? I came in at least once a day. It would have cropped up in conversation wouldn't it? "Who?" I asked.

The priest nearly choked as his drink seemed to go down the wrong way. He pulled a napkin off the table and patted at his mouth. "You wouldn't believe me, Sam. I'm sure she will tell you all in her own time."

A while later we had just about finished our food. My bean-burger had initially tasted of stale cardboard. Spliff suggested that I remove my nasal dressing. Tentatively I peeled back the micro-pore and swore as he laughed at my discomfort. After a bit of inquisitive prodding I yanked the dressing down from my nostril. The pain was excruciating. My friend was quite beside himself with mirth as I bit down heavily on a napkin to prevent myself from screaming the Borough down.

Fortunately, the repair work to the inside of my nose appeared to have done its job and, as the pain began to subside, I was able to eat my food without bleeding over myself. I rolled the bloody dressing in the napkin and stashed it in my coat pocket for disposal later.

As I wiped the red stains from around my nose,

Spliff asked, "So what happened to our fanged friend then? You never got back to me."

While tucking into a plate of food that could now be fully identified by taste, I apologised for not ringing him, explaining the events with Nightingale and Marcus in Dave's shop and how I had then made the most of being paid which had indirectly led to one elephant's tampon up my nose this morning.

As Spliff skewered the last remaining sliver of his steak I asked him, "So what's been wrong with your day then? Something has to be pissing you off to bring out the lady-boy desires."

The portly cleric harumphed. "The bloody Arch-Deacon's been on my back again."

I smiled. "Now there's an image."

"Quite," he muttered around the steak. "He's always on my case, that one."

"Which baptism did you forget this time, then?"

"Ha bloody ha. You know that wasn't my fault. They booked the wrong day."

"At least it wasn't a funeral."

"Who the hell do you think I am? Father Ted Bloody Crilley?" He wiped his mouth and grinned. "I love that episode. The hearse sticking out of the grave, bloody hysterical."

I nodded. Spliff and I used to watch *Father Ted* when we were students. If you haven't seen it, it's about three dysfunctional Roman Catholic priests on a god-forsaken island off the coast of Ireland. Absolute bloody genius. You have to see it. My favourite is the one where Ted and Dougal (the younger of the three priests) enter the *Eurovision Song Contest* with a little ditty named *My Lovely Horse*. Look up the video on YouTube – you will

201

be laughing for the rest of the week.

"So what's his holiness been whinging about this time then?" I shoved the last two chips in my mouth. Plenty of ketchup. My stomach was loving me once again.

"The usual," Spliff moaned as he poured himself another gin.

"Parishioners or Parish?"

"Parish."

"Oh."

We sat in silence for a small while. This was a serious matter. As you've probably noticed The Reverend James Francis MacIntyre is not your normal, run of the mill priest. He is the archetypal square peg that the Church tries from time to time to hammer into an unforgiving round hole. His first parish was an absolute disaster. There was the aforementioned baptism, but there was also his inability to keep a control of his paperwork or his libido. As a result, he was moved to somewhere that had been perceived as a safe option. Luneside University was looking for a new chaplain about ten years ago and the Vice-Principal at the time was a good friend of the then Arch-Deacon. As a result, a deal was done and Spliff was placed out of sight and out of mind until such a time that is was felt safe to release him back into the diocese.

Anyway, as with all things, time marches on and, as Spliff settled more and more into a campus life where his little eccentricities were either accepted or overlooked, administrations changed. Both the benevolent Vice-Principal and the Arch-Deacon moved on to pastures new, leaving the lonesome priest to the not so tender loving care of their successors. Admittedly, he did blot his own copy book with the new V-C when they first met. After shaking hands with his new boss' wife he innocently asked when the baby was due. The V-C rather acerbically pointed out that his wife was not, in fact, pregnant. Ouch.

As for the new Arch-Deacon, he was a younger, more vibrant man who liked to keep in touch with the parishes and his clergy. As a result, Spliff was continually having new parishes shoved under his nose for his approval. The hint was as obvious as a villain in a Disney cartoon – It's time you were moving on.

The problem was, Spliff did not want to move.

"Apparently there's this nice little place out by Blackburn." The sorrow brimmed over his words. "It has a rose garden."

Spliff loves his gardening. He has single-handedly crafted a mini Eden out of one of the more neglected corners of campus. In the spring it is awash with flowering bulbs and cherry blossom. In the summer the scent of roses drifts by you on the warm breeze. In autumn the bright reds of leaves lazily drifting to the ground are a joy to see. I sometimes feel that if people really wanted to get to know the real Spliff then they should look past his brash, camp exterior and spend just an hour or two in his little corner of paradise.

"Have you been to see it?"

He shook his head. "No. Just photos. He e-mailed them to me this morning. It does look rather sweet."

There was a touch more silence. Spliff was my best friend but there were times like these that I really struggled to say the right thing so I just kept quiet. There was the big part of him that would always be the bombastic Bohemian, but there was always that little voice that kept whispering about that nice, quiet country parish that he ought to try out and settle down in. Somewhere he could put down roots. Somewhere he could grow up in.

"I'm investigating a poltergeist," I finally volunteered.

"A poltergeist? I assumed it was a plastic surgeon offering back street nose jobs."

"You know what 'assume' spells."

"Oh stop that. You'll get me thinking about Richard Gere."

I smiled. This was the Spliff that I liked best. The one full of banter and insults. The distracted, depressed one disturbs me. I find it hard to handle. "It's at a local high school."

"Which one?"

"Saint Edmund's."

He nearly choked on his gin.

"What is it?" I asked.

"Not Ballcrusher's school?"

"Pardon?"

"Lindsay Wetherington," he explained, "terrifies the local clergy. She arrived three years ago and turned the place upside down. She chucked out all the governors and installed businessmen and cronies who all see the world the way that she does: driven by results. It's true that the school excels academically, but, my God, she runs the place with a rod of iron. You step out of line and your knackers are on the chopping block." He smiled at me over his drink. "You okay Sam? You're suddenly looking a bit pale."

"I'd rather hold on to my testicles, that's all."

"I could always hold them for you, if you'd let me,"

Spliff winked.

I shook my head. "You're bloody incorrigible. Now, back to the poltergeist?"

"Okay," he sighed dramatically, "if you insist. You reckon it's genuine? Not just laddish pranks? I got called to a pub once where they claimed there was this ghost knocking at the bar every night at eleven p.m.. The owner was shitting himself. So I turned up to investigate. They told me the story. Every night, bang on eleven, there would be three hard raps that sounded like they were coming from upstairs. So, that night, we sat waiting and whilst the owner sat concentrating on listening for the knocking I sat and concentrated on the young barman and the regulars all of whom kept looking at their watches, the wooden ceiling and the long broom behind the bar. Needless to say the poltergeist never showed up again."

I chuckled. "Bet you got some free drinks too after that."

"Damn right I did."

I described the incident in the IT lesson and Spliff let out a low whistle. "Wow! That sounds quite nasty."

I nodded in agreement. "I know. It could have been a lot worse, I guess. The question is 'Where to start?'"

"Find the source, I suppose," the priest suggested. "Most poltergeist manifestations are normally centred around an individual..."

"Usually an adolescent," I finished. "I know the drill. However, that school is full of hormonal teenagers, all of them with their own bucket-loads of angst. It's a needle in a haystack."

Spliff leaned back in his winged chair and frowned

at me. "Oh Samuel! Really! Surely it's obvious?"

"What?"

"For the incident to occur the way it did, the child was nearby."

I tapped my fingernail against my teeth as I thought this over. "You think they were in that lesson?"

He nodded. "Then there is the fact that some pieces of work were left on the wall."

Daylight dawned. "If I had worked hard on something, I would not want to destroy it. I think I need to see that classroom again tomorrow."

Come the next morning I was feeling decidedly chipper. The new case was starting to entice me. I did not seem to be in any sort of personal danger for a change: no crazed Satanists, no lurking vampires. It was really quite refreshing. What was more, the morning had that crisp, fresh autumnal feeling that makes one feel glad to be alive. The sky was bright blue with only a hint of cloud and light breeze blew any traces of last night's beverages out of my head.

I even managed some breakfast - the most important meal of the day you know – and even those constant bells were somewhat diminished.

I just knew it was going to be a good day.

You can see where this is going, can't you?

"What do you mean you're not going to help me today?"

John dropped his eyes to his scuffed shoes and carefully ground a piece of dirt into the tarmac path. "I... I'm sorry Sam. I want to. It's just..." he trailed off.

I gave an exasperated sigh as dark clouds gathered on my perfect day.

"Oh, come off it, lad. You owe me more than this," I snapped. "Grow a pair and tell me what's going on? Is it Wetherington? Has she got it in for me?"

"No!" His big brown eyes lifted up to mine and I could see the pain in them. I cursed myself for being too hard. He was only fourteen, after all. "It's not her," he said. "It's... it's Mum."

I frowned. That I had not been expecting. "Your mother? What's she got to do with all this?"

John turned to walk down the path to school. I kept pace with him. "She doesn't want me spending time with you."

I opened my mouth to say something, but no words came for a second. I was totally bemused. What was going on here? I was definitely missing something. Nothing new there. It seemed to be my general state for the week. Then I managed, "How does she know about me?"

"I was telling her all about you last night. About what you do and how great you are. I said that I wished I had a dad like you." He paused. Stopped walking. He looked back up at me. He was actually crying. "Sam, she went mental. Absolutely mental. She started screaming and shouting. She actually threw things around the room. She smashed an old ornament that she's had for years. She loved that little thing. It was cut glass, you know. Then she knelt down on the floor and started to pick all the pieces of glass out of the carpet. I tried to help but she told me to stay away. She said that I would get hurt. Really hurt. I said that it was only glass and I would be fine. Then she looked at me and she looked so sad, Sam, and she said that she didn't mean the glass. She said that she meant you. I asked her why but she just ignored me and carried on trying to clean up the broken glass. I tried to talk to her some more but she just ignored me so I went to my room and stayed there until the morning. I couldn't sleep and I finally heard her come to bed about three. She never stays up that late. Her job's too important to her to be tired in the morning."

The bells were ringing loud in my ears once more. I absent-mindedly rubbed the heel of my hand against the side of my head. My spidey-senses were tingling. There was something... something I was missing here. "What's her job?"

"She's a journalist."

The autumnal breeze whipped through my trench coat and my blood ran cold. In my head I saw another pair of brown eyes, female ones, twinkling with delight as they opened a carefully wrapped parcel. My voice cracked as I asked, "John, what was the glass ornament?" then I jumped out of my skin as a heavy hand clamped down on my right shoulder. "Jesus!" I swore as I turned to the intruder. A large brick wall of a man was stood there beaming at me.

"Mr Spallucci," he stated, rather than enquired. "I believe I have the pleasure of your presence in my gym class."

My mouth gasped like a goldfish drowning in the air and I turned to say something to John, but he had sailed off amidst a sea of blue blazers and school bags.

It was an impressive sports hall. I was rapidly realising now just how much things had changed since my day. First, there had been all the high tech computers, then the assortment of quality instruments and now this. Again, the room was bright and airy, hardly a whiff of stale jock strap. There was enough room for a small football pitch on the sprung wooden floor which was marked out in different colours for various activities. Basketball hoops lined the walls and cricket nets were tied up on opposing sides.

"So are you going to stand there gawping or are you going to help out?"

I turned and faced the brick wall on legs. He was tall, affecting rippling muscles and a highly polished bald head that sat atop a hooked beak of a nose. "Excuse my manners - forgot to introduce myself," The PE teacher thrust out his right hand. "James Dean. Pleased to meet you."

I shook his hand as he crushed my fingers tightly then raised an eyebrow. "James Dean?"

He shrugged. "We can't pick the names our parents choose."

"Tell me about it," I grinned. I was fast warming to him.

"So you going to ditch the hat and coat and want to grab a ball?" He motioned over my shoulder to a pile of orange basketballs.

I grimaced and started to back-pedal. "I don't know. I've never really been the sporty type. Besides I'm no teacher."

"Who said anything about teaching?" he beamed with big, white teeth. "This is fun!" He winked then grabbed a ball which he flung at my chest. Hard!

The boys were piling in and I had been thrust a fait accompli. I regarded the blank face of my orange nemesis which was staring blindly up at me and I grinned. I heaped my coat, my hat and my suit jacket at the side of the hall then went and stood next to James.

"So what's the plan?"

"Simple. I blow this whistle and they start to run." He turned and flashed the big grin again. "Then we hit them with the balls." He blew the whistle and a big cheer rose up from the class as they started to zig-zag around the hall. He was good. Very good. Within the first few seconds he had bagged three lads who then made their way to the edge of the hall out of harm's way. I managed one quite quickly too but he was a short, fat lad who wasn't looking where he was going so I could hardly be proud about it - but hey, a hit's a hit, isn't it? After that it got a bit trickier. My god, they were fast. Talk about greased lightning. They were obviously used to this warm up and ducked and dived from whatever angle I threw my ball at. It was becoming embarrassing as James notched up more and more victims and I was stuck with just the one.

There was a moment when I should have scored a second but the most curious thing happened. I threw my ball straight and hard. It was targeting in on the legs of a thin-looking boy with greasy brown hair. I was about to whoop with joy when suddenly the ball curved away from his legs. I darted after the ball and whipped it up and threw it once more at the same boy. He glared at me through his greasy fringe and the ball fell dead at his feet.

Very interesting: I thought. I walked over, picked the ball up and made to say something but James' whistle blew. "Okay people," he shouted, "enough warm up. Now line up."

The greasy-haired boy walked away and took his place in the line. I examined the ball briefly before depositing it in the basket with its cousins. I decided that

I needed to have a chat with the lad later, after the lesson.

After the warm up, James had the class divide into five groups of five and positioned them around various wall spaces with plastic footballs. "Right gentlemen, penalty taking is the order of the day. You know the drill. Off you go."

So it was that the members took it in turns in goal while the other four queued up to kick the ball at them. Repetitive but simple. James watched them for a while then nodded in satisfaction and motioned for me to come and join him on a bench. "That'll keep 'em busy for half an hour or so. Time for us to have a sit down," he smiled. He fished into his kit bag and pulled out a bottle of Lucozade which he offered to me. I politely refused (the caffeine content plays havoc with my ears) and he drank half the bottle in a few quick glugs. "Rumour has it you're a ghostbuster," he said after a little while during which he had obviously been mentally choosing the correct words. "Is that right?"

"In a manner of speaking. It's not just ghosts I investigate."

He nodded. "So you're here because of our little problem then?" As he spoke he never took his eyes of the kids. He looked like a shepherd watching for a wolf amongst his sheep.

"I was called in yesterday morning. You seen anything out of the ordinary in your lessons?"

"These are teenage boys," he laughed. "There's nothing ordinary about them. They're a breed unto themselves. Once those hormones kick in, they're all over the place. One minute they're all macho and hardman, the next they're running down the hall pretending to be a rubber duck!" He smiled as he continued to survey his charges. "I love 'em to bits. They keep me on my toes and keep me young, you know?"

"I think they'd drive me mad. I prefer a bit more order in my life." I winced as one poor unfortunate took a shot exactly where a boy would least want one. His mates laughed and he was about to show them the V when he caught his teacher's eye and relented. "So apart from adolescent vagaries, how about anything supernatural?"

"Yeah, I've seen stuff," the bluff, down-to-earth sports teacher growled. "Stuff I can't explain. I've seen good rugby players suddenly brought down when there was no one near them. I've seen a lad sent to casualty when the vault he was using collapsed. We stick to balls and mats now. They're less likely to break a finger, you know?"

I winced again. "Does there seem to be a pattern to when these things happen?" I asked.

He nodded. "Why do you think I'm not letting these lads out of my sight? It's always with this class. Every lesson over the last two weeks something has happened with this group of lads. That's why I came and grabbed you this morning before her ladyship sent you off on some cock-and-bull PR fiasco."

"You're not a fan of your exalted leader then?"

He pulled a sour face. "She gets the job done I guess, but she's far too image conscious for my liking. You've only got to take one look at the governors to see that."

My eyes followed his and I tried to take in the faces of the boys as they continued to shoot footballs at each other. I'm no good at telling most teenagers apart, but there were certain faces, builds and hairstyles which I recognised from the IT lesson the day before, one of which was the greasy-haired lad who had avoided my ball. It was now his turn in goal and he seemed to be having a hard time of it. One by one, the other lads kicked the ball at him and, with each ball, the boy flinched and cowered. His partners looked somewhat exasperated. I saw them gesticulate for him to put more effort in, but he steadfastly shook his head before crouching down in a sitting position against the wall.

James grunted and headed over to the boy. I followed behind. "Billy!" he called out. "What's going on here?"

"Make them stop, sir. Make them stop," the boy whined, pulling at his lank hair with his long, spindly fingers.

"Make them stop what, lad?"

"They're picking on me again, sir. Make them stop."

James looked at the other lads and raised an eyebrow. "Boys?"

The four lads looked genuinely gobsmacked. "We done nothing, sir!" one of them protested. "He just won't get the ball."

"They keep kicking it at me!" the greasy-haired boy shouted. "Make them stop!"

James rubbed his large hand over his bald scalp. "Mr Swarbrick," his voiced sounded weary, exasperated, "they're supposed to be kicking the ball at you. You're in goal, lad."

The boy just continued to rock on his heels as the other pupils stopped their target practice and gawped at

213

the peep show that was unfolding. I could hear the occasional throw-away comment and snigger.

"Make them stop, sir! Make them all stop," Billy pleaded again. "I don't like it. I don't like it."

James let out a deep sigh and bent down towards the boy. "Come on, Billy, let's get you out of here." He took hold of the boy's arm to pull him up.

Billy dropped his hands from his face and his eyes shot up at James Dean full of murderous intent. "Take your filthy hands off me," the boy snarled.

As the PE teacher's mouth opened to scold the boy I suddenly felt electricity charge the atmosphere and I was sure that we were not alone in the sports hall. I looked up at the rafters of the immense room and laid a hand on James' shoulder. "I think you'd better do as he says," I whispered.

"Why?"

"Just take a look up above you."

The teacher's eyes followed mine up above us where a mass of black, leathery wings flapped and fidgeted in the rafters and ten small, black faces peered down at us with sharp, beady eyes.

People often ask me what it's like to suffer from tinnitus. Well, there's two reactions or descriptions that I tend to hand out. There's the obvious one: it's bloody annoying. Those sodding bells never shut up. Not once. Not ever. They are always there, ring-a-ding-a-ding-a-ding. Constantly. Permanently. Incessantly. There is no softening them. There is no subduing them. They are there when I wake. They are there as I go about my daily life. They are there when I go to sleep. They are there in my dreams.

Most people look shocked and ask "How do you put up with it, you poor thing." I just shrug and say, "I get on with it. It's no big deal."

Then there's the other reaction I give. Admittedly this is normally if I'm having a good day. I tell them, "They're my constant companions. They are always there for me. They will never betray me. They will never walk out on me. They sing with me when I'm happy. They cry with me when I'm sad. In the deepest, darkest fear in the middle of the night they are there to remind me that I am not alone and they will sit and comfort me. When I'm being pissy or narky then they will be there to scold me for my stubbornness. They are my closest friend and my strictest teacher. They warn me when I am starting to feel ill. They relax me when I feel bored. But most of all they remind me and constantly tell me of one thing more than anything else. One thing that each and every one of us on the face of this planet should remember and hold precious to the day that breath finally escapes their lungs for that final, fatal time.

I am different.

Then people normally look at me quite shocked and there is that awkward little silence as their regimented mind tries to assimilate this profound credo that they had least expected. Then, when they think they understand everything about me, they have the damned audacity to say the most stupid thing in the world. "I wish I could hear them, then I would know what you're going through."

I look them straight in the face and sigh as for the umpteenth time I explain that no, they would not want them, because for all the wonders I have just spouted I would happily be rid of the little bastards in an instant.

As I looked up at the ceiling of the sports hall, I realised with dread that I had been the foolish people who so badly wanted to empathise with me. I had wanted to get into the mind of the individual with the poltergeist and see what made him or her tick.

Be careful what you wish for Sammy, I thought as I rolled out of the way of the vanguard of small, black imps that now swooped down out of the rafters and bombarded us. The next succession of events was somewhat of a blur, so please bear with me if this sounds rather garbled. It is, after all, not every day that one gets attacked by ten black imps dragged up from the paranoia of a dysfunctional teenage boy.

First, the obvious happened, they dive-bombed James Dean. The teacher was the focus of the boy's wrath so the imps swarmed all over him. The man's muscular arms batted frantically at the little dervishes, trying desperately to detach them, but it was in vain. They nimbly avoided any attempt to remove them. They just dug their claws in and flapped their wings in a cacophony of bat-like thrumming.

Next, there was a shout from one of the other boys as he hurtled out of the gym. Whether he was just running in fear or in an attempt to raise the alarm, I neither knew nor cared. I had to remain focussed on the matter at hand: how to safely remove the imps from the teacher. It was as I wracked my brains over this that I remembered the basketballs. "Throw me one!" I shouted to the group of on-looking boys as I pointed hurriedly at the basket containing the orange balls. "Quickly!"

One of the lads darted to the basket and grabbed one, then lobbed it straight to me. I snatched it to my chest, turned and hurled it towards the black melee that encompassed Dean. There was a cross between a bleat and a shriek as one of the imps momentarily detached itself before diving back into the fray. I nodded to myself. They were corporeal, which meant...

"They can be hurt!" I screamed. "Grab more balls!"

The students dived for the basketballs and suddenly their teacher was the centre of the most absurd game of dodge ball that I have ever witnessed. Ball after orange ball pounded towards him knocking imp after imp off. Each time they peeled off they dived back in, but the balls were relentless. The boys obviously cared for and respected their teacher. They were not going to give up. After a few seconds, it became obvious that the imps were reattaching themselves at a slower rate. They were tiring.

I grabbed my trench coat and wrapped it around my arm then dived into the fray. A violent hissing noise filled the inside of my head as leathery wings rained abuse down upon me. I stumbled and staggered under the weight of the blows from the imps and the occasional stray blow of a wayward basketball. But I stayed focussed. I had to reach James Dean. I reached out and latched my bare arm around his waist, then, with my coat for protection I swatted at the black furies, pounding at them until they began to retreat.

The clouds of black that had enveloped me and the teacher began to part but the hissing inside my head grew louder and louder. It sounded akin to my tinnitus, but far more extreme. It sounded alien, invasive.

"Stop this!" I bellowed at the flying creatures. "Stop this now!"

And surprisingly, they did.

I wished at that moment that I had brought a pin

with me just to see if you really could hear one drop at such a time, but fancy was soon overtaken by the new noises in my head. It had turned from a violent hissing to a bewildered chattering sound mixed with the sweetest singing I had ever heard. The imps flapped their wings casually and hovered about three metres off the ground. They cocked their heads to one side and stared at me in what could only be described as wonder. As they hovered there, I noticed that their skin seemed to shimmer iridescently in the bright lights of the gym. It seemed almost insubstantial. *Curious for a creature that could be hurt by a basketball*, I thought.

I gave Dean a quick glance. He was scratched and somewhat battered, but otherwise he appeared okay. Then I turned my full attention back to the imps. "Thank you," I said, relief flooding through my voice. "You had no need to attack him. He meant the boy no harm."

The boy.

I turned to see where Billy was, but he had gone. He had left the gym. I cursed, quietly at first then loudly, as I looked back up to the imps and realised that they too had fled the scene.

"Mr Spallucci! Really!" came the strident tones of the tempest that was Mrs Wetherington, her court shoes clacking on the hard gymnasium floor. "I shall have no such language in front of my pupils." She eyed the scattered basketballs and the scuffed gym teacher then turned on her heels. "My office. Now!"

"I believe that you have had an eventful couple of days, Mr Spallucci."

I nodded. "You could say that. It's certainly not

been like my old school days, that's for sure."

Mrs Wetherington's face looked sour enough to be the essence of the harshest lemon. "Quite," she managed through pursed lips. She steepled her fingers together and regarded me with a superior air. "Would you mind telling me just what was going on in my gymnasium?"

I described the ten black imps, how they had attacked James Dean and how the boys had pelted them with basketballs allowing me to get in and rescue the man. For the moment I left out the connection with Billy Swarbrick.

"This all sounds somewhat unruly," Wetherington sneered. "Not becoming of this establishment. Basketballs indeed!"

"It was the safest way to distract the creatures without hurting Mr Dean," I explained.

The middle-aged woman harrumphed and asked, "So have you come to any conclusions yet, or is this all proving to be a waste of your time and my budget?"

I ignored the insult. "What can you tell me about Billy Swarbrick?"

The head sighed deeply and sank back into her leather office chair. "Year nine. Constant under-achiever despite excellent grades in his first two years here. He will play havoc with our value-added come the end of key stage three."

"Value-added?" I frowned, unsure that I had heard right. "You have to tax the pupils?"

I was given one of those 'oh, you stupid mortal' looks that you normally only receive from librarians as she went on to explain the terminology. "Value-added is the phrase used to describe how a child has progressed.

If they come in poor and they respond well to the education that we give them allowing them to perform well at the end of key-stage, then the school is seen as having given good value for that child. If, however, they are perceived to go backwards or stay stationery at the end of key-stage then that is bad value. In short we have wasted our time and our money on them. Our systems here are faultless as long as the child wishes to put the effort in, Mr Spallucci. Billy Swarbrick has recently started to under-achieve. If anything, he has actually started to go backwards. He should be a high flyer, considering his background. Instead, he has continually shut himself off from the rest of his peers and alienated himself from the teaching staff. He is bad value."

I grimaced. It was so cold, so clinical. How could she write a boy off whose life was really just starting to blossom? Then I twigged on something that she had said. "You mentioned 'his background.' What do you mean by that?"

"Billy is the son of Hector Swarbrick, the chair of governors here," she beamed radiantly.

Realisation slapped me across the face like a cold, wet tuna fish. "By Hector Swarbrick you mean the owner of the *Lancaster Chronicle*?" I groaned. No wonder the local journalists had not dived on the story. The centre of the piece would have been the son of their own boss. Which surely meant...

"Has Mr Swarbrick ever mentioned to you about anything happening around Billy at home?"

Wetherington locked me in a stare cold enough to freeze every Bunsen burner in the school. "Hector is a fine, upstanding man and a rock upon which this establishment is firmly seated. He and his wife are constantly involved in school life as well as being fervent fund-raisers. Not only this, but they are personal friends of mine." This last statement sounded more like a threat than a fact. "Now would you mind telling me why you are so interested in their son?"

I suddenly realised that I was walking across very thin ice and the wrong word or interpretation could give me an extremely chilly dunking. "I have reason to believe that the so-called poltergeist activity is centred around Billy."

"You have evidence for this?"

The ice under my feet started to creak.

"Both of the lessons that I attended which suffered activity were attended by him."

"I'm sure there were other pupils who also attended both of those classes, Mr Spallucci."

A large crack was shooting towards me.

"I'm sure there were, Mrs Wetherington, but in PE, the activity with the imps was focussed on the person who could have been seen as a threat directly to Billy – namely, Mr Dean."

Wetherington's icy gaze held me fast. "I do not like where you are proceeding with this, Mr Spallucci. Are you saying that the son of the chair of governors is possessed?"

Very cold water splashed at my ankles and my legs trembled.

I shook my head. "No, not possessed. I feel that he is troubled. You said yourself that his grades have slipped and that he has become withdrawn. I feel that something has pushed him over the edge. Perhaps something at home..."

She did not let me finish. As the ice separated and

the frigid depths dragged me down, Wetherington stormed at me that I was obviously a fraud and a slanderer whilst she stamped over to her office door and bade me leave with haste.

As the solid oak slammed behind me I felt chilled to the bone, and not just from the mental metaphor that had enveloped me. The boy was in trouble and was obviously in need of help. The other boys in the gym had not been taunting him. They just seemed to have been exasperated by his weirdness. Had John and his mates been discussing this trait of Billy's personality in front of the glass window? Had Billy been making his way up the stairs to the study room and overheard them? Right then I could have done with my young friend to give me more information, but that was out of the question down to both his head teacher and his mother.

His mother.

With the glass figurine.

I found my hand sliding around my Zippo in my pocket, my thumb affectionately stroking its relief pattern.

I told myself to stop getting distracted by vague coincidences and to concentrate on the matter at hand. Right now I had to help out Billy. So, if there were problems in his life it seemed most likely that they were coming from home. I was about to walk out of the school when something struck me. I still hadn't revisited the IT suite. In all the swift-moving events of the morning I had completely forgotten about it. I checked that Wetherington could not see me and I headed for the stairs.

I slowly opened the door to the IT suite. The

corridor was surprisingly quiet and had that eerie sense that buildings get when there is no one around and you are somewhere that you shouldn't be. What with my previous experience of this room, I had a certain amount of the heebie-jeebies.

It was empty of pupils and relatively tidy now. There was not much mess at all, just the usual detritus one would expect from a classroom: discarded pens, paper and the eponymous shoe. Whenever I entered an empty classroom as a child there was always a discarded, muddy shoe in the corner. It conjured up this image of children the world over hopping home after losing a shoe and devising some lame excuse as to where it had vanished: a dog ate it, my friend ate it, aliens ate it.

What was most definitely still in disarray, though, was the display board at the back of the room. Many pieces of work were still missing and a lot of what was left behind hung in tatters. There were, however, four pieces which were stapled neatly to the wall at perfect right angles. I walked over and peered at them. They were very precise pieces on databasing, spreadsheets, web-links and e-mail. All of them bore the same student's name.

Billy Swarbrick.

If I needed any more proof, this was it, but how was I going to find his address, and quickly? Having witnessed the furious apparitions in the gym, I had the feeling that things were spiralling out of control for the young Mr Swarbrick.

I was checking my watch as I made for the main door of the school (it was just coming up to lunch) when a female voice called out, "Mr Spallucci?"

My shoulders sank. What was it now? Who else had I offended? "Yes?" I turned and saw the receptionist waving a brown envelope in my direction.

"I was given this to post on to you, but you don't seem to have left yet..." She let the sentence drift off implying my guilt.

I stepped over towards her desk and took the envelope. My curiosity was piqued as I thanked her. I decided that discretion was in order and I kept it firmly shut until I was out of the school grounds. Inside was a note written in a firm, masculine hand. It read:

"You will get nowhere with the ice-maiden. She's far too interested in appearances and, as you have probably found out by now, the Swarbricks are friends of hers.

So, as long as you tell no one where you got this from, Billy lives at 12, Sefton Close out in Slyne. Don't expect a warm welcome, though. His father's a pompous arse!

Thanks for your help this morning.
James Dean"

I grinned as I pocketed the letter in my trench coat. I climbed up into the life-boat that had just cruised up to rescue me from my icy plunge and set sail for Slyne.

Slyne-with-Hest is a small village to the north of Lancaster. It is surrounded by fields and populated by those with enough capital to do so: jewellers, bankers, accountants, retired builders. It's not the sort of place that I ever seem to frequent, so my knowledge of the local geography was sketchy at best. I had my local map gripped in one hand as I turned my VW Polo Classic off the A6 down Throstle Grove and I had to swerve to avoid an oncoming four-by-four being driven by a dapper gentleman and his twin-set-and-pearls wife. I crunched into the hedgerow and swore as I stalled. The four-by-four just ploughed onwards and left me in the gutter. My ageing Polo restarted on the third turn-over and I dragged it out onto the road again. I made a mental note that it was due for one of two things: a major service or scrapping. I had been driving it since my twenties. It was the first thing I had bought after my dad had died but it was a 1983 vintage and was starting to show signs of its age. At some point someone had shunted it up the rear in a car park and now an intermittent leak meant that passengers on the back seat inevitably got a wet back-side when they sat down. As a result, I always carried a supply of black bin bags in the boot for the rare occasion that I ever had anyone else in the car with me.

Sefton Close was just down the road on the left. It was a relatively new-built area: a reclaimed derelict farm that had been replaced with twenty red-brick detached houses. They all had pristine lawns out the front and ivy up the walls. Their owners obviously intended their residences to look rural, hiding the fact that they themselves had grown up and made their money in more urban areas.

The road was quite narrow so I bumped my car up

onto the kerb outside number 12 and turned off the ignition.

"Here goes nothing," I muttered as I opened the driver's door and swung my legs out. As my scuffed shoes crunched their way up the gravel path I could hear a very large dog bark maniacally from somewhere close by. I had stopped off at my office and partaken of a bit of Dutch courage before driving out to Slyne and now it was close to four o'clock and the evening was just starting to stake its claim on the sky as it is wont to do at this time in autumn. I reached the door and found no doorbell, just a large, ornate knocker which I grabbed and rapped three times. The dog barked even louder. Great, I thought, death by mauling, dribbling or crotch sniffing. Don't get me wrong, I love dogs, it's their owners that frustrate me. So many seem to see them as little babies that need pampering and spoiling. I know where that leads to. I've seen *It's Me Or The Dog* on daytime television. Even the fluffiest little fur-balls can go psycho when not given any boundaries.

There was a scuffling from behind the door and the sound of yelping as the pooch was dragged away by an unseen owner. I heard a door slam and light footsteps approached. The door opened and I was greeted by a slightly built woman in her mid-forties. Her hair was brown, turning grey, her eyes were green and her dress was plain. I could tell immediately from the way her eyes twitched nervously as they looked me up and down that she was a woman on the edge. "Can... can I help you?"

"Mrs Swarbrick?"

"Yes? Who are you?" The dog continued to bark in the background. There was the sound of large paws trying desperately to shred a kitchen door.

"Sorry to bother you, but my name is Sam Spallucci. I am investigating certain incidents at your son's school. May I come in?"

"School?" Her eyes glazed over and I could see tears welling up. "Oh god! What has he done? Please tell me he's not hurt anyone!" she wailed.

"I don't think the doorstep is the place for this sort of conversation, is it?"

She considered this for a split-second then opened the door wider and let me in. The inside of the house was as I had imagined: spacious. The wide hallway was floored in a light-coloured wood laminate giving it an open feel as it led onto an open-plan kitchen-diner (I had been mistaken as to where the dog had been shut in, then), three more doors and a sweeping staircase. It was from behind one of the doors that the dog was going frantic. Mrs Swarbrick noticed my gaze wander towards the noise. "Don't mind Dooby," she said. "He just gets excited. We'll go through to the living room."

I followed her through the nearest doorway into a room that stretched the length of the house and commanded a large glass patio door that overlooked the local countryside. Outside, the sky was getting darker. She flicked a light switch on the wall and subtle lighting illuminated the room. A rich carpet cushioned the soles of my shoes as I walked into the middle of the room past an enormous plasma screen television. "Is Mr Swarbrick home?" I asked.

She shook her head. "He will be soon. He's fetching Molly from ballet class."

"Molly? Is that Billy's sister?"

"Yes." The woman stood, obviously unaware of where to take the conversation, so I explained why I was there.

"Mrs Swarbrick, are you aware that there have been a number of incidents concerning Billy's lessons recently?"

Silently, she nodded her head.

I drummed my fingers against my teeth. This was like trying to get a pearl out of a delicate oyster without breaking the shell. "You asked before if he had hurt anyone." Her green eyes shot up to me, tears running down her face. "Let me reassure you that's not the case." Her shoulders sagged as a touch of relief washed over her. "However, you seem fairly certain that he is the centre of these matters even without me saying so. Why is that?"

She was about to answer when the door slammed behind me and a male voice roared, "Who the hell are you and what are you doing in my house?" Mr Swarbrick was well-dressed, tall, bespectacled and very, very grey. He stormed into his living room, his finger out in front of him, pointing accusatorially.

I opened my mouth to speak but Mrs Swarbrick beat me to it. "He's from the school, Hector. There's been more trouble."

Swarbrick's face turned murderous. "Spallucci," he growled. "Lindsay rang me at work and warned me he might show up here. Get out! Now!" He stamped over to me and grabbed the collar of my trench coat. I acted instinctively and thrust my forearm against his, causing him to topple backwards, pulling me with him. We landed on the floor in an unceremonious heap and, as I pulled myself away, I saw a small, brown-haired girl standing wide-eyed at the doorway. "Daddy!" she shrieked and ran to her father. The dog's barking grew louder and was joined by the sound of footsteps running down the wooden staircase.

This was rapidly turning out to be very messy. "Mr Swarbrick," I began, trying to placate him, but he was having none of it. He drew himself up, rounded on me, drawing back his fist and I braced myself for another bleeding nose.

It never happened.

"Stop it."

The voice was quiet but penetrating and had come from Billy. Hector Swarbrick's clenched fist remained frozen next to his face as the lights in the living room dimmed. There was the sound of a pitiful wail from Mrs Swarbrick and then the familiar feeling of air crackling around us like in a thunderstorm. I felt a breeze start to waft across my face and my eyes glanced around the room. A watercolour that hung on the far wall was starting to bang on its hook. A rug by the patio door was flapping up and down. A china vase was rattling on a small table.

"Billy!" I called out. "No!" but it was no good, the boy's eyes had glazed over and he was no longer with us. I felt a pulse of air shove into me and I was sailing across the room towards the patio door. I landed hard, but unhurt. The same could not be said for Mr Swarbrick. The water colour picture dropped with a crash from the wall before he was lifted off his feet and slammed up in its place. The air around his wrists and his ankles shimmered and four of the imps appeared, fixing him rigid in position. The newspaper magnate's eyes bulged with terror behind his glasses and a dark stain spread down his immaculate grey trousers. I winced in embarrassment and tried to reach him but found my feet pinned down by two more of the little fiends.

Then things started to fly.

It was another game of dodge ball but this time Swarbrick was the target and the projectiles were a lot harder: TV remotes, books, the water colour painting and the china vase. They were all whipped up into the air and smashed into the terrified man as Billy's rage grew in intensity.

Then, as the small table on which the vase had once rested rose from the floor, Molly broke through her fear and ran to her captive father. The table sliced through the air and caught her square on her back, pounding the small girl to the floor.

"Molly!" Billy's scream echoed through the room. All levitating objects, including his father, crashed to the ground and the imps vanished. For a moment the boy stood aghast, staring at the limp form of his sister, then he turned and pelted upstairs. His mother threw herself on her daughter and wept as she cradled the little mite in her arms. Swarbrick sat stunned and slouched against the wall.

I crawled over to Mrs Swarbrick. "Here, let me see," I said.

She protectively pulled the girl closer to herself and turned her back on me.

"Please, I can help," I tried.

The woman was slowly rocking back and forth. I placed a hand on her shoulder and waited. She stopped rocking and turned back to me. I reached over and placed two fingers on Molly's neck.

Her eyes flicked open. "What you doing?" the little

girl asked.

I smiled. "Checking that you're still with us. Apparently you are. How do you feel?"

"Okay. Just sore." She looked up at her mother. "I love you, Mummy."

Mrs Swarbrick said nothing and just hugged her tighter. I stood up, ignored the man of the house and chased upstairs after Billy.

As I pulled myself up the polished wooden stairs of the suburban house I wondered to myself as to what was going through the mind of the teenage boy who had shut himself in his bedroom. He had so much power and so little control. In his anger he had inadvertently hurt his kid sister and the thoughts going through his head right now must be coming from a dark, terrible place.

I had been to many such places as a teenager especially when my dad had been sick. I had lain awake night after night praying that he would get better, praying to God on High to make the arthritis miraculously disappear. Then I would wake in the morning and he was still the same, hunched, in pain and spiteful.

When my father's body finally gave in, my hope in miracles were buried in the ground along with him. All hope was lost. I was on my own – me against the universe – a small ant in a sea of sand, desperately trying to grab purchase on an ever shifting ground that threatened to suffocate me at any moment.

But I never gave up hope in a loving God. Even on his death bed my father had been an avid believer. He had kept his rosary and his bible by his bedside even when his fingers were too gnarled to count the beads or turn the pages. They were there to comfort him in his own dark places.

So I carried on my own journey and, as I prepared myself for the selection process for the Anglican priesthood, I continued to study. I studied hard. At first, just those subjects that were expected of me. Then, after my encounter with Gerald and after my graduation, those subjects which my heart craved. Those which would bring me true knowledge of the unseen universe. That which is all around and under our very noses but which we do not see because our minds will not allow us to comprehend it. So slowly, painfully, I peeled away the constraints of the logical mind and I explored the finest details of the world of the paranormal; from ghosts to zombies, from phantoms to mystics, from possessions to... poltergeists.

I took a steadying breath and knocked lightly on Billy's door. What this boy needed right now was not necessarily answers but reassurance.

There was no reply. I knocked again. "Billy. It's Sam."

There was still no reply. Also there were no little black imps to throw me down the stairs. I considered that a bonus. "Can I come in?"

I waited.

"Molly's fine, Billy. She's just a bit sore. She's with your mum right now."

The door handle turned and the side of Billy's face peered out at me under his lank, dark hair. His face was red with crying. It seemed to be my day for upsetting adolescent boys. I stood and waited, cap in hand. After a little while he nodded and opened the door up then went and sat down on his bed.

As I sat down next to Billy, the old mattress

sagged under my adult weight. I noticed that it hardly gave an inch under the teenager. He was as light as a feather – skin and bones. "Thanks for letting me in, Billy," I began. "You know we need to talk, don't you?"

The lank-haired lad nodded mutely and clasped the sleeves of his long-sleeved top tight in his screwed up fists. His eyes stared intently at the floor space between his feet.

I looked around the room. When I had been his age there had been posters on the walls of various pop bands and musicians: mainly Madness and The Specials with a smattering of Mike Oldfield or Tom Waits as my tastes had developed. There was just one decoration on Billy's wall: a poster of the solar system. Other than that, the walls were bare. There was a book case in one corner and a tatty looking wardrobe that seemed to be held up with duct tape and a prayer in the other. Besides the bed, there was no other furniture, not even a desk or a chair.

It was pitiful. I stored my boiling anger for a more appropriate time.

"You like astronomy, Billy?" I asked.

Again, a silent nod.

"I think it's fascinating, all that stuff out there. We must be so very, very small mustn't we? Just little specks of dust on one of nine planets in the..."

"Eight." The quiet voice cut my ramblings dead.

"Pardon?"

"Not nine. Just eight." Billy lifted his head and his dark eyes looked me in the face for the first time. They were ripe with sorrow and hurting. "Pluto is not a planet. It is a dwarf planet, along with Eris and Ceres. It is situated in the Kuiper Belt past Neptune."

233

"I didn't know that, Billy," I said. "Your knowledge is better than mine, I guess."

"The Kuiper Belt is full of objects," he continued, animation edging into his voice, "over a thousand at last count. Some of them may have moved, you know? Into the solar system? Triton may have been there once and Phoebe too." Excitement was starting to edge into the sad eyes. I decided to pursue the matter.

"I recognise the names," I lied, "but I'm not sure what they are. Why don't you enlighten me?"

"Triton is the largest moon of Neptune and Phoebe is an irregular shaped moon of Saturn," he explained, his hands lifting from his lap and drawing invisible lines in the air as if painting images of the celestial bodies that only he could see. "They may have originated in the Kuiper Belt, but the greater gravitational pull of the planets could have attracted them, so they were drawn into orbit around them. That happens a lot you know," his eyes flickered back down to his lap, "and not just to planets."

I heard a slight thud and noticed a book slip over on the bookshelf. I ran the nail of my index finger over my teeth. "Is that what happened to you Billy? Did some things gravitate in on you?"

A silent nod gave me the answer I was expecting.

"Why don't you tell me about it?" I pressed, my voice calm and soothing. The last thing I wanted was a reprisal of the events in the sports hall or with Molly. "Perhaps I can help?"

"No one can help me," he whispered as another book fell over on top of the previous volume, a puff of dust whispering up into the air. "I don't deserve any help."

I frowned. "Why would you believe that, Billy?"

"Because I'm a bad, bad, boy." The poster of the solar system smacked against the wall and I wondered if I could actually hear the faint flapping of wings, or was that just my fearful imagination?

"I don't think you're a bad boy, Billy," I reassured him. The poster settled slightly. "I also have a very open mind. I've seen a few weird things this week already, and not just at your school."

Billy looked back up at me, curiosity on his face. "Really? Such as?"

I rubbed the back of my neck. What should I say? Satanists and vampires? The kid was screwed up enough already, but I didn't want to break his fragile trust just as the foundations were starting to set. "Let's just say that, in my job, I've experienced enough to know that the things that are happening around you may be considered to be abnormal by most, but they are intrinsically part of you now."

Billy nodded, slowly, tentatively.

"I also know that you need to control them before you really hurt someone. But then I think you realise that already, don't you?"

Billy nodded again, this time a lot more firmly. "How can I do that?"

"Let's start from the beginning, shall we?" I suggested. "Tell me when it first happened. Was there a trigger?"

Billy paused for a moment. He stood and walked over to his bedroom door and, after checking that it was shut tight turned his back to me and lifted his baggy top. The sight of the faded belt mark on his back made me feel sick. I had guessed that his father was a git, but

235

this... This was intolerable. "Your dad?" I asked, just to make sure.

Billy lowered his shirt and nodded. "He gets stressed at work and he and Mum argue lots. And I mean lots." He sat down on the bed again and started to intently study his finger nails. "He first hit me a few weeks back. He was laying into Mum. Verbally laying into her – calling her lazy and stupid. She was in the kitchen, just taking it, crying. I flipped. I told him to lay off of her and let her alone. He turned on me and slammed me up against the kitchen door, screaming at me that it was none of my business and that I ought to be grateful for everything he did for me, everything he bought for me. He was the one who brought the money into the house, not that lazy little tramp. I didn't know what to do, so I ran out of the room crying and came up here. I lay down on my bed and cried so hard that my tears felt like drops of fire. I was scared. I was confused.

"I was so angry.

"Then as I got more and more worked up things started to twitch on the bookshelves and the lampshade started to sway. That brought me up sharp and I jolted in fright. Then a book flew across the room and whacked the wall. I hurried over and picked it up. I was scared that Dad would have heard it and come up to hit me, but he didn't. He was still busy shouting at Mum.

"It was late by that point, so I got myself to bed and tried to sleep, but all I could think about was the book flying across the room. I must have dozed off eventually, I guess, 'cos the next thing I knew was Molly shaking me and calling me to wake up. She was whispering loudly in my ear and she sounded scared. I opened my eyes and saw why. My room was a tip. Stuff was everywhere. Books all over the floor.

"'What happened Billy?' she asked me. I said I didn't know and she helped me tidy up and promised not to tell Dad. After breakfast I went to school and, well, you sort of know the rest. Little things happen all the time - things moving and stuff - but whenever I get stressed or feel like I'm being picked on," he made an explosion shape with his hands, "Ka-blooie!"

"Like the window on the staircase?"

He nodded. "I was heading up to the study room when I heard voices. I couldn't make out specifics but I heard my name and I heard laughter." He shrugged.

"Ka-blooie," I surmised.

"Ka-blooie," he agreed.

I drummed my fingernails against my teeth. The poor kid. What a life? A bully for a dad and adolescent paranoia at school. There was something else though, something that didn't quite fit. Something that he hadn't told me yet.

"What are they?" I asked.

The look of fear on Billy's face confirmed my suspicion. "What are who?" His eyes darted back at me from under his lank hair.

I sighed. "Billy, everyone seems to think this is a *poltergeist*," I accented the word with finger-quotes, "but you and I know it's no such thing, is it?"

The boy fiddled with his fingers and studied the floor. "I... I don't know what you mean."

"Poltergeists are an external phenomenon expressing internal anger and angst. They are unexplained noises and telekinetic activity surrounding a certain individual."

"Yes," he interrupted, "that's right. That's what's

been happening to me. A poltergeist."

I shook my head. "That's what it looked like originally, but that incident in the gym..." I waited, hoping he would finish the sentence. He didn't. Instead his eyes lifted and fixed on the wall behind me. I swallowed. Hard. "How many are there, Billy? I'm guessing ten. Am I right?"

He nodded.

I turned, very, very slowly so as not to appear threatening, and there they were, just as they had appeared in the gym, ten black imps, each about thirty centimetres in height, clinging to his wallpaper, their beady eyes scanning me with curiosity. Just as in the gym, their skin seemed to flicker in the light.

"Hello," I said, keeping my voice level and calm. "Now, you should really know by now that I mean Billy no harm. You have been watching us after all, haven't you? What I'd really like to know is what you actually are. Obviously you aren't a poltergeist. That is an invisible phenomenon. And this imp stuff..." I shook my head. "Sorry, not buying that. I thought this shimmering business was the lights in the gym before, but here you are flickering like a torch with a dying battery. You're generating this image just for the benefit of strangers. Why don't you just show your real selves? You know I won't hurt you."

There was a quiet chattering as the imps seemed to discuss the matter then one of them let go of the wall and hopped down onto the bed. It chicken-hopped across the duvet and pulled itself up in front of me before reaching out a black, spindly hand towards me. Instinctively I reached out with my considerably larger paw and touched one of its tiny fingers with the index on my right hand. The imp's mouth widened into a large smile and bright lights pulsed vibrantly across its skin. Its stature reduced somewhat in bulk and the black, leathery surface washed away into a bright iridescent sheen. Dainty clothes fashioned from a glowing fabric adorned its delicate, humanoid form and light butterfly wings thrummed behind it.

I couldn't help myself from grinning back at the little creature and its evolving companions as they floated down to join it.

"My God, Billy," I whispered in absolute awe. "They're fairies. They're bloody fairies!"

A number of the diminutive creatures covered their mouths with tiny hands and their wings shuddered delicately.

I frowned. "Are you laughing at me?" I asked, then smiled as their little faces peered up at me, radiant in a bathing light. "I'll let you off as you're so cute," I said, causing some of them to chuckle again. Others jumped up from the bed and circled around my head before flying over to Billy and alighting on his shoulders. They reached out and stroked his hair affectionately before bending over and whispering in his ears.

"They think you're funny," the boy explained, a smile starting to form on his face for the first time since I'd met him. "I guess they kinda like you."

"The feeling's mutual." For a short while, all I could do was sit and watch the little figures gambolling around the teenager's bedroom. It was truly amazing. I couldn't make out if they were male or female, they all seemed somewhat asexual – pixie-like, I suppose. There were the gossamer wings and the light coloured robes they wore, but they seemed to look like they had rainbows streaking through their light coloured hair. "Do they have names?" I finally asked.

Billy shook his head as one sat in his hand, its head inclined curiously to one side. "If they do, they've never told me. They're not the greatest of communicators."

"But they do talk, don't they? I mean, one just whispered into your ear."

Billy pulled a confused face. "It's a bit more complicated than that, I think," he explained. "It's more like telepathy. I'm more aware of the sounds they make in my head than an actual voice."

I recalled the burst of sonorous tinnitus I had suffered earlier and understood what he meant. "I heard something when they were flying round in the gym. I guess it was them." I sighed deeply. They looked so happy here in Billy's bedroom.

I heard a sniffing noise and looked up at Billy. He was crying.

"They hurt Molly," he murmured through the tears.

I nodded. "It was an accident, Billy. You know that, don't you?" I reassured him.

"All the same, she's my kid sister. It could have been worse, too!" he wailed. The fairies stopped flittering around and hovered nervously, all their eyes on him. One of them floated over and held one of his fingers in its tiny hand. It tugged gently and smiled up at him. "I know you're sorry, but it's not safe for you to be here anymore. I think you need to go."

The light from the fairies dimmed slightly as they considered this, then, as one, they turned their faces towards me, their heads inclined in question. I started, aware at where this was heading.

"Oh no!" I exclaimed. "No way. As cute as you are, I don't need little pixies in my life right now. I can look after myself, thank you."

One of the little folk hovered up in front of me and shook its head then clicked its fingers. A bright, white disk hung in the space between us. Craters pitted its surface where rocks from space had impacted. Ice trickled down the river of my spine as I regarded the full moon. Another fairy drifted up to the bedroom's curtains and pulled them back revealing the night sky. There hanging in the gloom was the same moon with a sliver still covered in darkness. Not much time. I had lost track. Damn it!

"You really think I'm in danger?" I asked the little creatures. As one, they nodded their heads. I considered the matter. I really did. They were obviously powerful, they had shown that over and over again, but did I want that power? Did I really?

Part of me really did. I could feel something deep down and animal hungering for the talents that they possessed and that was a problem. A big problem. Once I started down that path where would I end up?

I shook my head again. "No," I stated resolutely. "I will manage on my own. It is time for you to say your goodbyes then leave."

So they did. They floated over to Billy, covered him in hugs and kisses, then, one by one, their little lights blinked out until there was just one left. This one, after it had said its goodbye to the boy drifted over to me and took one last look at the apparition of the full moon, then regarded me once more.

"I said 'no' and I meant 'no'." My voice was firm but there were cracks at the edge.

The fairy gave a little frown and twiddled its fingers in the air. As it vanished, the picture of the moon dissolved and, for an instant, I was sure that the shadowy outline of a winged dragon hung in the air before melting into nothingness.

The quiet hung heavy in the room. I walked over to Billy and placed my hand on his shoulder. "You did the right thing," I said. "You did the right thing." Whether I was saying this to him or to me, I was not too sure.

That evening, I went home, drew the curtains blocking out any trace of moonlight, opened a fresh bottle of Jack D and turned on some Tom Waits very loud. The hard, raucous lyrics filled my ears, releasing the tension from my muscles and the alcohol from the whiskey soothed my battered nose.

Power is a terrible thing. It can turn good men into monsters. My dad told me that before he died. We were sat watching some politician or other on the television and he turned to me and said, "Sammy, innocent people voted for that bastard. Worst mistake they ever made. He walked in with smiles and manifestos, promising to right the wrongs and do good for the nation. Then a few years later he was oppressing workers and squashing the minorities. He wasn't always bad, Sammy. It was the power that corrupted him. It's a cancer, a growth, a malign tumour that feeds off your insecurities and totally consumes you. Never be like him. Promise me."

So I promised him. There and then I promised that I would never be like that politician. I would never grab power when it was presented to me. I would walk a straight path and keep my nose clean.

The next day the centre of my universe was dead

and my life was shredded by the claws of bad luck, but I've always clung to what he said: power corrupts.

So, as the whiskey heated my heart and the music nourished my soul, I drifted off into a deep sleep which was inhabited by dreams of fairies and dragons, mythical creatures that ran and did my will, protecting me from the beast that stalked the night in the light of the full moon, its heavy footsteps accompanied by a ragged breath and the stench of decay.

The next morning was another bright, sunny autumnal affair. I ate cereal in the living room as I watched people scurry around Dalton Square on their way to work and I drank a coffee as I listened to a bit of morning news on Radio 4: more doom and gloom about the Middle East.

Nine o'clock came and I was entering the office of Lindsay Wetherington, invoice in hand. There were no rebuttals. There were no put downs. There wasn't even an awkward silence. She politely took the bill and promised that I would receive a cheque within seven working days and actually thanked me for my help in the whole unfortunate matter.

I was actually starting to smile when I left her office. She had obviously talked to Swarbrick after my visit out to Slyne the previous evening. The conversation would have gone something along the lines of: Spallucci came, hell broke loose, it's all sorted now, pay him off.

Yes, power, that was the thing. Those with power crave it so much that they will do whatever they need to cling to it and if that means paying off a minor inconvenience which could turn into a major aggravation, then so be it.

I was leaving the school when my smile faltered. There, walking down the drive, was Billy, his bag slung low over his back as is the fashion and a nasty, red bruise circling his left eye which is not quite the norm. He saw me and actually smiled before bounding over. "Hello, Sam," he grinned from behind the bruise. "How are you?"

"Seemingly better than you," I observed. "What happened?"

He shrugged. "The official story is that I walked into my bedroom door last night."

"And the unofficial?"

He shrugged again.

"Bloody hell, Billy... I'm so sorry."

"It's okay," he said. "I've had worse. But better than that, I didn't retaliate. I just took it. He can't win if I just take it. And others can't get hurt." A bell rang from somewhere in school. "Look, I gotta go or I'll be late. Catch you around, okay?"

"Sure," my voice cracked. What had I done? I had removed this boy's only line of defence and he was grateful for it. I looked at my watch. It was only nine thirty and I needed a drink. I fished out a Lucky and headed back into town, towards my office. As I left the school premises my phone buzzed in my pocket. I fished it out and read the message, "Get here now. Important. Spliff."

Ah well, another crisis. At least he had a decent drinks cabinet.

The Case of The Werewolf of Williamson Park.

I was guessing that Spliff was at his place. This meant that I had two options: either go back to my office and grab my car or walk over to Luneside University. It was quite a walk out to the Quay but I decided that I could use some fresh air and I loathe it when people drive needlessly through town, so I decided to put my best foot forward and head off on Shanks' Pony.

It was about nine-thirtyish and the main throng of traffic in town had subsided - the school run was over and those subjected to the daily grind were safely ensconced inside their workplaces for the morning – so the walk through the west side of town would be quite pleasant. I like to walk as much as possible, which is not as much as it should be these days. When I was younger, I was always up in the Lakes climbing over hills and ambling along winding rivers. These days... well it's work, isn't it? It just gets in the way. You have the best intentions to do something. You get all the gear ready. You even go as far as making a packed lunch to take with you: hummus sarnies, crisps and a few flapjacks in my case. Then you get the phone call and you drop everything to sort out whatever it is that needs sorting and bang goes the day. The boots get put away and the sandwiches end up as a light supper later that evening to save wasting them.

So now I relish any chance I get to walk whenever it may be, even if it is just across town to see a friend whose idea of a crisis is that one of the students may have looked at him a bit funny.

Thirty minutes later and I had walked through the Infirmary grounds, over the canal, along Dallas Road, down onto the Marsh and through the rear gates of Luneside University. As I climbed the stairway decked with Saint Andrew's flags, I could hear such shouting and swearing that one might hear from Richard Dawkins if he was confronted by a small child who just wanted to believe in a higher purpose. I knocked once on Spliff's door and let myself in.

"Where, the bloody hell..?" One of the funniest things I find about Spliff is the way his accent regresses whenever he gets fraught or stressed. Normally, he is quite clipped and precise – a refined gentleman's accent with the lilt of heather plucked fresh from a verdant Scottish glen. However, as he was busy emptying the contents of a sideboard onto the piles of detritus that lay strewn across his floor, his deep Scottish brogue sounded more like it was forged from a viciously barbed highland thistle that had sprouted from the drainpipe of a Glaswegian tenement. "Och! Where the frig is the wee thing? Ah only had eet yasterdee!"

"If you're looking for your sweet innocence, I think it skipped out with your virtue and eloped off to Gretna many years ago," I smiled as I leant in the doorway. I

246

had not thought it possible for Spliff's living room to be even more untidy, but apparently I had been wrong. It looked like it had been played in by a baby tornado who had then thrown a strop when it had been told it was time to go home. Every drawer was emptied and discarded in a pile, their contents heaped up on the rug in the centre of the room. There were jackets and trousers piled on his red leather sofa like it was Harrods on the first day of the sales. One pile of shirts moved ominously and, as I walked over to my friend, I veered away from it, knowing that a black, furry ball of bile and hatred lurked underneath waiting to pounce on a passing pair of shins.

"Ha, bloody ha," Spliff grumbled without even looking up from his search. "If ye canna help then just piss off, will ya?"

"What you lost?"

The dark-haired priest stood up from his task, peeled his glasses of his bearded face, anxiously rubbed his brow and said, "A small, white card about so big." He gestured a small rectangular shape with his spectacles.

I cast my eye around the catastrophe that was his living room. "And this card is important because..?"

"It just is!" he snapped, kicking at a pile of trash. "Now are ye gonna help me look for the frigging thing or not?"

"It might help if you tell me what the card is?"

His eyes studiously peered into the depths of the amassed detritus. "It's an appointment card," he mumbled.

"For what?"

"For tea with the frigging Queen! What th' hell does it matta, Sam? Just help me will ya?"

I sighed. He was really rattled. "When was the last time you had it?" I asked.

"Last night. It was in ma jacket pocket."

"Have you..."

"Of course I've bloody well looked there, ya eejit! You think I'm simple or something?"

"Okay, okay." I raised my hands in a pacifying manner. "I'll just check it again to make sure for you. Err... Where is it?"

Spliff motioned over towards the moving pile of shirts. The sleeve of the jacket protruded from underneath them and twitched expectantly. Great. "On second thoughts, I'm sure you checked it thoroughly. Where were you when you put it in the pocket?"

"Drinking a coffee and eating ma supper last night."

I nodded slowly. "What were you eating?"

"Sam! What the frig does it matter?" Spliff threw an old diary across the room which hit the far wall with a thud. "I don't need to know what I was eating, do I?"

"Humour me," I said.

"Jam," he replied.

"On toast?"

"No, just jam."

I safely stifled a smirk. I did not want anything being thrown at me. Instead I warily made my way over to his kitchen. As I did, I noticed the occasional red marks dotted on the carpet between the piles of stuff. "Was it strawberry jam, by any chance?"

"Raspberry. Look, what's this frigging obsession with ma dietary habits?" He stood up, placed his hands on his hips and frowned at me as I tapped a small waste bin with the toe of my shoe. I could see a red mess lying at the bottom.

"And you used a spoon to eat this sweet delight last night, then? Like any other member of the civilised culture that we live in?" I crouched down on my haunches, grimaced and reached into the bin. It was like putting my hand into the mouth of a sleeping hippo with really bad tooth decay. I won't describe it any more. I'll just leave you with the image, okay?

Spliff opened his mouth to say something more abusive, then stopped mid-stride. "Oh," was all he could manage.

I stood up brandishing the once white appointment card. It was now red, sticky and somewhat smeary in nature. I smiled as I held it out towards him by my fingertips. "Yours, I presume?"

"Bloody hell, I remember now." Spliff replaced his spectacles and peered across the room at the card. "I had the munchies but couldn't find a clean spoon, so I..."

"Yeah. I think I get the picture." I frowned as a logo leapt out from the card. "Spliff, this is a hospital card." I tried to make out the department, but it was obscured by some pulverised raspberry. "You okay?"

He smiled and took the card from my relieved fingers. "Course I am. Bloody Archdeacon wants me to have a physical before I go and look at this new post, that's all. You up for a drink now? I'll just ring for a taxi."

At eleven we were walking through the doors of the Borough just as Grace was opening up. "Hi, guys!" she smiled. "Be right with you." The young red-head fastened the doors into place then whipped quickly around the pub, giving the tables a quick wipe-over, setting out beer mats, and picking up any rubbish that had been missed the night before.

"Come on, little dust-devil," Spliff called out as he settled himself in his chair. "It's like the Kalahari over here!" His eyes were twinkling, the coarse brogue had been smothered once more by the Armani scented pillow of refinement and he seemed his normal, good-natured self. At least on the surface.

I removed my hat and coat. As I took my seat, I contemplated the jammy appointment card. While we had been waiting for the taxi, Spliff had meticulously wiped the conserve from its surface, read and re-read the details on it and stowed it safely into his wallet. Nothing more had been said. No banter. No derogatory comments. No idle chit chat.

It was done, finished, forgotten.

Something was wrong, I knew it, but I also knew that my best friend was not the sort for relinquishing such details in a heartbeat. There would be a time and a place for gentle probing and now was not it. He would be automatically on the defensive. Judging by his mania this morning, the appointment was at some point today. I would let him go through with it, then in his own time I would let him get round to telling me what was the matter. If I pushed him I would just be met with, at best, bluster, more likely, abuse, or worse still, ice-cold silence.

Grace finally finished her opening up routine and brought our drinks over. "At last," Spliff said, "I thought they had instated prohibition."

The bar-maid chuckled and smacked him lightly on the shoulder. "Behave, you. So, you both, like, hungry?"

"Ravenous, my dear. Bring me a bull, horns and

all," the priest beamed.

I smiled quietly.

"Sam?" Grace asked. "The usual?"

"Yes please, and a Valium for my friend."

She giggled. "Don't know about the drugs, but I think I could slip you some extra salad, if you wanted."

"Thank you."

"Pah!" Spliff snorted as she left us. "Sheer favouritism, you know. You're the only one who gets extras."

"Don't be daft. It'll just be stuff left from yesterday."

Spliff sat back in his chair and pensively stroked his small beard, his blue eyes twinkling in the light from the outside morning.

I sipped my whiskey. "What?"

He said nothing.

"What!"

My friend's mouth spread into a wide grin. "Never you mind, Samuel. Just you enjoy your lunch."

Chance would be a fine thing as someone walked into the Borough who was going to ruin my appetite.

She was mid to late forties. Her hair was light brown with definite streaks of grey. Her skin had the appearance of someone who smoked far more than was good for them and her manner was one of someone who was highly strung. The woman walked straight up to the bar and called over to Grace who was on her way back to the kitchen having just delivered our food to our table. "Excuse me," the woman asked. "I'm looking for Sam Spallucci."

"Bang goes the peace and quiet," Spliff moaned.

I shot him a warning glance which the priest

dutifully ignored. "I'm over here," I said, rising from my seat to greet the woman. She turned without even thanking Grace and walked straight over towards me. "How did you know I was over here?"

"Your landlord," she explained. "He was fixing something in your stairwell and he said that I would probably find you over here at this time of day." Her eyes quickly scanned the half-empty glasses then focussed back on me.

Good old reliable Harry, I thought to myself. Always looking out for me.

"I tried your mobile the other day," she continued, "but hung up when I was bounced onto your voicemail."

I recalled my phone going off during the IT lesson at Saint Edmund's. "Sorry about that," I apologised. "I was sort of in a sticky situation at the time. Listen, we were just about to eat. Would you care to join us?" I gestured to an empty chair and she sat down seemingly placated.

"Thank you for the offer," the woman said, "but I can't say that I'm hungry."

"Why's that, might I ask?"

She took a deep breath, summoned all her reserve, then came out with something that almost made Spliff choke on his gin: "It's my brother. He's a werewolf."

Her name was Simone Hawkins. She and her brother, Nathan, worked in the mini-zoo at Williamson Park. She had thought that they lived a normal, quiet life. Neither of them had felt any compunction to settle down with a significant other so they had globe-hopped around quite a bit together touring first Europe, then more remote parts of the world. Last year they had decided to set down some roots and had taken jobs looking after animals up at the park. They shared one of the small, terraced old mill-houses in Moorlands. Their life was typically uneventful.

Until her brother had dropped a bombshell last night.

Apparently, while they had been travelling in Egypt, he had been bitten by a wild animal of some description. At the time they had not given it much thought; it had not been serious, just a nip and he had been up to date with all the relevant shots and vaccinations. There had been no infection, no complications. At least he had thought so until one lunar month later... He had hidden his secret from her, going away at the time of the full moon and keeping himself somewhere solitary and away from people. Aside from a few sheep, he had killed no living creature.

Now, however, things had started to change.

Over the last month, Simone had seen her quiet younger brother become more and more outspoken. He had become prone to terrible rages and outbursts of violent temper. On more than one occasion he had been cautioned for these outbursts at work and he was in danger of losing his job. Then, last night, he had confessed to his hidden nature. He was a wolf dressed in human skin and at the apex of this cycle he would finally give the beast full rein. He would not hide. He would not skulk away on a deserted farm like an outcast or a pariah. In two nights he would transform in the park itself and then he would rampage around under the all-seeing full moon ridding the place of drunks, vandals and druggies. He was going to wage a one-wolf vendetta on those he saw as being pollutants to the place that he loved the most.

Simone had been horrified. She had not known what to do until, later that evening, she had seen a news report about a local investigator in the paranormal.

"I was on telly?"

"Yes, the evening news. Didn't you see it?"

I shook my head. "Spliff?" I asked.

He shrugged. "Sorry, busy having a life," then he turned to Simone. "Do you have proof that your brother is a werewolf, or is it all just his word?"

Simone's eyes shot venom at Spliff. "He's my brother. Of course I believe him. We've grown up together and been through so much."

I held my hand up to pacify the situation. "Just one thing. Why was I on the telly?"

"Police are investigating something about you being abducted earlier in the week," she explained. "Surely you should remember something like that?"

"It's been a long week," I shrugged.

She sighed, gathered herself together and made to get up. "Perhaps I'm wasting my time here," she said. "I think I'll leave."

"No, please, sit down," I urged. "Seriously, I have really been having one of those weeks. Of course I'll investigate your brother."

"Seriously?"

"Seriously."

There was a somewhat tense silence until Simone gave a deep sigh then finally conceded, "Okay, but can we go and talk somewhere a bit more private?"

I gave my lunch a quick glance of longing and my stomach growled. "Of course we can. My office is just across the square."

I could just about feel the nerves rolling off Simone as she hovered nervously in my office. "Do you want to sit?" I asked, trying to set her at ease. She nodded, quickly, and settled herself on my sofa. "You look like you could use a drink," I observed, reaching into my filing cabinet. "Whiskey?"

"Yes. Thank you." Her voice sounded fragile, as if the slightest noise would cause it to splinter into tiny shards. I poured two reasonable measures of Jack and handed her one. She sipped tentatively at the glass. "I understand that you are not a charity, Mr Spallucci, and I am willing to pay whatever it takes to stop my brother." She gave a little snort and sipped some more whiskey. "Brother," it was the saddest sounding word that I have ever heard. "My brother is a kind, caring, introvert man. What I have now is no longer my brother. He's dead. Long dead."

I sat, drinking my bourbon, and let her continue. The woman obviously needed to talk.

"When we were kids, I used to care for him. If he fell over and grazed his knee, I was the one he came to. If the kids were picking on him at school, I was the one who told him that they were just jealous. Our parents had very little time for us. We were left to our own devices – latch-key kids, as it were."

"I know the feeling. My parents fought a lot and I had to entertain myself."

Her dark eyes peered up at me. "Did you have any siblings?"

I shook my head. "Only pebble on the beach. I was kind of late coming."

The dark eyes continued to look up to me. "May I

ask you something a bit personal?"

I smiled. "That depends on how much it will make me blush."

"I don't think you'll blush at all," Simone smiled back, her teeth perfect and even. "It's not *that* personal."

"Fire away, then."

"You don't look typically Italian. Your hair and your skin are lighter than one would expect."

I laughed. "Ah! That old chestnut."

Simone waited patiently for me to explain.

I downed the whiskey. "It's a bit of a convoluted story which needs back history filling in first." I looked down at those dark eyes and perfect teeth and pondered something inside. Ah what the hell, it had been a long week. "Perhaps, when I've sorted all this out, I could explain it all over dinner? If you don't think that too improper, that is?"

Simone gave a delicate laugh that sounded like a crystal waterfall. "No, it's not too improper, and yes, I'd love that."

I grinned like an idiot. "Great! Brilliant!" My heart was pounding and my synapses were tap-dancing in my brain. "So, now we've organised our social life, I guess you'd better tell me a bit more about your brother."

The laughter vanished from her eyes and melancholy settled itself down once more in its comfy chair. "I'm not sure what else there is to say."

"Do you have a photo of him? That could help me quite a bit."

Simone rummaged in her hand bag and pulled out a neat, red purse. "I have one in here. It was taken while we were in Egypt. Here you go." She handed it over and I took the photo gratefully. There standing in front of the immortal sphinx was a tall, bearded man with long, flowing, sand-brown hair. I had to admit that he looked half wolf already.

"Thank you. Do you mind if I hang on to this?"

"Of course not. To be honest, it's rather painful to look at right now. The happy times just..." she petered out as the tears finally took hold. I grabbed a tissue from a box on my desk and passed it over. "Oh, silly me. I'm so sorry. I'm sure you don't need this," she fussed as she dabbed at her large, dark eyes. "Look. I'd best be going. I'm sure you will be able to take care of everything."

I assured the poor woman that I would and saw her out of my office then closed the door and leaned heavily against it. I took a few deep breaths as I tried to assimilate the situation. My mind raced back a few days to my meeting with Dave and the other vampires. "The Bloodline have eyes everywhere. They will know and they will come after you. Soon," Nightingale had warned. I needed to be prepared. I needed to defend myself.

Also, I had a date! Wow, I certainly hadn't seen *that* coming.

But right now I had to focus on stopping an insane lycanthrope and for that I knew I would need certain equipment.

I headed out to see the only man I knew that could help me right now:

Uncle.

Let me tell you about Uncle. Since the Credit Crunch hit and we were all royally screwed by bankers, lawyers and over-priced plumbers, the pawn-broking business has risen in ascendancy and undergone a beatific transformation. The sharp-suited salesmen and the glamorously attired women that we see enticing us with catchy slogans on television may not go by their age-old title and they may not all have a set of three shiny, golden balls hanging from outside a dusty shop-front, but they are pawn-brokers none-the-less whether they just advertise "Cash For Gold!", "Cheques Cashed Here!" or other such niceties of modern life. They are the like that have not really been a daily necessity since our fathers' or (depending on your age) grandfathers' day. They are the vermin that rise up out of the sewer to feast upon the shit that we have blindly let ourselves be dragged into whilst spending the money that we do not really have from employment that is as stable as the foundations of the well-photographed Tower at Pisa. They are the opportunists of old, the drivers of fast cars that would no sooner blink than drown a five-year-old in the spray from their Merc as they speed down the country lane to their lodge meeting where they will quaff fine brandy, smoke fat cigars and proclaim how wonderful things really are and how it's a shame that those damned liberals got rid of the glorious workhouses because they really did fulfil a valuable task in their day, keeping the riff-raff of the street...

Hmmm...

I seem to be ranting once more. I do apologise. I sort of hate the little shits.

So, yeah, these are the modern pawn-brokers, the fly-by-nights who rise and fall with empires built on sand, feasting on the detritus and decay that they themselves have encouraged us to wallow in. They have made the profession less about pawning something against a debt that you will be able to redeem on payday in order to get by and pay off the 'leccy bill and more about sacrificing your house, your life and your first born child in order to position the latest 3D goggle box in the corner of the room for five months until it is obsolete and needs replacing once again.

Then there are the Uncles of this world.

If prostitution is the oldest profession, then Uncle's is the second oldest. After ancient man had enjoyed a jolly good time with an ancient lady of the morning, noon or night, he would have normally realised that he had not a bean to his name and no manner of transport to get him back home. Now, the wheel having only just being invented, it was still an expensive form of transport, but being tuckered out from a number of hours of intense activity, our ancient man was far too shagged out to walk home, so he would have fancied a ride in one of these new-fangled carts. So it was that, as he stood scratching his Cro-Magnon head, he would have heard a polite cough from behind and would have turned to see a short, stooped elderly man smiling at him and paying particularly good attention to our man's hunting knife that was stashed in his belt.

"My boy," says the old man, "that is a very fine knife."

"Indeed it is," replies our man, "fat lot of good it will do me today as I have no means of getting home in time to go hunting."

"Ah, but that is such a pity," sympathises the old man. "For sure you will go hungry tonight and your status in the tribe will diminish."

The old man waits whilst our not so bright caveman takes a while to ponder this fact. "Perhaps I could sell my knife?" the caveman wonders, eyeing the blade's fine flint edge. "It would fetch at least a goat."

The old man scratches his chin as if mulling this possibility over, then sadly shakes his head. "But, my boy," he observes, "you are a hunter, not a knife-maker. How would you feed yourself without your knife and no knowledge of how to make a new one? A desperate conundrum I think, don't you?"

Our ancient man sighs, "What am I to do, old man? I am lost! If only there was some way that someone would lend me a goat against my knife until tomorrow when I could return with payment from my own stock at home!"

The old man smiles and kindly puts an arm around our, not-too-bright hero and says, "Come into my cave, my boy, and let me see what I can arrange for you. By the way," he adds, "are you familiar with the word *interest*?"

And so it has been for time immemorial. Again and again, people have found themselves between a rock and hard place, be it an unexpected baby, the sudden desire to elope with the neighbour's daughter or even a very big, scary man called Vinny. In these moments of crisis they turn to the one place where they will never be scorned, where help is always at hand (albeit coming at a price and with variable rates), and where their precious goods will be kept safe for a fixed period after which they will be sold to reclaim any defaulted debt.

My dad knew all about these type of pawn-brokers. The one where I grew up was Dad's third home. His second home was the bookies, which is why the pawn-broker could only manage bronze. Every Saturday afternoon I would accompany my dad to the local pawn-broker where each week he pawned his pride and joy; his trumpet. His father had scrimped and saved to buy him that instrument when he had been just a kid and he was never going to let it find its way into a stranger's hand because of a bad debt on the gee-gees. No, first he would pawn the trumpet, then he would take the cash and wander up the street to the bookmakers where he would trust his cash into the hands of a six-year old.

"What shall it be today then, Sammy?" he'd asked me. His pale, grey eyes twinkling in the smoky fug of the bookies. I'd look the betting forms up and down and, as usual, I would choose the horse with the silliest sounding name: *My Cousin's Strumpet* or *Four-legged Glue Pot*, that sort of thing. Then my dad would laugh his deep, baritone laugh, run his fingers through his prematurely white hair, and call out to the girl behind the counter, "Wendy! He's picked a winner again," before placing the bet.

Every week he did this and every week we won. Not just once or twice, but three or four times. I'm not convinced that he always went with my selections, but he always told me that he did and there we would sit, cheering as my horses came in before grabbing his winnings and sauntering back down the road, a couple of swells hitting the big time. We would pay his debts, collect his prized trumpet then go home via the tobacconists where he would buy himself a Cuban cigar, me a bag of pick and mix and my mum a box of Black Magic.

Good days. Very good days.

Before he got ill.

So it was that these warm, sepia memories filled me with a satisfying familiarity as the brass bell above

Uncle's shop door tinkled and I stepped through into a rose-tinted part of my childhood. The painful memories of my dad's last days tried to claw at me and drag me down, but I fought them off with a stick sharp enough to fatally wound a mammoth and found myself smiling with genuine pleasure as the old man bustled up behind the counter.

"Samuel!" he smiled. "It's been a while, my boy. How are you?"

I looked through the toughened safety glass that ran the length of the counter and smiled to myself. Yes, Uncle was one of nature's constants. Dickens would have adored him – a complete stereotypical pawn-broker. He wore his Jewishness with pride; small round spectacles perched on the tip of his long nose and a black skull cap fastened securely on his fine, greying hair. He was adorned in a Scrooge-like housecoat over a bulky green woollen jumper that provided much needed warmth to his fragile frame which had shrunken with the onset of old age. His gnarled, arthritic fingertips were stained yellow from the burning tar of countless cheap, self-rolled cigarettes.

"I'm not too bad, Uncle. How are you?"

"Oh, Samuel," he waved a nicotine-stained hand in mock affliction, "it would take me from now to the hereafter to tell you of my woes and ailments. This body gets no younger, you know? My heart flutters, my prostate burns and my kidneys ache. I tell you, my boy, it will be soon that one of these mornings I shall wake up dead! Then what shall I do? Who will run my business? A worry, it is. Such a worry." He slipped me a conspiratorial wink and rubbed a finger against his cheek. "But enough of such pleasantries. I think that you have need of my services, yes? What is it this time, Samuel, hmmm? You have drunk your savings away again, is it? Or perhaps..." he paused dramatically, "Yes, perhaps you have need of capital to bail out that heathen priest friend of yours. Yes, I bet it is that, isn't it?"

I chuckled lightly. "No Uncle. I am neither broke nor at the beck and call of Spliff."

The elderly man's brown eyes twinkled in the dusty half-light. "It is not money you seek, you say? Well, well, well. Perhaps you have need of other services, I feel. Services that might be best discussed in private?"

I heard a dull click and the counter door swung outwards.

"Well come on, Samuel. Make with it. I am old, you know. I do not have all day. I might be dead this afternoon."

I smiled and entered behind the counter before following Uncle into his back room.

Five minutes later and the air hung heavy around us. I sipped nervously at a small cup of the strongest brewed coffee known to humanity and waited. It was all that I could do. Uncle was never one to be rushed. He always weighed up the situation thoughtfully and meticulously. He sat there in front of me, his eyes staring straight out in front of him, the flames from the log fire dancing on the lenses of his small spectacles and his arms involuntarily pulling the housecoat tight about him as if an unwelcome chill had just seeped into the room.

As I waited, I let my eyes flit around the old man's parlour. I had been back here a number of times, but every time I ventured into the inner sanctum I always found something new to fascinate me.

Today my eyes rested on a thing of pure beauty. It was a length of lacquered brass twisted round on itself, narrow at one end and bell shaped at the other, inserted with three mother of pearl inlaid valves in the middle. I longed to hear the resonant sound of the trumpet sing out in the stillness of the room. Instead all I could hear was the crackling of the fire and the ringing of faulty inner ears.

"It is a nice piece, yes?"

I jumped slightly. I had been unaware that Uncle had been watching me. "Yes." My voice croaked in surprise and I sipped some pure, unadulterated caffeine to soothe it. "My father had one almost identical."

The old man nodded. "You have not got your father's instrument?"

"No." I shook my head and looked back up at the trumpet hanging from the wall.

"Where is it?"

"I... I don't know. He has been dead some time now."

Uncle picked up his coffee cup, tipped some of the drink into the saucer and slurped it up. "Your father is dead and you do not know where the thing is that he treasured? Most peculiar... like so many other things."

"Uncle," I took a breath, "I didn't come here for a trumpet."

He shrugged before setting his cup and saucer back down on the rosewood coffee table. "You know I came over from Poland during World War Two, don't you, Samuel?"

I nodded. A large Polish community had established itself here during that period. They had settled and were an integral part of Lancaster's diversity.

"I was very young back then. Ten or twelve, I think. So many years have passed, you know? It is hard to keep track." He leaned back into his winged chair and let his eyes dwell on the crackling flames that snapped and spat in the hearth. "It was my father's brother who got me out. My *uncle*." He smiled at the word. "It was a hell of a journey, across war-torn countryside and taking our chances across borders, but that is another story, my boy. Let me tell you about something that occurred on the day that we left.

"Our village had a youngish rabbi. I can't remember his age, but my father always joked that his beard must have been false as he was not old enough to spit let alone shave. Anyway, as the war dragged on and anti-Semitism grew, our rabbi became more and more introverted. He would be seen less and less at public functions, those that there were and they were few and far between, I am sure you can imagine. Rumours spread that he was sick, and not sick of the body, you know? When people went to visit him, he would barely open the door to his guests, but what they saw was a shadow of a man. He was gaunt and thin, his hair unkempt and he rarely wore more than his pyjamas.

"Then one day, the order came through. *The* order. You know what I mean?"

I nodded soberly. The final solution.

"As the trains rolled into the village and the stormtroopers herded us like cattle into the market square, the young rabbi burst out of his house dressed in dirty, foul-smelling rags and brandishing some sort of spray of herbs. I did not know what they were or how he had managed to obtain them, but the flowers were yellow and the leaves bright green. They smelt almost as pungent as he did. He rolled into the square and positioned himself between the soldiers and the terrified villagers. His eyes rolled with that movement that is only used by those whose sanity has deserted this realm and he shouted out, 'I have you! I have you now! You will fail in this atrocity!'

Needless to say, the Germans shouted at the young man to be quiet and their guns clanked and clattered as they levelled them, nervously training them on him. Looking back, the soldiers were probably even younger than the rabbi and very much aware that, although they had the weapons, we vastly outnumbered them. They would not want to provoke a riot by gunning down the village's holy man.

"But he refused to be quiet. 'This is your day of doom! This is the day of wrath! You think you can destroy our nation? Do you? Pah!' He waved the bitter-smelling herbs at the soldiers and spat at the men in uniform, 'Great powers protect us. Greater powers than most would admit to. One of them came to me and told me this would happen. He said that you would herd us like your heathen swine to the slaughter. Well it will not happen. We are not pigs! He has told me of great things. He has told me how he built the Great Temple of Solomon, of how he commanded creatures of far superior strength than you. He told me how to control you!'

"His eyes seemed to lose the listlessness of insanity and burned with the ire of rage. Standing tall and pointing at the soldiers he declared, 'Do my bidding in the name of the Hidden One! Do my bidding in the name of Asmodeus!'"

Uncle paused and sipped some more coffee from

his saucer. I realised that I was literally sat on the edge of my seat and remembered at that point that I needed to breathe. "Well?" I asked, "What happened?"

Uncle gave another one of his little shrugs. "They shot the crazy son of a bitch." He pointed to his forehead. "Pop! Right there, between the eyes. Then all levels of hell broke loose. The riot, that the soldiers had so wanted to prevent, erupted like pus from an inflamed boil. There was shot after shot as villagers started to fall down dead. Those who did not die in the first volley charged the soldiers and tried to overpower them. Some succeeded, most died. I felt a pair of hands grip my shoulders and drag me away down an alley. It was my uncle. As we ran, I glanced back over my shoulder and saw a most curious sight. There, in the shadowed doorway of the dead rabbi's house stood a figure clad in black. At first I thought he was a German officer, but then I realised that he wore no insignia - just black, sharply cut clothes, and he was watching the massacre. Watching it and obviously enjoying it. A wide smile was spread across his pale-skinned face. Then he casually ran his fingers through his dark hair, turned and walked away, unhindered by anyone at all. No one charged him. No shot struck him.

"It was as if he could not be seen by anyone except for me.

"It was as if he were *hidden*.

"Then my feet were running so fast that my brain was struggling to keep up. Thoughts of crazy rabbis and dark strangers had to be cast aside in favour of desires to live and escape." He finished his coffee and settled back into his armchair.

We sat in silence as I tapped my finger tips on my

teeth in thought, then finally, I asked, "This is all very well and good, Uncle, but what does it have to do with my request?"

He threw his hands in the air. "Oy vey! What are you? A schmuck? You come in here asking for silver bullets for this little toy," he waved at the pistol that lay between us on the coffee table - the one that I had removed from the John O'Gaunt studios on Monday, "and I tell you a story about a rabbi who consorted with demons only to wind up dead and you do not see the meaning of the cautionary tale? Samuel, Samuel, some things are not meant to be tampered with. They are there. We all know that. We feel them in the shadows, we hear them in our nightmares, but they are best left hidden, out of sight. If they were to be brought out into the light of day, what evil would they wreak on us? What destruction would they bring? My boy, I do not want to see you ending up like my young rabbi." Tears were close to brimming over from his eyes. The old boy really meant it.

I chose my next words very carefully. "Uncle, I appreciate, your concern, but I have reason to believe that this werewolf wants me dead. I don't know why, but I have it on good authority that I am a marked man. I just want to defend myself."

"Defend yourself?" he harrumphed. "This sounds more like a pre-emptive strike, my boy. And who told you that wolfie was gunning for your blood, eh? A reliable source? Someone you can trust?"

"A vampire." I cringed. The words were out before I could stop them.

"A vampire? A vampire? First a werewolf, now a vampire." Uncle leant across and grabbed my hand.

"Samuel, Samuel, do you not see what trouble you are getting yourself into here? Please, I beg you. Let it be, my boy."

I shook my head. "I can't, Uncle. There's something set in motion and I have no desire to be crushed under its momentum. Please, help me."

The old man's shoulder's slouched in resignation. "Silver bullets, you say? The stuff of fancy, I feel. I will see what I can do, but I make no promises, you hear?"

I nodded my appreciation.

He picked up the small gun and tossed it over to me as if it was hot enough to burn his fingers. "Now take this little balloon-popper and get out of here," the pawn-broker growled. "I will bring something of more use round to your office later. Go! Before I change my mind."

Spliff has always been one for research - even more so than me. When we were at university he was the one who would go missing for days on end, chasing up the slightest lead on some obscure cult that existed for a few months on some far-flung Polynesian island, just to confirm that the human psyche was capable of looking at a blade of grass in a certain manner. It was during this period that he started to put the weight on. Now, I'm not saying that my best mate is fat, far from it, but he is, you know, portly. He looks like he lives too much of the high life when in fact he spends most of his time just eating out and microwaving convenience food in order to let him get on with his reading. When I first knew him, back in our fresher's year, he was pencil thin, but as the book addiction grew, so did the waistline.

Now me, on the other hand, I have always felt a tad uncomfortable trawling through the fusty archives.

Not that I have anything against the books themselves. Like I've previously commented, I was always one for hiding off with piles of them. However, when I was at university, the ones that I wanted always seemed to be guarded by those ageing librarians with medusa stares. You know the sort. You will be innocently browsing through the stacks for whatever takes your fancy at the moment when the nape of your neck twitches and you feel them there, somewhere. You glance over your shoulder and observe that you are alone, but that twitching little rodent inside you can sense them as clear as if they were coiled up on the top shelf waiting to pounce down on you. You grab the book and hurry to the desk with your heart in your throat only to be greeted by a knowing look that says, "Oh yes, I know all about you. I know I am far, far superior to you in every way and one day, when your back is turned, you will be mine..."

Or perhaps it's just me.

Anyway, these days the information that you seek is more or less at your fingertips. Give me Google any day. The whole cyberspace explosion is a wonder to me. These days we can chat to someone in Australia whilst watching re-runs of *Father Ted* when we should be looking up train times to Preston. It is amazing! This stuff had only just been spawned when I was a student. The whole computer thing was mainly still the realm of pale-skinned, greasy-haired individuals who lurked in a darkened technology lab referred to as "The Pit". Normal people either did not want to or were not able to understand what it was these tech-heads were talking about when they babbled such incoherent phrases such as PC, internet and network. And as for apples? Well they were just fruit, weren't they? But today....

Well, it really is amazing, isn't it?

So, when I got back from Uncle's and after wrapping the pistol up in a tea towel then stashing it in the bottom drawer of my filing cabinet, I booted up my laptop and settled down at my desk for some research. As Google found me the site for Williamson Park, I poured a large whiskey and lit up a Lucky. With two clicks I had read all the facts about its location; "...situated in a commanding position overlooking Lancaster City Centre ...approximately 5 minutes from junction 34 of the M6 motorway," its main attractions; "sundial... Ashton Memorial... Butterfly House... Mini-Zoo," and its visitor's centre opening hours; "10am – 5pm April to September, 10am – 4pm October to March."

Now, why would I need a big, dusty book and a hard stare for that?

After jotting down my newly acquired information I clicked on the link about the mini-zoo. I was greeted with bright, cheery pictures of various exotic reptiles, small, fluffy mammals and brightly coloured birds. Then, at the bottom of the page shone a flashing link that really caught my eye: "New this season: Driver Ants!"

"What the hell are they?" I mumbled as I clicked the link; "Ants in cars?"

Not quite. Driver ants were in fact the famous ants found in Africa that were known for eating anything that got in their way. They could strip a carcass in seconds, carrying every tasty morsel back to the colony and their queen. "Nice one for the kiddies," I grimaced. Well, I supposed it was a handy way of disposing of any dead rabbits or guinea pigs from the fluffier side of the zoo.

As I scanned the page of the mini-zoo, a couple of

pictures leapt out at me. There, showing crowds of enthusiastic primary school kids around the birds and the reptiles were the Hawkins siblings. I clicked on a photo of Nathan Hawkins smiling up at a white parakeet that was perched on his shoulder and studied it in Photo Viewer. Was this the face of a werewolf or just a crazed individual? My eyes looked him over for any tell-tale signs. Sure, he was a bit bushier than the average guy and he looked like he shunned the normal niceties of brushed hair, but the guy worked with animals, and in my experience, this was a standard uniform for those whose best friends had more than two legs. I'd been to the cattery with Spliff to pick Dante up a number of times. When you're dealing with animals, then social niceties such as the absence of aroma de cat piss or an immaculate makeup regimen are not a requirement.

Hawkins looked like just a normal guy.

I needed more first-hand details. I had to head up to the park.

A downright miserable mood settled itself on my shoulders as I stomped around Williamson Park in a futile fug looking for clues that either weren't there or had been dragged off by the resident rabbits to the deepest depths of their labyrinthine warrens. What on earth was I supposed to find to suggest that a werewolf worked here? Paw prints? A ragged scrap of fur? Wolf droppings? It was ridiculous and I knew it. Even if Hawkins was a werewolf, how was I supposed to confirm the fact?

I looked at my watch. It was just after seven and the light was starting to fade. I let out a deep sigh and fished into my pockets to pull out my cigarettes. I tapped out a Lucky and, as I lit it, a voice from behind commented, "They really are very bad for your health, you know."

I spun round and stared at a teenage boy with scruffy, dark hair wearing a grey hoodie, a small backpack slung over his shoulder. "You!" I shouted, almost dropping my ciggie.

Alec grinned and darted off across the park. I took up pursuit, my trench coat flapping behind me like the wings of a rather out of breath bat. He raced past the small lake and over the gravel area in front of the Ashton Memorial. He made it look so effortless. My lungs were already starting to burn as I pounded my legs across the unforgiving surface in an attempt to keep up with him. His young feet swept him nimbly up the brow of the hill by the children's play area to the cafe and mini-zoo. My feet, however, tried to fold together and trip me up on the grass. I refused to let my treacherous limbs confound me and carried on running in a staggering lope as best as I could.

When he reached the zoo, Alec turned and grinned at me. The little git was enjoying this! I ground to a halt, my chest burning hard, as the steep incline took its toll and I staggered slowly up to the top. I tried to gesticulate in an annoyed manner with the ciggie I still held between my fingers. Instead, my poor lungs gave up and I doubled up gasping for air. After a few ragged deep breaths, I was about to swear profoundly at him when I noticed that his hand was pointing to something on the wall of the zoo. Then, just as he had behind the Sugar House a few nights previous, he vanished into thin air.

"Sod! I hate it when you do that!" I dragged myself

over to the zoo and crouched down to where he had been pointing. I was rather glad that the park was empty. If anyone had seen me they might have thought that I was a dog piss inspector or something. I mean, why else would someone be inspecting the side of a brick wall about thirty centimetres up from the ground.

At first I saw nothing, but then I realised that the encroaching twilight and raised blood pressure was dimming my vision. I peered harder and saw something etched into the wall. I ran my fingers over it. Yes, there was definitely something there.

I looked even closer. There was a circle scraped into the brickwork and on each side radiated out three straight lines. It looked like a child's picture of the sun. There was one difference though. This "sun" had been painted in with green paint which was chipped and was beginning to fade.

I drummed my fingers against my teeth and grimaced. What the hell was this? Why did he want to show it to me? I stood up. "So what the hell is that supposed to mean?" There was no reply. "Look, I know you're still here," this was somewhat of a guess, albeit a logical deduction that he would want to make sure that I understood his message, "so why don't you just come out and explain it?"

There was a soft breeze behind my right ear and a hand fell on my shoulder. "You really should read more books, Sam," said a young male voice, then everything changed.

I was warm, really warm. Instinctively I went to undo my shirt collar and take off my trench coat.

My hand passed straight through my neck. "Okay,

that's weird," I muttered. I lifted my fingers in front of my face and gave them a quick wiggle. They were quite transparent, as was the rest of me. I was aware of my outline and my physical form, but I was quite insubstantial, like something composed from a clear gas. "Well I guess that's kind of cool. Now where am I? Ah." I looked up the street where I was standing and saw a row of sphinxes lining a rather grand looking, sandy boulevard. "I guess we're not in Kansas anymore, Toto."

So, I was in Egypt, psychically if not physically. The question was, *when* in Egypt? Modern day or a touch earlier? I went for a casual stroll down the boulevard feeling rather amused when I realised that I left no footprints in the sand. When I reached the first of the sphinxes I ran my hand through its giant paw. The stone looked smooth to the touch and the edges were sharply chiselled. It was fresh, new. I guessed that I had travelled back in time. The next question was "Why?"

"What do you want, Alec?" I mumbled. "Why have you sent me here?" I continued to walk down the boulevard. It then struck me that it was dark. A full moon hung in the night sky. My stomach automatically felt rather sick. "I've got a very bad feeling about this."

There was a huge building down the end of the street and in front of it stood an imposing statue. From my distance I assumed that it was of Anubis. I could make out the jackal-head that identified the statue as the god of mummification and the afterlife – a big player in the Egyptian Pantheon. However, as I drew closer, I realised that I was wrong.

Terribly wrong.

Whereas Anubis had the sleek face of a jackal, this idol was adorned with a canine head that sported a

275

somewhat more ragged look. Wild fur was sprouting from its scalp and a short, snarling muzzle was bejewelled with an array of vicious-looking teeth. The werewolf stood bare-chested, its arms held out in an aggressive display of raw power and round its stone neck it wore a medallion, a round, green stone that seemed to shine in the bright moonlight.

I suddenly wanted to be somewhere else very quickly, even more so when I became aware of movement. All around me, things were stirring in the shadows: big, sleek, stealthy things which imbued the warm night air with a taste of menace. I started to back my way down the boulevard as one by one the werewolves emerged into the light of the full moon. They ignored me completely and made their way to the base of the statue. There must have been dozens of them. I lost count after about thirty or so, panic had devastated my ability to use numbers of more than one digit. Then, as one, they raised their heads to the sky and howled.

I tried in vain to cover my non-corporeal ears with my insubstantial hands. The sound was sickening to the core, an ululation that would fill anyone lower in the food chain with dread. I had seen enough. I wanted to leave this place. I needed to leave.

Then it was cooler again. Much, much cooler and I was standing, shivering in front of the mini-zoo at Williamson Park, Lancaster. It was a cold, October evening and the wolves were far, far away – a distant memory.

I turned and faced the young psychic, words failing to form in my lips.

"That must never happen again," he stated, then vanished once more.

276

I left Williamson Park somewhat shaken and despondent. What was it that I had experienced? Had I actually travelled back in time or was it a waking dream, some sort of vision? I didn't know. All I could be sure of was one certainty, that the boy named Alec was exceptionally gifted and incredibly powerful. He didn't seem malevolent, quite the opposite. He had helped me out how many times now? Three? But he did not hang around much. He just popped in, did his thing, then vanished like Will O' The Wisp. There was something about him that disconcerted me.

Something? Who was I kidding? There was a bundle of stuff too vast to count. The boy was a complete mystery, but as long as he was a help, not a hindrance, I could hardly criticise him. I would just have to accept him for what he was; a Mona Lisa smile, an enigma.

Then there was the content of what he showed me. Ancient Egypt at the mercy of werewolves? Well that never made the history books, did it? I enjoy my history programmes, especially the archaeology ones and I have not yet seen Zahi Hawass or Robert Richmond standing over the mummified remains of a lycanthrope. So, surely, if it happened, then it must have been a short period, a flash in the pan. The Egyptians were good at erasing people from history, look at what they did to both Hapshetsut and Akenahten. They were both seen as an affront to the natural order of the kingdom so their monuments were desecrated and defaced. As far as their successors were concerned, they never existed and they would not exist in the afterlife, either. Perhaps that was the same with the werewolves? Perhaps their reign of fear was short and not so sweet, then they were overcome and the page of papyrus that they occupied was cast into the four corners of the Sahara?

And what was that medallion, the green stone that shone so bright in the darkness of the night? I thought about the symbol drawn on the side of the mini-zoo. Were they one and the same? Was it a relic that meant something to the werewolves? It had to be, surely? Their leader was wearing it after all.

I needed more information. That meant research. More bloody research. As I walked across Dalton Square I cast my eyes up to the clock tower on the Town Hall. Its baleful eye shone yellow in the darkening sky and told me that it was getting on for ten o'clock. Was it that time already? How long had I been out of it in the park? It had only seemed like minutes. Suddenly I felt oh so weary and I longed for a warm bed to keep out the cruel autumn chill, but research is a cruel mistress and she must be served.

You really should read more books, Sam.

I snorted as I stomped up the stairs to my office and let myself in. Sod that! I clunked the door shut behind me and, as the laptop booted up, poured myself a drink. Then, as Chrome loaded, I selected something loud to keep my concentration alert and, as my eyes grew heavier from trailing legions of hearsay regarding lycanthropes around cyberspace, Tom Waits' gravelly voice intoned that it was time to sail for Singapore. When Uncle Vernon was as independent as a hog on ice, I read that the oldest werewolf story dated to just 1591 in Germany and was a man called Stubbe. By the time the Big Black Mariah came rumbling across my speakers, I had found that the Greeks believed Zeus had turned the King Lycaon into a wolf and this was thought to be at the origin of the word lycanthrope, coming from the Greek words lykos (wolf) and anthropos (man). As some men did it for diamonds, my mind boggled at the various theories that were extrapolated as to how one became a werewolf, the most common being infection from another werewolf's bite.

It must have been when Tom was telling me to hang down my head in sorrow that I realised I had started to snore. I jerked up suddenly and intuitively looked around. My office. I was just in my office. There was no sand, no fur, no god-awful howling. I rubbed my eyes, drained my bourbon and rose stiffly from my chair to stretch. My spine creaked and cracked - it felt so good. I poured another drink to soothe the aches and licked my lips. I reached over to my discarded trench coat and rummaged in a pocket to pull out a packet of cigarettes. As the white packet slid out, something glinted and tumbled out, bouncing on the carpet. I frowned and stooped to pick it up. It was the silver pendant that Melanie Brande, that sweet-talking cherub (note the sarcasm) had been wearing when she and her co-stars had tried to sacrifice me. Was that only a few days ago? It seemed a lifetime away. I dangled the little chimera in front of me, its two heads – one goat, one lion – seemingly glaring at me with a spite synonymous of its erstwhile wearer as it swished its serpent's tail.

My mind was numb with werewolves. I fancied a little change. While horses came down Violin Road, Google instructed me that Chimera was a beast from Ancient Greek mythology which was slain by Bellerophon whilst the hero rode the winged horse

Pegasus. The last thing I remembered thinking before sleep took a firm grasp of me and led me into the wonderful world of Nod was, "That wasn't in *Clash of the Titans.*"

There was the beating of wings. The wind was whipping across my face as I clung onto the person in front of me for grim death. "We'll soon be there," came the gravelly voice of Tom Waits from over his shoulder. The smell of dark bar rooms, musty perspiration and cheap aftershave crawled up into my nose.

"Where are we going?" I shouted across the deafening beat of Pegasus' snowy white wings.

"To Singapore. We have to stop it."

"The Chimera?"

He turned his head and his sharp eyes bored into mine. "Not exactly," he growled and the wind left my lungs as his callused hand sharply shoved me off the back of the flying horse.

Okay, so I was dreaming. That was okay. I had fallen asleep listening to Tom Waits and reading about the Chimera. It all made sense up until the point where the drunken bastard had pushed me off the bloody horse. Why had he done that? No matter. This was a dream. I would just stretch my arms out, flap them like wings and...

Continue to fall.

The atmosphere screamed past my face as I maniacally flapped my useless limbs like a demented Wile E Coyote. I had been thwarted by a phantasmagorical Roadrunner once more. I was going to plummet to the bottom of the canyon and no amount of Acme product was going to save my neck. The desert floor was racing up to greet me and try as I may, I could not get my arms to work. I could not fly. I should be able to fly.

I shut my eyes and turned my face away from impending disaster as I could start to make out sharp rocks and boulders below, then suddenly I stopped and hung still in mid-air, before starting to move horizontally.

My arms had worked. I was flying.

I made to flap them only to find that movement was impossible. They were being held fast by a number of small hands. The fairies glistened iridescently as their tiny wings beat in a furious manner to keep me aloft. They seemed so vibrant compared to the wasteland that surrounded us. There was a large booming noise and the air around us shuddered. We rounded a corner and I saw the source of the disturbance. There, atop a bleak hillside fought two massive dragons. One was obsidian black with huge, gnarled wings and the other was blood red with seven heads. Primal screams shrieked from their fang-lined mouths as their claws slashed relentlessly into each other. Huge clods of blood and gouges of skin and scales flew across the valley beneath them. Wherever the debris fell, the land burst into immutable flame. The heat from this was intense and scorching. I felt as if I was stood at the brim of an erupting volcano that was spewing out lava.

The fairies set me down in the valley beneath the battle. I turned to protest, but they had vanished. Instead I saw two large armies stood facing each other. Surprise, surprise, I was in the middle. On one side stood an army clad in the purest white. The mid-day sun shone off their beatific faces and their wings fluttered in the breeze. Unmistakably angels. On the other stood creatures the like of which I had never laid eyes on before. They were roughly humanoid in shape, but were totally featureless. What heads they had seemed to be sunken into their shoulders as they were possessed of no kind of neck. Their limbs were long and gaunt and seemed to be the colour of wet clay.

Then darkness fell like a suffocating duvet and the armies changed. Where once stood the faceless creatures, prowled a restless pack of werewolves, their coal-black eyes darting left to right, seeking prey to devour. Where the angels had been, was a group of soberly clad vampires, their pale skin devoid of emotion in the light of the full moon.

I had seen enough and I tried to run but, once again, I could not move. My arms were tied to two stout poles. I tugged and grunted but they would not come free. Instead the cords dug deep into my wrists. I looked the poles up and down. Each of them had an object dangling from its top; green hemispherical stones that pulsed rhythmically in the night like a pair of living hearts. Green vapour teased its way down from the stones and encircled me. It smelt sweet like incense in a church or bread in my mother's oven. As I inhaled the smoke, I felt every sense in my body sharpen. I had been dead before I had known the stones and now I was truly alive. I longed to hold them in my grasping hands, to draw them together and mend their brokenness.

There was a whisper of movement and I knew a vampire stood behind me. "Oh, Sam," came the sad, sad voice of Dave. "How could you?"

Then I was alone, my arms and legs were still bound firm, but now I was lying on the hard floor of a darkened room at John O'Gaunt Media. I craned my neck and saw the ubiquitous pentagram once more. This time there were no crazed actors, but on the wall was a lilac coloured banner. It was emblazoned with a large golden "T" shape that was entwined with two snaking wavy lines.

Footsteps approached and Alec knelt down next to me on one knee. He was holding a small brass bell that was adorned with a jersey cow on its handle. He was ringing the bell back and forth and the tinkling noise was starting to fill my ears. "Why am I not surprised to see you here?" I moaned, laying my head back on the cold, hard floor.

"Oh, there are far more surprises yet to come," smiled a voice I had not heard before.

I lifted my head back up and saw that Alec had been replaced by a stranger. He looked about my age, had dark hair and was dressed in a black denim jacket which bore two small, round badges: one was a CND symbol, the other bore the word "Prefect". As he smiled down (and might I add it was not a very nice smile) from beneath a pair of dark sunglasses a kind of warm penumbra emanated around his person and in the lenses of his glasses I saw two items reflected; a chalice and a sword.

"Who are you?" I asked as the ringing from the small brass bell (which I now recognised as being an ornament on my mother's mantelpiece) started to rise higher and became more and more insistent.

The stranger peered down at me and removed his glasses. Where pupils should have been, fire danced in his eyes. "We," he said, "are one."

For the second time that week my drunken

slumber was harshly broken by the discordant hammering of my accursed nemesis, the confounded creation of Alexander Graham Bell. My eyes creaked open and checked my watch: ten-fifteenish, give or take a blur. I lifted my head off my desk and my legs pivoted me round on my chair. My arm shot out towards the phone which my hand fumbled from its cradle.

"Hello?" I croaked.

The voice on the other end was clear, so at least I had it the right way up this time, but my brain was still trying to catch up with my body. "Sorry, could you repeat that please?" I asked.

"Sam? Is that you, you sound awful?"

My forehead creased as I tried to place the voice. It was brisk, well-clipped and had the slight trace of an accent. Indian accent? "Jitendra?" I asked. "Yeah, sorry. I'm fine." I stretched my free arm and yawned into the mouthpiece.

"You don't *sound* fine," the DCI observed. "Listen, if this is a bad time, I can call back later." I smiled slightly. There was genuine concern in his voice.

"No, seriously, I'm fine. Just woke up. Late night. A case thing. I didn't know you guys worked on a Saturday." I paused. "It *is* Saturday, isn't it? I've kind of lost track."

"I'm a policeman, Sam. Always on duty, you know?"

I chuckled raggedly into the mouthpiece, "Yeah, you and me both, apparently." I coughed harshly and my eyes scanned the room for a source of liquid. My mouth felt like the backside of a camel in a sand storm. I spied an open bottle of Jack Daniel's, grabbed it, swigged it, and started to feel somewhat better.

"Okay, if you say so." I heard a rustle of paper at the other end – the rearrangement of notes. "I thought you ought to know that we've just about got what we can out of your abductors."

My mind was blank. There was a stilted silence. Abductors? I was still here - I hadn't been abducted.

Jitendra could obviously read my morning confusion. "The satanic cult? Baines and his little playmates?"

"Oh, yes." My fingers played with the silver necklace that lay next to my sleeping place. "Yeah, sorry. Like I say. Late night. What's going to happen to them?"

"Well, obviously, they will be standing trial, but we need a bit more meat on the bones yet. Needless to say we're starting to probe into their backgrounds and lives, but we will need some more information from your good self. I thought we could meet next week?"

I nodded. My head started to hurt. I rummaged in a drawer for some aspirin. "Sounds fine. Sounds good." I wrestled with a tub and washed two pills down with a swig from the bottle of whiskey. "Oh!" Inspiration hit.

"What?"

"While I've got you, I could use a bit of a favour."

There was a short pause. "Depends on the favour."

"It's to do with this case I'm working on. I could use some info on a suspect. I need to know if he has any previous."

"Okay. Shouldn't be too hard. As long as you're discreet with your sources."

I downed the rest of the whiskey. My stomach started to feel warm and relaxed. "Your secret will remain safe with me. You shall be as nameless as the woman at the house of Simon the Leper."

"Pardon?"

I chuckled down the phone. "Mark 14.9. Just look it up."

"Sure." His voice was hesitant. "When do you need the information?"

I thought about the big white disc that was going to rise that night. "This afternoon?"

"You don't ask for much, do you? Should be alright. What's the individual's name?"

I told him and said that Hawkins had a sister called Simone and that they worked at Williamson Park. We arranged for Jitendra to come round about two and, after hanging up, I shambled off for a shower. Five bracing minutes later, I was almost passable for human. I was clean and smelt of whatever chemicals in the shower gel were trying to pass for flowers and spice, but my head still churned; not so much from alcohol abuse but from the desire to learn more about the case. Hawkins was still a mystery to me and I was loathe to sit on my hands until Jitendra came round in about three and a half hours. That moon was rising tonight and I was far from prepared to meet whatever was going to present itself.

It was at that moment that inspiration hit from one of the other major organs of my body. My stomach noisily reminded me that I had not yet eaten. My eyes watched the long hand of the station clock tick round to the seven. Ten thirty-five – too late for a decent breakfast, too early for a proper lunch. I could grab something on the hoof in town.

Of course! Bob! I would go and grab a burger from

Bob with a dressing of information. Burger Bob had his own little business in the centre of town selling grilled produce of questionable definition and heavenly taste. He was privy to all sorts of gossip and I was sure I had seen him touting his wares up at the park from time to time. I grabbed my hat and my coat then headed off to feed my stomach and my head.

I love Lancaster on a Saturday. It really buzzes, you know? The street market is out and people mill around all over the place. It's great just weaving your way through the crowds picking up snippets of conversation, watching the shoppers and savouring the smells of fresh veg and freshly cooked food.

The food aromas have two main sources. The first is around the former fountain in Market Square. The smells here are the firmly traditional blended with the distinctly exotic. Along with the vendor selling freshly baked bread and the huge veg stall with all manner of legumes, brassicas, potatoes, onions and fruit (English and foreign), there's Indian food, Chinese food and a guy who sells falafel and other such delights. The other culinary epicentre is down where Cheapside meets Church Street.

This is the realm of Burger Bob.

Now, I'm no meat-eater and I really don't like the smell of it cooking (the bacon thing does not work with me at all), but I take my hat off to Bob. He always has a string of clientele backed up the way queuing for his "Locally Produced Hand-Cooked Burgers." I dutifully joined the end of the line and waited for my turn to shuffle itself up before ordering my little dose of heaven in a bun served with a garnish of reliable information.

287

You see, the thing with Bob is that he has been here for time immemorial and, as a result, he sees things come and go that others miss. Also, while people wait for their food, they talk to him and, while he grills that little piece of sustenance, he listens. He listens intently, stores it away and is able to recall it with incredible detail.

"Sam!" he called out whilst deftly flipping a trio of his burgers over and reaching for two more. "Good to see you. You hungry?"

"I sure am," I said, "on two counts."

Bob looked me up and down, nodded appreciatively and tossed a kidney bean special on the grill along with some chopped onions and sliced tomatoes. The beanie goodness sauntered enticingly up towards my nose and my stomach growled hungrily in response. I felt like I hadn't eaten for a week.

"It'll just take a couple of minutes," he said as the customers in front of me headed off with their burgers. "You'd better be quick."

"You've catered for things up at the park, haven't you?" I asked. "Quite a few times, am I right?"

"Sure." He pressed down gently on my burger, easing out a seductive hiss. "They always get me in for things during the summer. They may know their flora and fauna, but when it comes to mass catering..." He let the sentence trail off as a mischievous smile filled his face and he chuckled to himself.

"You ever meet a guy called Nathan Hawkins?"

He nodded. The smile vanished as he flipped my burger.

"And?"

"You wanna stay away from him, Sam. He's trouble."

288

"What kind of trouble? *My* kind of trouble?"

Bob shrugged. "You hear stuff, you know?" He grabbed a white bun and sliced it down the middle. "Weird stuff. He can be sweetness and light on the surface, but underneath..." He squeezed a generous squirt of mustard into the bun, "there's something quite sour."

"Specifics, Bob."

He lifted the edge of my burger to see if it was ready. "Well, summer just gone, there was an incident when a young girl was messing around in the small animals' section. Little kid, yeah?" He flipped my burger into the bun, topped it with the grilled veg and closed the bread lid down. "Just a kid, about six or seven. Well, he went ape shit. Now, I know we all have bad days, but Hawkins..." Bob handed me the burger. "Like I said; sour. Oh, damn it!" A blast of loud pop music blared out from across the other side of the pedestrian precinct. "I thought she wasn't here today!"

I bit into my burger and smiled as I watched the source of the chef's ire. There, next to a large CD player was a young woman in her mid-twenties, made up to perfection and dressed like she was off to attend an executive meeting.

However, executives don't jiggle up and down in the street to Abba's *Dancing Queen*.

"Hey! Betty!" Bob yelled at the top of his voice, waving a spatula in the air. "Knock it off will ya? You'll piss me customers off!"

Betty was oblivious to Bob, just as she normally is to everything else. Betty, or Boombox Betty as locals know her, is widely considered to not just be a sandwich short of a picnic, but a completely empty hamper. Every day she will stand over the road from Bob and every day she will dance to her heart's content to whatever music grabs her fancy.

Like I said, today it was *Dancing Queen*.

I know it really gets to Bob, the poor guy has to put up with it every day, but it does make me chuckle seeing him get so irate over something so innocent. Right now he was reeling off expletives that would make Roy Chubby Brown blush. I decided that I would get no more information, so I wandered back up Cheapside, chuckling to myself and devouring my burger of the gods. I paused at Horseshoe Corner and mentally checked myself. Here I was in the middle of a potentially horrific case and I was finding time to laugh. Was I becoming numb to the situation? Was this week starting to mould itself around me like a snugly fitting glove of everyday reality? Surely not? I shrugged and finished the burger then tucked the napkin into my pocket after wiping my lips clean. As I weaved in and out of the Saturday shoppers and street evangelists of Penny Street, I studied the faces of those who bustled past me, oblivious to my presence. I was just another random Joe in the crowd. I was no one special - another face on a chilly autumn day in Lancaster. These people had no idea what I had been through this week. They were oblivious to what might face me this evening. All they were concerned about was finishing their weekly shop and getting home to the warmth and love of their family homes. Those who had families, of course. Those who didn't... I thought about my empty flat above my office. I had been alone how many years now? Fourteen years? Fifteen, was it? I had lost track. It seemed like only yesterday that Caroline had said we were finished and that she could never, ever love me.

She had said that *no one* could ever love me.

Dull clouds blotted out my bright mood and I thrust my hands into my coat pockets. One of them found my Zippo. My thumb slowly traced the outline of the pyramid that was moulded in the brass finish. I grunted as a burning sensation washed across my chest. I decided it was heartburn from eating the burger too quick and continued back up Penny Street. Enough of these thoughts about the past, I told myself. It was dead and buried. It couldn't touch me anymore.

By the time the afternoon approached two o'clock, the lighter had exhausted an entire packet of Luckies and I had finished off the open bottle of bourbon.

There was a quick, efficient rap at the door. "Come in!" I called out from my desk. The door opened and the brown-skinned figure of Detective Chief Inspector Jitendra Patel strode in attired in a commanding air of no-nonsense authority. He was wearing an immaculately pressed grey suit that complemented his skin tone perfectly. His shoes were pristinely polished with a complete absence of the slightest smudge or stain and he held a leather document wallet under his left arm.

"Good afternoon, Sam." Polite. To the point.

"Thanks for coming," I said and gestured towards the sofa. "Would you like a drink?"

"Coffee please," he replied, his eyes scanning every intimate detail of my office. I tried not to glance at the bottom drawer of my filing cabinet. "You really have got a lot of..."

"Clocks," I finished for him as I made my way over

to the kitchenette area next to the main room of my office. "I know. It's a thing of mine." I opened the fridge and frowned. "How do you have your coffee?"

"Black, no sugar, please."

I breathed a sigh of relief and flicked the kettle on. "Thank God for that. I don't have any cow's milk at the moment. I don't drink it myself and tend to forget about it. When I buy it, it doesn't get used and goes off."

He nodded. "Perhaps you ought to invest in some little catering pots of UHT milk? Less wasteful."

I nodded in agreement. "Good idea."

"Besides, when it's in coffee no one can really tell the difference," Jitendra continued. "They *say* they can but..." he shrugged. "People always like to appear knowledgeable."

The kettle clicked off and I poured the boiled water onto the coffee granules. "I can't believe we're discussing the benefits of long life milk." I brought the mugs over to the small coffee table and sat on the sofa next to the policeman. "Is that the normal discussion topic at your place?"

He smiled and sipped the warm drink. "You'd be surprised what we discuss, Sam. *X Factor*, *Coronation Street*."

"Not *CSI* or *Hawaii-Five-O*?"

Smiling, he shook his head, then placed the mug back down and proceeded to open the wallet. "Far too depressing watching sun-tanned models prancing about without a care in the world. Have they never heard of budget constraints when they write those things? This fellow, however, would be a cause of much discussion if my colleagues knew you were interested in him."

I let out a low whistle as Jitendra placed a rather

large manila folder on the table. "My God, it's half a tree."

"And that's all I've been able to find so far." He slipped a thick ream of A4 sheets from the folder and began thumbing through them. "Mr Hawkins has been exceptionally busy. As far as I'm aware he has gone under at least three pseudonyms, so I am hypothesising that there are more out there that remain to be, as yet, uncovered."

On the top sheet were mugshots of a twenty-something male with roughly brushed, light brown hair and bad acne. "What's his racket?"

"Well there's the usual: GBH, drunk and disorderly, petty theft. The sort you see every day in every town. However, there's some more unusual things." Jitendra pulled out a group of papers that were clipped together. "When he was sixteen, Hawkins was a member of a group that spent most of their time sat in a field waiting for a flying saucer to come and take them away."

"He's a ufologist?"

The detective shrugged. "Oh, it gets better. Obviously, the little green men did not show, so two years later Mr Hawkins was living in a commune dedicated to living their life apart from modern society."

"That's not so bad. I have a certain amount of empathy with that."

"Yes, well I'm hoping that you would not use the commune as a front for taking the members' savings and ploughing them into a lucrative drug-supply ring."

"Hawkins was behind it? He was only eighteen!"

Jitendra shook his head. "No. He was just a disciple, so to speak. The ring leader went down for a good amount of time. Hawkins was cautioned and treated more as a victim than a criminal. However, that changed two years later when he turned up in Surrey heading a new-age church prophesying that the end of the world was nigh and everyone who was not with him would be blown to smithereens when the world exploded."

I groaned. "A doomsday cultist. What happened?"

Jitendra studied the notes. "The usual: allegations of fraud and abuse, lengthy investigations, dawn raid, trial and imprisonment."

"He's done time?"

"Eight years. Looks like he got out on good behaviour and promising never to set foot in Surrey again."

"So that takes us to when?"

"About eight years ago, then he dropped off the radar for a few years."

I nodded. "His sister said that that they travelled around for a bit: Europe, Egypt."

"That would explain the gap. Then, a little while back, he moved up here and got a job as an attendant at Williamson Park. Since then, he's been as clean as a whistle."

I skimmed through the pages of the reports. The early years certainly made interesting reading, just as Jitendra had illustrated – Hawkins had been a serial cultist, meandering from one group to another, stealing to fund his habit and beating up those who tried to stop him. Then, after his conviction and subsequent incarceration, he had emerged as a reformed character. He had seemed to get his act together. After the travelling abroad, he had moved up north with his sister and taken the job at the park where he diligently lived his life as a model citizen. The police records on him dwindled to nothingness about twenty-four months ago. The man seemed totally clean.

The turbulent past did not match the idyllic picture that his sister had so graphically drawn for me, nor did the present day promises of redemption and good behaviour gel with the uneasy feeling owned by Burger Bob. I drummed my fingertips against my teeth and various clocks ticked in the silence of my office as I tried to piece the two characters together.

"You look perplexed."

"This just doesn't fit," I said, looking through the papers once more, almost hoping to find something recently which said, "This guy is nuts!"

"Are you going to enlighten me as to why you are so interested in the man?" Jitendra asked, finishing his coffee. "I presume it's related to a case."

"His sister came to see me yesterday morning. The description she gave of how he is now doesn't exactly fit with the image these recent reports give of him. The earlier stuff... yeah, bang on, but these," I waved the offending articles in front of me, "are a completely different man. A reformed man. The man she described to me... was a psycho."

Jitendra leant forward. "Sometimes appearances can be deceptive."

I looked at him. His eyes were peering off to a place that mine could not follow. "Now, that sounded heartfelt," I commented. "Care to unload?"

The policeman rubbed his fingers over his clean-shaven jaw. "You have something a bit stronger than coffee?" I reached into my filing cabinet drawer, making sure I didn't draw attention to the bundled-up tea towel, and hooked out a fresh bottle of Jack Daniel's which I cracked open then poured into the two mugs. Jitendra sipped gratefully at his. "I've worked bloody hard to get where I am, Sam. Bloody hard. My dad wanted me to follow in the family profession."

"What was that?"

"A sodding shop-keeper," he growled. "Please come again! Have a nice day!"

I laughed at the very passable impression of Apu off *The Simpsons*. "I take it that the family business wasn't for you, then?"

He sipped more whiskey. "It wasn't a job. It was a bloody stereotype! I told him that. I said that I wanted none of it, that I wanted to do my own thing. I had a brain and that I wanted to use it. He told me not to be so stupid. He said that this country was blinkered and that I would never come to anything on my own. He said that perhaps, if the shop wasn't for me, then perhaps I ought to be a doctor. A doctor! That's even worse! What else could he suggest? A role in a seventies' sitcom as the poor Indian sap who doesn't understand innuendo and gets himself in all sorts of saucy scrapes? Pah! So I told him what I was going to do. I laid it on the line and I told him that he wasn't going to stop me."

"What did he think to that?"

"Not much. We haven't spoken since I left home. Parents! Waste of space. They just fill you with neuroses and hold you back."

Inside of me something shivered with cold.

"Anyway," he continued, "I studied. I did well. Very well. Top of my class in Psychology. Took a masters in Criminology then applied for the Force. I rapidly went from strength to strength. I started at the bottom. I insisted on it. I didn't want to be one of those uni boys who waltz in and lord it over the rank and file. God no! You see them looking down their noses at the guys on the beat and it sickens you. The uniforms have no respect for them either and I wanted to make sure that any respect I received had been well and truly earned. In order to do this, I needed to see the job from both sides of the desk. So I slogged my guts out on the beat and patrolled my way up into CID where I really got myself noticed. I had the highest conviction rate of my station. People were whispering hushed things about me in the corridors. Meetings were being held to discuss my glorious future. I was on the up, a rising star. I was to be a model of the new police force for the twenty-first century: a multi-racial body, a tolerant and inclusive office.

"Then I was appointed as DCI here. An external appointment to lead the department down the golden paths of glory."

He paused a moment and sipped his drink, steeling himself.

"On my first day I was shown to my office by a young constable. She must have been no more than twenty if she was a day – straight out of training. She was all smiles and compliments. She had heard all about me. She was excited about working with me. She hoped I liked my office. She was sweetness and light.

"Just after she left and closed the door behind her, I realised that I had left my briefcase in my car. I opened the door and made to go fetch it when I heard the young girl saying to her friend, "Just settled the new DCI in. Seems quite nice for a Paki.""

I winced.

"Sometimes, for all the work you put into things, Sam, a leopard just cannot change its spots. You think that it has become a nice fluffy little tabby, but then it turns around and slashes you right across the heart."

We were silent again as we both finished our drinks. I topped them up and we drank some more, surrounded by the ticking of clocks and the occasional hoot from a car out in Dalton Square.

"So what is it that Hawkins' sister has said about him?" Jitendra finally asked.

"She said that he's a werewolf and tonight he's going to go on the rampage around Williamson Park."

For a moment the detective sat, mug in hand, his eyes fixed on me and his face impassive. Then, all of a sudden, he threw back his head, slapped his thigh and my office was filled with deep, braying laughter. "My God, Sam," he roared, wiping tears from his eyes, "that's a corker. Absolutely priceless. You had me going for a second there." His laughing subsided as he brought his mirth under control. After a few composing breaths he asked, "Seriously. What is it you want with this chap?"

I was silent and sipped some more of my drink before fishing out a fresh pack of Luckies. I flipped my Zippo and popped a cigarette in my mouth, saying nothing.

Jitendra looked at me in complete astonishment. "You're serious. You're bloody serious!" He stroked his chin and stared at me. "You have got to be kidding, Sam? Surely you can't be taking this at face value? Sure, Hawkins likes his little groups, shall we say? But a werewolf? She's winding you up, or perhaps she's out to cause trouble for her brother?"

"If she wanted to cause trouble," I replied, drawing heavily on the fag, "then perhaps she would tell your lot that he's up to his old tricks? That would sound more realistic, surely?"

Jitendra shook his head. "Perhaps, but a werewolf? Come on. That stuff doesn't exist, does it?"

I thought back to a vampire sinking their sharp teeth into my wrist. I recalled an exsanguinated body behind the Sugar House. I considered Nightingale's warning. "I've seen a lot of stuff this week that you would not believe, Jitendra." I inhaled deeply and finished the Lucky, stubbing it out in the ashtray on my desk.

He stood up and smoothed out his expensive suit. "Okay, this is insane. You're being taken for a ride, Sam." He pointed to the files on the coffee table. "You can borrow these. Read through them and I think that you'll see sense. The man was a whacko, but now he's clean. His sister is out to spite him and is just reeling you in. I've got to head off, but if you need me, call, okay?" His eyes narrowed on me. "Don't do anything stupid."

I nodded acceptance at the official warning and let him out of the office then stood thinking. As the clocks ticked and my ears rang I thought over the evidence in front of me. Jitendra may have been sceptical but his previous words rang true: "The leopard does not change its spots." Hawkins was up to something, whether he was a werewolf or not. True, he may be a cult junkie, but then again...

I needed to take precautions.

I needed Uncle to get here with my silver bullets. I picked my phone off its cradle and dialled in the number of his shop. After about twenty rings I hung up and checked the mantle clock on the window-sill. Three in the afternoon. The old bugger must have shut early. I drummed my fingers against my teeth and shut my eyes. The whistling in my ears chased the tumbleweed around my brain. I had nothing, absolutely nothing. I was getting nowhere fast, to walk a well-trodden cliché.

I opened my eyes, lit up yet another smoke and dragged a pad and pen out of the desk, deciding to write down everything that I knew in the hope that it would give my brain some thinking space. At the moment it seemed to be cluttered up with half-truths, vague myth and speculation.

I stared at the paper. Where to begin?

At the beginning of course.

One. I had been told by vampires earlier that week to watch for the full moon. I had helped the Children of Cain and now the Bloodline of Abel would be gunning for my blood.

Two. Yesterday, I had been approached by one Simone Hawkins (potential date, although now part of me was starting to reconsider the sensibilities of that) who said that her brother was a werewolf and intent on going nuclear at the next full moon.

Three. The next full moon was tonight.

Four. Hawkins had history. A colourful past of cults and violence.

Five. Hawkins worked in the zoo at Williamson Park. He was rumoured to still be violent.

Six. I had encountered something mystical regarding Alec at the park. I had seen a vision where werewolves were prowling around in Ancient Egypt whilst being curiously missing from the history books.

Seven...

I paused and drummed my pen on the pad. Was

there a seven? I sat and finished off the Lucky, slowly ground it into an ashtray then lit another. The roasted smoke filled my mouth and I blew its tobaccoey flavour out of my nostrils.

Yes, there was a "Seven."

Seven. I was on my own and the sky was starting to darken outside. In about an hour, the moon would rise and I would find out, for sure, what was truth and what was fiction. I would see if Hawkins was just a lunatic with delusions of primeval shape-shifting or whether he would be coming for my jugular.

I got up, walked over to my filing cabinet and opened the bottom drawer. There at the back, wrapped in the red and white tea towel was the revolver that I had snatched from the John O'Gaunt studios earlier that week. Had it only been Monday? It sure had been a full week. I turned the gun over in my hand. I had never used one of these before, but it looked fairly simple. Finger on trigger and don't peer down the business end. It looked like there were still bullets in there. I tentatively pushed a catch on the side and the front end dropped down. Yep, there they were, six little packages of death and destruction.

Not silver, but they would have to do, for now. I snapped the gun shut and shoved it into the pocket of my trench coat.

The sky was starting to dim on a mid-October afternoon and I had somewhere else to be.

Normally, I enjoy a quiet, leisurely stroll through Williamson Park with the sun dappling the paths through the autumnal leaves and the gentle breeze wafting the smell of woodland to my nose, but that October evening my skin was crawling worse than a beach at crab-mating season. As I made my way up the gravel path from just opposite Christ Church on Wyresdale Road, my eyes were scanning the darkening shadows, straining to discern anything that might be animal rather than vegetation.

Specifically, anything that might be rather large, furry and full of teeth.

I tried to walk stealthily but the cruel gravel betrayed my every movement. I felt like I was a herd of elephants trying to tip-toe through a corn-field. My heart was dancing a polka in my chest and stress was pulling the ropes of cathedral bells in my ears. I absentmindedly rubbed the side of my head as I approached the first clearing in the park. I don't know it's real title but I always think of it as the fairy ring. It's a circular grove of trees that stand over a small hillock which is surrounded by rough seats fashioned from preserved tree trunks. I swung my legs over one of the trunks and seated myself down, trying to calm my heart and still my chiming ears. As I let my eyes wander around the ring of trees I thought about Billy Swarbrick's diminutive friends and wondered if they ever came here to dance in the still of the night. They had shown me an image of the full moon. They must have known about the werewolf.

Werewolf.

Damn it! Just last week I would have scoffed at the idea. As you can probably tell, I'm not the sceptical kind of person. I have seen so much stuff over the years – that's why I ended up in this profession – but the idea of a real-life lunar shape-shifter? The idea would have been insane. Such notions were the product of old-time superstitions and fears.

Just like vampires.

Vampires like the ones I had met just earlier that week.

So if there really were vamps then that suggested that there had to be...

My train of thought stopped mid-ramble and that mammalian instinct that stems from once having been a small monkey at the bottom of the food chain kicked in. The hairs on the back of my neck stood proud and to attention like a band of subconscious sentries, all the saliva drained from my mouth as it absorbed back into my body, and my bladder performed a little dance as it tried to decide whether it needed to empty itself thus making me lighter and able to run quicker.

I was being watched.

I was being hunted.

Slowly, trying desperately to blend into the shadows of the umbrella of trees, I lifted my eyes to the foliage that surrounded me. There was no sound. There was no movement. There was only instinct. It was there, I knew it.

Carefully, shakily, I rose to my feet, a hand steadying itself against the gnarled, upright trunk of a tree. The bark felt electric to the touch. Every crack, every ridge stood out against my soft fingertips. My breathing slowed and my eyes travelled from tree to tree, from bush to bush trying to spy my stalker.

There on the opposing side of the fairy ring was a gap between the trees. A muddy slope led up to a higher level. Broken branches and snapped twigs littered the way up. In the gathering gloom I could make out decaying leaves scattered about the woody flooring.

There, in the midst of the dying leaves, stood a

furry paw. A very large, furry paw. I was frozen to the spot as my eyes travelled up an incredibly thick front leg that was clad in rough, greying hair, over a shoulder that rippled with pure sinew and muscle, across a thick neck maned in predatory camouflage, past two sharp, pointed ears to a pair of dark, abyssal eyes that were fixed directly on me.

It was the teeth that broke my stasis.

In an instant I had transformed from Greek statue to African gazelle. I bounded across to my left, further into the park, my shoes crashing against the gravel path as I tried to place a distance between me and the wolf that would be akin to the distance between the Earth and Alpha Centauri.

Shit! It was real!

It was here!

It was after me!

As I rounded a curve in the path I allowed myself a glance over my shoulder. The wolf was nowhere to be seen. I should have felt relief, but that scared monkey inside of me recognised the reality that the predator was, in fact, hiding, lurking in the gloomy shadows. I groaned as I realised where I had run into. In the light, summer evenings the park is used as an open-air theatre, with different stages set at different locations. I had just run into one such area. On either side of the gravel path were high rising banks with seats sunk into the earth. Trees obscured my vision at the top of both slopes. The only way out was back the way I came or down the other end of the impromptu stage. It was a rat run and I was the little lab rodent scurrying through the test with the big, furry scientist looking on from above, hidden in the foliage. No doubt a dissection would follow shortly.

I shoved my hand into the right pocket of my trench coat and pulled out the appropriated pistol that I had brought for protection. True, the bullets weren't silver, but surely they were capable of some sort of damage? One foot after another I edged down the path, all the time my eyes scanning the horizon of the high, obscuring tree line.

I glimpsed a movement. The pistol rang out. There was an echoing silence, but no ethereal howl of pain.

Damn! A bullet wasted. I tried to recall how many this thing had. Were there five? Yes, I was sure there were five more.

I walked further.

Movement. Up above. Yes, definitely movement. I raised the gun as I approached the end of the rat run. I could see a tremor in the leaves. Was it the wind or was it my hunter? How could I be sure? I kept moving one foot after another. One foot after another. Just keep moving. Just keep moving. Distance is our friend.

Then, with a roar, the leaves revealed their secret and the wolf leapt down the banking. I ran for the end of the stage area and fired wildly behind me. A high yelp cut through the crash bang of the gunshot. I glanced quickly and saw the wolf rise up backward, one shoulder wrenched behind him. I had winged him.

I made good my advantage and pelted hell for leather across the open grass towards the Ashton Memorial.

Now, when you think of a memorial, you might imagine a little blue plaque on the side of a house - Joe Bloggs, inventor of the toffee-chocolate machine was born here, that sort of thing - or, at the most, a grand statue commemorating some glorious victory over peasants whose greatest crime was to hold a pitchfork in self-defence. The Ashton Memorial is the mother of memorials. It is an entire building. Hewn from white marble and standing God-knows-how high, crowned in a green copper dome, it can be seen from most parts of Lancaster. It was built by Lord Ashton in 1909 and was probably a memorial to his late wife. It is a must-see for all visitors, tourists and investigators being pursued by a slavering beast.

I charged across the gravelled area deciding that the memorial would give me the high ground and a clear view.

I bounded up its fine stone steps two at a time until I reached the first level. I turned and saw my hunter stalking with deliberate menace out of the trees. I had to admit that, in the light of the full moon, he looked quite marvellous. Low to the ground, his eyes still fixed upon me, even at this distance, his limbs working in complete harmony despite a slight limp from his left foreleg. He was the ultimate predator. Part of my mind, the part that wasn't shrieking at me to run for my life up towards the top level, was saying, "Thank God that there's only one!"

I reached the top level of the stairs and approached the building itself. I tugged frantically at the glass door. Locked, obviously. I reversed the pistol in my hand and smashed the hand grip through the glass then reached inside and unsnapped the latch. I flung the door open and threw myself over the threshold. He would be behind me soon. I had to make a plan.

Stairs. More stairs. Stairs were good.

There are viewing areas on the outside of the memorial up towards the roof. To reach these, one has to climb one of two small, tight staircases. I chose the nearest one, ignoring the "No Entry. Exit only." sign and darted up them. I spiralled up with the stairs as they took me to the first landing and I climbed out onto the balcony. I was now facing the other side of the memorial, towards the butterfly house and the mini-zoo. There was a modicum of safety for now. The wolf had to come up to get at me. He could not fly and I doubted that, with his wounded leg, he would be able to climb up the outside of the memorial, besides I had a good view of the exterior walls and there was no way he could creep up on me, unseen.

I stood in the silence of the cool, October evening. All I could hear was the pounding of my heart, the gasping of my breath and the ringing of my tinnitus. There was no other noise - no heavy animal breathing, no brushing of fur against stone, no clicking of claws against steps. Just silence for what seemed like an age.

I brushed something off my shoulder.

It was replaced by more of the same.

Dust. A light dust was falling on me.

From above.

The little monkey inside me expired as I looked up and saw something large and hairy clinging to the next balcony up. The werewolf had gone up the other stairs and taken the access way to the next level. He had me in his sights.

As I lifted the pistol, I saw his legs bend and his muscles tense in the white moonlight. Then, as my third attempt to use the handgun sent a bullet flying off harmlessly into the night, the wolf was sailing through the air down towards me.

I didn't think. I just reacted in a manner of self-preservation. I shoved my hands out in front of my face and, when I felt the impact of a toothed killing machine, I twisted around and the weight of the wolf was gone. A second or two later there was a blood-curdling thump.

I realised that my eyes were closed tightly shut. I dared to open them and peered down over the precipice. The werewolf was laying immobile on the mosaic pattern of the red Lancashire rose that adorns the courtyard between the memorial and the butterfly house.

I must have stood for about a minute panting heavily, willing my numbed legs to move. Eventually they obliged and I tore down the stairs, almost sending myself for a burton as I did so. As I ventured out of the memorial I could still see the pile of fur and fangs lying immobile on the ground. I raised the pistol and tried to hold it steady with two shaking hands while I made my approach. There was no movement. None whatsoever. Nothing was twitching. I could not discern any rise and fall of breathing.

Nothing.

I leant closer and poked it with the muzzle of the gun.

Still nothing.

In the light of the moon I moved round towards his head and took a better look. "My, grandma..." I began, then its eyes flicked open and all I knew next was nauseating blackness.

Sometime later I came to. Normally, I'm a sluggish waker, the effects of sleep grip me tight and try to pull me back down into the comfy duvet of somnolence. However, on this occasion, the little bunnies of panic were jumping up and down outside their warrens and insisting that we skedaddle.

My eyes shot open and the first thing I noticed was that my head hurt like hell. The second thing was also that my head hurt like hell - which meant that I still had a head. I checked the other extremities. Two arms, two legs, crown jewels; all still intact. The scared bunnies dragged me wobbling to my feet. The world was dark and spinny.

No. Wait. The world *dark*. I *was* spinny. Certainly in no fit state to take on a creature that had survived a fall from the top of the Ashton Memorial then had beaten the crap out of me with one solid blow.

I had to get out of there and recoup.

I had to escape.

I don't remember much about getting the hell out of the park. Adrenalin pumped through my heart and bells rang shrilly in my head. About midnight, I crashed into my flat, ransacked my medicine cabinet for some paracetamol and some betahistine. I poured a large whiskey, downed it, poured another, lit a Lucky and crashed into my armchair.

I was alive. I was alive. I had met the bloody werewolf and survived.

I sipped at the second whiskey and revisited that phrase. It made no sense. Why had he not killed me? Blood drained from my face as I leapt from the armchair, ignoring the wobbling floor, stripped my clothes off and stood naked in front of the mirror in the bathroom, a cigarette hanging from between my lips. Nothing, not a scratch, let alone an infectious bite. There was just a bruised swelling starting to emerge on the side of my head. I decided it would match the ones that were fading around my nose, then dressed again and made my way back into the living room. I was just considering how this made no sense whatsoever when I saw the long parcel propped up against the wall. I had obviously missed it when I had staggered into my flat. I drew heavily on the cigarette and approached the object with caution. It was about forty centimetres long, wrapped in brown paper and tied with string. This was no present from Father Christmas. A scrap of paper was tacked to the wrappings. I snatched it off and read:

"Samuel, silver bullets at such short notice is a no-no, but this little item should serve you just fine. I do not know if you have used one before, but they are straightforward enough. Flick the switch at the back of the barrels and they open up for you to insert the cartridges which are laced with silver. There is a safety on the side. I suggest you use it so you do not blow your balls off.

Uncle.

P.S. The lock on your door is about as useful as a pork chop at a bar-mitzvah!"

I managed to smile for the first time that evening and carefully unwrapped the parcel. It was a short, stubby firearm with two barrels that ended at carefully filed apertures: a sawn-off shotgun, the favoured weapon of thieves and hoodlums the world over. Reggie Kray would have loved it. There was a *thunk* as a smaller package tumbled out of the parcel and onto the floor. I picked it up and opened the little box. There were a number of cartridges inside and another note in Uncle's scrawled cursive handwriting.

"These contain a high amount of silver as well as the usual shot. They are expensive. Don't waste them!"

I smiled again and in five minutes I had worked out how to load the gun and turn the safety on and off. I was now a bona fide werewolf hunter. I could track him down and shoot him dead.

My spine crawled. Was that what I wanted? Did I want him dead?

No. Of course not! What was I thinking? Here I was imagining myself as some sort of big game huntsman, when in fact my prey was a normal man. Well, as normal as anyone can be who changes into a wolf once a month and desires to eat up half of Lancaster in a feeding frenzy.

I was no killer. The gun had to be the last resort. But what else could I do? I could not capture him. Even if I did, what would I do with him? Have him neutered and kept as a guard dog? True, it would save having a new lock fitted on my door, but the practicalities...

Then it struck me. I fished Jitendra's card out of my pocket and dialled his mobile number. Surprisingly he picked up after two rings.

"Hi, Sam. I've been waiting."

Jitendra met me at the park. He was leaning against a black four by four, his hands in his pockets in an attempt to defend himself against the insidious cold night air. When he saw me approaching in the yellow glare of the harsh street lights he stood up sharp and stalked over.

"Damn it, Sam. What happened to you?" He reached out with a gloved hand and turned my head to peer at my swollen cheek.

"I told you on the phone. I got hit by a pissed off werewolf."

Jitendra left out short, exasperated breath. "Don't start with that crap again or I'm off home. There's no such thing as... What the hell is that?" he yelled as I drew the sawn off shotgun from out of my trench coat.

"Protection," I explained, coolly checking that the safety was still on. At least I hoped that I seemed cool. My heart was beating faster than that of a teenage boy as he watched his first porn video in a darkened bedroom.

The whites of the policeman's eyes were stark against his brown skin as anger swept over his face. "Sam, you do realise I ought to arrest you on the spot for this? Do you?" His face was close to mine and he spoke in an aggressive whisper. I remained stoic, silent. "Well? What do you expect me to do? Be your Sancho? There's no damned windmills up there! Are you going to shoot a man in cold blood? That's murder."

I breathed slowly. I had expected this and all the way up East Road and Wyresdale Road, I had carefully prepared a little speech. It had sounded convincing to me. I just hoped it sounded convincing to the man who kept handcuffs on his person and could throw me in a cell then leave me there to rot. "This time last week, I would have been the man stood in your shoes," I said slowly, carefully selecting every word before it left my mouth. "I would be saying, 'Shit! What's all this?' But in the last seven days I have been abducted and almost sacrificed by Satanists, played nanny to a newly created vampire, stopped irate fairies from causing havoc at a local high school and now, to top it all, I have been attacked by a creature which stepped straight out the pages of *Little Red Riding Hood*. Now, I'm not sure what I was expecting when I set up shop, but let me tell you it was none of this. Perhaps I was thinking that there might be grannies convinced that their dead husband was moving cutlery around the house and that was why they could never find a teaspoon when they needed one. Perhaps I thought that there would be a neurotic teenager who had convinced herself that everyone was being mean to her because the wart on her little finger meant that she was a witch. Perhaps there was a whole lot of other mundane, trite and easily explainable stuff which I thought would present itself to me. What I did not expect was to be stood at the end of the week outside the local park with a sawn-off shotgun that was loaded with cartridges laced with silver readying myself to blast someone who does more than hump your Aunt Ethel's leg or chase postmen when the moon is full. My life has changed, irrevocably. Now, so has yours. So you have a choice. You can either try to take this gun off me and lock me up - and believe me when I say that I will not go without a fight - or you can come with me and help do anything that needs doing.

"What will it be?"

Jitendra's eyes went from my face to the gun to the park then back up to my face. "Sod it!" he swore and stomped off into the park.

My heart stopped racing. Just a fraction.

We walked in silence for a short while until Jitendra turned to me and asked, "I'm guessing you have a vague idea as to where we're going?"

In all honesty I hadn't even considered the matter yet, but not wanting to look like a total muppet I said, "I think it would be logical to start where I left off."

"In front of the butterfly house?"

I nodded.

So, on we traipsed, through the gloom of the park. It was now the middle of the night and the canopy of trees rose over us blanketing out stars, clouds and even the baleful, all-seeing eye that was the full moon. I gripped the shotgun tight, my finger resting on the guard around the trigger. The last thing I wanted was to fire off involuntarily because my hand was shaking. I was too aware that any sharp noise could alert the wolf to our presence.

That was, if he did not already know that we were there.

I quickly booted that thought from my mind like a drunk cast out of a family-friendly pub. It could not be indulged. It was not worth thinking about. The idea that the creature was there, in the woods, his head low, his eyes sharp and his dagger-like teeth exposed from under his wide, slavering lips as he stalked us silently, purposefully...

Stop it, stop it, stop it. "That's crazy talk. You'll get us both killed!"

"Pardon?" Jitendra stopped, his eyebrow raised.

"Oh. Did I say that? That was supposed to stay inside my head."

My companion gave something that almost passed for a smile as we reached the open area in front of the memorial. "Looks rather exposed, wouldn't you say?" he noted, his eyes scanning the trees that encircled the area. The big, dark trees with all their handy hiding places.

Everywhere I looked there seemed to be wolf-shaped shadows. Between the trees, behind the benches, over by the pond. I really knew how a small rodent felt. "We've got to cross it," I said, reluctantly.

Jitendra nodded and set off purposefully across the tarmac. After a second's hesitation, I scurried over behind him trying to ignore any ominous movement. We climbed the stone stairs and it was only after we rounded the building that he seemed to proceed with added caution. He motioned for me to hang behind him in the shadows and whispered, "So this is where you say you last encountered the werewolf?"

"If by encountered you mean *got knocked senseless by*, then yeah, that was here."

"Wait here," he commanded with no room for discussion and walked slowly out over the rose-tiled esplanade. He circled a couple of times then crouched down and ran his fingers over the ground, nodded and walked back over to me. "Well there are certainly signs of a scuffle there," he said.

"You don't say?" My voice was ladled full of tasty sarcasm which he chose not to digest.

"More importantly," the DCI continued, there is evidence of blood and it trails off in that direction." He pointed towards the entrance to the mini-zoo. "Do you think your wolf is an exhibit? Sharing a run with the rabbits perhaps?"

I looked him hard in the eye under the light of the moon. "You're still not buying this, are you?"

"Let's just say that I'm keeping an open mind, shall we?" He stretched an arm out towards the mini-zoo. "Lead on MacDuff."

I swallowed and looked over towards the attraction. My stomach was lurching behind the shotgun that I had clasped tight to my middle. I so did not want to do this. I thought of my bed, my lovely warm bed and a soothing bottle of Jack Daniel's that could keep me company into the early hours. Then I thought of a splintering crash as a blood-lusting hell hound smashed through my door and pounced on top of me, ripping out my throat as my screams evaporated to a damp, squelchy nothingness.

I really had no choice, had I?

I sucked it up, grew a pair the size of beach balls, and led the way over to the zoo. Jitendra was right, there was a thin train of blood dribbling its way across the floor. It glistened a path in the light of the moon all the way to the main glass door of the entrance. The door hung open, still in the quiet night air. I peered in and saw nothing but a darkened gift shop. I gripped the gun even tighter and nodded for Jitendra to pull the door back. As the door swung silently open, I inched my way in, foot after hesitant foot, slowly swinging the shotgun around the small room. It was soon obvious that the scariest thing here were the prices for the touristy knick-knacks. Jitendra lay a silent hand on my arm and pointed to the other side of the room. The door leading through to the main part of the zoo was also open. I nodded and we made our way over there. Once more, the DCI opened another glass door and we stepped back out into the night.

The door brought us into an open courtyard behind the butterfly house. In the middle stood a large, round aviary, its occupants apparently fast asleep, and down the far side of the courtyard lay the newly renovated bird-house and mini-beast building. Looking down at the floor, the trail led off to this new construction. We continued our hunt.

I froze as my foot crunched on top of light-coloured gravel that paved the courtyard.

"Quietly," Jitendra mouthed.

"Duh!" I mouthed back as I continued to walk, albeit somewhat more cautiously, telling my feet to imagine the old *Kung Fu* trick of walking on rice paper.

After what was in fact a few seconds, but seemed like a number of hours, we made it across the treacherously noisy path in one piece. Once more we found another door (this one solid, not glass) that was ajar. Darkness was recumbent on the far side. Jitendra pushed the door open to the bird-house and the gloom inside was even blacker than that which was outside. I hesitated.

"Go on," he mouthed.

I stared into the blackness of the room and my feet froze. They were not for moving.

"Go on!" Jitendra mouthed more urgently, then, when it was apparent that I would not be budged, he edged past me into the darkened building.

I sighed. I couldn't let him go in on his own, so I followed in behind. The vague light from outside gave me a glimpse of large aviaries similar to the one that I had seen in the courtyard. They reached from floor to ceiling and ran parallel down a path towards the door on the opposite side of the room which I guessed led to the mini-beast house.

Then it all went black.

The door had closed shut.

There was no breeze. It had not closed on its own. Shit.

There was a small click and a thin beam of light shot out from Jitendra, who had obviously brought a pocket torch. Mine was probably still lying somewhere discarded in the John O'Gaunt studios. I made a mental note to nip into town on Monday and buy a new one. That was supposing, of course, that I did not end up doing a good impression of a tin of Pedigree Chum in the next few minutes.

"This is DCI Patel of the Lancaster Constabulary," he proclaimed with unnerving authority. "Please show yourself."

Nothing stepped into his torchlight, instead there was the unmistakable sound of heavy breathing and was that fur brushing against the metal cages or was it just my panicked imagination? My hands flexed on the shotgun. "Nice shotgun," I thought to myself. "Friendly, safe, protective shotgun."

"Do not play games with me." The detective's voice was calm and steady. I was totally in awe of him for keeping his nerve. Had I tried to speak right now I would have squeaked higher than a castrati on helium. "Show yourself." He swept his torch slowly around the room. All it found was cages of sleeping birds.

The rustling stopped. Was it behind us or was it to the side? The dark was confusing my senses somewhat. That, and the blind panic of a sprinting heart.

Then I definitely heard something. It sounded like

gravel being rolled back and forth across a rain-drenched tombstone by the mushy, bleeding end of a severed arm. I wanted to cry as I recognised it for what it was. The sound of laughter; cruel, evil laughter.

"You do not scare me, Mr Plod," came the guttural voice, dripping with contempt. "You are nothing to me. It is the investigator that concerns me."

Then there was the sound of swift movement and a thud followed by a clattering as Jitendra's torch scuttled off across the room. I swore loudly and survival instinct took hold. My legs aimed for the door through to the mini-beast house and launched me in its direction. Three long strides took me there. I held the gun in one hand and scrabbled for the door handle with the other.

Where was the bloody thing? Where was it? I ran my hand over the smooth wood at waist height but found nothing. It had to be here. There had to be one. As I searched frantically for my hope of salvation, I was aware of the cacophony of chirruping and twittering as the birds protested at my rude disturbing of their sleep. "Screw them!" I thought, "I need to get out of here." Then my hand lit onto something hard and round. I twisted it clockwise and it turned. Footsteps, strong, hard footsteps approached from behind me. As I flung the door open, light cascaded into the bird-house. I risked a glance backwards and saw the werewolf approaching. He was pacing forwards on his hind legs dragging the inert form of Jitendra by the collar. I lifted the gun up horizontally and fired. The blast was deafening in the enclosed environment and I almost dropped the bloody thing in fright, but I gripped on tight and legged it into the mini-beast section without looking back to see if I had hit the wolf or not. I slammed the door behind me and leaned heavily, waiting for the inevitable thump of the werewolf pushing against it.

The seconds passed.

I waited.

Nothing happened. Had I shot the beast? Had I killed it?

Or was it playing with me?

I quickly took in my surroundings. The room was not that brightly lit, but in comparison to the black hole that I had just escaped, it seemed like seventh heaven. Vivariums were dotted around the edge of the large circular room and there, in the middle, stood Williamson Park's latest, greatest additions, the driver ants. As my heart started to apply the brakes to my blood-pumping I had to admit that it really was quite a spectacular sight. The colony was enclosed in a circular glass case that stood about three meters tall. Glass tubes ran off from the core at various angles and travelled around the perimeter of the mini-beast house. I could make out tiny figures scurrying along these carriageways with leaves and debris on their tiny, powerful backs. The ultimate workers.

But I did not have time to stand and stare. I had to formulate a plan. A plan, yes, a plan. I needed a plan.

No. I needed a miracle.

"Sam? Is that you?"

I started at the sound of the female voice and my face must have shown such surprise as Hawkins' sister stepped out of the shadows. "Simone? Is that you? What are you doing here?" He must have abducted her, I told myself. Brought her here under duress to witness his horrific cull.

But I knew I was wrong.

There wasn't a mark on her.

Crap!

The door pushed hard against my back and I was sent tumbling into the room. Hawkins stalked into the room, in his malevolent lupine state, still dragging Jitendra behind him. There wasn't a mark on my pursuer. The wild blast from the shotgun had obviously missed. I staggered to my knees and brought the twin barrels round to bear on the huge form of the wolf. I had to take care. There was just the one cartridge loaded now and I knew that I would never stand a chance of reloading it with the spares in my pocket.

The wolf, however, was *also* taking care. He dumped the unconscious but not bleeding policeman by the entrance to the mini-beast house and circled behind the ant colony. "There's no escape, you know, Spallucci," his gravelly voice rumbled. "You will die here."

"I've already heard that once before this week, so you'll have to excuse me if I wait and see just how this pans out." I was impressed with myself: humour in a time of crisis. I must have been getting bold.

"The Bloodline of Abel will squash you like a fly, Sam," Simone declared as she too circled around the ant colony. "They have such power. You are totally insignificant."

"So insignificant that you had to get me here to feed me to Fido?" I asked, pointing towards the werewolf with the gun, whilst trying to circle around the display towards Jitendra who was most definitely breathing and, was that his finger moving? "It all seems rather elaborate to me."

"Even a little thorn can dismount a great leader

should it get stuck in the horse's leg." She really seemed to be enjoying the sound of her own voice. And I had actually thought she wanted to go out on a date with me! So much for luck with the opposite sex.

"So Scooby-doo here is a great leader, is he?" I glanced over to Jitendra. Yes, there was definitely movement there, just a little, as if for my eyes only. "Where are his soldiers?"

"The Bloodline are scattered, in hiding." Hawkins growled. "They await their command from one who can lay his claws on that which will unite them."

"And what would that be? A nice bowl of tripe?"

"The Potency." Simone positively glowed as she said the word. A gleam normally reserved for religious zealots filled her eyes as she continued; "It will give such power that has never been seen since the time of..."

"Enough!" roared Hawkins. His eyes fixed on mine. "Time to die," and, as he let a long howl rise from his snout, I felt something hard whack against my wrists. I yelped as my hands dropped the gun onto the floor, then grunted as Simone hit me in the throat with a metal pole before kicking the gun out of reach. As Hawkins started to stalk around the far side of the ant colony to join his sister, Simone brought the pole down on the back of my neck, causing everything to grey and my knees to buckle. I bit my lip and forced myself to hold on. If I blacked out now I was a dead man. I focussed on two distinct things: terror and hope. Terror was personified by the sharp claws that the wolf was flexing from underneath his grey fur. Hope came in the form of Jitendra rising to his feet and focussing his attention on the shotgun that lay discarded out of sight from the werewolf. He dived towards the weapon and swept it up in his hands before taking aim around the ant colony. I took a split second to admire his agility, then I cursed his aim as he let rip a blast which pounded a hole into the ceiling above the werewolf rather than in the chest of the ducking lycanthrope.

A deep, rumbling chuckle rose from the mouth of Hawkins and, darting back, he lurched forwards clipping the DCI with the back of his hairy paw. Jitendra crashed into the wall and slumped to the ground. This time he was truly out for the count rather than just stunned.

I swore as the werewolf's head turned and he focussed all of his venomous attention back onto me. I cast my eyes around as he stalked forwards. I was quickly running out of options. The shotgun was lying discarded by Jitendra's limp hand on the far side of the room and, as well as being far from my grasp, it was empty. Could I drag myself up from my prone position, scramble across the room, snatch the gun from behind the werewolf, load it, aim it and fire a killing shot? I thought not.

Hawkins saw the panic in my eyes and continued to chuckle as he took a mighty leap that sprang him up onto the glass casing at the middle of the ant colony. Beneath him, frantic worker ants clambered up and down the glass with valour to assure themselves that the colony was not under attack. The wolf lowered his head and, through a frothy leer, growled, "And now, Spallucci, it's your turn."

"Not a chance," I whispered, harshly, my bruised larynx screaming in agony. I pulled the revolver out of my trench coat pocket and held it firm in front of me with two hands.

Simone drew back nervously behind her brother

for protection, but the werewolf just continued to laugh. "You are such a slow learner, Spallucci. Do you not remember that feeble toy cannot kill me? Look. Look at my arm." He thrust his shoulder forward. New fur replaced that which I had grazed earlier in the night. "I am immortal to human weapons. Only a silver weapon can stop my heart from beating and cease my brain function."

"Really?" I asked, pulling back the hammer on the gun. "Then I guess this is just really gonna sting." I fired off three shots in quick succession. With the first, his left kneecap exploded, causing the werewolf to slump down onto one side on top of the glass enclosure. He would have screamed in agony had the second shot not removed half of his face. Simone shrieked as blood and brains splattered her, then the third shot covered her shouts as the glass casing beneath Hawkins shattered from a bullet impact, causing the disfigured wolf to tumble in amongst the ants.

Very pissed off ants, might I add.

As they scurried over him and started to eat at his broken flesh, Hawkins gurgled through what remained of his mouth only for the noise to gag tight on a swathe of ants marching into his gouged orifice. His arms flailed around trying to grab a purchase on the sides of the enclosure, but all they could do was scrabble in vain and slide down the clear, unforgiving surface.

I should have grimaced at the carnage. I should have been sickened by the sight of an immortal creature being digested by insects. Was he still alive in their guts? Was he aware of his tortuous fate?

But I didn't care. All I could think of was the relief that he was not going to get up from the insectile feast.

I pulled myself up from the floor, avoiding the occasional splinter of glass. My back cracked and I winced as I straightened up. I ignored the gruesome sight of the feasting driver ants and limped over to Jitendra's still form. I placed my fingers on his throat and found a slow, steady pulse. Unconscious but alive. No doubt he would wake with a severe headache.

I picked up the shotgun, fished two fresh cartridges from my coat and reloaded it before firing a shot into the rapidly decreasing remains of Nathan Hawkins. Just to be sure.

I froze as I heard a foot crunch down on a piece of glass behind me.

"You bastard!" Hawkins' sister hissed. "You utter bastard!"

I turned round and stood to face the harpy. Her face was screwed up in anger and tears flowed freely down her twisted face as she waved her pole weapon unsteadily at me. "I presume you're talking to me?" I asked.

"Of course I'm talking to you, you fuck-wit!" she spat venomously. "Look what you've done!" She pointed at the ant display. Hawkins was now nothing but a pile of bones – human bones. There was no trace of the wolf. "He was a wonderful man. He had such vision," she wailed.

"He was an utter lunatic with delusions of grandeur and a severe murderous streak," I countered. "What was I supposed to do? Let him kill me? I think not." As far as I was concerned I was done here. I showed her my back and made to rouse Jitendra.

"You think you're so clever don't you?" Simone continued. "You think you're so smart. Pah! You know

325

nothing. Wait until they find out about you, then you'll know what true wisdom is. Then you'll see real power. The power of the Bloodline!"

I stopped shaking Jitendra's shoulder. He was still out cold. Instead, I contemplated her words.

"What do you mean?"

She raised her head and looked down her nose at me with utter contempt. "The Bloodline of Abel. They are everywhere, Spallucci, and when they find out about you, they will descend upon you and devour you."

"Bloodline of Abel?" I mused. "So they will come and rip me to pieces then?"

She nodded enthusiastically. "Oh yes. They will tear you limb from limb and dine on your vile entrails."

"How appetising. But they don't know about me yet? So who's going to tell them?"

"Well, I will, of course. They must know of this profanity that you have accomplished here. They must know of your vile deeds. They must..."

Her words were cut short by the sound of my shotgun firing its second deadly cartridge. Her eyes opened wide and she looked down at the gaping wound that pumped blood out of her chest, then she collapsed onto the floor. I stepped slowly up to her, looked her straight in her disbelieving eyes and watched impassively as her life drained away.

She would have set a pack of werewolves onto me.

It was self-defence.

It wasn't murder.

It was self-defence.

It was.

I've never really believed crime writers when they say that a dead body weighs so much, but now I can genuinely testify that it is absolutely true. As if trying to dispose of Simone Hawkins' body wasn't bad enough, I had to contend with the driver ants. I had seen what an efficient job they had performed on the werewolf and I had no desire to be their pudding. So it was with much grunting, care and precision that I hauled the deadweight into the massed colony to serve as their second course.

I should have felt sickened as they stripped away her flesh and devoured her insides, nausea should have risen in my gorge at such a repulsive act of feasting, but it didn't, not one bit. I felt nothing.

No revulsion.

No remorse.

No guilt.

It was self-preservation, plain and simple.

As the second body was steadily devoured I turned to the unconscious form of Jitendra. He had certainly experienced his share of misfortune that night. I crouched down and shook him, calling his name. Slowly he started to come to.

"Sam?" he croaked. "That you?"

"Yep," I said, reaching into a pocket and fishing out my pack of Luckies. They were somewhat battered but sufficient. I offered him one and he shook his head then winced. I lit myself a cigarette and helped him sit up.

He gazed morosely at the shattered colony. "What a mess."

I nodded. "We ought to get out of here."

He frowned. "I'll have to call it in. What happened?"

I paused, smoking my Lucky. "An accident," I finally stated.

Jitendra's dark eyes regarded the trail of crimson blood on the floor that smeared itself towards the colony before turning back to me. "An accident? You call that an accident? I see two dead bodies and a swarm of flesh-eating ants."

I shrugged. "They were threatening us, climbed up on the glass and it gave way. Your shot with the shotgun must have clipped it and weakened it."

The detective closed his eyes in despair. "But that's not what really happened is it?"

"How would you know? You were out cold."

We sat silently for a little while longer.

"Sam."

"Yeah?"

"It really was a werewolf, wasn't it?"

"Yeah."

"Let's get out of here," he said.

So we did.

It was about two o'clock on Sunday morning by the time that I got home. After leaving the carnage behind us, we walked out into the cool night air and Jitendra called the incident in. A couple of squad cars were pulled up by the mini-zoo within ten minutes. Within half an hour a forensics team had arrived. I answered a few questions: I had asked DCI Patel to accompany me on a case, the deceased had been armed, they dropped their weapon, DCI Patel fired a warning shot with the deceased's weapon, the glass must have been damaged, chow down time for the ants.

As the officers went about their business Jitendra

and I sat quietly by ourselves on the stone steps of the Ashton Memorial. "Two questions," he said.

"Shoot."

"Hawkins mentioned two things in there. The Bloodline and the Potency. What are they?"

"I don't know," I answered honestly. "I'm guessing that the Potency is some sort of object of power." My mind recalled the green stone hung around the Egyptian werewolf's neck and I made a mental note to follow that image up later. "The Bloodline... Well, while you were taking your second nap, Simone referred to the Bloodline of Abel as if it were a group of werewolves."

Jitendra's eyes were horror-struck in the night. "A group? Here in Lancaster?"

"No. Not here. The sister and brother were working entirely on their own." I hesitated for a second. Should I tell him any more about my encounter with the vampires? He was a good man. A trustworthy man. But could he take so much information right now? Could he grasp that there were Children of Cain as well as a Bloodline of Abel hiding out there in the shadows? I looked him directly in the face and studied his square, ordered features.

"What is it?" he asked.

"Nothing. I just need to go home." I stood up and began to walk down the steps, leaving Jitendra behind to clean up the mess.

Epilogue.

It's now early on Monday morning. I have sat at this laptop for God knows how long. I haven't eaten or drunk anything - the thought of food makes my stomach turn. I have smoked countless packs of Luckies and I can barely see my hands in front of my face. I really ought to open a window to let the smoke out.

My back hurts and I need to move around, but I feel somewhat unburdened. That was my first week on the job; warts and all. There have been lunatics, vampires, fairies and homicidal werewolves. Quite a baptism of fire, don't you think? Have I gotten the worst of this job out of the way in the first seven days or is it just a precursor of things to come? I don't know. I guess we will have to wait and see.

Oh. There's someone knocking at the door. Back in a mo'.

It's now three in the afternoon. The air in the office is clear, but the fog in my head is dark and heavy.

Things have gotten much worse than I could have possibly imagined.

The person at the door, it was Caroline.

Sam will return in
Sam Spallucci: Ghosts From The Past.

A.S.Chambers

Author's notes: fact & fiction.

First, thank you for reading my book. I hope you enjoyed it. Second, I felt that I had better say a quick word or two about the Lancaster that belongs to Sam. I say the Lancaster that belongs to Sam, because that is what it is, really. It is sort of a side-step away from the city where I live and write; certain things are the same, certain things are different and others are completely made up.

Dalton Square:
The place where Sam lives and works surrounded by his multitude of clocks and empty bottles of Jack Daniel's is, to a point, an exact reproduction of the real-life location.

The Borough does indeed exist, as do the seats where Sam and Spliff normally imbibe their individual tipples whilst watching the world pass by. It is a rather fine hostelry, recommended by CAMRA and always accommodates an excellent selection of real ales some of which it now brews itself and are in fact vegan (Sam would be very happy, I am sure).

The Paradise Dragon, alas, is a fiction. However, it is based on an equally excellent Chinese restaurant called the Fortune Star. I have eaten there many, many times and suggest that, should you visit Lancaster, you eat there yourself. The owner is lovely and she is always very accommodating and welcoming.

White Cross/John O' Gaunt studios:

A little mixture of fact and fiction here. The White Cross Business Park does indeed reside across the A6 from the Royal Lancaster Infirmary but, whereas TV studios were located there in Casebook, in reality there are workshops and offices, among which is an office for BBC Radio Lancashire. To the best of my knowledge, it's presenters are not, and never have been, abductors or Satanists.

The Sugar House:

Indeed, the Sugar House is a student-run night club behind the old Gillow building. It has been going donkeys of years now and I even went there twice when I was a student. Once I was very drunk and the second time I was on a date. I'm sure it is enjoyed by those who frequent it but, like Sam, it's not really my cup of tea.

Luneside University:

This is probably the biggest fiction in the whole book. It does not exist, apart from in my, and now your, imagination. There are two universities in Lancaster: Lancaster University (situated south of the city at Bailrigg) and the University of Cumbria (situated near the centre of the city in Bowerham). I decided to mash the two up a bit and locate them next to the river Lune in an area of the city which, when this book was first conceived, was occupied by the derelict remains of the old Williamson linoleum works.

Dave's shop:
Now, any fantasy/sci-fi fans who have lived in Lancaster for a long time will know that there did indeed used to be such a shop on North Road. It was a fantastic place that was crammed full with little gems from almost the entire universe of fantasy and sci-fi. Sadly, it closed down a few years back and Vexed Vampire was, in part, a little tribute to this shop passing. I am hoping, however, that its real-life proprietor was not left half-vamped on Caton Road.

Edmund Campion School:
There is a school on Ashton Road, but not the one in Paranoid Poltergeist. Ripley Saint Thomas is such a huge gothic edifice surrounded by rambling grounds that it is practically screaming out for a ghost story and I could not resist adapting it for my purposes. All the staff in the story are completely fictitious but I am sure that we have all come across teachers like them at some point in our times at school, from the bullying class teacher to the hard-nosed PE teacher and the incredibly strict head whose glare could wither a perpetrator at twenty paces.

Cheapside/Lancaster City Centre:
The vague layout I have sketched throughout Casebook is more or less accurate. I feel that I just need

to say a quick word on Boombox Betty and Burger Bob, both of whom are vaguely derived from real people.

I did not grow up in Lancaster. Like so many, I was a university import. Where I did grow up, however, had its own version of Boombox Betty and, just like in the book, every Saturday morning she would stand outside the Arndale centre and dance away in front of her ghetto blaster. She was a wonderful sight to behold and I just had to use her. I will be using her again at a later date so Betty fans, stay tuned.

Cheapside in Lancaster does indeed have a chap who sells burgers on the street corner, but then I don't think it is unique here. These sort of street venders are in just about every town and city throughout the world. I thought it would make sense for him to be Sam's man on the street and a convenient source of information as well as good, tasty food.

Williamson Park.

If you have ever driven up the M6 past Lancaster, you will have seen the Ashton Memorial rising above the canopy of the trees from this Victorian masterpiece. Just about wherever you go in Lancaster, you can see its green dome. I kept the layout of the park exactly as it is in real life, but I did take liberties with the mini-zoo in order to incorporate the driver ants which were inserted as a way to kill off a murderous lycanthrope.

Spliff and Grace:

The Reverend James Francis MacIntyre and Miss Grace Darling are both entirely fictitious beings as well as being the two creations that I have enjoyed fashioning the most during my time writing Casebook. As a result, they have both taken upon themselves personality traits and quirks of many old friends and people (some of whom are sadly no longer with us) who have touched my life in really positive ways. On rare occasions real-life situations have and will probably continue to seep in; just don't ask me which they are because my lips are sealed. Just hope that, one day, Spliff will settle down and finally feel at home and that the special someone in Grace's life will finally wake up and realise where the young Miss Darling's affections lie.

ASC February 2018.

ABOUT THE AUTHOR

A.S.Chambers resides in Lancaster, England. He lives a fairly simple life measuring the growing rates of radishes and occasionally puts pen to paper to stop the voices in his head from constantly berating him.

He is quite happy for, and in fact would encourage, you to follow him on Facebook, Instagram and Twitter.

There is also a nice, shiny website:
www.aschambers.co.uk